Sparrow

By Sara Mack

Diana –
Here's to second
chances ♡

Sara Mack

Sparrow

Dedicated to

CJ and The Peanut

Table of Contents

The Past

~

Chapter One
August 2004

"Dude. Just go talk to her already."

My head snaps to the right. "What?"

"I said go talk to her." Kevin starts reeling in his fishing line. "I'm only fourteen, but I know a nice piece of ass when I see one."

I slug my younger brother in the shoulder.

"Ow! What was that for?"

"Watch your mouth. If Gram hears you, she'll yell at me."

Kevin shifts his pole to his left hand and rubs his shoulder with his right. "Why would she yell at you? Besides, she's at the house."

I glance behind me and up the hill that leads to our grandparent's cottage. Gram is hidden inside, but I know she'd freak if she heard Kevin swear. I turn back to the fishing pole in my hands and cast my line. "Because she'll think you learned that language from me."

Kevin snorts. "I did learn it from you."

I shoot him a scowl and shake my head. "Just watch it."

A shriek and a splash pull my attention to the left again. Two of the three girls who suddenly appeared this summer are standing on a wooden raft about thirty feet into the lake, grabbing their sides, and shaking with laughter.

"Looks like your girl got tossed," Kevin observes. "Maybe you should go and see if she's all right."

I want to. Bad. But for some reason, I can't bring myself to speak to her. Every time I consider it, I imagine the worst. I'll introduce myself, her friends will giggle, she'll blow me off, and I'll slink away with my ego shattered.

"Kyle," my brother says as Mystery Girl's head pops above the water, "seriously. Dragging me down here to 'pretend fish' for the last four days is getting old."

"We're not pretend fishing," I grumble.

Kevin rolls his eyes. "You and I both know we'll never catch anything with all the noise they're making. I'm not stupid." He starts to reel in his line again. "It's not a coincidence they're out swimming at the exact same time you want to fish."

Damn. I should have come down to the dock by myself. I thought it would look less conspicuous if I brought Kev with me.

Refusing to own up to the fishing charade, sarcasm rolls off my tongue. "Nothing is keeping you here. Maybe you should head up to the house and finish that Monopoly game you started with Gram. I'm sure that will be *way* more entertaining."

Kevin shrugs. "Hey, I'm not gonna argue. I'd rather stare at tits than Park Place any day."

I slug his shoulder again.

"Geez!" He leans away from me.

"Your mouth is going to get you in trouble."

"Like you're not doing the exact same thing!"

I'm so guilty.

I sneak a glance to my left as the object of my interest arranges herself on the raft. Wearing a neon yellow bikini, she lies down between her friends on her back, knees bent and pointed toward the sky. Her chin follows, tilted toward the sun.

Every year for the past six years I've spent the summer at Buhl Lake, and every summer it's only been my grandmother, Kevin, and me. Never has anyone close to my age shown up. Now that I'm sixteen, I was dreading our annual trip with Gram. I expected more of the same: fishing, riding the quad, helping with chores, and eating dinner at precisely four o'clock each day.

That changed a week ago.

It was early Monday the first time I saw her. I crept down to the dock around five a.m. wearing my ratty gray sweats and an old hoodie. A big bass lives in the lily pads between Gram's place and the neighbors, and I decided to try and catch that fish.

About a half hour into my quest, I heard a strange pounding sound. Confused, my eyes panned the lake and, lo and behold, I saw Mystery Girl making her way to the water, taking the wooden steps two houses over. At first I thought I was seeing things; no one has used that place in years. She tiptoed her way to the end of the rickety dock and threw her arms open wide, inhaling deeply. Her move took me by surprise. I do the exact same thing every time I come up here – minus the throwing my arms out part. The smell of northern Michigan is distinct, especially by the lake. It's damp, yet clean and woodsy. There's nothing else like it, and experiencing that smell always lets me know I've truly arrived.

Briefly stunned, I took in every inch of her...her long legs, her plain white tee tucked into tiny denim shorts, her wavy, honey-brown hair that hung to her lower back. I was too far away to see the color of her eyes, but I couldn't miss the curve of her face and her expression, as if she were enthralled to be here. I swear to God my stomach knotted as I stared at her.

Her eyes roamed the lake, drinking it in, until they fell on me. She caught me gaping, but I couldn't look away. She didn't appear shocked to see me. Instead, she curiously tipped her head and gave me half a smile – I think. It was still somewhat dark, and the sun was just beginning to creep over the horizon. Before I could offer a wave or a cocky grin, a deep bark shattered the silence and ruined the moment. At least, I think it was a moment.

Mystery Girl quickly turned, leaving the dock and shushing the gray and white Husky that barreled toward the lake. "Samson! Quiet!" She snagged the dog by the collar and pulled him back toward the house.

And I haven't caught her eye since.

I'm off my game.

Kevin jabs my ribs. "Man, this isn't like you. You're never nervous around girls."

I snort and shrug him off, although what he says is true. Back home, I never have a problem talking to girls or finding a date, not that I mess around with everything on two legs. I'm selective and too involved with football to worry about female drama. I usually do the homecoming thing; maybe take someone to a party now and then. For whatever reason, there's always a girl or two willing to go out with me. I see the same pattern being repeated with Kev;

he's a regular ninth grade lothario. There must be something in the Dayton family genes.

"Like you're one to talk," I tease him. "Why aren't you over there, Casanova?"

He gives me a sly smirk. "I wouldn't want your woman falling for me. Bros before hos and all that."

I shake my head and laugh. "Glad to know you have my back."

"Always, dude."

We continue to fish, and I sigh. For reasons I don't understand, I need to man up and talk to this girl. She could leave at any time. Then, the rest of my summer would suck. I don't want to spend the next two weeks beating myself up over a missed opportunity.

~~~~

The following afternoon, I skipped the fake fishing because, let's face it, it's not getting me noticed. I decide to take out the quad instead.

Several dirt trails wind through the empty property surrounding the lake, cutting through fields and curving between hundred-year-old birch, pine, and maple trees. I know these trails like the back of my hand; I've been riding them since I was a kid. Years ago, my dad used to take me riding with him, and he'd let me drive. The memory is bittersweet. That was before my parents divorced and our family went to hell.

Today, I take the trails a little faster than I should, kicking up huge clouds of dust in my wake. We haven't had a lot of rain, and the fire danger has been set to high since we arrived. It doesn't take long before I'm covered with dirt from head to toe. I stop the quad just long enough to wipe the grime from my helmet visor before I'm off again. I round a few tight curves and fishtail in the soft dirt before I spot a figure walking the trail in the distance ahead. I'm confused; people don't usually wander this far from the lake on foot. Maybe their machine broke down. I kick it up a notch and tear up the path, scanning the side of the trail for an abandoned bike or quad like mine. I don't spot anything, and when I look forward again, I'm completely surprised.

Mystery Girl hears my machine and glances over her shoulder. She stops in her tracks, watching me skid to a stop as I slam on the brakes. The cloud of dust that followed me continues forward, covering us both.

She starts to cough, and I curse under my breath. *Nice first impression, moron.*

When the haze clears, I flip my visor and ask, "You lost?" Not, are you okay, or can I help you, or my name is Kyle, I think you're hot. No.

I am an idiot.

She clears her throat, then crosses her arms and sticks out her hip, drawing my attention to her little black running shorts. She's all legs.

"Eyes up here, buddy."

My focus snaps to her face, and she's pointing two fingers at her soft brown eyes. She smirks. "That's better."

Feeling awkward, I shift my weight, suddenly uncomfortable in my seat. "So, are you lost?"

"Yes," she says and sighs. "Sam ran off, I can't find him, and now I'm all turned around."

"Sam? Your dog?"

She shoots me a curious look, but doesn't ask how I know her pet's name. "Yes," she says again. "He disappeared while we were packing to leave."

My frown is instantaneous. Did she just say leave? I knew I was too late.

"Hello?" She waves her hand in front of my face, and I realize she's stepped closer. "Can you help me? I can cover more ground on wheels."

Hell yes, I can help you. "Sure." I hop off the quad so she can climb on, then unfasten my helmet and hand it to her. "Put this on."

She gives me a questioning look. "Why?"

"Safety first. What if you fall off?"

She scrunches her face in the cutest goddamned way. "How about you don't drive like a maniac so I won't fall off?"

Feeling more confident, I flash her a grin and step up on the quad, swinging my leg over and forcing her to scoot back on the seat. "I make no promises. You'll have to wear the helmet *and* hang on tight." Mentally, I congratulate myself on my smooth line.

"You're an ass," she says as I hear the chin strap click into place.

Okay, maybe that line wasn't so smooth.

She slides forward, her legs hugging the outside of mine. She wraps her arms around my waist, and her touch forces me to swallow. My heart starts to beat double time. This day just got a shit ton better.

Before I start the quad, I try to think of the most likely places Sam would go. He's probably digging holes around the lake, or maybe he saw a squirrel and decided to chase it. Wait. I look over my shoulder. "Sam's a Husky, right?"

"No, he's an Alaskan Malamute."

That settles it. "I know exactly where he is."

"You do?"

I nod decisively and start the quad.

Across the lake from our place lives old Mr. Grant. He keeps chickens, and I'd bet any amount of money that Sam figured that out while exploring. I can't remember how many times Mr. Grant has been over to our cottage complaining to Gram about losing another chicken to a coyote. If any dog has a wild tendency like a coyote, it's Sam.

It takes us about twenty minutes to get from where we are to the other side of the lake. I decide to take the longest route possible and maintain a steady speed because, hey, I've got a cute girl wrapped around my body and I don't want to scare her. But, then again, I kind of do. The thought of her holding me tighter sends inappropriate feelings to certain parts of my anatomy.

When we pull up into Mr. Grant's driveway, I see I was right. Sam is here. He's sitting like a perfect little puppy, next to who I assume is Mystery Girl's father. The man tries to apologize over Mr. Grant's escalating voice and flailing arms. Over to my right, I notice the yard is littered with brown feathers. It looks like a pillow exploded.

"Shit," Mystery Girl whispers after I cut the ignition. She rips the helmet from her head and jumps off the quad, the warm feeling of her body gone and immediately missed.

Mystery Girl's father notices his daughter and hands Sam's leash to her. "Get him out of here," he says with a defeated sigh as he reaches for his wallet. "How much do I owe you for the chickens?" he asks crotchety old Grant.

Uh oh. Chickens plural? Gram will be hearing about this for weeks.

Mystery Girl – I really need to get her name – walks up to me with Sam trotting happily ahead of her on his lead. She hands me my helmet. "Thanks for your help," she says. "I need to get him out of here before he causes more trouble."

She gives me a small smile and walks away.

She walks away.

My mind races. I can't let her go. What if I never see her again?

"Wait!" I hop off the quad and jog a few steps to catch up. "I'll walk you back."

She gives me a sidelong glance and tries to hide a knowing smile. "Do you think I'll get lost again?"

"The probability is high," I say and shove my hands in the pockets of my dusty jeans.

"Kyle!"

I turn around as Mr. Grant hollers my name.

"You can't leave this contraption in my driveway!"

"I know, Mr. Grant! I'll be back in a few minutes!"

He mutters something unintelligible, and I'm sure Gram will hear about this, too.

"So, your name is Kyle," Mystery Girl looks at me with one eyebrow raised.

I mirror her expression. "And yours is?"

"Addison." She smiles. "Addison Parks."

I smile back at her. "Kyle Dayton."

She nods, and we walk in silence. Any minute we'll be back at her place and then it's goodbye. I will my brain to think and form sentences. Time is slipping through my fingers.

Out of the blue, Addison says, "I know you've been watching me." She meets my eyes without a hint of shyness. "I've been waiting for you to make a move."

Is she serious? I thought she couldn't have been less interested. I have no excuse for my actions, or lack thereof, and I don't know what to say.

"Did I mistake your interest?" she asks candidly.

"Um, no," I mutter. Damn, this is awkward.

We fall silent again, and I try to think of something to change the topic of my lost man card. "Who are your friends?" finally tumbles from my mouth.

"Ashley, the blonde; she's my best friend. The brunette is my older sister, Meagan."

"Ah." I nod.

More steps. More silence.

"Do you come up here very often?" Addison asks, pulling Sam away from a rotted, hollowed out stump at the side of the road.

"Every summer," I tell her. "Usually June through mid-August; I have to get back for football camp before the school year starts."

Addison laughs.

"What's so funny?"

She doesn't elaborate. Instead, she shakes her head and asks, "What position do you play?"

"Tight end."

She raises her eyebrows and slows her walk, falling behind me a step or two. I shoot her a confused look as she blatantly stares at my ass. "What?"

She catches up to my side. "I can see why."

This girl is something else. She's cute and feisty. I like it.

We make it to the edge of the property where she's staying, and I see the loaded bed of her family's pickup truck parked in the driveway. "You're really leaving?" I ask, trying not to sound disappointed.

"Just for a few weeks. My parents bought this place; we'll be up again in late September."

While this is great news, I'll be home by then. I won't be back at the lake for another year.

"Well, Kyle, it was nice to finally meet you," she says as we stop directly behind the truck. She lowers the tailgate and nudges Sam to jump up. The dog obliges, and she slams the tailgate shut. She turns to me. "My only regret is that you didn't grow a pair and come over sooner."

My mouth falls open, and I immediately shut it. I rearrange my expression to look smug. "I'll have you know that everything has grown just fine, thanks."

She tries to suppress a grin by biting her lip. I suddenly get the urge to do the same thing.

"Addison? Is that you?" A woman's voice is calling her from the front window.

She turns. "Yeah, Mom."

"Come take care of this laundry."

"Where's Meagan?" she asks, slightly miffed.

"In the shower. C'mon, we need to get moving."

Addison starts to back away. "You heard the lady." She shrugs. "Guess I'll see you around."

I step forward to rub Sam's head, which is hanging over the tailgate. Honestly, all I want to do is get closer to this girl and keep her from leaving. "I'm sorry I didn't come by sooner."

She stops walking, returns to me, and stands on her toes to meet my eyes. "Lesson learned. Don't forget it."

To my surprise, she reaches up and runs her fingers through my hair, trying to tame the windblown mess it's become from riding without my helmet. It's useless, and she gives up. Stepping back, she stares at me.

"What?" I ask, my heart pounding.

"Are your eyes gray or blue or green?"

"They change," I say. It's the truth. Sometimes they're more one color than another, but they are a mixture of all three. I have my mother's eyes.

"Hmm," she muses and searches my face. Without another word, she backs away, then turns and heads to the house. I round the truck to watch her, and when she steps up on to the front porch, she faces me again and flashes a smile. "Don't be a stranger next summer."

Chapter Two
June 2005

In the months following my departure from Buhl Lake, Addison's last words seared into my brain. *Don't be a stranger next summer.* Those words held so much promise. Of what, I wasn't exactly sure. But I could wonder.

Okay, maybe fantasize is a better word. Wonder sounds too clean. Depending on the day, my thoughts weren't very pure. Hey, I'm a seventeen-year-old guy. Sue me.

I used her invitation to my advantage. If something stressed me, her words would sound in my mind and I knew I could get through whatever it was. Whether it be pushing through pain on the football field or taking on a few extra chores at home, I worked toward the ultimate goal. Another day down, another day closer to Buhl Lake. Don't get me wrong; I didn't dwell on Addison *every* day. Time passed as it typically does; I spent equal time with both parents, hung out with friends, nearly failed English, and went on a few dates. I didn't spend a year pining for Addison Parks...but she never left my mind, either.

Now, as I follow Gram's tan Buick La Sabre up I-75, I curse the fact that she refuses to drive even one mile per hour over the speed limit. I'm anxious to get to the cottage.

"In a hurry?" Kevin snorts from the passenger side of my truck.

"Shut up." I scowl.

He laughs and throws back the rest of his Monster. I told him about my run-in with Addison because he ripped into me about using all the gas in the quad that day. We have a bet as to when her family will arrive at the lake. My guess is next week. He says she's not coming at all.

Dick.

I turn up the radio to an obnoxious volume and Sevendust blasts in my ears. As I count each mile marker we pass, I'm convinced my jog is faster than Gram's driving.

My brother rolls down his window and tosses out his empty can.

"Hey!"

Kevin shoots me a sarcastic look and yells over the music. "You yelled at me yesterday for leaving my empties on the floor! What am I supposed to do?"

"Not throw them out the window!"

Last fall, my dad and I found a black '92 Ford F150 for dirt cheap. It was in rough shape, but I fell in love with it. Dad helped me with the repairs, but my mom was furious. She thought I needed a safer, more reliable vehicle. Regardless, the interior is in decent shape, and I want to keep it that way. I only yelled at Kevin so he would pick up his shit, not assault people on the highway with flying objects.

"Where's your common sense?" I ask.

"Where's yours? You're bent on getting up north to see a girl you don't know. Who says she'll even want to hang out with you? I mean, *if* she shows up." He grins.

I decide to ignore my brother. If I don't, I may punch him.

The trip takes us a half hour longer than it should and, as we round the lake to our cottage, we pass Addison's place. It looks empty, and Kevin shoots me a confident smirk.

~~~~

Days later, I drag the palm of my hand over my tired eyes. I'm starting to re-think my bass catching strategy. I'm still after that fish from last summer; maybe pre-dawn isn't the best time to bait him. I know he's still around because I saw him jump out of the water twice yesterday. He's probably floating under the lily pads now, watching and waiting for me to give up.

I glance to my left and stare at Addison's place, willing her to appear. Kevin hasn't forgotten our wager, and I'll be damned if I'm paying that kid fifty bucks. I need that money for my truck. I

18

haven't lost the cash yet, but I am starting to feel uneasy. What if he's right and she doesn't show? I'll never hear the end of it.

Eventually the sun rises over the tree line, exposing a fine haze that blankets the lake. The mist lets me know the water is warmer than the air, and I consider swimming today after cleaning out the cottage gutters. It's not an exciting activity, but it's one of the reasons Kevin and I are here. Ever since grandpa died a few years ago, our summer vacation has turned into an adventure in home improvement. Gram doesn't live here year round, and she needs our help to maintain the place. I don't mind lending a hand; the thought of my tiny, seventy-year-old grandmother on a ladder makes me uneasy.

My stomach growls, and I decide to call it quits. I reel in my line and stand, then take a step toward the pole holder attached to the dock. As I do, I hear the familiar pounding of footsteps down wooden stairs. My head snaps up.

Addison is making her way to the lake, just like the first day I saw her. She steps to the end of the dock, closes her eyes, and breathes in the northern air. She wraps her arms around her waist and stands completely still.

My first thought is an ecstatic, *She's here!* The second is a self-satisfied, *Take that, baby brother.* The third is, *Should I jump in the lake so she notices me?*

I decide against throwing myself in the water and stare at her instead. It's possible I could do that all day, every day. Her hair is longer and lighter than I remember, and her tan skin is offset by the white sundress she wears. It's held by thin shoulder straps, and it falls just above her knee. My eyes wander to her sandals and then back up her body again.

Before my thoughts wander too much further, she opens her eyes and locks them on mine. Her teasing words echo across the lake. "You should take a picture. It would last longer."

I answer with half a smile. "I don't have a camera."

She turns her body toward me and jerks her head toward the hill. "Mailbox?"

Confused, I ask, "What's at the mailbox?"

Her face lights up. "Me."

With that one word, she takes off running. She heads off the dock and up the stairs without a second glance. Convinced it's a race, I drop my fishing pole and sprint after her, pumping my legs as fast as I can for this early in the morning. I make it up the hill, reach the corner of our cottage, and continue past it toward the garage to find that she hasn't arrived yet. Stopping to catch my breath, I realize I don't know if she meant my mailbox or hers, so I decide to head down the road.

It doesn't take long before I see her walking toward me. I pick up the pace and can't help but notice how confident she looks. This girl is on a mission. What it is I don't know, but she seems pretty determined.

When we're steps away from each other, I open my mouth to say hi and her body crashes into mine. She wraps her arms around my neck and pulls my face toward hers, planting an all-consuming kiss on my lips. My hands wind around her waist and rest on the small of her back as I try to make sense out of what is happening. I have no idea why she's kissing me, but I'm not going to stop it. Her mouth slides perfectly against mine, and I don't have time to think about anything other than how good she feels in my arms.

A minute or two passes before Addison steps back. She hangs on to my neck and looks up at me with a playful expression. "Have you missed me?"

~~~~

Later that evening, Gram sends me to the garage to make sure it's locked up for the night. It sits separate from the house, out by the road, and we don't want any animals making themselves comfortable again. Last summer, a raccoon and her babies took up residence in the rafters after someone – Kevin – left the side door open. After Mr. Grant trapped and relocated the family, my brother and I cleaned up the huge mess they made. It was nasty and not something I care to repeat, although the baby raccoons were kind of cool. Kind of.

Just as I pull the locked door closed, I hear tires crunch against the gravel of our short drive. When I step around the corner of the garage, I find Addison behind the wheel of her dad's white Chevy.

"Hey." I smile as I approach the driver's side.

"Hey yourself." She smiles back. "I decided I need ice cream. Want to join me?"

"That depends." Of course I'm ready to jump in the cab with her, but I pretend to be indecisive. "Where you headed?"

She gives me an incredulous look. "Mooney's. Where else?"

Now there's a girl after my own heart. Mooney's carries hard ice cream, the real stuff, not that processed soft serve crap.

"I'm in." Taking a few steps back toward the cottage, I holler to Gram that I'm leaving, then round the truck to climb inside. When I close the door, I glance at Addison and notice how tiny she looks driving this four-door, extended cab beast of a vehicle. "Do you want me to drive?"

She shoots me a sarcastic look and rolls her eyes. "Please."

We drive with the windows down and classic rock on the radio. The stations are limited this far north, but I don't mind; I actually like a lot of older music.

"So, what's your favorite flavor?" I ask.

"Of ice cream? Anything involving chocolate. You?"

"Rocky road."

She smiles. "Sugar cone or waffle?"

"Definitely waffle."

She nods in agreement. "Do you work from the top down or lick around the sides?"

Her question catches me off guard. My hormone driven mind can only process the word lick. "Are we still talking about ice cream?"

She laughs. "Yes."

"Sides, then."

When we come to a stop sign, she looks me and raises an eyebrow. "And if I wasn't talking about ice cream?"

I knew there was a reason I liked this girl. "It varies. Can't be too predictable, you know?"

She smirks. "Good answer."

As we make a right turn, "Living on a Prayer" starts to play. Addison immediately reaches for the volume and turns up the music. As she sings every word, I watch her out of the corner of my eye and follow along in my head. I know the words too; my mom is a big Bon Jovi fan. When the song gets to the chorus, Addison looks at me and theatrically sings. She looks so carefree that I join in. When John gets to the part about taking his hand, I reach out toward her and she starts to laugh.

So do I.

We make it to town and when we pull in to Mooney's, it appears everyone had the same idea as Addison. There's a line.

As we wait side by side, I feel compelled to hold her hand. I haven't stopped thinking about her kiss from this morning, and I just want to touch her again. What she did was bold, and I wonder what made her do it.

"So." I try to act casual. "You kissed me this morning."

She looks up at me innocently. "Yep. I was there."

"Why?"

She shoots me a confused look. "Why was I there or why did I kiss you?"

I shake my head. "What do you think?"

We move up in line and then Addison meets my eyes. "I'm not a very patient person."

What does that mean?

We're next at the counter, and I watch Addison scan the selections. I spot the Superman ice cream and consider getting it; it's the only flavor I would eat when I was little. I choose my standard rocky road instead, just like we discussed in the truck. I don't need my lips stained blue. Addison gets two scoops of chocolate brownie chunk and takes a huge bite as soon as it's given to her. I'm impressed that she actually eats, not like some girls who order nothing but a side salad. That always confused me. If we're going out to a restaurant, eat, damn it! I didn't bring you here to look at the food.

When it's time to pay, Addison won't let me cover her dessert. It's annoying, but I don't make a big deal about it. We make our way back to the truck and sit on the bumper, enjoying our cones.

Halfway through, I can't take it anymore. "What did you mean you're not a patient person?"

She catches a drip of ice cream with her thumb. "You took your sweet time talking to me last summer. If you hadn't found me looking for Sam that day would you ever have spoken to me?"

The back of my neck gets hot. I don't want to appear embarrassed in front of her, but she's got me there. "I was working on a plan."

She sighs. "You didn't need a plan. Why do guys overthink things?"

My eyebrows shoot up. "Why do guys overthink things? Why do girls?"

She ignores me and breaks off a piece of her waffle cone. "I want to spend time with you; I want to get to know you. I kissed you because I don't want to wait for you to figure that out."

I try not to grin, but I can't help myself. "Well, thanks for the hint. I really enjoyed it."

She smiles. "So did I."

Deciding I don't need the rest of my ice cream, I stand and toss it in a nearby trash can. When I return, I sit closer to her and say, "I may need a reminder from time to time, though. So I don't forget how much you want to see me."

She arches an eyebrow, then leans forward to leave a chocolate kiss on my lips. "I think that can be arranged."

Chapter Three

"So," Addison says as she wraps her hands around my arm and leans against me, "my parents want to meet you."

"That's a coincidence," I say as I move Sam's leash to my right hand. "Gram wants to meet you."

Her eyebrows shoot up in surprise. "Which meeting should we have first?"

We stare at each other for a few seconds and then answer in unison. "Gram."

She giggles and I laugh, but it's nervous laughter. My past relationships were never long enough to warrant a formal parent meeting; the introductions were a quick hello and goodbye. As we walk and I think about it, my relationship with Addison definitely fits the short category. We've only hung out a few days, but we've spent every spare minute of those days together. I should have seen this coming; I'm sure her mom and dad want to make sure I'm not some creep corrupting their daughter.

Addison's fingers slide down my arm to grab my hand with both of hers. It's crazy how my body registers her every move; I even find myself aware of her proximity when we're not touching. Whatever is going on between us is happening fast, and it's something I've never experienced with any other girl.

"I think we should take the canoe out later," she says as we walk. "I didn't get a chance to use it last year because Ashley and Meagan were afraid we'd tip."

"Speaking of," I say, "where is your sister?"

"At home, getting ready for college." She rolls her eyes. "It's all she can talk about. I'm sick of hearing about Michigan Tech."

"What's wrong with Michigan Tech?"

"It's not the school." She shrugs one shoulder. "I'm just tired of listening to my parents fawn over their golden child."

We stop walking to let Samson explore the side of the road, and I catch Addison's eyes. "I'm sure you're exaggerating, but I'll play along. Why is Meagan the favorite?"

She frowns. "Because she's going to college to major in pharmacology; she'll have a *real* career, as my mother says. I don't want that."

"What do you want?"

"To dance. Professionally. I've already been working some scholarship leads; I want to get in to Julliard."

I'm impressed. Unlike Addison, I have no idea what direction I'm headed. I don't know what school to go to or what to major in, and my grades won't qualify me for any financial help. My high school offers a small athletic scholarship, but my chances of earning it are slim at best. "That's amazing. You dance?"

"I have since I was four. Ballet, mostly, but I take modern dance, too."

I nod approvingly. "I should have known."

"How?"

Stepping back, my eyes run from her hips to her ankles. "I knew those legs were lethal for more reasons than one."

She playfully punches my arm, and I jump back, smiling. "Hey, you were staring at my ass last summer."

She bumps her shoulder against me as we start to walk again. "Yeah, well. It's the only thing I could see from a distance besides your black hair. Maybe it's a good thing we didn't meet until I was leaving."

"Why's that?"

"Because I got an up-close and personal look at those color-shifting eyes." She scrutinizes my face, and I stare at the light freckles on the bridge of her nose. "More green than blue today," she decides.

"And that's bad?" I ask. "That you saw my eyes, I mean."

"A girl can get lost in those eyes," she says matter-of-factly. "I bet the panties melt off the girls back home."

My laugh sounds like a bark. "That doesn't happen!"

"Really? There's not a line of girls beating down your door?"

"No." I shake my head. "I go out on a few dates now and then."

"So, no girlfriend?"

"No. Do you honestly think I'd be making out with you if there were?"

She shrugs. "I would hope not."

"Well, just so you know, I don't believe in cheating."

When I was twelve years old, my father had an affair with Lydia, the dental hygienist at his practice. They're married now, but I never understood, even as a kid, why he couldn't have left my mom first, before he started messing around. While I'll always care about my dad, I don't like what he did. Our family is broken because he couldn't keep it in his pants.

Addison disrupts my thoughts by reaching for Sam's lead. I stop walking to hand it to her and when she takes it, she stands on her toes and rewards me with a slow kiss that goes from sweet to sexy in seconds. I set my hands on her waist to steady her and a deep understanding takes root in my brain: if we do nothing else in the coming weeks but walk Sam and kiss, I'll be a happy man.

When she steps away, I ask, "Was that for not having a girlfriend?"

She smiles. "Yeah."

"I take it there's no boyfriend back home either?"

She shakes her head. "He dumped me."

I can't stop myself from frowning. The idea of her dating some jerk doesn't sit well with me, which is absurd because I've only really known her for a few days. "When?"

"After prom."

So, he's a complete asshole. "How long had you guys been together?"

"Only a couple of months." She starts to walk again, tugging on Sam's leash to get his attention. "It wasn't that big of a deal, really."

I have the urge to punch this guy I've never met. We walk a few feet and then she looks me in the eye. "I can tell you're irritated. Trust me; he didn't break my heart. I'm happy it ended."

Okay, good. My shoulders relax, and I wind my arm around her waist. As I lean over to kiss the top of her head, I catch the scent of her shampoo. Her hair smells like strawberries. "I'm glad you weren't hurt."

She leans into my side, and we circle the lake, ending where we began.

~~~~

Two days later, I pray that I put on enough deodorant to mask the smell from the sweat in my armpits.

Addison's father glares at me as he passes the tossed salad. Her parents requested my presence at dinner because Addison and I got caught red-handed. In our defense, we were only kissing. Yes; I kind of had her backed up against the side of my truck, and yes, her legs were kind of wrapped around my waist. But, that's only because she jumped from the bed of the truck and I caught her. It was entirely her fault that she was wrapped around my body. Deciding to walk forward and pin her against the door...well, that was my idea.

"Kyle." Beth, Addison's mother, pulls my attention away from her agitated husband. "Addison was telling us you live in Fenton."

I clear my abnormally scratchy throat and respond, "Yes, ma'am, that's right." Our addresses were one of the first things Addison and I exchanged when we met up again. She lives south of me, in the Waterford area. It's a town I've never visited, but I plan to, if her parents don't take out a restraining order.

"That's, what, about a half-hour away from us?" she asks her daughter.

Addison nods, her mouth purposefully stuffed with grilled chicken. She's just as uncomfortable as I am, yet I can't help but notice how good she looks, even with puffy food-filled cheeks.

"You'll be a senior this year, too, then?" Beth asks me as she takes a bite.

"Yes, ma'am, that's right." Apparently those four words are all I'm capable of saying.

"What colleges are you considering?"

Robert, Addison's dad, startles me. His voice sounds deep and rough, like the man swallowed rocks for breakfast. I don't know if that's his natural tone or his 'I'm-fucking-pissed-as-hell-keep-your-hands-off-my-daughter' tone. It's the only voice I've heard him use, mainly because the first time he spoke to me was when he growled to put Addison down.

I use my standard answer to the college question. "I'm looking at a few."

"What will you major in?"

I don't have an answer. As I push some rice around my plate, I realize I'm being interrogated; I should have expected nothing less. I don't want to give Addison's parents another reason to dislike me, so I find some fake confidence and meet Robert's eyes. "I'm torn on that as well."

"Between what, exactly?" he presses.

My mind races as I consider lying. I should probably say I want to be a doctor or a lawyer. Instead, "My father is a dentist and my mother is an accountant, neither field interests me," comes out of my mouth. "My main goal is to play my hardest this fall and earn a football scholarship."

This piques Robert's interest, and his face relaxes a bit. "Really? What schools are scouting you?"

Shit. That's not what I meant. Addison gives my knee a reassuring squeeze under the table, and I decide to lie. I'll confess to her later, in private.

Forcing a self-deprecating laugh, I say, "Coach doesn't like me to talk about it. He says it will jinx the season. None of the scouts want word getting to the other schools, either; I'm sure you understand."

Addison's dad gives me a curt nod. "Impressive. I get the sense some big names are looking at you. Big Ten schools perhaps?"

My mouth opens but nothing comes out.

"Rob, leave the boy alone," Beth interjects from the opposite end of the table. "He said he can't talk about it."

I shoot her a grateful glance.

"Has Addison mentioned Julliard?" she asks me.

A smile I can't contain breaks across my face. I look at Addison. "Yes. There's no doubt in my mind she'll get in."

Addison blushes and stares at her plate.

"I don't doubt she will be accepted, either." Beth reaches for her wine glass. "What I do doubt is her ability to make a living as a dancer. Maybe you could talk some sense into her, Kyle, since you have your choice of colleges. As an athlete, you know you can't rely on your body forever. I feel she should minor in dance."

Addison's brown eyes flash. "Really, Mom? You're going to bring this up now?"

"We're on the topic of colleges," Beth says innocently, "and Julliard is quite expensive."

"I told you I'm looking into scholarships. I'm willing to take on the loan debt."

"But, you'll need a co-signer without a job. Your father and I aren't..."

"Beth."

All eyes swing to Robert and his baritone voice. "Enough."

Addison's mom lets out an exaggerated sigh, and she levels her eyes at her daughter. "I love you. I only want what's best."

Addison's shoulders sag. "You've said that before."

Uncomfortable tension hangs in the air and a knot forms in my stomach. I want to hold Addison and tell her she can do whatever she damn well pleases. Instead, I sneak another piece of chicken to Sam, who has been sitting by my chair the entire time I've been here. I don't want Addison's mother to think I dislike her cooking, but my appetite has disappeared.

Dinner is finished in relative silence. Addison stands to help her mother clear the empty dishes from the table, leaving me alone with her father. My nerves jump into overdrive at being scrutinized by such an intimidating man.

He runs his napkin over his mouth and then tosses it on to his plate. Crossing his arms, he leans back in his chair. "So, Kyle. I guess now would be the appropriate time to tell you I own a gun."

I swallow and rub my sweaty palms against my cargo shorts. I thought this only happened in the movies. "Yes, sir."

"I don't like what I saw today, mainly because I remember being your age. I know what's going through your mind," he says. "Addison is my baby. If you hurt her, I hurt you. Understand?"

I nod.

"My daughter has a bright future ahead of her, be that in dance or whatever else she decides to do. She doesn't need anything getting in her way, if you know what I mean."

I don't know what he means. Does he think I'll be too much of a distraction if I stay in her life? Or does he think I'm not good enough for her, period?

He sighs and reaches into his jeans pocket, then shocks me by flipping several condoms on to the table. I stare at them wide-eyed. What the hell?

"This doesn't mean you have my blessing or I condone what you're doing," he says as he rubs his hand over his face. "But I know I can't stop it and I don't want her pregnant."

Holy shit! Is this a test? If I take what he's offering, it's like admitting we're sleeping together. Which we're not. I won't lie; I've thought about it. Imagined it.

"Mr. Parks," I protest, "Addison and I...we're not...we haven't..."

"Doesn't mean you won't," he cuts me off. "How many more weeks are you up here?" He shakes his head. "Take them. Trust me. I'm thirty-six years old. Addison's sister is eighteen. You do the math."

Now I feel obligated to take them. My fingers shake as I cover his offering and slide it off the table into my hand. I stuff the condoms in my pocket just as Addison and her mother return from the kitchen.

"Ready for dessert?" Addison asks.

Since I had to meet her parents tonight, we decided she should meet Gram too, and knock out all the introductions at once. Gram's making apple pie.

"Yes," I say eagerly and stand, bumping my legs against the bottom of the tabletop. They feel stiff from sitting; my whole body is coiled with tension.

"Then let's go."

She rounds the table and grabs my hand, pulling me toward the front door. Given the conversation I just had with her dad, I don't feel right touching her. At least, not in front of him. I pull my hand from hers and offer it to her father in an awkward gesture. "Thank you for dinner."

He shakes my hand and his brown eyes lock on mine, silently confirming he's not above killing me. I give him a nod so he knows I understand.

As I walk past Addison's mother, I tell her the same thing. "Dinner was great. Thank you."

"You're welcome. Feel free to come by anytime." Her forced smile tells me she's saying that to be nice.

Once we're outside and off the front porch, I fill my lungs with the cool evening air and let it out in a rush.

"That completely sucked," Addison says as she grabs my hand. "I'm so sorry. You looked miserable."

"You have no idea. Did you know your dad owns a gun?"

"Jesus." She rolls her eyes. "He threatened you old school, didn't he?"

31

I nod. As we walk toward my place and Gram, I replay the evening. "Oh, hey," I tell her when we're halfway there, "I want you to know, no colleges are scouting me. I went with your dad's assumption because I thought it might make him hate me less."

Her eyes light up. "Well played."

"You're not mad?"

Addison's face twists. "No. You did what you had to do. I don't care that you're not being scouted. I don't care what college you go to or what you major in; hell, I don't care if you even go to school."

"Really?"

She stops walking and faces me. "All I care about is that you're happy. As long as you follow your heart, who has the right to say what you do is wrong? Take me, for example. I want to perform for a living because I feel complete when I dance. That feeling can't be wrong. Just like the way I feel when I'm with you; no one can tell me that feeling isn't real."

A slow smile stretches across my face as I pull her body against mine. "Thank you."

"For what?"

"For liking me with the full knowledge that I have no direction."

Her free hand curls around my neck. "You're easy to like."

I realize I feel the same way. It hasn't taken long for Addison to weave herself into my every thought. "You're easy to like, too."

Her smile matches mine before my lips meet hers.

Chapter Four

Days later, I spend the morning scraping old paint off the deck railing. Even with Metallica blaring in my ears from my iPod, I picture Addison's face. You would think we might need some distance after all the time we've spent together, but the opposite is true. I go to bed thinking about her. I wake up thinking about her.

I'm whipped.

What's funny is I don't care. I knew things were happening fast when she first arrived, and I thought it might be because everything was new. But here we are, weeks into the summer, and I'm still excited to see her each day.

Glancing over my shoulder, I check on Kevin to make sure he's still scraping. I swear that kid hates any kind of manual labor. He can talk and write for hours; I usually have him help me with my homework. Me, I like using my hands. I don't have to concentrate as much and it's easier to daydream.

We work in silence with our ear buds in place until lunch time, when Gram appears with two plates of sandwiches and chips. She hands me my peanut butter and jelly, and I notice she's cut the bread down the center.

"Gram," I groan. "I'm seventeen. You don't have to cut my food."

She sets her hands on her lower back. "Oh, leave me alone. It's a habit."

"I like my sandwiff cut," Kevin says around a mouthful. "You can keep doing it for me."

What a kiss ass I think.

Gram lovingly pats his shoulder.

"You two are moving faster than I expected," she says as she looks over the deck. "We'll have this thing repainted in no time."

"That's only because Kyle wants to spend every minute with Addison," my brother teases. "He's working so fast I'm surprised he hasn't scraped his fingers off."

I glare at him. "You only think I work fast because you're so slow."

"I'm not slow! You're just worried your girl might find something better to do without you."

"You're just jealous you don't have a girl."

"Boys." Gram tries to give us her stern look which isn't stern at all. "Stop it. You're acting like kids."

"But we are." I grin. "You cut my sandwich."

She walks over to me and swats my arm. "I'm heading into town. You two are eating machines." She steps toward the sliding door. "I should be back in an hour or two."

Kevin and I nod.

After finishing my lunch, I stand to get back to work. My brother, however, needs more to eat. As he heads inside, he asks, "You want anything?"

I shake my head no.

As I reach for my ear buds and pick up my iPod, I hear a familiar voice.

"Anyone home?"

I spin around. "Hey."

"Hi." Addison smiles as she rounds the deck. "What are you doing?"

"Getting rid of this old paint. What are you doing?"

"Coming over to ask you out."

She makes it to the steps and my pulse picks up. "I thought we already had plans."

"We do." She walks toward me and wraps her arms around my waist. "But, I thought of something fun."

Everything we do is fun. "What might that be?" I ask.

"It's a surprise. Come over to my place at eight. You'll see."

This will be my first time inside her cottage since the dinner from hell. "Are your parents going to be home?"

"Yes, but don't worry about them."

"Do you need me to bring anything?"

"Nope, just you." She squeezes me tight then backs away. "I'll see you later."

"That's all I get?" I complain. "A hug and a goodbye?"

She laughs. "I'd stay, but I have to help my mom clean. If I'm not back soon, she might change her mind about tonight."

"Fine." I pout.

Addison leaves the way she came, throwing a wave over her shoulder just before she's out of sight. I pick up my iPod, turn on the music, and slow down removing the paint.

I need something to pass the time until eight o'clock.

~ ~ ~ ~

"Where did you get this?" I ask as I step inside the tent.

Addison zips the door closed behind us. "It's my parent's. My dad used to take Meagan and me camping when I was younger."

I look around the nylon room. Addison has pitched a tent in her front yard; two sleeping bags lie on the ground and an electric lantern glows in between. "So, we're having a sleepover?" I wiggle my eyebrows.

"I wish," she says. "No; I thought this would be a way to spend some time alone. My parents agreed as long as you leave by ten."

I look around the room again. Damn curfew.

"You think it's lame," she says and starts to unzip the door.

"No!" I reach for her and pull her close. "I think it's awesome."

"You do?"

"I'm tired of having Gram and my brother for an audience."

Because the atmosphere is more relaxed around my family, we spend the majority of our time at my cottage. If we're not taking a walk or riding the quad or going for ice cream, you can usually find us on my grandmother's couch – with two other sets of eyes in the room.

"Good," Addison says. She takes my hand and pulls me down to sit on one of the sleeping bags. "I don't care what we do in here. I just wanted to be alone with you."

I smile and take her other hand. Now, we're facing each other with our fingers intertwined. We sit in silence for a few moments, but it's not awkward. I run my thumbs over hers, and she watches me.

"What did you think last summer?" she asks. "When we first met?"

35

I take a few seconds to come up with an answer. How honest should I be? Let's face it; I had a lot of *thoughts* when we met and afterward. "I thought I was an idiot for not talking to you sooner," I say.

She bites her lip. "I was kicking myself for not talking to you, too."

"Why didn't you?"

"Meagan told me I had to make you work for it." She shakes her head. "I shouldn't have listened to my sister."

I chuckle. "No; you shouldn't have."

We're quiet again until she confesses, "I thought about your eyes all year."

"You did?" I'm surprised.

"Yeah." She blushes. "Is that weird?"

"Kind of."

She lets go of my hand and pushes my knee. "Thanks a lot!"

"I didn't mean you're weird!" I grab her hand back. "I meant it's weird to be thought of that way."

She looks confused. "What way?"

"I don't know. Like, at all."

"Come on." She looks doubtful.

"I told you before. I don't date a lot. It's strange to have someone be honest with me."

In the few relationships I've had, none of the girls told me how they felt. We didn't have in-depth conversations about my eyes or what we wanted to do after high school. They were movie and dance dates that usually ended with a kiss or, if I was lucky, more.

"Well, I think about you a lot," she says. "More than I probably should."

I grin. "We have the same sickness. I've never thought about another girl so much in my life."

She looks shy at my admission. I don't know why. She has to know she's hot. Not only is she pretty, but she's fun to be around. She's always up for anything, and she can be a sarcastic wise ass like me.

Scooting back on the sleeping bag, I pull her toward me. I lay down on my back and she moves, curling against my side. She fits there perfectly.

"I wish we were really camping," she says.

"Me too."

"Meagan and I used to have so much fun with my dad," she says. "Then, he started getting these killer migraines. He still does. He never knows when they're going to hit, so he decided we should stay out of the woods for extended periods of time."

"That sucks. Didn't your mom take you?"

Addison shakes her head. "She's an indoor girl."

I run my fingers over her arm. "What else do you like to do? When you're at home, I mean."

"Dance mostly," she says. "I'm in class four nights a week." She lifts her head to look at me. "We put on two big shows every year; one of them is in December. You should come." Her eyes light up. "I'm a senior this year, so I'll get a solo."

She wants to see me six months from now? "I'll be there."

Her smile gets bigger. "What else do you do other than football?"

"As far as sports go, that's it."

"Can I come and watch you play? I can pretend to scout you." She giggles.

"Hey!" I squeeze her to my side.

"Seriously. I'll bring a clipboard and everything."

The image makes me laugh and she joins me; I wouldn't put it past her to do just that. Secretly though, I'm excited by the thought of her sitting in the stands and watching me. Cheering for me. My mom and dad make it to some of my games, but that's to be expected. Addison doesn't have to support me and realizing she wants to makes a smile break across my face.

I decide to tease her. "What would you be scouting me for? Do you recruit for a team?"

"Yes." She pulls her body up higher on my chest. "Team Addison."

My eyebrows shoot up. "How big is the roster?"

"Only two people." She leans closer. "We're super selective when it comes to the players."

Good to know. "When do tryouts start?" I ask.

Her eyes leave mine and travel to my lips. "How about now?"

I pretend to mull it over. "Hang on. Let me check my schedule."

I start to sit up and she laughs, pushing me back down. "Just kiss me," she says.

Can do.

My mouth catches hers, and for the first time her tongue searches for mine. I tip my head to help her find it while my free hand makes its way to the back of her neck. This is the deepest kiss we've shared and I don't want it to end; I want it to move on to other things. Unfortunately, her parents are steps away.

When she pulls back, I'm a little winded. "How am I doing so far?" I ask.

"With what?"

"My tryout."

"Really good. I'd say you're the number one draft pick."

"Excellent." I set my forehead against hers. "I really want a spot on this team."

She laughs. "Bribing the scout helps."

"How so?"

"Keep up the long walks and the sexy smiles. Kisses like that last one work, too. Oh, and don't forget to occasionally work in the yard without a shirt. That's a surefire winner."

My eyes get big. "You've been spying on me!"

"All the time."

Have I mentioned how much I like this girl?

Without warning, I reach for her side and tickle her ribs. "No!" She laughs as she tries to roll away. "Stop!"

I do – for a second. She rolls on to her back as I hover over her. "What makes you think you can get away with stalking me?" I tease.

"I won't do it again. I promise." She grins.

"Liar." I smile and start to torture her again.

"Ahhh! Not my sides!"

Addison has nowhere to go inside the tent, so it's easy for me to catch her. She wiggles and laughs beneath my hands as she tries to retaliate, but I'm only ticklish on the bottom of my feet.

"That won't work," I say as she giggles.

"You have to be ticklish somewhere!"

I catch her wrists and pin them beside her head. "That's for me to know and you to find out."

She meets my eyes as she catches her breath. "Gladly."

Wow.

I'm in the middle of kissing her again when her dad interrupts. "Addison!" He must be standing on the front porch.

She pulls her mouth from mine. "Yeah?"

"I can see you."

38

Immediately I release her hands and sit back on my heels. I should have realized our shadows could be seen with the tent lit from inside.

"It's just a tickle fight, Dad." She rolls her eyes.

"Don't test my trust," he warns.

Silent seconds pass before a door slams. I let out a breath. "He does not like me," I say.

"It's not you." Addison sits up so her face is level with mine. "It's guys in general. He didn't like my old boyfriend. Why would he like my new one?"

I do a double-take and she notices. Scrunching up her nose, she asks, "Too fast? We don't need labels; I was just trying to explain..."

I cut her off. "It's okay." Tucking a piece of hair behind her ear, I ask, "I take it I made the team?"

She laughs. "I guess so."

"That was a quick draft. Are you sure?"

"Positive."

Yes!

We spend the rest of our time curled together, talking about everything from school to music to more serious topics. I confide in her about my dad and Lydia; I don't know why, it just comes out. She tells me more about her parents and their opinions regarding her future. When her father reappears to inform us it's time for me to leave, I don't want to go. I could spend all night talking with Addison. She's the first person I can see myself doing that with; even our silences are comfortable.

"I'll see you tomorrow," I say as I step out of the tent.

"Are you still working on the deck?" she asks.

I nod.

"Don't be surprised if I show up to help. Will Gram mind?"

When Gram first met Addison, they hit it off immediately. Gram welcomed her with open arms and an open heart; they shared plenty of laughs at my expense while eating apple pie. Kevin used his big mouth to inform everyone of my nervousness when I first laid eyes on Addison last summer, which led to her informing both of them how inarticulate I was when we finally did meet. After I walked her home, Gram told me she had a good feeling about our neighbor.

"Hang on to that girl," she said. "She's spunky and fun and gorgeous. Reminds me of myself at that age."

I told her she wouldn't have to tell me twice.

"Of course she won't mind," I answer Addison's question. "Gram loves you."

She smiles. "I like her a lot too."

I take a few steps, then turn around. "Sleep tight," I say.

"I'll try. I'm pretty sure I'll be up thinking about a certain someone."

I feel like throwing my fist in the air. *Perfect.*

Chapter Five

Winding her arm around my grandmother's thin shoulders, Addison gives her a quick hug. "Good morning, Gram." She drops an overstuffed backpack by her feet and then plops into one of our kitchen chairs.

"Mornin' honey," my Gram says and pats her hand. "Ready for the big trip today?"

Addison smiles. "I think so."

"What did you put in there?" I ask, stepping from the kitchen into the small dining area. I kick her backpack and then hand Gram her coffee mug. "We're hiking. You're going to have to carry that."

Addison narrows her eyes at me. "I can handle it. I assure you." She looks at Gram. "I think he's giving me a hard time. He shouldn't do that this early in the morning."

Gram nods as she sips. "I agree." She turns on me. "You be nice."

I step back in surrender. "I'll get my stuff and we can head out," I say to both ladies.

Today, I'm taking Addison hiking at Tahquamenon Falls in the Upper Peninsula. Not only will we be alone, I thought it would be nice to get out of town for a while. I've only been up to the falls one other time, back when my parents were still married and I was six. It's a vague memory, but I do remember the loud, rushing water. I also remember Kevin being four and crying about a dropped popsicle. Why my mind hangs on to that, I don't know.

Speaking of my brother, I nearly run him over on my way to the bedroom we share to grab my pack.

"What's your hurry?" He yawns and pulls up his shirt to scratch his stomach caveman-style.

"Addison and I are outta here," I say and bump past him. I snag my backpack and start to head downstairs.

"Ah, hiking day," he says and frowns. "You know, I've been stuck entertaining Gram this whole time while you're off screwing around. Did it ever occur to you that I might need to get out of here once and a while too?"

"So?" I shrug. "Take the quad and hit the trails. Or take the boat out."

"That boat motor's been leaking oil for two summers." He crosses his arms. "You know I'll get stranded in the middle of the lake."

I shoot him an evil grin. "Make sure you take the oars."

He lunges at me and tries to catch me in a headlock. I'm not in the mood to wrestle and I dodge him, heading for the stairs. I take them two at a time and make it back to the kitchen in seconds, with Kevin hot on my heels. "Stop," I tell him and shove his shoulder.

Gram peers at us over her mug. "What are you two doing?"

"Kevin's acting his age," I say and shove him again. He slugs me in the arm. Addison laughs.

"See. She thinks I'm charming." Kevin winks at my girl.

"She does not."

"Addison," Kevin rounds the table, "tell your boyfriend that you want both Dayton men to escort you to the falls today."

My mouth falls open. "What? No way!"

Addison raises her eyebrows and looks between Kevin and me. Kevin kneels by her side and gives her the most dejected puppy dog expression he can muster.

"You look demented," I tell my brother. "That's not going to work."

Addison tilts her head and studies the slightly younger version of myself. Kev has my dark hair, but he wears it shorter than I do, and his eyes are always the same shade of gray. His face is more angular than my own, but you wouldn't be able to tell that by the way he has it twisted. Addison places one hand beneath his chin and squeezes his cheeks, so his lips pucker.

"Now he looks like a demented fish." She grins at me.

Both Gram and I snort with laughter as Kevin scowls.

"Aw." Addison releases his face. "Don't be upset. You're a cute demented fish. Of course you can come with us."

Now I'm the one making a face.

"Sweet!" Kevin jumps to his feet. "Give me five minutes."

"Make it ten," I grumble. "You need to shower, and I don't want your smelly ass in my truck."

"Kyle!" Gram snaps.

"Sorry, Gram. But he reeks." I narrow my eyes at him. "In more ways than one."

Kevin shrugs me off and bounds up the stairs.

"Addison," Gram says, "did you see what Kyle planted out front? He transformed that whole dead area; it looks so much better." She turns to me. "You should show her."

I gesture for Addison to follow me. It might be the only time we get alone today, thanks to my brother.

We head out the front door, and I point out an area by the porch where Gram has battled a dead patch of grass for years. "All I did was buy some plants."

"Are those hydrangeas?" Addison asks as she heads down the stairs and bends to sniff to the blue flowers.

"Yeah." I move to stand beside her and explain the other bushes I've tried to arrange artfully. "There's a Painter's Palate and a rhododendron in the back. Those get pretty big."

"How do you know?"

"Because the tag on the pot said so."

Addison takes her time to look over the plants, touching the leaves on each one. "What are these?" she asks, looking down at the ground.

"Begonias," I say. "Pink is Gram's favorite color."

Addison's eyes meet mine. Her expression softens and she stares at me, as if just realized I'm standing here. "It's beautiful, Kyle."

Before I can tell her she only likes my work because she likes me, she says, "Oh! This can be your first picture."

"What?"

She reaches into her jacket pocket and pulls out a camera. "I bought this for you."

I take the small silver Kodak from her and turn it over in my hand. "Why?"

"Because I told you a picture would last longer and you said you didn't have a camera." She grins.

"You got me a camera so I'll stop staring at you?" I'm surprised she remembered what I said.

"Absolutely not. You can keep doing that."

She shows me how to turn it on, where the batteries go, and where the memory card is. Then she steps out of the way. I take a picture of Gram's plants, then make her stand in front of them to take another.

"Here." She reaches for my hand and pulls me next to her. "Let's try to get the both of us."

I hold the camera at arm's length as she presses her cheek against mine. I press the shutter and we look at the result. Half our faces are cut out of the frame.

"Okay, let's try that again."

She kisses me this time and, again, the picture ends up being just our chins. After several more tries, we're laughing like little kids. I can't take a decent picture to save my life.

"Are you two ready?"

Kevin's voice forces us to turn around. His hair is damp, he's dressed, and he's raring to go. He must have taken the world's fastest shower. Begrudgingly, I follow him into the house where we gather our things, say goodbye to Gram, and promise not to speed.

~~~~

Unlocking the front door, Addison flips the light switch, and tosses her backpack on the floor. "My feet hurt."

My arms circle around her from behind. "You should have worn better shoes." Her red Converse don't look like they offer much support.

"I guess I didn't think we were *for real* hiking. I thought we'd be walking along a scenic overlook or something." She sighs under my arms and leans back against my chest. "I'm beat."

Her head rolls to the side and I take the opportunity to push her hair off her neck, exposing her skin to my lips. She wiggles and laughs, then turns around and places her hands on my shoulders. "I take it you're not tired?"

"I haven't had you to myself all day." Suspicious, I glance around the room. "Are you sure your parents are gone?"

"Did you see the truck in the driveway?" she asks. "They said they might go out for dinner."

She pushes against me and moves my body toward the kitchen, where there's a note on the counter. *Out for dinner and a movie. Make sure to bring Sam in. Remember, no visitors after ten.*"

"I take it by visitors they mean me?" I ask.

She nods and presses her lips into a thin line.

"What happens after ten? Do you turn into a pumpkin?" I tease.

"Worse." Her expression changes and she leans into me dramatically. "A vampire."

I grin. "You don't look very scary."

"It's not my appearance you have to worry about."

She kisses my chin and then her breath is hot against my neck. She bites me and a jolt of electricity shoots up my spine. That has to be the hottest thing any girl has ever done to me. Ever.

When she leans back, her eyes dance. "Did you feel that?"

Yeah, in my pants. "Are you trying to kill me?"

She looks surprised. "I didn't hurt you did I?" Concerned, she starts to inspect my neck.

"No," I laugh. I'm not about to admit other parts of me ache.

A loud whine at the back door pulls our attention away from one another. "I think Sam knows we're here," I say.

We leave the kitchen and walk into the living area where a sliding door leads to a deck. Through the glass I can see Sam pawing at the door handle. He jumps up when he sees us, excited.

Addison opens the door to let him in and he rushes past his owner, straight to me. I bend down and rub my hands roughly along his sides. "Hey, buddy."

He licks my nose, and I lean away with a laugh.

"Do you two need some time alone?" Addison asks with a hand on her hip.

We both look at her. "What? He likes me."

She kneels down to pet Sam, too. "I know. I'm glad he does."

Sam licks Addison's cheek, then pads off toward the kitchen in search of his food dish. She stands and grimaces. "Ugh."

"What is it?"

"My stupid foot."

"Which one?"

She holds her right foot out toward me and, since I'm already crouched down, I grab it and remove her shoe, then her sock. Looking over her toes and her heel, I find the problem. "You've got a nasty blister." It looks like the back of her shoe rubbed her skin away and it's bleeding a little.

"Great," she sighs.

I let go of her foot, and she pulls off her other shoe and sock. "C'mon."

I follow her as she hobbles down the hall. At the first darkened doorway, she stops and flips on a light. "Make yourself comfortable. I'm going to get a band aid."

I find myself staring at Addison's room. It's tiny. Beneath the window sits an unmade twin size bed with tan sheets and a purple comforter. Shoes and piles of clothes are scattered on the floor; I think I spot one of Sam's rawhide bones sticking out from under the bed. Across the room, I find a dresser with one of those TV/DVD combos sitting on top. I walk over to it and pick up the small stack of movies placed there.

"Do you want to watch something?" Addison asks from behind me.

I look toward her as I sort through the DVDs. "*Footloose, Dirty Dancing,* and *Strictly Ballroom,*" I say as I make a face. "I'm sensing a theme here."

"Hey!" Addison reaches out and grabs the next movie. "*Flashdance* is a classic."

"Isn't that about a stripper?" I take it from her hand.

"You haven't seen it?"

"No. Why would I?"

"Have you seen any of these?" she asks.

When I shake my head no again, she says, "We should watch *Footloose.* It's about a guy who dances. Maybe it will inspire you."

I snort. "I highly doubt that."

Addison takes the DVD from me and puts it into the player. I really don't want to watch this movie, but I want to spend time with her. If watching this is what she wants to do, I'll suffer through it.

Once we've shut the door, hit the light, and arranged ourselves around one another on her bed, Addison pushes play on the remote. The opening credits roll, and I'm subjected to a bunch of random feet wearing bad '80s shoes dancing to the song

"Footloose." Addison's back is to my chest, and I frown over her head. This is going to suck.

About a half hour in, as Ariel plays chicken with a train, I start to fall asleep. My lack of interest in this movie, coupled with our hike, has worn me out. Plus, Addison's body is warm pressed against me. I barely register her move until her lips find mine.

"Hey, sleepyhead," she says.

My eyes pop open. "Hey. Sorry." I blink.

"You're not into this, are you?"

"The movie?" I glance over her head to see Kevin Bacon start to dance inside a barn. "Ah..."

She laughs. "It's okay." Her mouth finds mine again and then she whispers, "Would you rather do something else?"

Um, yes. I respond with a lazy smile. "What did you have in mind?"

She pushes herself up until she's sitting on her knees. Her hands find the bottom of my shirt and start to lift it as she leans in toward me again. "How about we start with getting rid of this?"

Sounds good to me. I prop myself up to catch her mouth with mine as she raises my shirt to my shoulders. I lift one arm, then the other, then break our kiss to help her pull it off over my head. She tosses it on the floor.

Her eyes follow her fingers as she trails them over my chest, around my ribs, and down my stomach to land on the waistband of my jeans. All my muscles tense as she moves forward and kisses her way back up the same path. When she reaches my shoulder, she slides one leg over my waist and settles herself across my hips.

Damn. Instantly, my jeans feel two sizes too small.

She sets her elbows on either side of my head, and I realize it's my turn. I grab her shirt and pull it off, coming face to face with her chest. The changing light from the television tells me her bra is pale pink, and I want to take that off too, but I'm not sure how far she wants to go. I mean, we've messed around a little, but nothing like this.

Instead, I decide to kiss her neck, her jawline, and her chin. My hands trace her spine, and I think she shivers.

"Are you cold?" I whisper beneath her ear.

She shakes her head and pushes herself upright. Her hands disappear behind her back and when I see them again, they're sliding her bra down her arms. My eyes must double in size because she quietly laughs, "This can't be the first time you've seen some of these."

It's not, but it's the first time I've seen hers. There's a difference. The way I feel about Addison...I've never felt this way about anyone before. Age and hormones aside, when I look into her eyes, I feel something deep and unexplainable. Something exciting and scary. Something I don't want to lose or, God forbid, screw up.

I allow myself a smile as I take her lingerie from her fingers and toss it over my shoulder. Before I have a chance to touch her though, she leans forward again, pressing her body to the length of mine and burying her head beneath my chin. We're skin to skin as I wrap my arms around her and follow the contours of her back. She has to be the softest thing I have ever felt.

As minutes pass and my hands continue to roam, I can feel her heartbeat accelerate. Soon, my pulse matches hers, and I find myself pressing my fingers deeper into her skin, kneading her muscles beneath the palms of my hands. Her lips find my shoulder and then my neck before landing on my mouth and kissing me hard. She grabs my hair and twists it in her fingers as our bodies move against one another. It's an awesome, yet excruciating feeling. I want the rest of our clothes off. Now.

Shifting my weight, I slide out from beneath her, and she rolls on to her side, facing me. I reach for the top of her shorts and unfasten the button, then feel her hands at my waist doing the exact same thing. *Good to know we're on the same page*, I think as I work my mouth against hers and my hand in between her clothes and her hip. She runs her fingers over me as she lowers the zipper on my jeans, and a surge of adrenaline snaps up my back. I clutch at her hip and groan as she smiles against my lips.

"Addison? We're home!"

Holy shit.

Instantly, our eyes lock. Addison pushes against my chest and whispers, "Get under the bed!"

Panicked, I do as I'm told. I scramble to the floor as Addison moves to the center of the mattress and quickly pulls the blankets over her. I lie on my back and scoot into the barely six-inch wide space; I have to press my cheek to the ground so my damn head will fit. Thoughts of her father demonstrating his marksmanship blast through my mind as my shoulders register carpet burn.

48

Just as I'm concealed, a ray of light appears across the bedroom floor. "There you are," Beth says as she opens her daughter's door. "In bed already?"

"The hike wore me out," Addison lies. "I decided to watch a movie. Why are you back so soon?"

Her mother walks into the room, and I see Sam's paws pass behind her ankles. He immediately puts his nose to the ground and makes a beeline straight for me. *No!* I silently pray. *Don't give me away!* Not only is it bad that I'm hiding; it will look even worse if I'm found half-dressed and hard.

"Your father didn't feel well after dinner, so we decided to skip the show," her mother explains. "How was your trip? Did you have a good time?"

"Yes."

Addison doesn't elaborate as Sam's nose inches closer to mine. I decide to hold my breath. There's not much else I can do.

"Is that all you have to say?" Her mother sounds impatient.

"Well, I got a blister on my heel. It's gross. Would you like to see it?"

Why in the world would she ask that? What if her mom says yes?

"Oh, no." Beth sounds disgusted. "Did you use the antiseptic?"

"Of course."

Just then, Sam's nose bumps against mine. He licks my face, and I can't do anything but slam my eyes shut and take it.

"Sam! What are you chewing on under there?"

"Oh, probably a toy," Addison says to appease her mother. I feel the bed move. "Sam! Go on; get out of there."

His face leaves mine, and I get the feeling Addison is pushing him away.

"Addison Renee!" Her mother's voice sounds shocked. "Are you sleeping in the nude?"

Christ!

"Mom, it's not a crime." Addison sounds exasperated.

Silence passes between mother and daughter, and I imagine Beth's eyes scouring the room for any trace of my existence. Nervously, I wait for her to find my shirt on the floor.

"Modesty is a virtue," Beth eventually sighs. "Please remember that."

I open one eye to see her feet backing away. "Do you want the dog in your room?"

"He can stay," Addison says.

Finally, I hear the door shut. It's like music to my ears. I start breathing again.

After a moment, Addison appears on the floor on all fours. "You're going to have to leave out the window." She grins.

"I'm glad you find this funny," I whisper as I start to maneuver my way out of hiding. "I have rug burn on my back and dog spit on my face."

She stifles a laugh and grabs my arm to help pull me free. "You're still hot though."

When I stand, I fasten my pants and notice she's wearing her shirt again. "Well, this is disappointing." I trace her collar with one finger. "You're dressed."

With a wry smile, she repeats her mother's words. "Modesty is a virtue."

I search the floor for my t-shirt and come face to face with Samson. "Dude, you almost got me in trouble," I quietly chastise him. "You're supposed to be my wing man." He tries to lick me again.

I find my shirt, pull it on, and then go to work removing the screen from Addison's window. Luckily, it's the same kind we have at our place, and all I have to do is flip a few clasps. I hand it to her as I step on to the bed, then hoist myself over the window ledge. Once I'm on the ground, I look back up.

"Good night," I whisper. "I'll see you tomorrow."

"See you tomorrow."

I start to walk away.

"Hey, Kyle?"

"Yeah?"

Addison places her hands on the ledge and leans forward. "Don't think we're not finishing this." She smiles.

I wink at her, then turn and walk away.

My sentiments exactly.

Chapter Six

"That's the only reason he likes you, you know."

I pull another piece of turkey from my sandwich and feed it to Sam. "He's a good dog," I defend my action. "He deserves a treat."

Addison grimaces. "Then you deserve to deal with his upset stomach." She grabs his collar. "C'mon beggar," she says and leads Sam away from me, his supplier. They walk to where I anchored a rope around an oak tree, and she leans over to tie him up.

I finish my sandwich in two bites and start to pick up what's left of our lunch. Tossing the garbage in a grocery bag, I notice Sam kicked up one edge of the blanket Gram lent us for our picnic. I kneel to fix it as Addison makes her way back to me. Her pale green sundress hugs her waist and brushes her knees; it's strapless and barely there. She smiles as she pushes her long hair over one shoulder, and I forget how to breathe for a minute. God, I'm lucky.

When she reaches the blanket, she pushes against my shoulders and falls forward, landing on top of me. I let out an "oompf" and she laughs as I catch her. She slides off my chest, settling into my side.

"I like this place," she says as she weaves her fingers through mine. "How did you find it?"

"By accident," I say. "I ended up here one day on the quad."

Two summers ago, I stumbled across this property. When I asked Gram about it, she said it used to be a working farm, complete with an orchard, cows, chickens, pigs, you name it. She said a friend she went to high school with used to live here, but his family moved and the place changed hands a few times. Years ago, lightning struck the barn, and everything went up in flames, even the house.

"I like the trees," Addison says.

"Me too."

Scattered around the property are several huge oaks, the shade from their branches keeping the grass low. Just beyond them is the crumbling cement foundation of the farmhouse, and beyond that lies the orchard. The fruit trees are still there, overgrown and unkempt, but perfectly aligned. The way nature took over makes the land look like a painting.

"Something draws you here," Addison says, looking up at me. "What is it?"

I shrug my shoulder beneath her and look into her eyes. "I don't know. It's neat." Then I smile, adding, "And secluded."

"Be careful." She arches an eyebrow. "Your ulterior motives are showing."

I lower my lips to hers. "I've got nothing to hide."

Our kiss is slow and deep, and I think we may be headed toward finishing what we started a few days ago. We haven't had much time alone since that night, since her father came down with a hell of a migraine. Spending any time at her place is forbidden until he feels better, so we've been hanging out at my cottage with my ever-present brother and grandmother. That's when I came up with the idea for this picnic, to get away.

Addison breaks our kiss. "I think it's more than that," she says.

"What's more?"

"Your reason for coming here." She looks around. "You have an eye for the outdoors."

I laugh. "Okay."

"You do," Addison says and pushes herself upright to sit beside me. "Think about it. I noticed the way you were mesmerized by the falls when we went hiking; I see how you look at this place now." She pauses. "The garden you planted for Gram is beautiful." She tips her head. "I think you were meant to be outside."

I stare at her. "You think I should stay outside? Like a mountain man or something?"

"No," she laughs. "I'm saying you should think about working outdoors. Like, for college."

Huh. I'd never considered that before.

"Besides," she says as she leans back over me, "I don't think I'd like you with a beard."

"Noted." I smile. "Never grow scraggly beard. Check."

Just as I try to catch her mouth with mine again, the song on the radio changes. Addison jumps to attention as the unmistakable opening chords of "Freebird" carry through the open windows of my truck.

"This is my favorite song," she says as her eyes light up. She quickly stands and backs away, offering me her hand. "Dance with me."

My response is skeptical. "I don't dance." Truth be told, I'm so bad at it, I'm afraid she'll stop seeing me once she finds out.

"It's not a waltz, Kyle."

True. It's Skynyrd.

She crooks her finger, gesturing for me to come here, and I obey despite my reservations. I wind my hands around her waist and pull her against me as we start to move in a circle.

"See? It's not that hard." Addison wraps her arms around my neck and tucks her head beneath my chin. "Every song has a beat. You just have to find it."

I sigh, letting her set the rhythm. She decides how fast we move; I'm only here for support. I always thought dancing was strictly a girl's show, probably because I've only been around it at school or at parties. Girls are either trying to get a guy's attention or trying to show off for their friends when they do. But, today, there's no one here but Addison and me. The longer we move the more I realize dancing can be something different. Something meaningful.

The music continues and Van Zant's voice starts to croon about never changing. I begin to wonder why Addison loves this song. It's about a guy who leaves a girl because he won't change.

"Why do you like this song?" I ask. "I mean, it's a classic, but the lyrics are horrible."

She lifts her head to look at me. "How so?"

"The guy loves the girl, but he won't change for her."

"Don't be so literal."

I throw her a confused look.

"The song is about being free," she elaborates. "Fly free bird?"

Again, I'm lost.

"I'm free," she says. "Just like the song. I can't change, and I won't change. I am who I am. I make my own decisions, damn the consequences."

Ah, I get it. "This is about your parents, isn't it?"

She shakes her head. "Not just them. It's about life, Kyle. Everything in life."

I can't help but smile at this amazing girl. I've never met another like her; she's strong-willed, confident, and hot as hell. She seems to have everything figured out.

"So, if you're such a free bird, what kind of bird are you?" I ask.

"It's a metaphor."

"I know, but what kind of bird would you be? I'd be a falcon. Or maybe a hawk. Something dark and dangerous."

"You are *so* not dark and dangerous," she scoffs. "You'd be more like a peacock."

"Ew. Why?" I make a face.

"Your changing eyes," she says simply. "And the fact that you have a, well, a..." She looks down at my crotch.

My jaw drops. "Seriously? You're basing my bird on my junk?"

She grins. "I guess that makes me a brown-eyed Booby."

I can't believe she said that. I start to laugh and she giggles.

"I refuse to be a peacock and you cannot be a booby," I say, laughing. "Pick something else."

She tries to be serious, but can't hide her smile. She glances over my head. "There," she says, "that tiny brown bird. I pick that."

I turn to look over my shoulder. "A sparrow?"

"Yep," she says confidently. "He's cute."

I study the bird. He hops along the tree branch and stops near the end, tilting his head toward us as if asking, "What are you staring at?" Another bird lands on his branch, and he ruffles his feathers, shooing it away. I turn back to Addison. "You're right. A sparrow fits you. You two are definitely little and feisty."

She smiles and the music from my truck picks up the pace; it's the middle of the song where the tempo changes. Addison steps away from me and picks up the beat, moving her arms and swaying her hips in time with the melody. The sun reflects off her hair, turning it a golden caramel brown, and I imagine her as a hippie, dancing in a field back in the '60s. She gives me an encouraging smile to join her, but that's not going to happen. Since I can't dance, I decide to break out my mad air guitar moves that are typically reserved for the privacy of my bedroom. She laughs and jumps in time with the music as I pretend to be Slash on tour with Lynyrd Skynyrd. If the dog is watching, I'm sure he thinks we've lost our minds.

Near the end of the song, Addison grabs my hands and starts to pull me in a circle. Our arms are extended between us as we spin faster and faster, ring-around-the-rosy style. When she lets go, she crashes on to the blanket, laughing. I follow and land beside her, breathing hard.

"That has to be the longest song on the planet," I say, trying to catch my breath.

"I think it is," she pants.

I roll on to my side and prop my head on my hand as Addison brushes her hair out of her face. It's a wild, tangled mess around her head. I try to help by tucking a piece behind her ear, and she smiles up at me. Her eyes lock on mine, and it's then that I know.

My world has shifted, and she is the center of it.

I knew I was falling for her. Hell, I think I fell for her the minute I saw her. But there's a difference between like and lust and love, and I've just figured it out. I liked her when I met her. I lusted for her the other night. But now? Now, I've fallen for her in the hardest way. We can be serious, and we can be stupid. I have no secrets from her, and she doesn't hold anything back with me. Yes, we just met. Yes, we're seventeen. But something inside me says she's going to be a part of my life. Forever.

"Why are you looking at me like that?" she asks.

"Like what?"

"Like you just noticed me for the first time."

I swallow, suddenly nervous. "Because I think I just did."

She lifts herself to her elbows and searches my face. "You had the forever moment, didn't you?"

My forehead pinches. "How –?"

"Because I had it last week." Her hand settles on the back of my neck, and she nudges me forward. "I had it when you showed me Gram's garden."

Her eyes soften, and I find myself getting lost in them. For the first time, I notice flecks of gold swim in their chocolate brown color. When I remember how to breathe again, I catch her mouth with mine. I explore the fullness of her bottom lip and the soft curve of her smile. She winds her fingers through my hair, holds me in place, and sighs as our kiss deepens. My hand leaves her waist, catches her knee, and pulls her leg over my hip. Her mouth disappears.

"I think I'm mooning Sam."

I peer down and, yeah, her short sundress is bunched around her hip, revealing her perfect, panty-clad backside. I can't help myself, and I grab it. She laughs.

"Technically, you're not mooning anyone." I arch an eyebrow as I run my finger just under the edge of her underwear. "You'd have to take these off first."

Mischievously, her eyes lock on mine. "I will if you will."

I have to bite my lower lip to keep from breaking out into a stupid grin. She really just said that.

To prove I'm up for the challenge, I slide her leg off of mine and sit up. I reach for the button on my shorts and unfasten it before Addison's hand flies out to stop me.

"Wait."

Damn it.

She curls her legs to the side and kneels. "Let's do it together."

Hell yes.

Now I'm kneeling, too. We face each other, inches apart. "Should we count to three?"

A small laugh escapes her, and she looks up at me from under her lashes. Her hands find my pants, finishing what I started, then slide inside and around my hips to land on my ass. I wrap my arms around her waist, pull her against me, and start to lift her dress to return the favor.

"Hey," she says quietly into my ear before kissing it. "I want you to know this isn't my first time."

My hands stop moving and I lean back to look at her. "What?"

She blushes, which is something I rarely see her do. "I just...I thought you should know. In case you wanted to change your mind."

The thought of her with another guy makes my stomach twist, although she did say she used to have a boyfriend. Did I really expect to be her first? She's not mine.

I kiss her forehead. "I hate the thought of someone else touching you." I pause. "But that would never change my mind about us. If we're being honest, it's not my first time either."

She scrunches up her face, and I wish I could read her thoughts. My past shouldn't be a deal breaker if hers isn't.

"Were you safe?" she finally asks.

"Absolutely." I tilt my head. "You?"

She nods. "The whole experience was a disaster, though."

"A disaster?"

She shrugs.

I lower my shoulders, so I can look her straight in the eye. "Then, why do you want to do this with me?"

A sly smile lifts the corner of her mouth. "Because everything is different with you. I can't get enough." Her hands, which still rest inside my shorts, pull me against her. "All you have to do is look at me and I know I'm yours."

I'm yours. Her words are a whisper against my lips, and there's nothing left to do but kiss her. I move my hands to cradle her face, devour her mouth, and plan on making this last as long as possible.

Chapter Seven

I roll on to my side and punch the pillow. Again. I can't sleep, and it's useless to try. Tonight is my last at Buhl Lake. In the morning, I leave for home and a week of football camp. In six hours, I head back to reality.

Reality blows.

Addison and I said our goodbyes earlier, when we took a long walk around the lake. We decided it best to get it over with to make things easier; although, I don't think the timing would have mattered. I'm still struggling to accept the fact that I won't be able to see her for the next two weeks. The lake spoiled us, and it's pissing me off. Why can't her parents leave early? Why won't they let her go home by herself? I volunteered to take her.

Oh yeah. That's why.

Her sister is also stopping by on her way to Michigan Tech. Addison's parents want her there to celebrate, to have one last family dinner before Meagan is buried under snow in the Upper Peninsula. Addison said she couldn't care less, but I have a feeling she misses her sister. Meagan comes up in conversation more than she would admit.

Kevin starts to snore, and I pull my pillow over my head to block out his wheezing snort. I hate that sound. If there is one good thing about going home, it's that I'll have my bedroom to myself again.

Suddenly, I hear two knocks in between Kev's nasal symphony. At least, I think I do. I move my head from beneath the pillow to listen.

Wheee-snark. Wheee-snark. Wheee-snark. Thunk-thunk.

There. That was definitely a knock.

I roll over and stare at the window opposite my bed. The moon is high in the sky, and the light shines through onto the carpet. Seconds later, a tiny fist appears and raps against the glass.

I untangle my legs from my blankets and spring to the window. Sliding it open, I hear rustling and a whispered curse.

"Shit!"

"Addison?" I press my forehead to the screen and look down. "What are you doing?"

She stumbles as she frees herself from the bush she's fallen into, and I fight the urge to laugh. She stands up and wraps the comforter I recognize from her bed around her body. "Hey," she whispers, giving me a small smile. "I need to talk to you."

"Obviously," I whisper back.

"Can you come out here?"

"One sec."

I close the window and sneak around Kevin, although a freight train could plow through the bedroom and he wouldn't hear it over himself. I snag a t-shirt off the floor and pull it over my head as I creep down the stairs and through the living room. Sliding the patio door open, I slip through and close it quietly behind me. When I turn around, Addison is waiting at the bottom of the deck steps. As I walk toward her, my bare feet register the cool dew covering the deck. That's the weird thing about northern Michigan; it can be eighty degrees during the day and fall to forty at nighttime.

When I reach her, she opens her arms and winds them around me, cocooning us inside the blanket. My hands find her waist and pull her close. She sighs against my chest.

"I can't sleep."

"Me neither."

I kiss her hair, then set my chin on the top of her head. I stare out into the surrounding darkness as minutes pass. We don't say a word; our heartbeats falling into the same rhythm.

Eventually, Addison speaks. "Don't go."

Her voice is shaky, which is odd for her. Concerned, I lean back and see a tear escape the corner of her eye.

"Hey." I wipe it away with my thumb. "Don't cry." *Please*, I think. I'm already depressed enough about leaving; knowing that she's upset will only make it worse. "We'll see each other soon."

She releases my waist and steps back, wiping beneath her other eye. "Are you sure?"

My forehead pinches. "Of course I'm sure. We talked about this." In two weeks, on Labor Day, I am to be on her doorstep at exactly noon. "Don't you trust me?"

She lets out a small laugh. "I want to."

"What's that supposed to mean?"

She sighs. "It's nothing."

"No. It's something." I take a step forward and reach for her. "Talk to me."

She gives me a wary look, and I grab her hand. "C'mon."

"Where are we going?"

"To the dock so we don't have to whisper." I doubt Kevin will hear us, but I'm not sure about Gram. I don't want to wake her and have to explain why we're outside in the middle of the night.

As I lead Addison down the hill and to the lake, my mind scrambles. I don't *think* I did anything wrong, but she's acting funny. She's never been emotional around me before. Then again, I've only known her for two and a half months.

The thought stops me short. It's not a long time. But, for me, it is. I feel like I've known her my whole life.

When we reach the dock, I take a seat on the bench and pull her onto my lap. She settles onto me and arranges the blanket over us, then buries her head against my neck. Inwardly, I groan. The warmth of her body pressed to mine is amazing. After tonight, it's going to be awhile before I feel it again. September can't get here fast enough.

"So?" I ask as we wind our arms around one another.

"So what?"

"Are you going to tell me what's bothering you?"

"You're leaving."

"I know that." I move my head to the side to look her in the eyes. "What else?"

She grimaces. "Landon."

Instantly, my jaw clenches. Who the hell is Landon? "Keep talking."

"Landon...he's the guy who left me after prom." She presses her forehead to my neck again. "He...we...he was my first," she explains. "We'd been dating for months. He kept asking, I kept stalling, and then, the night of the dance, I caved." She pauses.

"The next day, he broke up with me." A snort of laughter escapes her. "He said I wasn't good enough."

Anger surges through my veins. What I wouldn't do for two minutes alone with this guy. It wouldn't take me any longer than that to beat the shit out of him.

My arms hold Addison tighter. "I'm sorry he did that to you."

"Yeah, well." She shrugs. "It was my mistake to trust him."

A realization starts to take over. "Please tell me you don't think I'm the same."

"I don't. You're completely different."

I'm confused. "So why...?"

She lifts her head. "When I couldn't sleep, I started to freak out. What if, after these next few weeks apart, you decide I'm not what you want? I won't be there to convince you otherwise. I've given you everything. What if you decide there's nothing left to come back for?"

She can't be serious. My eyes lock on hers. "Addison Renee." I recall her middle name from the night we almost got caught half-naked in her room. "I thought you had the forever moment."

"I did."

"Okay, then. Stop worrying."

She stares at me. "But, you never said it."

"Never said what?"

"That *you* did." She purses her lips. "You never said you had that moment too."

She's right. When she asked me about it, I confirmed her question with a kiss, not words. I thought kissing her would mean more. I guess I was wrong.

I lean forward, so we're nearly nose to nose. "I had the moment."

A slow smile creeps across her lips, and I decide to plant a soft, full kiss on them. "Nothing will change how I feel about you."

Once I say those words, her body relaxes in my arms. Her full weight falls against me, and I realize how tense she really was. I had no idea she was so stressed over this. I decide to lighten the mood.

"Do you know why my feelings will never change?"

"Why?" she asks sleepily.

"Because this," I slide my hand down to cradle her ass, "fits in my palm perfectly."

She rolls her eyes and lets out a small laugh. "I hope that's not all it takes."

"It's not," I reassure her as I run my hand down her leg to her knee. "These legs help." I zero in on her neck with my mouth next. "This doesn't hurt either," I murmur against her.

She tips her head so I have an easier time making my way to her ear. "You just want to make out with me."

"Always."

Our lips meet, and we kiss until they feel swollen. It's as if we're trying to cram the next two weeks in these last few hours. I want Addison to know how much I care about her; I want to brand her with my mouth so she won't forget. It's then that I know I need to tell her. She didn't understand what my actions meant before; she needs words.

"Hey." I pull myself away from her. "I need to tell you something."

She studies my face as her breathing slows. "Don't say you love me."

I want to. I've never told anyone before. "Why not?"

"Save it," she says. "I want those words to be the first out of your mouth when I see you again."

I don't fully understand her reasoning; girls confuse me. Addison less so than others I've known, but still. "Are you sure?"

She nods and gives me her sly smile. "If we save it, seeing you will be like Christmas. The anticipation will be worth the wait."

I narrow my eyes, trying to read her. My gut tells me she wants another reason to ensure I will show up on Labor Day, despite my admitting to the 'forever moment.' I decide to drop it and pull her toward me. She settles her body against my chest. "I'll get in trouble if I sleep here," she says.

I let out a heavy breath. "I know."

As much as I don't want her to get yelled at, I want her to stay. I want to spend the night wrapped around her on this uncomfortable wood bench, surrounded by nothing but the water and the stars.

"Make sure you call when you get home," she says quietly.

"I will." I kiss the top of her head. "Don't forget to head up to town."

Addison and I both have cell phones, but we haven't used them because there is no signal at the lake. We've spent the majority of our time here together; there was never a need for them. Now, she will have to drive into town to get reception if we want to talk.

Minutes pass and she doesn't move to leave. I glance down and notice her eyes flutter closed. The longer I look at her, the steadier her breathing becomes. She's falling asleep. I know I should wake her, but I don't want to. If her parents find us together in the morning, oh well. Her dad might aim his gun at me, but I don't think he'd pull the trigger.

I take that back. He'd definitely fire a warning shot.

Regardless, it's worth it. The moon is high in the sky, and the light reflects off Addison's face. Her skin looks softer than usual, and here, relaxed in my arms, she looks fragile and innocent - two words I would never use to describe her while she is awake. When her eyes are open, she's strong and confident. Instantly, I'm thankful I get to see every side of her.

My eyes feel heavy, and my gaze jumps to the lake. The water is still, like a sheet of glass. It's calm and peaceful.

Just like I feel right now.

Chapter Eight
September 2005

I hate speed limits.

Heading south on the expressway, I meticulously weave around slower traffic. It seems everyone is out for a leisurely drive today. Not me. I have an important appointment at exactly twelve o'clock. One I've been looking forward to for fourteen days.

There is no way on this earth that I will be late to see Addison. None.

As I change lanes to move past a putzing Toyota, the text she sent yesterday afternoon pops into my thoughts. A stupid grin breaks across my face.

Addison: *Finally home. How many more hours?*

Me: *23. But who's counting?*

Addison: *I'm dying over here.*

Me: *Do you need mouth to mouth? I'm self-certified in CPR.*

Addison: *I know ;)*

Me: *Seriously. I could come over tonight.*

Addison: *I wish. Dad says he has a surprise for us and we'll probably be out late.*

Me: *It better be something good to keep you away from me.*

Addison: *Right?! I've never missed anyone so much.*

Me: *I miss you too, Sparrow. You have no idea.*

After I arrived home from Buhl Lake, I had a week of football camp, which meant getting up at six a.m. every day to make it to the high school by seven. As I mechanically fed myself Rice Krispies each morning, I would stare out the kitchen window that overlooks our backyard. The birdfeeder I made years ago in shop class hangs just outside of it, and the only thing that would show up to eat were sparrows. Lots of them. They reminded me of Addison, and I took their presence as a sign that she was thinking about me. When I told her about the birds, she said that was sweet and most likely the truth. I nicknamed her Sparrow after that.

I finally arrive at my exit and glance down at the directions Addison wrote out for me. After a few more miles, I end up at the entrance of a swanky subdivision called Glendale Oaks. The winding roads are lined with impressive brick homes that sit on manicured lawns with sprinkler systems. I inwardly cringe at the thought of her visiting me. My house is a three bedroom, one-story ranch with white siding and black shutters. These houses look like they have in-home movie theaters and bowling alleys.

At last, I find her address and turn into the paved drive. I park, turn off my truck, and stare at the structure before me. Three car garage. Fenced in yard. Wrap-around porch. Professional landscaping.

Nice.

Despite my excitement to see Addison, I exit my truck slowly. My heart rate picks up as I make my way to the front door. A weird lump forms in my throat, and I realize I'm nervous. Unpleasant thoughts start to creep into my brain. I've only been here about ten seconds, but my subconscious is tapping me on my shoulder and whispering in my ear. It says I'm not good enough to be here.

I press the doorbell and wait, listening to the chime on the other side of the door. Almost immediately, I hear Sam's bark from somewhere deep inside the house. I didn't notice until now, but I've really missed that furry guy, too. I glance around the porch absentmindedly and rock back on my heels. Call me arrogant, but I expected Addison to be waiting outside, anxious to see me. I thought she'd be in my arms as soon as I got out of my truck. That's how I envisioned it, anyway.

I press the doorbell again and hear Sam's bark. Minutes pass, and the nervousness I felt in my chest spreads to my stomach. Why isn't anyone answering the door? There is no way Addison would forget I was coming. We talked about it yesterday.

Immediately, I pull my phone from my back pocket. No new messages or missed calls. I find Addison's number and dial it. I get her voice mail and hang up. A strange mix of worry and anger starts to take over. No one is home, which means she's with her family somewhere. Do her parents despise me so much that they would purposefully make her leave the house today?

I step to my left and peer in the window, cupping my hands around my eyes so I can see inside. My eyes search what looks like a den. Newspaper is spread on the coffee table, and a glass half full of something sits beside it. I can see down a hallway and spot what I think is the entrance to the kitchen. It's then my eyes catch a blur of white fur and realize Samson isn't in the house. He's in the backyard.

Quickly moving off the porch, I head toward the fence gate I saw when I first pulled in. I yank the handle, and it's not locked. Closing the door behind me, I yell for the dog. "Sam? You back here?"

Sam comes barreling around the side of the house, nearly knocking me down when he reaches me. I kneel, rubbing him roughly behind his ears and down the sides of his body with both hands. "What's going on boy? Where's your family, huh?"

He licks my face and acts happy to see me. Standing, I head to the backyard. When I round the corner, I come upon a stamped concrete patio full of furniture. An outdoor bar and grill sit to one side, and on the opposite end sits what looks like a custom made dog house. Sam's bowls are set in front of it, full of food and water. Addison and her parents must have left this morning.

Now I'm pissed. I reach for my phone again and text her.
Did you forget something?

She could have at least let me know to come later. It's not like her not to talk to me. Instantly, I blame her parents. Did they take away her phone? I eye the patio furniture and make up my mind. I'm going to park my ass in one of these chairs until they bring her back home.

~~~~

Hours later, my cell buzzes in my hand. I nearly jump a foot off the chair, and Sam jerks his head away from my leg. I glance down to see my mom's name on the screen. Frustrated, I answer.

"Hello?"

"Kyle? When are you coming home? You have school tomorrow."

I'm irritated and it causes me to snap. "I'm not twelve years old."

"Listen young man," my mom says. "You still live under this roof. You play by my rules."

Silence.

"I expect you home within the hour," she says adamantly. "Understand?"

Reluctantly, I agree and hang up. I look at the time on the screen. It's almost eight o'clock. I've been sitting on Addison's deck for eight hours with no sign of her. No phone call. No nothing.

I push my legs off the chair I've been lying on with Sam. He gets up with me, and we both stretch. I don't know what to do. My feelings vacillate between anger and a worry so deep it reaches my bones.

I look at Sam and he tilts his head, giving me a sad whine. I don't know if he knows something I don't or if he's picking up on my nervous vibe. I do know that I don't want to leave him here alone.

It's then that I make up my mind. I crouch down and meet his eyes. "Listen," I say out loud. "I have to go, but I'll be back to check on you." Concern for the dog will give me an excuse to come back tomorrow, unless I talk to Addison tonight.

Sam bumps his head against my hand, and I feel terrible. This whole day has been a disaster. Two weeks of anticipation for this?

Giving Sam's soft fur one last rub, I will my body off the deck and toward the front of the house. The dog follows close at my heels and when I make it to the fence, I turn around. "Stay. I'll come back. I promise."

Despite everything inside of me screaming not to leave, I slip through the gate and make my way to my truck. I can hear Sam's high pitched whine and his paw scratching the wood fence. The sound makes the back of my throat ache. My hands clench into fists and when I reach my truck, I punch the driver's side door. An insane pain shoots up my arm, and the skin across my knuckles breaks. Blood starts to ooze down the back of my hand as I flex my fingers.

Goddamn it! What happened today?

~~~~

Sitting in class the following morning, I can't focus. All I can do is stare at my bruised hand and will my phone to ring. Addison hasn't returned my calls; she hasn't responded to my messages.

I'm worried sick.

The bell sounds, ending third period, and I robotically make my way toward my locker. I throw my history book inside with more force than necessary and slam the door shut. Behind me, a large part of the student body rushes past on its way to the cafeteria. Reluctantly, I join the herd, even though food is the last thing I want right now.

With that thought, I immediately change direction. Pushing sideways through the crowd, I pick up my pace and head down the sophomore hallway to the student parking lot. I'm not going to lunch.

I'm going to Addison's.

Just as I reach the double doors, I hear Kevin at my back. "Where are you going?"

I glance over my shoulder and keep moving. "Think about it."

My brother gives me a concerned, yet knowing look. "You can't ditch. If coach finds out, he'll bench you first game."

"I don't care."

I make it to Waterford in record time; it's much quicker in light midday traffic, when everyone is at work. My tires squeal as I turn into Addison's driveway, and when I park, the house looks exactly the same as I last saw it. I jump out of the truck, leaving the door open, and head to the front porch. With each step I take, my anxiety builds. I can't shake the feeling of déjà vu.

I pound on the door, then peer in the windows again. Everything remains untouched from yesterday. I repeatedly ring the doorbell. No one answers.

It's then that I realize I haven't heard Sam's bark. I head off the porch, to the fence gate, and let myself inside. When I round the back of the house, my eyes roam the yard to find everything the same.

With one exception.

Sam and his food dishes are gone.

I walk over to the chair I sat in the day before and stare at my hands in disbelief. An hour later, I'm still doing the same thing. Addison's laugh echoes in my mind; her smile dances through my thoughts. I remember the feeling of her kiss and her body against mine. Was this summer a lie? It couldn't have been. Where is she? Why won't she talk to me? My mind starts to jump to conclusions and assume the worst. Are her parents that cold-hearted that they wouldn't contact me if she were hurt?

With heavy steps, I make my way to my truck and start the engine. I back down the driveway slowly, with my head and my heart full of confusion.

That was the summer I fell in love with, and lost, Addison Parks.

The Present

~

Chapter Nine
October 2013

Eight years later

Rounding the all-too-familiar corner, my new baby slows. Not because she wants to, but because I make her. Lifting my foot off the accelerator, my truck gently rolls to a stop. It sits idle, in the middle of the dirt road, as I stare out the open window.

Everything looks the same.

Overgrown, but still the same.

My eye catches the small garden I planted by the cottage all those years ago. It's not little anymore. The rhododendron has taken over, nearly choking out the hydrangeas. I always reminded Gram to cut it back in the fall, but she refused. She said she wanted me to do it; she said didn't want to mess it up and ruin the bush.

She was trying to get me to come back here.

I blink, and the ghost of a girl I once knew appears. She stands in front of the plants, just like she did the day we went to the Falls, and she smiles at me. I focus on her face, a face I remember all too well, and when the wind blows, she's carried away. Dry fall leaves swirl where she stood, and I take a deep breath.

I've only been here five minutes and my mind is already fucking with me.

Releasing the air trapped in my lungs, I turn the steering wheel and pull into the gravel drive. I knew coming to the lake would be hard, but for different reasons. No, I'm not stupid to think the memories of that summer wouldn't surface. I just thought they would take a day or two to fully resurrect themselves. It's been a long time, and I have more important things to do than take a walk down memory lane.

As I sit and wait for Kevin, my eyes unwillingly land on the front door of the cottage. Any minute I expect Gram to burst forth, all smiles and hugs mixed with harsh words for me. Words that say she's happy to see me *here* and not at home. Words that say she needs my help and she's been waiting. Words that say "Dinner will be ready at four o'clock."

The door remains closed.

The longer I stare at it, the more it starts to blur around the edges. I clear my throat and focus on my phone, picking it up off the seat to find out where my brother is. I will not cry. The first time I did was two weeks ago.

At Gram's funeral.

~~~~

"How many do you want?"

"How many can you carry?"

As dusk settles over the lake, Kevin and I decide to call it a day with the decision making. Neither of us has answers for the questions we ask, and I, for one, am getting a headache. We're supposed to be sorting through Gram's things, boxing certain items to take back home, leaving others, and throwing useless stuff away. The problem is neither of us knows where to begin or what our mother wants us to bring home from this place. She never gave two shits about it before, but suddenly, when it was revealed that Kevin and I inherited the joint, she wants us to bring home memories.

Of what?

It's not like she can't come up here whenever she wants. Her sons own the place, or will as soon as the estate is settled. While she deals with her mother's affairs back home, we're up here, standing in the living room, lost. Yes, the cottage and its contents are technically ours, but neither of us wants to throw away anything of Gram's. Who are we to decide what to keep and what to donate? It's frustrating and not a task that's going to get finished in the few days we've taken off work.

I glance at Kevin, who has his head stuck in the refrigerator. When he backs up, he kicks the door shut. He holds up both hands, revealing a case of Budweiser in one and a six-pack of Corona in the other. He smirks. "This should get us started."

I grab a lighter out of the kitchen drawer and make sure it works by flicking the switch. A blue flame dances before my eyes. "I agree. Let's get lit."

We wander down to the fire pit near the water's edge with our supplies, plus two plastic patio chairs. As I carry them in front of me, I stare at the ground so I won't trip down the hill. I think about how drunk I want to get and imagine stumbling back up to the house later. I probably should have brought a flashlight.

When we reach the pit, I set the chairs near one another as Kevin places the beer on the ground. He begins piling logs in his arms from a nearby stack, and I head off into the brush to find some tinder. Not thinking, I walk to the left and, through naked tree branches, my eyes fall on Addison's cottage. In the hazy twilight it looks vacant, almost haunted. Gram told me Addison and her family disappeared from the lake just like they disappeared from their home. Just like she disappeared from my life.

Momentarily still, I think back to the countless times I called her cell in that first year, just to hear her voice tell me she was unavailable. I'd be lying if I said I didn't pray that she would pick up every time I called. Her voice was eventually replaced by an electronic one, telling me the number had been disconnected. I can still remember the way I felt in that moment – like a boulder had crushed my chest.

The memory tempts others, and I will my mind not to go there. I was in a dark place for a long time, a place where I felt betrayed, denied, and lied to. A place full of hurt and worry. I was an egotistical kid who didn't get his way; a kid who didn't understand.

I still don't understand.

Crouching down, I begin to gather sticks, dry leaves, and pine needles. It's been a rough week. I need a beer.

Or twelve.

Before long, Kev and I are feeling much more relaxed as we watch the flames of the bonfire dance in front us. I feel hypnotized by the orange colors, probably because I'm buzzed and the heat is making me tired.

"It's weird, isn't it?" my brother asks. "I can picture Gram sitting in the living room, waiting for us to put out the fire and come to bed."

I give him half a smile. She was always worried we would burn the place down. "I know. I keep expecting her to yell out the window to wrap it up."

He laughs. "Me, too."

Silence reigns as we think about Gram. I hate that she had a heart attack; I hate that she was ripped from us so suddenly. The only thing that keeps me sane is the thought that she's with Pop again.

"Oh," my brother says, simultaneously remembering and swallowing. "Did you get the Schuster contract? The old man finally signed."

I nod as I drop my empty can by my chair and lean over to grab another full one. "Yeah. I checked my email while I was waiting for you." The wireless reception at the lake has greatly improved over the years. "What did you have to give up?"

He gets cocky. "Ten percent."

I shoot him a suspicious look. "That's all?"

Kevin settles into his chair with a smug expression. "That's all."

"After the hell he put us through? He settled on ten percent?"

"It's called the art of negotiation, my brother. You could learn a thing or two from me."

Kevin takes a swig of his beer and my eyes narrow. He loves to rub it in that I will never possess the skills he has.

After the first year of trying to run my own landscaping company, I realized I needed some serious help. The horticulture, design, and creativity I could nail with no problem. It was the client schmoozing and number crunching I couldn't get a hold on. I needed someone to handle the business side of things. My work spoke for itself, but I needed to build a client base. I needed a clone, someone to promote my business so I could stay on-site. Kevin fit the bill. Pair his analytical mind with his smooth talking, and you've got a lethal combination. There is no one I can trust more than my brother. He's family.

And my best friend.

Despite my reminiscing, I respond to his statement with a sarcastic, "Whatever. You may be able to sell ice to Eskimos, but you suck at telling time. Why were you so late today?"

He raises an eyebrow suggestively over his Corona. "I got tied up with the new girlfriend."

I shake my head. Knowing my brother, he probably means literally. "Is this the hot blonde?"

"The same."

I haven't met Kevin's new girl yet. If I remember right, they met just before Gram died. "I take it things are good?"

At first he gives me a sly smile, but then it turns more reserved, almost shy. This is a new look for him. When it comes to discussing women, he's usually pretty sure of himself. After a few moments, my little brother sighs and says, "She's...different."

My eyes grow wide with surprise. He's used a lot of words to describe the girls he dates, but 'different' has never been one of them. "How so?"

He concentrates on the Corona bottle in his hands, scratching at the label with his thumb. "I don't know how to explain it. I've never felt this way before." He pauses. "It's like I'm not breathing unless I'm with her. She's my air." He looks at me. "You know?"

My face falls because, unfortunately, I do know. I want to ask him if he had the forever moment, but I stop myself. Obviously those don't exist. That feeling is just a sick trick your heart plays on you when you're infatuated.

When I don't answer his question, he mumbles, "I think I'm in love with her."

My face pinches in doubt. "Are you sure? You guys have only been dating for what, a couple weeks?"

Kevin tosses me an irritated glance. "Have you ever heard me talk about a girl like that before?"

"No."

"Then I'm sure."

"Kev," I lean forward and rest my elbows on my knees, "all I'm saying is to give it some time. It seems pretty quick to fall that hard."

He lets out a sarcastic snort.

"What?"

"You of all people..." He shakes his head then gives me a pointed look. "You're the last person who should be giving out relationship advice."

That hits a nerve. "Excuse me?"

He raises his bottle to his lips then looks at the fire. "Never mind."

"No." He can't drop something like that and expect me to forget it. "What are you trying to say?" I know I don't have the best track record when it comes to women, but I have learned a thing or two. Let's see Kevin smooth talk his way out of this one.

He takes a deep breath, realizing he should have kept his mouth shut. He slides to the edge of his chair, so he's closer to me. He's sets his bottle on the ground and says, "Let's start with Monica. Exhibit A."

Oh, here we go. "That's not fair. She moved away for college. Not my fault." Monica and I dated briefly when I was nineteen. "We weren't even together six months."

"But," Kevin holds up a finger, "she was your first serious relationship after Addison."

My body tenses at the sound of her name. It shouldn't affect me after all these years, and I get defensive. "I would hardly call what Monica and I had a serious thing. We messed around."

"What did she say to you before she left, though? What was a deciding factor in her move?"

I can't believe he remembers this. "She said I didn't love her." It's the truth. I didn't.

"Okay. Now we can move on to Courtney."

"Seriously?"

"You dated for two years! I think she qualifies as a relationship."

I concede with a nod, but protest, "She left me. I didn't leave her." I remember the day she broke it off, telling me her parents had set her up with a family friend. She had been seeing Eric for a few weeks, and I never even realized it. She wasn't lying when she said I didn't pay enough attention. I didn't.

"Courtney was sick of putting up with your shit," Kevin says. "You never focused on her."

"I was twenty-two! I wasn't ready to settle down." Not that I cheated on her, but if the guys wanted to go out, I went with them. If there was a game on, I'd watch it. Plus, I was beginning to put some real effort into starting up the business. "What else you got?"

My brother sighs. "What about Jen?"

His question takes me by surprise. He can't possibly know about Jen; she just packed the last of her things yesterday. "What about her?"

"She moved out."

"How do you know?"

"You forget we were friends before I introduced you."

Evidently Jen's been talking to my brother behind my back. I'm curious and pissed at the same time. "What did she say?"

"She said she tried, Kyle. She really tried."

I can't control my sarcasm. "Last I checked, moving out isn't trying."

"What did you expect?" Kevin holds out his hands. "Every time she told you she loved you, all you would say was 'me too.' She needed to hear it. After three years, she needed to hear it. Even I understand that."

"Okay, Dr. Phil," I scoff and stare at the can in my hands. Even though what he says is true, I don't like the idea of my baby brother lecturing me. It's too soon. Jen literally left twenty-four hours ago. Pair that with Gram's death and having to confront my memories at the lake, and I'm having a pretty shitty October.

"Maybe if she's gone you'll realize what you had."

My eyes snap to Kevin's. "Do you think I wanted her to leave? I asked her to give me some time to figure things out, but that wasn't good enough. She wanted a bigger commitment and an immediate answer. When I couldn't give her one, she threw Gram's death in my face; she said losing someone close to me should make me realize life is short."

Apparently Jen neglected to tell Kevin that part. He's looks confused and blinks at me.

"I wasn't going to let her push me into a proposal."

Kevin runs his hand through his hair and leans back in his seat. "All she said was that she felt she'd wasted her time. That she cared about you more than you cared about her."

That may or may not be true. I toss my empty can into the fire and watch the flames lick up the sides. I know I care about Jen a lot; we have fun together, and I would never want to see her hurt. But the truth is, I don't think I love her. Not enough for what she needs, anyway.

"Listen," Kevin's voice sounds quiet. "I shouldn't have brought it up. I just hate to see you repeat the same pattern."

"What pattern?"

"The one where you're with someone great, but you keep them at arm's length until they give up and leave you."

His words place a heavy weight on my shoulders. "Yes, every girl I've been with has left me. Thanks for pointing that out, asshole."

Kevin lets out an annoyed sigh. "It's just...I've been thinking a lot about the future since Gram died."

I face him. "Is that why you think you're falling in love?"

He shrugs. "It probably has something to do with it. Regardless, I know I don't want to be alone. When I'm sixty, I'd rather be with Ashley than sitting here with your wrinkled ass."

A snort of laughter escapes me. I can picture us, old and grumpy, sitting in this exact same spot.

"Don't you want that?" he asks. "Don't you want to share your future with someone?"

Now he's getting sappy. It must be the alcohol. I decide to appease him and nod yes because I'm done with this conversation. I came out here to get hammered and forget, not to have a conversation about love and my romantic shortfalls. I can't tell him my future is hard to see because, years ago, I gave it away. I gave to the girl who was *my* air.

Then, she vanished.

Without giving it back.

~~~~

Two days later, I stand in Gram's garage scratching the back of my head. What am I going to do with all this stuff? This place is packed like Home Depot circa 1920. Some of the tools I can use for work, but others are ancient. I silently wonder if I can get ahold of those guys from the television show *American Pickers*.

I decide the best way to tackle this job is to divide everything into piles. There are things that should stay here, since Kevin and I are going to keep the place. Last night, during dinner, we discussed the possibility of selling it. After weighing the pros and cons, we decided that Gram would haunt us if we ever got rid of the cottage. Plus, if the business grows, we could possibly have two locations. One back home and one based at the lake.

Working from the floor up, I start with the lower shelves on the workbench that spans the entire back wall of the garage. I should have worn a hazmat suit. Spider webs cover everything; there are mouse traps with congealed food stuck to them and droppings everywhere. Some animal has made a nest in one of the corners; I'm pretty sure it's a mouse or a chipmunk. Whatever it is, it's going to be pissed when it comes back because I just threw away its home. I feel kind of bad about it, but then again, its nature. Go live outside.

After making decent progress, I'm sweating despite the fall weather. I wipe my dirty hands on my jeans and my forehead on my sleeve, then stand and stretch. I need to get some air moving in here. I walk toward the aluminum garage door and lift it, hanging on to the bottom when it's completely open. Sunlight blasts my face from the outdoors and bounces off the windshield of my new truck. She's a 2013 black Ford F250, and if I can say I'm in love with anything, I'm in love with her. I needed a commercial vehicle for the business; I was sick of paying someone else to deliver material when I can pick up things myself. The truck is perfect; we go everywhere together, and she never asks about my feelings.

"Hey."

I turn around. Kevin is standing in the doorway holding our old fishing poles.

"Where did you find those?" I ask.

"In the utility closet. Ready for a break?"

"Yeah."

We head down to the dock and sit on the edge like we used to years ago. I purposefully ignore the wood bench behind us as I inspect the deteriorating wax worm on my hook. I know if I look at the bench too long I'll see Addison sitting there – just like I see her sitting at Gram's table or standing on the cottage deck. If I turn my head to the left, I know I'll see her walking down the steps from her old place.

I cast my line with more force than necessary. These memories are starting to piss me off. They need to stay buried where I put them. It's been too long.

"Are you trying to reach the other side of the lake?" Kevin asks.

I reel in my line a bit. "My technique is rusty."

He shoots me a skeptical look.

We fish in silence. I'm not sure what he's thinking about, but I'm studying the opposite shoreline. Despite avoiding this place, I have to admit the scenery is awesome. The leaves left on the trees are at their peak fall color; red, orange, and yellow swirls reflect off the water. The wind blows, lifting a patch of lily pads, and their color changes from green to burgundy. Staring at the plants reminds me of the bass I never caught, and I reel in my line to cast in a different direction. Not that the fish is still around.

Over the next hour we catch some small Blue Gills and let them go. When Kevin closes up shop, he says, "I'm hungry. I'll order a pizza and pick it up if you buy."

"Whatever," I say and stand. "Want me to take that?" I gesture toward his pole.

"Sure."

As my brother goes inside to wash up, I head to the garage to put away our gear. I stare at the piles of tools I created earlier and groan. I guess there's no time like the present to get back to work. Approaching a pile I know I'll keep, I pick up a few items and carry them to the bed of my truck.

Over my shoulder, a deep bark interrupts the silence. Depositing the tools, I glance to my right and see a white blur of fur round the curve in the road. Tentatively, I walk to the end of the drive to meet it. The dog picks up his pace when he sees me, even though he favors his left hind leg. I kneel down to greet him, hoping he has tags.

It's when our eyes meet that I know.

No. Fucking. Way.

Sam rushes forward and when he makes it to me, he tries to lick me to death. He gets in a few good swipes before I lean back and snag his collar. Obediently, he sits so I can read his tags. This can't be happening. My eyes refuse to focus for a minute, but when they do, my mind is blown.

"Sam?" I look him in the eyes again. He barks and pants, appearing to smile. I can't think straight, so I rub up and down his sides, noticing how thin he feels beneath his thick fur. He lies on his back, and I go for his belly. His eyes close, loving the attention, and I find myself smiling down at him.

"There you are."

My head snaps up. Standing just a few feet from Sam is the one person I never thought I'd see again in this lifetime.

Addison tips her head. "Hi."

My heart trips over itself in disbelief. Slowly I stand, willing my legs to hold me. "Sparrow?" I whisper.

She looks down at her feet and then back at me. "Hey, Kyle."

Chapter Ten

My mind is having a hard time comprehending her presence.

I used to imagine what it would be like to see her again, to hold her and discover the truth. I would weave silent stories about what I would say, what she might say, and how she would apologize and tell me she loved me. But, as time went on, it became obvious that I was torturing myself with something that would never happen. I forced my mind to come to the only conclusion that would allow me to let her go: she was dead. She had to be. Google and I had an intimate relationship; I couldn't find one shred of evidence that she still existed. First her phone was disconnected, then her house was foreclosed on. Next, it was sold. Her name didn't appear in any search I tried. After years of wondering, I finally had to push her away as best I could.

And now, here she stands, as if I saw her yesterday.

"I didn't expect you at the lake this time of year," she says.

My forehead pinches. I didn't expect to see her ever again. "You mean in the fall?"

She nods.

"It's been a long time since I scheduled my vacations around football camp."

The comment comes out more sarcastic than I would have liked, and Addison loses her smile. She bites her lower lip and studies her shoes.

"I'm sorry," immediately falls from my mouth. I sidestep Sam and walk toward her slowly.

"No." She meets my eyes. "It has been a long time. That was a stupid thing to say." She takes a steadying breath. "It's really good to see you, Kyle."

Still baffled that she's here, I stop walking a few feet in front of her. "It's good to see you too," I murmur. We stare at each other, searching for words, and my hands itch to touch her. My memory hasn't done her justice; even after all this time she still takes my breath away.

Addison wears a pink and white baseball cap; her hair is pulled through the back in a ponytail. It's the same shade of honey-wheat that I remember, and I can tell she wears it long by the way it brushes her shoulders. Her eyes appear to have more gold than brown in them, and she's wearing a plain white fitted tee and low-rise distressed jeans. The clothes hug her every curve; it's hard not to notice she's grown up. Gone is the seventeen year-old girl I once knew and in her place stands a twenty-five year old woman. She looks amazing, almost vibrant, her skin still holding a hint of her summer tan. Her cheeks are flushed pink, probably from my sarcasm, and she looks as if life has treated her well.

I wonder what she sees when she looks at me.

"So, are you here with Gram?" Addison asks, breaking my train of thought and looking past me toward the cottage. "I'd love to see her." Her eyes snap to my face and she smiles. "That is, if she remembers me."

I shove my hands in my front pockets. "No, Gram's not here." Gazing at the ground, I clear my throat. "She's gone."

"Gone where? Did she head into town?"

I shake my head and lift my gaze. "She passed away."

Addison's eyes get big and she steps closer to me. "Oh, God. I'm so sorry. When?"

"About three weeks ago."

She reaches out, like she's going to hug me, but then changes her mind and wraps her arms around her waist instead. "That's so sad. She was such a sweet lady. How are you holding up? How's Kevin?"

"Kevin's inside." I glance over my shoulder. "Gram left this place to us; we're trying to organize. Would you like to come in?"

She gives me a sympathetic look. "I wouldn't want to intrude on your family time."

"Trust me; it's not an intrusion," I say. "It's a welcome distraction."

Addison appears to consider it. My pulse quickens. In my mind I develop a rationale; if I can get her into the house, I can stop her from disappearing again.

"Add?"

A male voice sounds from the road, pulling our attention away from one another. Sam sits up and barks as Addison waves the guy over.

As he walks toward us, I assess him. His dirty blonde hair is neatly styled, and he's dressed in a preppy polo and jeans. *Catalog,* I think and smirk at the name Kevin and I use to describe pretty boys. He's probably got an inch or two on me height-wise, but we're pretty comparable when it comes to muscle. Working outdoors with heavy equipment has kept me in better shape than when Addison and I first met. This guy looks solid too; but more manufactured, like he pays for his fitness at the gym.

"I see you found him," he says to Addison, then looks at Sam. "For an old dog with a bad hip he sure manages to run away a lot." He smiles in my direction. "I hope he didn't cause any trouble."

"No, no trouble," I say.

The guy moves closer to Addison and drapes his arm around her shoulders. Instantly, my body reacts and tenses.

"Derek, this is Kyle," Addison introduces us. "Kyle, this is Derek. My husband."

The word 'husband' rolls off her tongue effortlessly, while I, on the other hand, am rendered speechless.

Derek extends his free hand to shake mine, and the gesture takes a moment to register. I blink to clear my thoughts and then complete the task robotically.

"Kyle is a friend," Addison explains. "Sam must have realized he was here."

"Cool." Derek smiles at me again and then looks at Addison. "Are you ready to get going? Our dinner reservation is at seven."

"Sure." Addison steps away from her husband's embrace. She snags the dog by his collar then looks at me. "I'm glad Sam found you instead of Mr. Grant's chickens." Her eyes light up at the memory.

All I can manage to say is "Right," because I'm still trying to wrap my mind around the fact that she's married.

"I really am sorry about Gram." Addison's face softens. "If there is anything we can do, please let us know."

"We?" I ask, confused.

"Derek and me. We're staying until Monday, if there's something you need."

My mind snaps out of its fog. There is something I need, and she should know what it is. I need time with *her*. I need an explanation. I think she owes me that.

"What happened?" Derek asks.

"Kyle's grandmother passed away," Addison answers. "Here's here with his brother to take care of the cottage."

Derek looks grim. "That's rough. My condolences."

"Thanks," I mutter as I try to figure out how to ask Addison when I can see her again.

Before I can open my mouth, Derek says, "I bet you guys need a break. Why don't you and your brother come over tomorrow and knock a few back. The game's on at one."

Kevin and I were already planning to watch the Michigan-Michigan State football game. My eyes lock on Addison and she gives me an encouraging nod. It's clear she wants me to say yes, so I do.

"Great," Derek says. "We'll see you then."

He winds his arm around Addison's waist and slides his hand into her back pocket. As they turn to leave, he tucks her possessively into his side, nodding his goodbye as she gives me a bright smile.

I want to stop them – stop her – but I don't. If I did, what would I say? How dare you walk away from me? It's clear she has moved on with her life, and it bothers me how much it pisses me off. This shouldn't hurt. Too much time has passed; I should just be happy that she's alive.

But I'm not.

When they make it to the curve in the road, Kevin's voice surprises me from behind.

"What the hell?"

I turn around and find his eyes locked on my departing visitors.

"Is that who I think it is?"

"The one and only."

"Are you shitting me?"

"Nope." I turn back around to follow his line of vision.

"What did she say?"

"Not much. But, I found out she's married."

"Married?" Kevin asks, dumbstruck. "For how long? Where's she been?"

I shrug.

"Jesus, Kyle! What's wrong with you? Do I have to speak for you in your personal life, too?"

I pin him with a hard stare. "Don't be a dick! I haven't seen her in eight years; I thought I was looking at a goddamn ghost."

My brother groans. "Well, when are you going to see her again?"

"Tomorrow." I turn to catch one last glimpse of their retreating figures. "We've been invited over to watch the game."

~~~~

The next afternoon, I shift a case of beer in my arms as Kevin and I wait for Addison to answer her front door. Kevin's eyes meet mine when we hear Sam bark and footsteps approach. He sends me a silent message. *I've got this, bro.*

Despite my asking him to stay out of it, my brother is convinced he will get every ounce of information worth getting from Addison and Derek today. I told him I could handle it.

Naturally, he disagrees.

When the door opens, Addison greets us with a relieved sigh. "You came."

Kevin steps forward and throws his arms wide. "Was there any doubt?" He catches her off guard and wraps her in a bear hug, picking her up off her feet and making her laugh. "Hey, beautiful," he says over her shoulder. "Long time, no see."

Addison's eyes lock on mine for a moment before Kevin sets her down. When he does, she takes a step back from him and smiles. "I'm just getting ready to throw the chicken on the grill. You like barbecued chicken, right?"

My brother holds his stomach and groans. "Are you kidding?"

She laughs again and pushes him toward the open door. He walks inside, and I move to follow.

"Hey." Addison playfully elbows my arm. "I'm really glad you're here."

All I can manage is an uncertain smile.

She nudges me over the threshold then shuts the door behind us. "Let's put that in the fridge," she says, eyeing the beer.

"Hold up." Kevin stops us and pulls one from the case. "Okay, proceed." He winks at Addison. "I'm going to introduce myself to your *husband*."

If I'm not mistaken, Addison blushes. "Derek," she calls toward the couch. "Our company is here."

Derek glances over his shoulder at us. "Hey, guys. You're just in time for the kickoff."

Kevin walks further into the living room, extending his hand to Derek. "Kevin Dayton."

Derek shakes it. "Derek Cole."

My brother pops the top on his can and makes himself comfortable on the end of the couch. I follow Addison into the kitchen. She opens the refrigerator and starts rearranging items so my beer will fit.

I decide now is the time to find my voice.

"So, your last name is Cole," I say. "No wonder I could never find you under Parks."

She stands up straight and meets my eyes. "You were looking for me?"

My brow furrows. "How could I not?"

Addison's expression softens, and she glances around the kitchen. "Here," she says, redirecting her attention. She pulls a pan of raw chicken pieces out of the refrigerator and hands it to me. She grabs two cans of beer and a bottle of barbecue sauce, then shuts the door with her hip. "How important is watching the game to you?"

"Not."

She nods. "Come help me grill."

I follow her out of the kitchen, through the living room, and out on to the deck where I have to step around an excited Sam. I whisper conspiratorially to the dog, "Hey, bud. I'll give you some chicken when it's ready."

Sam parks himself next to my feet as Addison rolls her eyes. She sticks her head back into the house and says, "Give us twenty minutes on the food, guys," then closes the patio door behind her.

Placing the pan next to the grill, I grab a large set of tongs that hang from the side. I start to add the chicken to the hot surface while Addison finds the basting brush and stands next to me. She squeezes sauce on to each piece and paints it as we work in silence. Her arm bumps against mine a few times, and when she finishes with the last leg, I close the top of grill and lean back against the deck railing.

Addison grabs the beer, walks over to where I sit, and settles her body beside mine. She hands me a can and then stares at hers, tracing the top edge with her thumb. "So." She pauses and looks up at me. "I owe you an explanation. Would you like the long version or the Cliffs Notes?"

One side of my mouth twitches. "I'll take whatever you'll give me as long as it's the truth."

She laughs sarcastically. "I couldn't make this up if I tried."

Intrigued, I set my can on the railing ledge and turn toward her. She tips her head. "Remember the last time we talked? When I texted you and told you my dad had a surprise?"

I nod. That conversation is etched into my brain.

Addison inhales and then shifts her gaze toward the lake. "My dad had been taking flying lessons; he got his pilot license in the mail the day we came home. His surprise was to take my mom and me on his first solo flight."

That's actually kind of cool. "Where'd he take you?"

"Up the coast of Lake Michigan. He grew up on the west side of the state."

"Did you have a good time?"

Addison shakes her head. She looks down and swallows hard. "The plane crashed, Kyle. My dad had a stroke and the plane crashed." Her eyes meet mine. "My parents died and I was in a coma for nine months."

All I can do is blink at her. In all the time I spent wondering what had happened to her, I never imagined this. A car accident, yes. An illness, maybe. Her parents relocating for work, definitely. But never her falling out of the sky.

With that thought I snap to. I can't believe she survived something so horrible. Instinctively, I reach for her, wrapping her protectively in my arms. I'm thankful she doesn't resist because I need to touch her, to make sure she's whole.

"How...? If I had known..." I stutter as I crush her to me.

"You couldn't have known," she says, muffled.

My arms tighten around her before I step back to study her face. "Are you okay?" Of the million thoughts racing through my mind, it's the first question that makes it out of my mouth.

"I'm fine," she says with a hint of a smile. "I've had a few years to process what happened. I also have a really great counselor."

"Counselor?" I frown.

"For the PTSD," she says like it's no big thing. "My nightmares are almost non-existent these days."

Holy shit.

"You have nightmares?" I ask. "How many?"

She sighs. "Like I said, not a lot anymore."

I'm concerned, and my face shows it. Addison notices and rolls her eyes. "Please don't look at me like that."

"Like what?"

"Like you feel sorry for me."

My eyes narrow. "You were in a plane crash."

"Yes."

"You were in a coma."

"Yes."

"That had to be terrifying."

"I've worked past it."

We stare at one another. Addison crosses her arms and sticks out her hip, just like she did the first day I met her. I remember how sarcastic and confident she was that day, when she told me I was an ass before she knew my name. As I look at her now, I still see that girl. But, as much as she may want to hide it, I also see a vulnerability that was never there before. Her mouth might say one thing, but her eyes say another.

"So, where have you been all this time?" I ask.

She blinks and her expression looks a little brighter. "I was living in the upper peninsula until a few years ago."

"Why up there?"

"To by near my sister." Addison walks over to the grill and raises the lid to check on the chicken. She finds the tongs and pokes a few pieces, then closes it again. "After the accident, when I got back on my feet, I moved in with Meagan. We got an apartment close to Michigan Tech; we waitressed while we went to school."

"Wait." I walk toward her. "You ended up at Tech? What happened to Julliard?"

She lets out a sarcastic laugh. "Unconsciousness does not lead to scholarships."

"But, that was your dream."

"It's hard to audition when you have to learn how to walk again."

I must look like a deer in headlights because she continues. "I have a pin in my hip and a metal rod in my leg." She pats her left thigh and smiles. "You can call me the bionic woman."

My eyes get wide. "That's not funny."

"Sometimes you have to laugh to get through the crazy," she states diplomatically. "It took me almost a year after I woke up to get my strength back. In the beginning, I couldn't even feed myself." She looks embarrassed. "Ask Derek; I was a hot mess."

My brow creases. "Why Derek?"

Addison lifts the top of the grill again. "He was my physical therapist."

As the information sinks in, I watch her pick up a chicken leg. She slices it open and pulls off a piece of meat. She blows on it, then holds it out to me. "Want to try?"

I open my mouth to ask how she can be so nonchalant, but she mistakes my move as an invitation. She pops the food into my mouth, and it takes me a moment to remember how to chew. I never thought I would see her again, yet here we are. She's feeding me grilled chicken while she explains how she cheated death. It's hard to think straight.

"Is it done?" she asks.

I swallow. "Yeah."

She faces the grill and turns off the gas. "I'll go get a plate for this."

As she starts to walk away, I grab her elbow. "Addison."

She meets my eyes.

"Why didn't you contact me? I would have been there for you; I could have helped."

Hurt colors her features for an instant then disappears. "I was broken when I woke up; more than physically. I wasn't the same person you knew." She takes a heavy breath. "By the time I felt sane again, years had passed since we had seen each other. It made sense that you would have moved on and forgotten about me."

Gently, I squeeze her arm. "I never stopped thinking about you. Ever."

She gives me a tiny smile, and her body relaxes beneath my fingers. She studies my face for a few silent seconds. I wonder what she's thinking.

"More blue today," she finally says.

"What?"

"The color of your eyes. They're more blue today."

I remember a similar conversation we had a lifetime ago, about my color-changing eyes. "Is that bad?" I ask.

"No." She looks wistful as she removes her elbow from my grasp. "They're just as amazing as I remember them."

Chapter Eleven

For the second night in a row, I can't sleep. Kevin, however, snores soundly from the bed beside mine.

When we first arrived at the cottage, my brother and I discussed sleeping arrangements. Neither of us felt okay staying in Gram's bedroom, so here we are, two grown men, sharing the same room we slept in as kids. I know I should man up and move to Gram's bed, but I can't bring myself to sleep there. It doesn't feel right. Besides, it's not my brother's snoring that's giving me insomnia.

It's a certain girl from my past.

For the hundredth time, I drag my hand over my tired eyes. It's useless to lie here and get a headache listening to Kevin. I throw the blankets off my body and sit up, staring at my brother through the darkness. He continues to snore, and I seriously wonder if he should get that checked. I can't believe his girlfriend puts up with it.

Stiffly, I wander downstairs and find myself in the kitchen. The clock on the stove glows green in the dark, informing me it's after two a.m. I flip the light switch by the sink and decide there's no time like the present for a bowl of cereal.

As I hunker down over my late night snack, my mind turns to today.

And yesterday.

And days well before that.

I can't stop comparing the girl I fell in love with to the woman I spent the afternoon talking to. They're so similar, yet different. Seventeen-year-old Addison was carefree and determined. She planned on following her heart, and you couldn't tell her otherwise. Twenty-five-year-old Addison still appears strong, but more resigned. Experience lives behind her eyes now. Years ago, when she would talk about dancing, she would light up. Now, when she talks about her job as a dance instructor, she barely glows. It's not what she wants to do and I can tell. Her husband, on the other hand, doesn't seem to notice. He thinks the job she was able to find when they relocated down state is perfect.

Thanks to Kevin, the questions kept coming during the game today. Apparently Derek was Addison's primary therapist when she was in the hospital. When her doctors determined she had brain activity, he was there; working her arms and legs after her injuries healed, so her muscles stayed limber. Derek was the first person she saw when she opened her eyes again. After rehab, he helped her study to earn her GED and, when she decided she was well enough to move in with her sister up north, he left his job at the hospital for another, to avoid a long-distance relationship. Now they're married; have been for five years.

The thought burns me. I know it shouldn't, but it does. I should have been the first person Addison saw when she opened her eyes, and I would have been had I known where she was. Does that mean we would be together now? I'm not sure. She said she was broken back then. But, a smug part of me would like to think Derek wouldn't have stood a chance had I been in the picture.

Don't get me wrong: I understand that ship has sailed now. Derek and Addison look happy, especially after she plopped her ass in his lap and spent the last quarter of the game pressed against his chest. My face twists at the thought. What I saw only brought up memories of her curled in *my* lap, on the last night we spent together at the lake. It was hard not to compare my past experience to this afternoon, especially when she kept catching my eyes with hers. I couldn't figure out if she was trying to tell me something or if she was just comparing grown Kyle to teenage Kyle, like I did to her.

With my spoon, I scrape the bottom of the bowl and realize I've tasted none of the cereal. Kevin thinks I should be able to move past Addison, now that I know she didn't willingly disappear. He says running into her again should bring me some closure. Honestly, it does and it doesn't. Maybe, in time, I'll be able to think about her without contemplating the what-ifs. The truth is, if she wasn't married, I would jump at the chance to get to know her again. Can I really blame Derek for wanting her? Despite Addison's condition when she first arrived at the hospital, he probably lost his heart then and there. I know I would have. As a matter of fact, I think she still has mine. Given the circumstances, I should probably ask for it back.

After the game, Addison gave Kevin and me a goodbye hug. She didn't mention getting together again. I'm not sure what I expected; she told me everything. Why would we *need* to see each other again? Kevin did manage to slide one of our business cards into her hand, saying if she ever needed anything done around the house to let us know. At least she has my number. I have to think if she wants to talk, she'll call. Unfortunately, I know better than to hold my breath waiting.

Tasteless snack gone, I place my bowl in the sink, turn off the light, and stare out the kitchen window. It faces Addison's cottage, but I can't see it in the dark. Regardless, I know it's there, and I know she's inside.

It's then the realization hits me.

I may not be able to see her or touch her, but I know she's there. Even though we've parted ways, she exists. Addison is alive, and she is safe. It's the only thing that matters.

It's the only thing that should matter.

~~~~

The following afternoon, Kevin and I pack up to head home. We've been at the cottage nearly a week, and it's time to get back to work. We made decent progress in sorting through Gram's things. Kevin has a truck load to drop off at the Goodwill, and mine holds what I salvaged from the garage for the business.

As I slam my tailgate shut, my brother's phone rings. He answers it for the millionth time today. "Hey, babe. I'm leaving in five."

I eavesdrop on his side of the conversation and frown. This Ashley is impatient.

"Three hours give or take. Yeah, I'm coming over." He chuckles, then almost growls, "Please do." His tone changes back to lighthearted. "Love you, too. Bye."

Christ.

Kevin catches me scowling at him. "What?"

"Love you too?"

He sighs. "I told you how I felt about her."

"You said you *thought* you were falling in love with her. When did that change?"

"Since we've been apart for five days. I miss her."

I shake my head and cross my arms. "I told you to slow down."

Kevin mirrors my pose. "And I said you should understand."

Now it's my turn to sigh. "It's not that I don't understand. It's just...you know how things turned out when I fell too fast."

"Well, I'm not you, and Ashley's not Addison." Kevin walks forward. "This is the real thing."

Is he insinuating that Addison and I weren't the real thing? Oh, wait. We weren't. At least, not after fate or karma or some other shit stepped in.

"Listen, I get it." I put my hands up defensively. "I want you to be happy, and if you want Ashley, then that's fine. I can't stop being your big brother, though. If this goes bad, don't say I didn't warn you."

Kevin grins and slaps me on the shoulder. "You'll see. You'll love her once you meet her."

I'll take his word for it.

We agree to meet at the office in the morning, then jump in our respective vehicles to head home. I take one last look at the place I avoided for so long and immediately know I'll return. Not only do we still have work to do, but this place is ours now. Gram wanted us to enjoy it, and I know she's watching. I won't let her down again.

As my truck winds its way around the lake toward the main road, I realize I saw next to nothing during my time here. I managed to make it into town once for groceries, but that was it. Unlike my brother, I don't have anyone to rush home to, so I decide to detour to the old farm property I used to visit on the quad. Since working outdoors is my life now, I'm curious to see how nature has taken over the place. I would be pleasantly surprised if someone bought it and lived there, even though I've never seen it up for sale. It's a great piece of land.

When I pull up to the farm, I notice a silver Hummer H3 parked crookedly in the grass. My eyes dart past it and find Addison, sitting on the edge of the farmhouse foundation with her knees pulled to her chest. My truck slows and my pulse accelerates as I debate stopping. I search for Derek. I don't see him, but that doesn't mean he's not here. Should I stop and say hi or keep going?

To hell with it. At this point, I have nothing to lose.

I park next to the Hummer, kill the engine, and glance at Addison through the windshield. She hasn't moved, and it doesn't look like she knows I'm here. Slowly, I exit the truck. I shove my hands in my back pockets and walk toward her. She probably came out here to be alone and here I am, ruining her solitude. I'm about ten steps away when she wipes beneath her eyes and turns to face me.

"Fancy meeting you here." She offers a weak smile.

Concerned, I close the distance between us and crouch in front of her. "Are you crying?"

She takes a shaky breath and sniffs. "Not anymore."

Her eyes are puffy and rimmed in red; it's obvious the tears have been falling for some time. My jaw tenses. "Whose ass do I have to kick?"

She lets out a clipped laugh. "No one's, but thanks for the offer."

"Are you sure?"

She nods. "Same issue, different day. I'll be all right."

Not that it's my business, but I want to know what the problem is. Does it have something to do with her nightmares? She said they were better. Suddenly, I'm worried it is related to her trauma, to her past. Just yesterday, she had to re-live it all to tell me what happened.

Did I push her into some sort of relapse?

"It's me, isn't it?" I ask and stand. "I'm sorry. I'll go."

Her face contorts. "What? No! Don't be an idiot."

I give her a wary look. "Telling me what happened didn't hurt you?"

"Hell yes it hurt," she says. "But, it's a familiar pain."

The fact that she has any pain, let alone a familiar one, doesn't sit well with me. I want to comfort her, but I don't know how. "I wish I could change things," I tell her honestly. "I wish I could make it better."

She sighs. "It's not up to you to make it better." She moves over on the cement she's perched on and glances at the empty space next to her. With caution, I take a seat. Together, we stare out over the empty yard in silence.

As my eyes roam, I take in the ancient oaks that still stand like towering guards over the property. Most of their leaves have fallen, but a few branches remain dotted with rusty red. To my left, the fruit orchard is the same overgrown mess as it always was, although you can still make out the perfect alignment of trees. Scattered beneath them, on the ground, are dozens of apples, well-rotted by now. Time stands still and my mind wanders. It creates pathways and designs flower beds; it constructs a driftwood arbor next to a manmade pond. My eyes land on the spot where Addison and I had our picnic summers ago. My mind switches gears. I see the place where we danced like fools, where she earned her nickname, where we –

"Are you thinking what I'm thinking?" Addison quietly interrupts my trip down memory lane.

I clear my throat. "Possibly."

My eyes meet hers, and I swear to God if she wasn't married I would kiss her. I *want* to kiss her. I want to tie more memories to this place by wrapping her in my arms, holding her against me, and erasing our lost years with my lips.

My shoulders tense at the thought. If I acted on my imagination, I'm sure I would get slapped. It wouldn't hurt anything but my ego. Or, worse yet, the chance to see her again.

Addison must read my mind because she moves, hugging her knees to her chest, and filling the space between us. The last thing I want is for her to feel uncomfortable, so I manage a crooked smile and say, "I was designing one hell of a landscape in my head. Why? What were you thinking?"

She gives me a knowing smirk and lightly kicks my leg with her foot. "I always knew you had a thing for the outdoors. Kevin gave me your card."

"I saw."

"I'm happy for you. You're doing something you love." She looks sincere. "I bet your work is amazing."

"Business is good." I shrug off her compliment. "Kevin does the talking, I do the design. It works like a charm."

"I'm sure it does."

Silence surrounds us again, and I hate it. It never used to be this way; Addison and I could talk for hours about absolutely nothing. Or, if we were quiet, it was a comfortable silence. Usually our bodies were wrapped around one another and there wasn't any need for words.

I almost resort to asking her about the weather, when an image of her face from yesterday appears in my head. I'm as curious now as I was then.

"Tell me about your job," I say, remembering how she looked less than enthused. "You're doing something you love, too, right?"

She gives me half a smile. "It really is a great opportunity. The pay is good; my boss is flexible. And the kids," her eyes finally light up, "they're so sweet. Watching them grow as dancers makes me want to burst with pride."

"But?"

She looks confused. "But what?"

"There's something wrong. I can tell. You don't talk about dance the way you used to."

She looks down at her knees. "You know my goals were tied to dance. I lost Julliard." She lets out a heavy breath. "I realize I should be grateful for what I have, and I am. I mean, it's a miracle I'm alive, let alone able to dance." She looks at me. "But, some days, I just want...*more*. You know?"

I nod. Despite everything we're blessed with, there's always something else we want. Hell, what I want is sitting right in front of me and I most definitely can't have her.

"What would be more for you?" I ask.

Her face lights up before she speaks. "I want my own studio," she says with real enthusiasm. "My own school. Where everything is my vision, from the shows to the lessons to the technique. Where I can charge what I want." Her face falls a little. "Classes aren't cheap where I teach. I've seen people turned away."

I'm confused as to why she can't have this. It doesn't sound like an impossible dream. "So what's stopping you? You should go for it. There would be a waiting list to get in, I know it."

She smiles. "Thanks. The truth is I've always wanted my own studio. Even when Julliard was an option, I always knew I would teach at some point. I've put money aside; I've been saving it, for when Derek and I found our permanent home. Now that we've moved downstate, I need to start looking for a building I can afford."

"Why haven't you?"

Her excitement fades. "Derek wants me to spend the money on something else."

What? After everything she's been through, how could he deny her any happiness? "What's more important than your studio?" I ask.

She offers me a hint of a smile. "A baby."

I was not expecting that answer. My stomach plummets, landing on the ground and splattering somewhere between my feet. "You're not...are you...?" I can't even say the word. *Pregnant.*

She shakes her head. "I can't."

"You can't what?"

"Get pregnant," she says softly. "The accident...I had a lot of internal injuries too." She tucks a piece of hair behind her ear. "The doctors removed the scar tissue, but things still aren't working right. Derek wants us to try in vitro."

A test tube baby? This subject is foreign to me. The only thought I've given to kids is how to protect myself *against* having them. As I look at Addison, it's hard to believe we're the same age and living such different lives.

"Is that what you want?" I ask, not sure I want to know the answer. "I mean, you're only twenty-five. Maybe if you gave it some time, it might work out." Yes, I'm trying to talk her out of this. Why, I don't exactly know.

Addison turns, sets her feet on the ground, and stares at her shoes. "I agree. I'd like to wait and see what nature brings instead of trying to play God." She looks at me. "Like you said, I'm twenty-five. Derek is thirty-one. I think we have some time. We've only been trying a year."

"So, I take it Derek doesn't agree?"

"He comes from a big family; kids are important to him. He doesn't understand why I would want to wait any longer." Her face falls, defeated. "It's not that I don't want kids. I just know that if we spend the money, it will take us years to save it again."

"How much does this thing cost?" I ask, perplexed. "Why can't you do the in vitro and look into the business at the same time?"

"It's expensive," she sighs. "Sometimes it takes more than one procedure to work. We have roughly twenty-thousand saved and most of it came from my parent's life insurance. One procedure would wipe that out."

Damn.

"That's why I brought Derek to the lake," she continues, "so we could get away and talk things through. It's the first time he's been here; the first time I've been back since I last saw you." Her eyes soften. "This place was magic for me once. I thought it could be again."

Her words hit me in the chest. I thought this place was special, too, before I lost her. I start to wonder what forces brought us back here, at the same time, all these years later. Then I realize she's not finding the magic she came looking for. "Is that why you were upset earlier?"

The tops of her ears turn pink. "You know what? I'm sorry. I shouldn't be dumping all of this on you. It's way more than you want to know. Forget it. Let's talk about something else."

I shoot her an incredulous look. "Are you kidding? I can't forget what you told me. You're going through something huge; you've *been* through something huge. If you need to talk, I'm here. I don't know how much help I'll be, but I can listen." I stop short of telling her I've missed her voice so much I don't care what she's saying. She could read the dictionary and I'd want to hear it. Twisted as it is, if talking about her issues with Derek keeps her here with me, I'm okay with that.

Her face fills with uncertainty. "You're sure?"

"Absolutely. Tell me why you were upset and then you can ask me something personal."

"It's not hard to figure out," she says. "I tried to talk to Derek this morning, and I didn't get anywhere. Instead of finding a middle ground, we argued. He still doesn't think we should wait." She bites her bottom lip. "I also told him about me and you; about what we used to be. I don't think it helped."

My mouth falls open. "He didn't know?"

She shakes her head. "He knew I was seeing someone before the accident, and he knew it was serious. I never gave him a name."

"Why not?"

"Would it have mattered?"

I guess not. I don't tell my girlfriends the names of my exes. "So, I take it he's pissed?"

"I would say shocked above anything else. He's more upset that I'm denying him offspring."

She has to be kidding. "Did he say that?" I ask. If he did, I may have to pay a visit to Mr. Cole. All Addison is asking for is time.

She shrugs. "Not in so many words." She turns her head and looks toward the oak trees. "I feel guilty for hurting him. I hate that we don't want the same thing right now."

Her eyes start to tear up again, and I want to stop her from crying. I know I shouldn't, but I reach out, grasp her chin, and gently turn her face back to mine. "Listen, I'm the last person who should be giving relationship advice. Just ask Kevin."

She smirks.

"But, you're entitled to your opinion. It's your life, too. Derek should understand that. If he doesn't, he's an ass."

Addison narrows her eyes and leans out of my hold. "You don't know him."

"You're right," I respond. "But, as my brother so rudely pointed out the other night, relationships won't work without give and take. I know. I follow a 'pattern'." I mimic air quotes for emphasis.

She laughs. "Does Kevin moonlight as a psychologist?"

"Just around the campfire."

She smiles again, and I'm happy to see it. I don't care that it got there at my expense.

Just then, a beep sounds and Addison reaches into the front pocket of her jacket. She pulls out her cell phone and consults the screen.

"Let me guess," I say.

"He's worried. I've been gone almost an hour." She frowns. "I should go."

As much as I don't want to send her back to Derek, I have no choice. Standing, I offer my hand to help her up off the hard cement we've been sitting on. She takes it, and I pull her to her feet. Without a word and to my surprise, she winds her fingers through mine. She leads me toward our parked cars, and I follow without an ounce of regret. Slowly, we walk side by side, holding hands, as if time never separated us.

I love every moment of it.

When we reach her truck, I open the door and help her up into the driver's seat. I don't want this to be the last time I see her, but my gut tells me her decision to hold my hand was her way of saying goodbye. When her fingers leave mine, my stomach feels hollow.

"Take care of yourself," I manage to say. "Promise me you will do what feels right."

She pauses from putting the key in the ignition and looks at me. "Always."

The way she says the word confuses me. It's almost as if she's talking about something else, other than her fight with Derek. My mind races. "Well, if you need someone to talk to, you know where to find me."

Before she can say anything, her phone beeps again and she rolls her eyes. "Gotta go."

I get it; if I were her husband, I'd be worried, too. I step back as she closes the door and starts the engine. She raises her hand, giving me a slow wave, and then looks over her shoulder to back the truck on to the road.

Standing with my arms crossed, I watch her leave, damning my heart for hurting again. Through the window our eyes meet, and I almost think she's changed her mind and decided to come back to me.

A short second later, she drives away. I'm left standing alone to wonder if I'll ever hear from her again.

Chapter Twelve

Exhausted, I toss my keys on the kitchen counter. I'm due a hot shower, a cold beer, and a long nap, in that order. For some unknown reason, Kevin bailed on me today, and I've been working my ass off since six this morning.

While I'd like to be angry with him, I really can't be. In our business, the fall season is the slowest for Dayton Landscaping. My brother and I tend to spend the time catching up on paperwork. Things get busy again in the winter months, when we offer snow removal services for homeowners and businesses. However, this fall my brother managed to secure a contract with Eden Gardens, a subdivision in Macomb Township. We're taking care of the fall cleanup for every lot in the sub, which means over 100 homes. My guys and I have spent the last few weeks winterizing sprinkler systems, cleaning up leaves, and trimming back common areas. It's a race to get everything finished before the temperature drops, and I'm dead on my feet.

But I also have more money in the bank.

I make my way to the bedroom and peel off layers as I go. Long-sleeve thermal: gone. White t-shirt: gone. I wad them into a ball and toss them on my unmade bed, followed by my sweaty socks. If Jen were here, she'd glare at me for throwing my dirty clothes where she sleeps. As I reach for the button on my pants to remove my grimy jeans, a realization hits me.

She's been gone a month.

Thirty days have passed since I was at the cottage.

It surprises me how fast time has passed. I pause, grateful for the extra business that has kept me busy. I don't think I could take my usual fall boredom; I'd be out of my mind sitting in this empty house replaying every decision I've ever made when it comes to both Jen and Addison.

I shed the rest of my clothes and make a vow at the same time. I haven't beaten myself up over them, and I'm not going to start tonight. What's done is done; the past is the past. Today is a new day and all that shit. It's time to get comfortable, and I'm not talking about getting cleaned up and lounging in sweats. I'm talking about my life, from this day forward. So I'm bound to be a bachelor. So what? I know guys who would kill for that life.

When I step into the shower, I hear my phone ring from the bedroom. I let it go to wash up, then hear it again when I get out. Curious, I wrap a towel around my waist and walk across the hall to find my cell. When I dig it out of my pants pocket, I have five missed calls from Kevin, all within minutes of each other. My first instinct is that something bad has happened, and an image of our mother appears in my head. I immediately dial his number.

"Where have you been?" Kevin answers before I can say anything.

"In the shower. What's wrong?"

"Nothing." I can practically hear him smile through the phone. "Everything's perfect." He pauses. "I did it."

"Did what?" I plop down on the edge of the bed. "Figured out you're annoying as hell?"

He laughs. "No. I proposed. Ashley said yes. We're getting married."

My jaw nearly hits the floor. "You what?! Why didn't you call me first?"

"So you could try to talk me out of it?" I picture his twisted expression. "No way. Ashley's the one."

"Kev," I start to reason with him, "you've only been dating a couple of months. I mean, she's a great girl, but don't you think you're moving a little too fast?"

My brother introduced me to Ashley soon after we got back from the lake. We went out to dinner and, at first, she was reserved and polite, almost boring. Later, after the main course and a few drinks, she opened up, revealing her quick wit and wicked sense of humor. I immediately liked her. She hung on Kevin's every word, and she's exactly his type; shorter than him, curvy, and very blonde. But, does their compatibility warrant a quickie wedding?

"This is why I didn't tell you," he huffs. "I don't need your shit. Can't you just be happy for me?"

"You're 23."

"I know."

"Why the rush?"

"I love her."

"Are you two in trouble?"

"Like how?"

"Is she pregnant?"

"No!"

I'm silent for a few moments, wondering how we came from the same gene pool. While I keep my feelings guarded, Kevin wears his on his sleeve. He's impulsive; I'm careful. While he listens to his heart, I pretend mine doesn't speak – especially when it brings up a certain married ex. Thinking of Addison reminds me that I've been in his shoes once, a long time ago, and I should cut him some slack. If he's feeling anything like I did back then, he's a total goner.

And maybe that's the point.

Take the chance. Own the opportunity. Make her yours while you can.

Before I can concede that he's probably done what's best for him, he sighs. "I want you to be my best man."

My free hand rubs the back of my tense neck. I want to be happy for him; I honestly do. "Okay," I say.

"Okay you'll do it?"

"Of course I will. If this is what you really want."

My brother snorts sarcastically. "No; I proposed because I'm confused."

"You know what I mean. I'll support you, even if you decide to walk out of the church at the last minute. We'll come up with a secret signal, and I'll meet you out back with a getaway car."

He chuckles. "Great. I'm glad we have that unnecessary plan."

One side of my mouth quirks up as I picture him wearing a tux and sliding across the hood of a car Dukes of Hazzard-style, saving just enough time to jump inside before I hit the gas to peel out of the parking lot.

"So, now what?" I ask. "Please tell me you're not getting married next week."

"No; we haven't set a date. But, we made plans for this weekend, and you're involved."

"How so?"

"Ashley wants to get all our friends together to celebrate."

Of course. "Where at?"

"Necto."

I'm familiar with the trendy nightclub; Jen and I went there once for her co-worker's birthday party. There were plenty of pulsating lights and pulsating bodies; needless to say I spent the night with my ass parked at our table.

"When?"

"Saturday. I'm not sure what time yet."

"All right." I sigh. "I'll make an appearance, but I don't know how long I'll stay."

If scowls made a sound, I'd hear Kevin's. "For once in your life could you just relax? Come out and have some fun."

"Yeah, yeah." I stand and glance behind me. "Listen, I've got to go." Since I answered the phone without drying off, my bed is all wet. "I'll see you tomorrow at work."

"Yep. I'll be there."

"Good. We need the help."

After I hang up, I toss my phone on the bed, wondering when my little brother got so mature. It's going to be hard to think of him as a settled, married man. I shake my head as I make my way to the dresser and find my well-worn sweats, the pair with the obnoxious hole in the knee; the ones Jen hated and wanted to burn. I finish drying off, lose the towel in a crumpled heap on the floor, and pull the pants on with a weird twinge in my gut.

~~~~

Saturday night rolls around faster than anticipated. I'd put off a bunch of errands, like grocery shopping and laundry, with how busy I'd been at work. When I discovered I had one pair of clean underwear that morning, it prompted me to suck it up and get shit done. Empty the trash: check. Wash dirty dishes: check. Buy food: check. Get haircut: check.

Now, turning into the parking lot of Necto Nightclub, I try to determine how short of a stay would be considered rude. Dance clubs really aren't my scene; I'm more of a sports bar kind of guy. I plan to say hi, introduce myself, have a couple drinks, and head home. I have a full day of football to watch tomorrow.

God, I'm boring.

I leave my truck with the valet and then walk toward the entrance, quickly texting Kevin to find out where he is inside. As I pay the cover, my phone vibrates in my hand.

Next to the bar, far side of the room.

The club is packed. I should have expected nothing less on a Saturday. Heavy bass pumps through the speakers as I pass through the crowd. I maneuver my way around the gyrating bodies and toward the bar. As I brush past one girl, I accidentally bump her arm. Some of the drink she holds sloshes on her hand, and she turns and pins me with an irritated stare.

"Sorry!" I apologize over the music and reach out to steady her arm by her elbow. "It's a little crowded!"

She studies me and her irritation disappears. She plasters on a flirty smile and steps closer, placing her hand on my chest. Before she can say anything, I step back and release her elbow, nodding my goodbye. The last thing I came here to do is hook up.

After a few more seconds of scanning the bar, I spot Kevin's waving arm next to Ashley's blonde head. I make a beeline straight for them.

"Hi!" Ashley enthusiastically greets me. She throws one arm around my neck in a hug while balancing some sort of red drink in her other hand. "I'm so glad you could make it!"

I pat her back awkwardly. This is only the second time we've met.

"Let me introduce you to the girls!" Her eyes sparkle.

Is she overly excited or just buzzed? I give Kevin a questioning glance, and he grins as she grabs my arm and pulls me forward.

"Ladies," she addresses a girl with dark hair and a red head sipping drinks as they lean against the bar. "This is Kyle. Kevin's brother and our Best Man."

The one with the raven-colored hair extends her hand and smiles. "Nice to meet you. I'm Nikki," she introduces herself. "Ashley's sister."

My eyes dart to Ashley, then back to Nikki. They look nothing alike. While my brother's fiancée is the all-American blonde, Nikki has exotic features and an olive skin tone.

"She means sorority sister," the other girl notices my confusion and elaborates. She elbows Nikki, then shifts her glass to her left hand and offers me a handshake as well. "My name's Tara. Also a sister."

I shake her hand and smile hello. Tara has cute freckles and gorgeous green eyes. "Thanks for clearing that up."

"These two will be in the wedding party," Ashley explains. "We're still waiting for my best friend – oh!" She stops short as something catches her eye. "Here comes the Maid of Honor now."

Ashley steps around me to greet the new arrival, and I turn my head to follow her. When I see who she meets, I forget how to breathe.

Addison lets go of Derek's hand and skips toward Ashley with open arms. They let out a girly squeal as they hug one another and jump up and down.

My eyes snap to Kevin and I walk up to him, turning my back on the girls. "Did you know about this?"

He shrugs and looks over my shoulder. "No. If I did, I would have told you."

There's a tug on my elbow, and I turn around to find Addison standing directly in front of me. She looks like she jumped straight out of my dreams wearing some sort of sheer, gauzy cream-colored tank top, dark, skin-tight denim, and knee-high boots. Her hair falls in long, messy waves, and when she speaks, I can't tear my eyes from her shiny, glossed lips.

"What are the odds?" she asks with a tiny laugh.

"About a million to one," I answer around the smile that breaks across my face.

She reaches out and squeezes my forearm, then walks around me to point at Kevin. "You," she says dramatically. "Here I was giving my best friend crap for moving too fast only to find out she's engaged to a Dayton." She shakes her head with a smile. "You had me all worried for nothing."

Kevin fakes an innocent look, then winks. "My apologies."

Addison opens her arms and gives Kevin a hug, saying something in his ear I can't make out. Whatever it is makes him grin and rock her body back and forth, squeezing her tight. When they step apart, Addison looks around the group and asks, "Do we have a table?"

"Uh uh." Ashley swoops in and grabs her hand. "No sitting; only dancing. I've been waiting all night!"

Addison rolls her eyes as Ashley tugs on her fingers. As she's led away, she asks Derek, "Get me a vodka cranberry, 'kay?"

My eyes fall on her husband, and he nods but doesn't look amused. His irritation makes me wonder if he doesn't want her drinking or if he doesn't want to be here, period.

Nikki and Tara follow the girls to the dance floor. As they pass us, Tara stops and asks Derek to keep an eye out for her boyfriend, John. He agrees, which leads me to ask Kevin who else he's expecting.

"Just Austin, and maybe Eli and Noah from work," he says as he flags down a bartender. Austin was Kevin's best friend in high school.

The bartender stops in front of us and my brother orders a draft. He defers to me and after I place my order, I look at Derek. "You need anything?"

"Thanks." Derek moves closer to us so the bartender can hear him. "I'll take a vodka cranberry and a Labatt Blue Light."

Within the next half hour, John arrives, as well as Austin and Eli. To my right, Derek carries on a steady conversation with Tara's boyfriend; it's obvious they know each other well and hang out often. To my left, Austin, Eli, and my brother are having a heated discussion about the show *The Walking Dead*. As I lean against the bar, I'm not into either conversation. My eyes keep gravitating to the dance floor. The way Addison moves mesmerizes me. I know it's wrong to admit, but it's the truth. The woman was born to dance; the way she moves coupled with what she's wearing...I can't believe her husband isn't paying her more attention. It's obvious half the guys in this place have noticed her; there's a group a few feet away from me staring at her now. I don't like it and start to feel protective. If she were here with me, there's no way in hell those guys would look at her twice. I'd make it very clear to everyone in this place that she was off limits and *mine*.

Just then, my married ex swirls her hips and runs her hand through her hair. The sight hits me hard as my mind wanders and imagines my hands clutching those hips. Her eyes catch mine, and I'm forced to look away. She's killing me and she has no idea.

I take a heavy breath and decide it's not healthy for me to face the dance floor. I'm either going to get caught staring or have words with her admirers. Turning away, I try to find a place in the zombie apocalypse conversation. The back of my mind registers the song change to Beyoncé's "Single Ladies" and, a moment later,

I catch Addison approaching the bar. She squeezes herself in between me and Derek, who John is still talking to, and reaches for her as-yet-to-be-touched drink. She downs it in three swallows.

"Whoa!" I turn toward her. "You might want to take it easy."

She smiles and runs the back of her hand across her lips. "I'm hot."

Really? I think sarcastically. *I hadn't noticed.*

She places her elbow on the bar and faces me. "I'll dance it off after this song anyway."

My gaze shifts from her to the dance floor and back again. "Why wait?"

She holds her left hand in front of her face and wiggles her fingers, the lights from the club reflecting off her ring. "I'm not a single lady."

My stomach feels like lead. *Thanks for the reminder.*

"So," she says and looks out toward the sea of dancing bodies, "see anyone you like?"

I frown. "I'm sorry?"

"This place is full of women." She gestures toward the dance floor. "Half of which are single or pretending to be." She gives me a knowing smile. "One of them has to have caught your eye."

My first thought is that I'm busted for watching her and she's trying to call me out on it. But, then, she starts to analyze different girls and try to find one that's right for me.

"How about the brunette in the corner? The one wearing the red heels?"

"No." I shake my head. "Too tall."

Addison shrugs. "She has killer legs, though." She looks around some more. "Okay. How about the petite girl over there with the pretty, dark hair?"

"No. I don't like short hair."

"It can grow!" she says with annoyance. She glances around again and then blatantly points. "Ooo! How about her? The blonde with the long hair and hot pink dress?"

I grab her finger to hide it before anyone can see. "Would you stop? No. Kevin's into blondes, not me. And that dress looks like she put on a t-shirt and forgot her pants."

Addison starts to laugh and it's contagious. I laugh with her, loving the sound of her voice.

She sighs. "Come on. There's not one girl in here who interests you?"

Why is this so important to her? I decide to make her happy and play along. "Fine. Yes. Someone has caught my attention." There's no need to tell her that she's that person.

Addison's face lights up. "You should ask her to dance." She sounds genuinely excited, like she's playing matchmaker. "Wait." She stops. "You don't dance." She bites her lip. "You should at least buy her a drink to let her know you're interested."

I give her a smirk and shrug off her advice. "I didn't come here to find the next Mrs. Dayton."

She rolls her eyes and turns to press her back against the bar. "Suit yourself." After a second or two, she asks, "It's crazy, isn't it?"

"What's crazy?"

"All of this." She gestures around us. "Do you remember who was with me at the lake the first summer we met?"

Now I do. My eyes widen. "Your sister and your best friend."

She smiles and nods. "Meagan and Ashley. Who knows what would have happened if I hadn't left that day. What if Kevin had met Ashley back then?"

"Who knows?" I shrug. "They probably would have fallen in love and be on kid number two by now."

"Or," she pauses, "at the very least Kevin would have had her number. You would have been able to find me after the accident."

Her words take me off guard; I'm surprised she went there. It would have taken me some time to figure that out. "Well, yeah." I hesitate. "That would have been convenient."

She laughs.

Out of the corner of my eye, I see Ashley and Tara waving to Addison to rejoin them. She pushes her body away from the bar and looks at me. "I'll be back. Ask Derek to get me another drink, would you?"

I want to ask her why she doesn't ask him herself, but she's out of earshot before I can. I glance at Derek and he's still talking to John. I wonder if he even noticed his wife was standing between us.

Moments later, John pulls his phone from his pocket and walks away to take a call. I'm just about to tell Derek that Addison would like another vodka cranberry, when he steps away from the bar as well. My eyes follow him to where he joins Addison on the dance floor, and she smiles as he approaches. When he reaches her, he wraps his hands around her waist as she winds hers around his neck. Although they remain feet apart, they start to dance, and it's clear Derek has moves. Like Backstreet Boy boy-band moves. They sway as one, as if they have rehearsed this routine, and my stomach knots.

Derek backs up and grabs Addison's hand. He dances and sings along with the song, which happens to be Justin Timberlake's "Mirrors". Addison appears shy as he mimics the lyrics and sings about how she's his reflection, his other half, and how no one else could stand beside him. It makes me want to punch something.

Like Derek's face.

I need a distraction. Maybe Addison had the right idea; I should find someone here to get lost with for a few hours. My eyes scan the room and inevitably land back on the Mr. and Mrs. Cole Show. Derek has moved behind his wife now, with his hands low on her hips. He kisses her neck, and her hands grasp his as she leans back against his chest with her eyes closed. His eyes are open though.

And locked on me.

My jaw tenses. I get what this is now. It's the territorial dance; the proverbial pissing match. Apparently he did notice Addison talking to me before; hell, he probably overheard our conversation. His hard stare tells me a few things:

One. I don't like you.

Two. You don't dance? Watch me, motherfucker.

And three. She's *mine*.

I hold his stare. He's right. He shouldn't like me; I was checking out his wife earlier. She is his. On the other hand, I haven't touched her and we were just talking. It was an innocent conversation. Which reminds me...

I turn toward the bar and flag down the bartender, knowing full well that Derek is watching. I order Addison's drink, and when the bartender brings it to me, I turn around and hold it up, blatantly showing Derek. Then, I set it on the bar. He needs to know he doesn't intimidate me.

His eyes narrow and I can feel the tension roll off his body from across the room. Yep. He heard our conversation all right. He's pissed.

Why?

Because I just bought a drink for the girl I'm interested in.

Chapter Thirteen

My cell rings and an unknown number flashes across the screen. I pick up the phone and touch 'answer' while turning the steering wheel with my left hand. "Dayton Landscaping."

"Kyle? I need your help."

My forehead pinches. The caller sounds like –

"This is Addison."

That's what I thought. My tongue starts to feel dry. I haven't spoken to her in a week, since that night at the club. Minutes after my silent exchange with Derek, I left. I didn't know what he might do, and I didn't want to make Addison uncomfortable or ruin Kevin and Ashley's night. I wonder if he said anything to her; if what happened is the reason for her call.

"Are you there?" she asks.

"Yeah. I'm here."

"What are you doing?"

"Driving." I slow at the next corner and make a right turn.

"Oh. Well, like I said, I need your help. Are you busy tomorrow?"

Hmmm. Let me consult my empty calendar. "No. What's up?"

The line is silent and I imagine Addison twisting her fingers together. After a second or two, she says, "My sister's husband can't make it to the lake to winterize the cottage. I have no idea what needs to be done. Can you come with me for the day? I'll drive."

Instantly, I'm suspicious. "Where's Derek?"

She sighs. "Working."

I get the distinct feeling I'm imagining this conversation. I pull the phone away from my face, glance at the number, and then put it to my ear again. No, it's a real call.

"I know this is out of the blue," Addison rushes to say, "but, I literally just got off the phone with Marc. He's tied up and worried the pipes are going to freeze. Derek's pulling a twelve hour shift and can't take off. You're the next person I thought of."

I'm confused. "Who is Marc?"

"Meagan's husband."

"And he usually takes care of the cottage?"

"Yes, and this year he can't. Will you come with me?"

Forget the pipes freezing; hell would have to freeze over before Derek would approve of Addison spending time with me. "Why can't your sister do it?"

Addison lets out an exasperated breath. "You know what? Never mind. I'll figure it out."

"Wait." I stop her. "Derek's okay with this? He knows you're asking me to go to the cottage with you?"

"No."

Well, at least she's honest.

"Listen." I brake at a stoplight. "I'd love to help, but your husband and I..."

"Don't like each other. I know."

She sounds so nonchalant about our mutual dislike that I begin to debate my options. I tap my fingers on the steering wheel as Rebel Kyle appears on my shoulder and cocks an eyebrow. He says if she doesn't care about Derek's feelings, neither should I. However, on my other shoulder, Moral Kyle sits, with his damn halo, and asks if I want her husband upset with her. I couldn't care less if he hates me, but Addison doesn't need a fight on her hands. Not over something like this.

Decisions, decisions.

Rebel Kyle shouts, *"Screw it! Let's go!"* while Moral Kyle gives me a disapproving glare. My shoulders slump as I choose the high road. "How about you call me when you get there? I'll walk you through everything that needs to be done over the phone."

Rebel Kyle flips me off.

"I have a better idea," Addison says. "Let me mention it to Derek. If everything's okay, I'll pick you up tomorrow morning. If it's a no go, I'll call you tonight. Deal?"

I give her my address.

~~~~

To my surprise, Addison never called. She sent me a text message.

Be there at 9 a.m.

Completely caught off guard, I abandoned *Late Night with Jimmy Fallon* to scramble around my place and make it presentable. I took care of the dirty dishes in the sink and cleared the kitchen countertop of empty bottles. I plumped the couch cushions. I vacuumed the carpet and made sure my dirty laundry was in the basket, not in a pile on the floor. I even put the toilet paper roll on the dispenser and wiped the bathroom sink clean of toothpaste and shavings. I have no idea if she will want to come inside my house, but, if she does, I'd like to make a good impression.

The next morning, I shower and dress in jeans and a navy blue Henley. Not my best attire, but not my beat-up work stuff, either. I want to look decent; however, I will have to crawl underneath a house. After a quick breakfast, I perch on the edge of the couch, waiting. I check the time on my phone repeatedly – 8:55, 8:57, 8:59 – and toss it aside. She's not even late, and I've all but convinced myself that Derek changed his mind and she's not coming.

Then, I hear a knock on my front door.

When I open it, Addison greets me with a small smile. "Hey."

I can't help but smile back at her. She's really here. She looks like a breath of fresh air with her pink cheeks, purple turtleneck, and puffy white winter vest.

"Hey." I open the door wide and step back. "Let me get my coat."

Addison follows me inside. I leave the doorway and jog over to the closet by the garage entrance. It's the end of November, and the temperature has dropped into the forties. I know it will be colder the further north we go, so I find my Columbia jacket. Slipping it on, I turn around to find Addison walking the perimeter of my living room. She stops in front of the shelves next to the entertainment center and runs a finger over my DVD collection, perusing the titles.

"Looking for something in particular?" I ask.

She meets my eyes with another smile. "No. Just trying to get to know you."

I walk toward her and reach over the back of the couch to pick up my phone. "You already know me."

"Do I?" She raises an eyebrow. "You haven't changed after all these years?"

"I don't think so." I round the couch to stand next to her. "My taste in movies is the same." I glance at the shelf. *Friday the 13th*. *The Dark Knight Trilogy*. *Anchorman*. *Stepbrothers*. *Talladega Nights*. "Okay. Maybe I have a thing for Will Ferrell."

She laughs. "I loved *Elf*."

She moves on, walking past my flat screen, the stereo, and the PlayStation. Her gaze jumps to the furniture and lands on my ratty, old, pea-green upholstered recliner. Stuffing leaks out of the arm rest, and there's a permanent dent in the seat from my ass. She shoots me a questioning look.

"What? It's my favorite chair," I confess. "I know it doesn't match." Jen gave me crap for keeping it when she picked out the gray microsuede living room set.

Addison nods in concession and then looks around again. "Your house is cute," she says. "How long have you lived here?"

I think back. "Almost four years. This place was really cheap." Back then, I was twenty-two. The fall in the housing market is the only reason I became a new homeowner. "It's not big, but it's enough for right now."

"Do you plan on moving?"

"Eventually." I walk toward her. "Someday, I'd like to build my own house."

Addison looks impressed. "Like, with your own hands?"

"No; I'm not that talented. I meant I'd like to choose where it goes. And have a say in what it looks like."

She nods, then smiles. "Can I see the rest of your place?"

I'm glad I cleaned.

I lead her down the short hallway and gesture toward the bedroom on the right. "My room," I say as she steps inside. She looks around, her eyes combing over the king-size bed, the dresser, and my computer desk, chair, and laptop. Standing in the hall, seeing her in such an intimate space – a space I've imagined her in – I get a heavy rush of adrenaline. It would be so easy to walk up behind her, wrap my arms around her waist, and bury my lips under her ear.

I inhale, then exhale. I've only been around her five minutes. *Get a grip, Kyle.*

"Uh, the bathroom is behind us," I say to distract myself and pull her attention away from my personal space.

She turns and leaves my room, peeks in the bathroom, and then points at the only other door in the hallway. "Spare room?"

I nod.

She pokes her head in my guest bedroom, which only serves as a catch-all for everything that doesn't have a place. There's a bin of old CD's, a couple of filing cabinets, an acoustic guitar, and boxes of things from my mom's that I never unpacked.

Addison zeroes in on the guitar. "Do you play?"

"Very little," I admit. "If it were a piano, my skill level would be chopsticks."

She laughs. "Then why do you have it?"

I shrug. "My ex played and she tried to teach me. I wasn't a very good student."

"Jen?" she asks.

My eyes widen in surprise. "How do you –?"

"Ashley told me."

"And she knows about my life how?"

"From Kevin."

I stare at Addison in confusion, and she nervously tucks a piece of hair behind her ear. She breaks eye contact and looks into the guest bedroom. "I asked, okay? Once I found out Ashley was engaged to your brother, I asked some questions." She meets my eyes again. "Okay?"

I cross my arms and lean against the doorframe, pursing my lips and trying not to grin. Addison's been asking about me.

Excellent.

She notices my reaction and rolls her eyes. "Don't get a big head about it."

"I'm not." I can't contain my smile. "But, just so you know, you can ask me whatever you want personally. I've got nothing to hide and I don't always trust Kevin's rendition of things."

Her shoulders appear to relax. "Good to know."

I lead her in the opposite direction. We end up in the kitchen next to my small dining table. "Well, that concludes the tour. Do you want to get going? Or would you like to look inside of my refrigerator?" I tease.

She playfully bumps my arm. "No." She shoves her hands in her vest pockets and glances around my tiny kitchen. Her eyes move along the top of the cabinets, which Jen decorated with fake plants to offset my manly display of international beer bottles. She steps back, leans against the countertop, and catches my eyes for a moment. Then, she stares at her shoes and shifts her weight from foot to foot.

If I didn't know any better, I'd say she was nervous.

"Kyle." She raises her head to look at me. "I lied."

My eyes narrow in confusion. "About?"

She opens her mouth to speak, thinks better of it, and then closes it again.

Shit. My mind starts to race. There are only a few things we've discussed. Did she lie about the accident? Or Derek? *Please let it be Derek.*

"The cottage," she sighs. "You don't need your coat."

"What?"

She lets out a heavy breath. "I came up with the story about the cottage so I could see you." She shifts her weight again. "My brother-in-law called yesterday to tell me he took care of everything. I twisted it into an excuse to call you."

No. Way.

I want to grin like a fool, but Addison's chocolate brown eyes soften and silently plead with mine. "Say something," she says.

"Sparrow, I..."

Her breath hitches at the sound of her nickname, and I mentally kick myself. It's probably not a good idea to call her that. I run my hand through my hair. "You told a pretty elaborate lie."

Her cheeks flush. "I'm so embarrassed."

She doesn't need to be. I give her a crooked smile and take a step toward her. "Guess what?"

"What?"

"I've been trying to figure out how to see you again, too."

Relief floods her features. "Really? Ever since the night at the bar I can't stop thinking about the wedding. I can't believe we've been thrown together like this. I don't want things to be awkward; there's a lot we need to talk about and..."

"Whoa," I chuckle. "Slow down. We've got all day."

"About that..." Addison bites her lower lip. "I have to be at work at two."

I shake my head as I take off my coat. "How did you think you were going to pull off this lie?"

She looks defeated. "At first I was only going to use the winterizing as an excuse to call you. You know, get your opinion on what needed to be done. Then, it morphed into wanting to see you, and I asked you to come with me. When you brought up Derek, I figured that was my out; I'd just call you later and tell you he said no. But, then..." She shakes her head. "I don't know what happened. I ended up texting you that I would be here."

I laugh. "Sparrow. If you're gonna make up stories, you need a better plan."

She doesn't laugh with me. Instead, I notice her eyes widen as she searches my face. My smile fades. Did I say something wrong?

"You called me Sparrow again," she says softly.

Shit. I did, and I didn't even realize it. "I'm sorry."

Addison stands up straight, pushing herself away from the kitchen countertop. We're about a foot apart when she looks up at me. It reminds me of how perfectly her body fit against mine; how when I would hold her, she fit against me like a puzzle piece.

"Don't apologize," she says. "I've missed hearing it."

I'm suddenly very aware of my breathing. Air rushes in and out of my nose. "Are you sure?"

She nods. "Derek calls me Add." She looks down at her ring. "I have a math function for a nickname." She scowls. "I hate math."

Laughter erupts from deep inside my chest. I can't help it. This whole situation has me tense and elated at the same time.

Addison laughs with me, and, after a moment or two, I gesture toward her vest. "Since we're not going anywhere, do you want me to take that?"

She nods and removes it, and I head over to the closet to hang up our coats. I'm kind of relieved we don't have to make the six hour round trip to the lake and back.

When I return to the kitchen, Addison is standing in front of my refrigerator with her arms crossed. Her eyes are focused on the few papers stuck there.

"Tell me about your business," she says when she realizes I'm in the room. She points to one of my several Dayton Landscaping & Design magnets. "How did you get started?"

I'm pleasantly surprised she wants to know. My other girlfriends didn't care. I don't blame Courtney; she hated the business. Probably because I spent 99 percent of my time trying to get DL&D off the ground. Jen never asked because she was friends with Kevin before dating me; I'm sure she knew everything she wanted to know about the company. As long as there was money in the bank, Jen was happy.

"Actually, you're kind of involved," I say and move around Addison. She gives me a questioning look as I open the fridge door and grab two bottles of water. "Want one?"

"Thanks."

I hand her a drink and lead us back into the living room. I take a seat on one end of the couch and Addison sits down on the other, facing me and crossing her legs beneath her. I set my bottle on a coaster as I figure out where to start.

"After high school, I didn't know what I wanted to do." I wink at her. "But you know that."

She nods. "Did you get that football scholarship?"

I'm surprised she remembers. "Ah, no." I lean back on the couch. "After you..." I hesitate, looking for the right word. "After you...left, I had to throw myself into something. I chose football. Except, I became a real asshole." I look at her. "I was angry. I picked fights; I took my aggressions out on the other players. Let's just say it didn't pay off."

Addison avoids my eyes and I notice her swallow. I don't want to make her uncomfortable, but her disappearance plays a big part in who I am today. "Do you want me to stop?" I ask.

She shakes her head. "No. Just...Kyle..." Her face falls. "I'm really sorry. If I could go back and change what happened, I would. I never would have gotten on that plane."

I move over on the couch and reach for her hand. She places her fingers in mine and I squeeze them. "It's not your fault."

Her eyes look glassy. "I made you an asshole."

I smile. "No, I made me an asshole. I didn't know how to deal with your leaving. I wasn't sure if your parents made you go, or if you got sick, or what happened. I was out of my mind, and I didn't know how to deal with it."

"So, you got into fights?"

"Usually. All it took was someone to say the wrong thing or look at me the wrong way. Then Kevin would step in and it was a big mess." I shake my head. "If I wasn't in class, I was in the office. It was a miracle I graduated."

Addison frowns. "Your poor mother."

"That woman is a saint." I move my hand to lace my fingers through hers. "She didn't know what to do. If I wasn't angry, I was depressed. If I wasn't depressed, I was moody. She tried everything she could think of to fix me, until the summer after high school. She was fed up and frustrated. When I refused to go back to the lake, she gave me an ultimatum. Go to college, get a job, or get out."

Addison lets out a small gasp. "You didn't go back to the lake? What about Gram?"

"Kevin went to help her. This October, after her death, is the first time I've been to Buhl Lake since..." Now it's my turn to swallow. "Since the summer you vanished."

Her grip around my fingers tightens.

"Anyway," I continue, "my mom was going to kick me out. I knew school wasn't for me, so I went job hunting. I found a help wanted ad for a landscaping company and your words came back to me." I smile. "You said I had an eye for the outdoors; that I was meant to be outside. So, I applied and I got the job."

Addison's eyes finally light up, and she grins. "I take it you used your experience to start your own company?"

"Yes and no. I got along really well with the owner of the place I was working for and kept bringing him my ideas. When I started at Brady Landscape, we only carried and delivered supplies. I wanted to design. The owner was near retirement, so he didn't want to take on anything new. When he finally did retire, none of his kids wanted the business. I took it over slowly, with his blessing, and expanded it to what it is today."

"That's amazing," Addison says sincerely.

I move my hand and lightly run my thumb across her knuckles, enjoying the fact that we're still touching. "Well, you had a part in it. If you hadn't said those things to me that summer, I'd probably be working in a gas station somewhere."

She laughs.

"So, what about you? Any news on your studio?"

She looks down and shakes her head. "I won't budge and neither will Derek. We've decided to shelve both our dreams for a while." She looks back at me. "No in vitro and no studio."

I want to tell her that's good; that she shouldn't have a baby with Derek. She should leave him if he doesn't support her goals. She should leave him and be with me.

I'm a selfish prick.

Instead, I say, "At least it's a compromise."

She gives me half a smile.

My phone vibrates in my pocket, and I let go of Addison's hand to pull it out and see who it is. I plan on silencing it until I see the text message from Kevin:

Noah had to back out. You're on for the parade.

I groan.

"What is it?" Addison asks.

I talk as I text my brother back. "Kevin put our company truck in the annual Christmas parade. Noah was supposed to drive and now he can't."

"Parade? Sounds like fun."

Sounds like a nightmare to me. I finish my message to Kevin. *No way. This was your idea. You drive.*

"How will you decorate the truck?" Addison asks.

My face twists. "We won't. We're just going to wash it and drive it. The logo is on the side."

"That's lame," she chastises me. "You at least need to put a wreath on the grill or something."

I roll my eyes. "It's advertisement."

"It's boring! People will think you accidentally got caught in the parade."

She may be right.

Kevin responds. *Can't. Ashley's birthday is that Saturday and we're skiing up at Boyne.*

I take a deep breath. Most of our crew is laid off during the winter months and called back depending on the weather. There are only a handful of guys I trust to drive the big plow truck. Who else can I call?

"Let me help." Addison grabs my arm to get my attention. "It will be fun. You can drive and I'll help you decorate the truck."

I want to spend time with her. So fucking much. I arch an eyebrow. "What would your husband have to say about that?"

Addison shoots me an "oh please" look. "Last time I checked, I'm an adult. I don't have to ask permission to be anyone's friend."

"Do you want to be friends?" I ask.

"Yes. Don't you?"

Of course I do. I'd rather be more, but that's not a possibility.

Since I don't immediately answer her question, Addison's expression turns serious. "Kyle. I lied to you yesterday, but I want you to know I won't do it again."

Is that why she thinks I didn't respond? Because I don't trust her? "I believe you."

"Do you promise never to lie to me?"

I can do that. "Yes."

Addison lets out a deep breath. "Good. The truth is, since we've met up again, my mind has been a mess. I've kept my memories buried for a long time; I thought I'd made peace with them and moved on. But now, they keep coming back."

I understand how she feels.

She shifts forward on the couch and drops her legs to the floor. "I need to show you something."

She reaches up and gathers her hair in one hand, pulling it over her shoulder. She turns slightly to the side and tips her head. "Do you see it?"

Uh...all I see is her smooth curve of her neck and know I want my lips there. I'm going to have to practice thinking friendly thoughts.

"It's behind my ear," she says.

I lean forward. What I see makes my heart skip a beat.

"At the lake last month you said you never stopped thinking about me. Well, I never stopped thinking about you." She turns around to see my face. "I got the tattoo to carry that summer with me. I put my memories of you into it. I thought if I couldn't carry them in my heart, I could carry them on my body. Outside, so they wouldn't hurt as much."

All I can do is blink at her. On her skin, etched in black ink, is a tiny sparrow.

"What does your husband think it means?" I ask.

"I told him it's me, before the accident."

I feel my face soften as words I shouldn't say slip from my lips. "Even after, you're still my free bird."

She gives me a knowing smile.

"When did you get it?" I ask.

"About two years after the crash. Just before I moved in with Meagan."

My face falls. "I wish you would have called to let me know where you were. God, I wish I knew what had happened. I hate that you felt you had to move on and forget us."

She meets my stare. "You had moved on. So I had to, too."

"What?"

Addison's eyes get big and she looks away. "Never mind."

"No." I shift my weight. "What do you mean I moved on?"

She closes her eyes. "I can't believe I'm telling you this."

"Telling me what?"

She sighs. "I came back."

There's no way in hell I heard her right. "Excuse me?"

Addison opens her eyes. "After I was better, Meagan asked me to move in with her and Derek wanted a more serious relationship. I was torn. I couldn't shake you, and I wasn't sure I wanted to live in the Upper Peninsula." She pauses. "Before I made any decisions, I drove to your mother's house. I felt like I needed to see you to help me decide. I had no idea if you would want to talk to me or if you would even be there, but you were."

I think I've stopped breathing.

"I saw you," she confesses. "From my car parked in the street. You were leaving the house with a girl; a pretty brunette. You opened the car door for her. You gave her an amazing kiss before she drove away; a kiss that told me I was a memory."

This is not happening.

"I meant what I said at the cottage. It had been two years since I saw you; it made sense for you to move on."

She was there and I didn't see her? How is that possible? "Why? Why didn't you get out of the car?"

"It felt wrong." Her eyes search mine. "You were involved with someone else."

My heart pounds. We would be together, right now, if she had gotten out of that car. I know it.

Instantly, I move closer to her. "That girl... Monica...we weren't serious."

Her face falls. "It's okay."

"It is not okay!"

She leans toward me. "That's why I'm not letting this get away from us. Not this time." She meets my eyes. "First Kevin misses meeting Ashley and then I screw up because I was hurt. I think it's a sign. No more missed opportunities."

I nod.

"So, I'll ask again," she says. "Do you want to be friends?"

I weave my fingers through hers. "You couldn't pay me to stay away."

Chapter Fourteen

"It's a small town parade, not the Rose Bowl."

Addison sticks her tongue out at me as she hands over four huge plastic bags. "I wanted to make sure I had enough. I didn't know how big the plow truck was."

Standing inside the doorway of the garage that houses nearly all of Dayton Landscaping's equipment, I take the bags from her. I start to look inside as she turns around and heads back toward her Hummer. "Where are you going?" I ask.

"I'll be right back," she says over her shoulder and picks up her pace.

Shrugging, I head further into the warehouse to set down the holiday decorations. I start to rummage through the first bag, searching for a receipt. There's no way I'm letting her pay for all of this. Her decision to spend time with me is more than enough; I've been geeked since I woke up this morning.

Who am I kidding? I've been geeked for the last week, since she lied to come over to my house.

The sound of nails clicking against concrete distracts me. My head snaps up to find Sam trotting happily in my direction, a big, red, velvet bow tied to his collar. His owner follows behind carrying a large thermos.

"Hey!" I kneel and pat my knee, calling the dog over. Sam meets my outstretched fingers for a good scratch. "This is a surprise. How have you been, buddy?" I'm talking to him like he'll answer.

"Whiny," Addison responds for her pet. "He wouldn't leave my side today; I think his hip is bothering him. I dressed him up for the parade. Do you care if he rides along?"

"Not at all," I say. "I've missed him." It's the truth. Sam and I have a connection I can't explain. We have since the first day we met.

When he's satisfied with his rubdown, the dog gets interested in his unfamiliar surroundings and walks away to check things out. I stand and wipe my hands on my jeans.

"He really likes you," Addison muses as her eyes follow Sam. "Did you have a dog when you were little?"

I shake my head. "I wanted one, but no. I had a goldfish. Mr. Bubbles."

A snort of laughter escapes her. "Mr. Bubbles?"

I fake annoyance. "Don't knock Mr. Bubbles. I won him at the county fair, throwing those plastic rings over bottle necks. It cost my mom $20 to win that fish."

"Awww." She smiles. "I bet Mr. Bubbles was great."

"Mr. Bubbles was awesome," I correct her. "What's that?" I nod toward the thermos in her hands.

"Hot chocolate. I didn't know how cold it would be in here."

"Well, you're in luck. The garage is heated."

Addison thrusts the drink at my chest. "Great. Let's get to work."

She skirts around me and heads toward the bags on the ground. "Okay." She starts to open them. "I got a big wreath and a small wreath. Some lights." She opens another bag. "Bows. Oh, some sleigh bells." Yet more searching. "A ton of garland and a few boxes of tiny candy canes."

My forehead pinches. "Why?"

"To hand out." She picks up a box and holds it in front of her chest. "Didn't you ever go to a parade as a kid?"

"Well, yeah."

"Didn't they give out candy?"

Oh. Well, yeah.

I walk over to her. "Guess you thought of everything."

She smirks. "I'm female. It's what we do."

I roll my eyes.

Addison glances around. "Which truck are we decorating?"

I jerk my thumb over my shoulder. "The clean one with the huge plow on the front."

She looks past me, then gets sarcastic. "Are you going to give me shit all day?"

I grin. "I'm a man. That's what we do."

She shakes her head and leans over, trading the box of candy canes for an armful of garland. "Here, take this." She hands the decorations to me and then finds the wreaths, holding one in each hand. "I think these should go on the front and the back of the truck. What do you think?"

"You're the brains behind this operation. You lead, I follow."

Over the next hour, we sit on the ground side by side and play with fake pine needles. We make easy conversation and work in unison; I wind the multi-colored strands of lights around the wreaths and the garland, and Addison adds the bows and bells. She asks about my Christmas plans. I tell her I'll spend the day as usual, with my mom and my brother. That said, I'm not sure how things will change with Ashley in the picture. She informs me that she and Derek will spend the week in the Upper Peninsula with her sister's family. Marc and Meagan have a two-year-old daughter, Livie, and it's obvious Addison adores her niece.

"You should see Derek with her," she comments as she arranges and ties. "He's a natural."

"And you're not?"

She shrugs. "I love to tickle her belly and make her laugh. I like to buy her cute things and spoil her rotten. But, when she's upset, I panic."

I know nothing about kids. "Does she get upset a lot?"

Addison raises her eyebrows. "Have you ever heard of the Terrible Two's?"

"Vaguely."

She laughs. "Everything is 'me', 'mine', and 'I do it'. If Livie gets frustrated, she throws a fit. Derek can always distract her, though."

"Speaking of," I snap the batteries into place at the end of a light strand, "what does he think about you helping me today?"

Addison gives a sidelong glance and continues to tie the bells. "He's not a fan."

I frown, even though I expected her answer. "Did you guys have a fight?"

Addison is silent for a few moments before she responds. Her focus is concentrated on one of the last few sleigh bells she's tying on to the garland. When she finishes, she looks at me. "I'd say it was more of a spirited discussion."

My frown deepens. As much as I want to spend time with her, I don't want her to argue with her husband. I know how upset it makes her, and that's the last thing I want.

"You shouldn't fight with Derek," I say.

"Oh, really?" she asks and drops the decorations. "At least once a week he goes out with his friends. I don't tell him he can't go, and I certainly don't tell him who he's allowed to see. I trust him. It's only fair I'm treated the same way."

I can tell by her tone the two of them have discussed this before. I have to take Addison's side on this one; what she says makes sense. If he's hanging out with friends, why can't she do the same?

Then, a realization hits. "You're using me," I say incredulously. "To get back at him for his guy's night out."

Addison's eyes get big. "No! That's not what I meant!"

I laugh. Honestly, I wouldn't care if she used me. The fact she's willing to argue with her husband about us speaks volumes. She must feel pretty strongly about our friendship to push him.

My ego likes it.

I wrap my arm around her and press her to my side. "Sparrow, you can use me anytime. I can be a shoulder to cry on, an alibi, or bar night revenge...whatever you need."

She lets out a tiny laugh. "Thanks, but I would never use you."

"You can."

"But I won't."

I raise my eyebrows at her playfully, questioning her sincerity, and she giggles. God, I love that sound.

After a moment, she moves out from under my arm. She picks up the truck decorations again, and then looks at me. Her smile fades into a smirk.

"Is there a problem?" I ask.

She doesn't answer. Instead, she reaches out and brushes her finger across my chin. "What's up with this?"

"What?" I run my hand along my jaw. "I thought chicks dig the whole five o'clock shadow thing."

"Some do," she admits.

"And you don't?"

"That's not what I said."

My eyes narrow, trying to read her. "Then, what are you saying?"

"It's just different. There's a lot more of you to get used to."

More of me? I look down at myself and back at her again. I'm in the best shape of my life. "What are you talking about? Are you trying to tell me I've let myself go?"

"Ah, no."

She blushes a little and looks away, getting to her feet. I think I hear her mutter 'just the opposite' as she gathers the garland in her hands. When her arms are full, she changes the subject. "A little help here?"

I stand, start to reach for the decorations, and stop. She thinks I look good. This is the perfect opportunity to give her more shit. Friends are supposed to joke around with each other, right? I cross my arms. "You think I'm hot."

"Kyle." She tries to give me a condescending look and fails.

"If we're gonna be friends, we have to be honest with each other. We promised never to lie." I lean forward. "You think I'm hot. Yes or no?"

She steps back and some of the garland slips from her grip. Instead of grabbing it to help her, I pretend to study the ceiling. "I'm not helping you until I get an answer."

Addison lets out an irritated sigh. "You're the one who needs my help, remember? I could walk out of here right now."

I meet her eyes and shrug, like it wouldn't be a big deal if she left. My action is a complete lie. It would be a huge deal. My day would be ruined.

"Fine," she huffs. "You want the truth?"

I smile and step closer, ready for her to fess up. Instead, she raises an eyebrow and gets cocky. "You can't handle the truth."

"Ugh!" I groan. "That was terrible! You are so *not* Jack Nicholson."

She laughs. "C'mon. If we don't get this stuff on the truck, we're going to be late."

~~~~

Shortly before five o'clock, Addison, Sam, and I are directed to our designated spot in the parade lineup. We're behind the high school marching band and in front of an antique fire truck. Once in place, I shift into park and leave my vehicle running to keep the heat on. It's the first weekend in December, and the temperatures have been in the twenties. A few inches of snow fell over Thanksgiving, and it's still hanging around.

There's a knock on the passenger side window, and Addison rolls it down. A chirpy woman wearing a fluorescent yellow vest and holding a walkie-talkie greets us. "Hi! Thanks for coming. Here's a schedule of the festival events, if you don't already have one." She hands Addison a piece of paper. "We'll get going in about ten, fifteen, minutes and end up at the high school. Any questions?"

Addison looks at me, and I shake my head no. "Nope, no questions," she tells the parade volunteer.

"Great. Cute dog," the woman compliments Sam as he tries to poke his head out the open window.

"Thanks." Addison smiles.

The volunteer walks away, and Addison looks at me. "You didn't tell me the parade was part of a festival."

"Kevin set this thing up; I didn't pay much attention." I lean over to look at the paper in her hands. "What do they have planned?"

She starts to read over the activities. "There's ice carving, caroling, a tree lighting ceremony...oh! Fireworks!" She looks at me, excited. "We should stay and watch those."

"You want to?"

"Yeah. I can't remember the last time I went to see fireworks."

Her answer strikes me as odd. "Don't you watch them on the Fourth?"

"Not usually."

Not usually? "I take it you and Derek aren't very patriotic?"

She chuckles. "No. He volunteers to work on the holidays for overtime. Memorial Day, the Fourth of July, Labor Day. You know, the ones that aren't big like Christmas. That way, his coworkers with families can have the time off."

Well. Isn't Derek a saint?

"I usually watch the Detroit fireworks on TV."

"You have different plans this year," I decide. "Fourth of July. Fireworks. You and me." I turn around. "And Sam."

She smiles. "It's a date."

I wish.

Minutes later, the parade gets underway. It's an uneventful process. We pass through town, and the band treats us to a repeated, three-song playlist of "Jingle Bells, "Rockin' Around the Christmas Tree," and "Louie Louie." The latter must be a staple, no matter what the season. We roll along slow enough to toss out the candy canes, and I'm secretly relieved Addison remembered to buy them. The streets are lined with families, and the fire truck behind us is passing out candy, too.

When the parade ends, I circle around town and find a parking space behind a local church. It's within walking distance of the community center, where most of the festival events are taking place. Once we get out of the truck and get Sam situated with his leash, we walk in the direction of the lights and crowd.

"Thanks for agreeing to stay." Addison bumps my arm with her shoulder. "I'm having fun."

"Me too." I smile at her. She looks ridiculously cute wearing a pair of fuzzy white earmuffs. "You know, you kind of look like a Muppet." I reach over and tap her ear.

She scrunches up her nose. "Thanks, but that wasn't the look I was going for."

"What were you going for? Sexy snow bunny?"

Did I just say that?

Addison chokes on a laugh. "No!"

She doesn't seem offended, so I raise an eyebrow. "Sexy Muppet?"

She looks at me in confusion. "Is there such a thing?"

"Are you kidding?" I pretend to be shocked. "Miss Piggy is crazy hot."

"Really?" She gives me a knowing look as we sidestep a group of people. "I thought Kevin was the one who liked blondes."

Shit. I try to come up with another female Muppet and draw a blank.

"What? Cat got your tongue?" she teases.

"I was just trying to say you looked cute," I say in defense of myself.

"Cute or sexy?" she asks with a smirk.

Damn. Why are you married?!

As we get closer to the activities, the smell of vanilla and cinnamon floats through the air. Vendors have set up concession stands along the sidewalk, and I see a sign for candied almonds.

This will be the perfect distraction. I stop walking and point. "You want?" I ask.

Addison nods enthusiastically. "Please." She looks at the sign tacked to the stand post. "Get hot cider too. A big one."

I step up to the booth to place our order as Addison leads Sam out of the way to wait. While the man behind the counter bags our almonds, I glance at Addison. She's oblivious to my stare as she messes with the bow on Sam's collar. Her presence seems too good to be true. When she crouches in front of Sam and rubs his ears, my head and my heart have a tug of war. My mind gives me shit for still wanting her, while the damn muscle in my chest refuses to let her go.

Gathering our snacks, I make my way over to her and hand her the cider. She tries to replace the cup in my hand with dollar bills.

"What's this?" I frown.

"I'm paying."

"No, you're not."

"Yes, I am."

"No, you're not."

"Yes, I am."

"No, you're not." I pluck the money from her fingers and step closer, tucking the bills inside her coat pocket. "It's my treat."

Addison looks up at me, annoyed. I wink at her, and she reluctantly relaxes. She takes the cider from my hand and tries to look stern again.

"Don't think you can do that and get your way all the time."

"Do what?"

"Wink at me with those damn blue, green, whatever-color eyes you have."

I smile. "You used to like my eyes."

She opens her mouth to say something then thinks better of it. She blows on the cider and takes a tentative sip instead.

"So, where do you want to go?" I look around. "The fireworks don't start for a while."

"Ice sculptures?" she suggests.

We turn and head down the sidewalk toward the growing sound of a chainsaw. From a distance, I can see the front lawn of the community center and three carving stations set several feet apart. The carver furthest from us is tearing into his block of ice; snow flies around him as he transforms the frozen water into a work of art. He must have started several minutes ago, because his ice is taking shape. From here, it looks like it could be a reindeer.

As we get closer, another carver is prepping his station to begin. He's a stocky gentleman, with a white mustache and a beard. He catches my eye for a brief second. Before I can tell Addison he reminds me of Santa Claus, he stops the two of us.

"Evenin'." He tips is hat. "Could I bother you for a little help?"

"Sure," I say. "What do you need?"

"A suggestion." He smiles at Addison. "I'm up next. What should I carve?"

Addison regards St. Nick skeptically. "You want me to choose?"

He nods. "Anything you'd like."

She tilts her head in thought, then looks at me. "What do you think?"

I shrug. "A Christmas tree?"

The carver immediately rejects my idea. "Too easy."

"A snowman?"

"Even easier."

"A wreath?"

Again, no.

"You're terrible at this," Addison teases. She turns back to the gentleman. "You want something intricate, right?"

"And unique."

Addison chews on her bottom lip for a second before her eyes light up. "I think I've got it."

She gestures for the man to come closer and she whispers in his ear. His eyes get wide for a moment and then he nods. "I think I can do that." He steps away from Addison, then looks at me. "Just so you know, I agree."

"Agree with what?" I ask.

Addison doesn't let him answer. "You'll see." She grins. "It's a surprise."

After putting on a pair of gloves and some ski goggles, the man begins his project. A crowd gathers to watch, and I'm awed by the carver's talent. It takes some serious creativity to look at a rectangular block of ice and bring a vision to life, especially with a piece of machinery like a chainsaw. I've handled a few in my line of work, and it has never crossed my mind to do anything artistic with them.

As minutes pass, it becomes clear Addison chose something with wings. The tips are the first features to emerge. At first I think she chose a bird, like a Christmas dove. However, as the sculpture starts to become more defined, I discover I'm wrong.

"It's an angel," I say before shaking some almonds into my palm.

Addison holds out her hand, and I give up my snack. "Yes, but what kind of angel?"

I wasn't aware there was more than one type, unless you count the Victoria's Secret variety. I doubt she asked St. Nick to carve an angel wearing lingerie, so I'm at a loss. "A heavenly angel?" I guess.

She just smiles and pops a few almonds into her mouth.

It's only when a little girl standing next to me says, "Mommy! It's a pig!" that I get it.

"He's carving Miss Piggy?" I ask in disbelief.

Addison laughs. "As an angel. I told him you thought she was sexy."

I shake my head with a smile. "I can't believe he agreed."

She shrugs. "You heard the man. He likes her, too."

When the sculpture is complete, the carver gets a round of applause from the spectators, including myself. After removing his goggles, he walks up to Addison and me.

"What'd you think?"

"It's incredible," Addison says. "It looks just like her."

I hold out my hand to shake his. "Nice job. You must think we're insane."

He takes off his glove to shake my hand. "Not at all. You'd be surprised what I've been asked to create."

"Like what?" Addison asks, curious.

The man rubs the back of his neck. "Let's just say I've been hired to do a few bachelorette parties."

My eyes get big and land on Addison's. What are women paying him to make? Giant dicks made of ice?

"Do you have a card?" Addison asks, her expression mischievous.

"Sure do."

The man reaches beneath his winter coat and into his back pocket. "Name's Rick. Just give me a call if you ever need anything."

"Thanks." Addison takes his information. "I just so happen to be in an upcoming wedding."

Rick laughs. "Well, I have a portfolio when you get to plannin'. Have a nice night."

He walks away and I pin Addison with a stare. "Please tell me you're not thinking what I think you're thinking."

"What's that?" she asks innocently. "I am Ashley's Maid of Honor. I do have to plan her bachelorette party."

"And you need an ice sculpture?"

She tries to suppress a smile. "That's for us girls to know and for you to never find out." She starts to lead Sam toward Rick's creation. "Come on. I want a picture."

Addison throws away her empty cider cup and makes me stand with Angel Piggy. She takes a few pictures with her phone until I make her join me. I take the opportunity to wrap my arm around her waist as she effortlessly takes a perfect shot on the first try. It reminds me of our summer up north, when I tried to take our picture and failed miserably.

"Do you still have that camera I gave you?" she asks, as if reading my mind.

I do, although, it's packed away in a box. After she vanished, I'd look through the pictures every now and again, to make sure I didn't imagine her. Over time, the batteries in the camera died, and I never replaced them. I took it as another sign that she was never coming back.

"Yes," I answer, just as the first firework bursts above us.

We both look up in time to watch the last sparks fade away. "Let's go find a better place to watch," I say and take her hand.

Addison lets me lead her around the back of the community center to where people have gathered for the show. Two more shells are launched into the sky, and the bright red and green colors light up the night. The crowd responds with "ooohs" and "ahhhs" as I find an empty spot big enough to accommodate us and Sam. Addison lets go of my hand to make the dog sit at her feet, and, despite wearing gloves, my skin feels cold in its absence. Would it be wrong to reach for her hand again?

Um, yes.

The next few fireworks are huge gold starbursts that fizzle as they fade. Following those are giant Roman candles that shoot fountains of sparks into the air. I catch Addison's eyes with mine, and we smile at each other. She turns her attention back to the sky and steps closer to me. As another shell explodes, I shift my weight and find myself closer to her.

As minutes pass, we repeat this little dance. Addison adjusts Sam's leash and moves to the side. I glance around the crowd and inch toward her. It's as if we're trying to be discreet, but each of us knows what the other is doing. One more step, and my arm will touch hers. Is that what she wants?

Because I do.

Tension grows as neither of us will commit to taking the final step. What little space remains between us sparks with electricity; the anticipation of who will move first is nearly tangible. As the show comes to a close with a rapid succession of bright colors and loud blasts, my pulse keeps time with the fast pace. Should I move or shouldn't I? Will I regret it if I do? Will I regret it if I don't?

My indecision is interrupted by cheers and applause after the last firework fades. As the crowd breaks around us, I turn toward Addison and give her a questioning look.

She raises an eyebrow. "Well, that was interesting."

Yeah. It sure was.

Chapter Fifteen

"Three, two, one..."

"Happy New Year!"

The crowd around me goes wild. Noisemakers bleat and confetti flies through the air. My brother grabs his fiancée for a deep kiss, and I look away.

Hello, 2014.

I raise my beer to my lips, but feel awkward as I realize I'm surrounded by kissing couples. Not only here in the sports bar, but on the TV as well. Images from Times Square are projected on every screen in the place. Public displays of affection don't usually bother me, but tonight, as I sit here trying to avoid the spectacle, I feel fidgety.

As Kevin and Ashley continue to kiss to ring in the New Year, I find myself uncomfortable on my bar stool. I shift my weight and clear my throat before taking another drink. When they asked me to come out with them tonight, I almost said no. Now, I wish I had. The gratuitous PDA around me is making me feel left out of the celebration. For the last three years, I've had a girl to kiss at midnight. This year, I don't.

And I can't keep the one that is off limits out of my head.

I haven't seen Addison since the parade. Even now, weeks later, my body still reacts when I think about the tension that radiated between us that night. It was like a magnetic pull, and I've never felt anything like it in my entire life. I keep replaying what happened in my mind, and I love it one minute and hate it the next.

The day after the parade, Addison sent me a text message. She told me she had a great time and thanked me for allowing her to get creative with my truck. I replied and told her I enjoyed myself, too. Days later, I sent her a message wishing her safe travels up north to see her sister. She responded and wished me a Merry Christmas, saying she knew I'd been a good boy, and Santa should treat me to whatever I wanted.

As if.

My brother and Ashley finally separate, and my sis-in-law-to-be turns and drapes her arm over my shoulders. She pulls me to the side for half a hug. "Happy New Year Kyle!" She pops a quick kiss on my cheek. "It's going to be the best year yet!"

I shoot her a skeptical look. "How can you be sure?"

"Because I'm marrying your brother, silly." She grabs the shot Kevin placed in front of her and downs it like a champ; although, I think the last five shots are starting to show. She slams the glass down on the bar and smiles at me. "May can't get here fast enough." She turns to Kev. "Right, babe?"

"Damn straight," he says and wraps his arms around her waist again. "In five months you'll be mine."

"I'm already yours," she giggles.

Pardon me while I puke.

My phone vibrates in my back pocket and I grab it, grateful for the distraction from Romeo and Juliet. A text message is displayed on the screen, and I feel a smile creep on to my face as I realize it's from Addison.

"Happy New Year! Have fun and remember – safety first ;)"

Apparently, she thinks I'm partying.

I hold my phone in the palm of my hand while I think of what to send back. I feel the need to tell her I'm not out screwing around. Ashley peers over my shoulder. "Who ya talking to?"

"Is that any of your business?" I ask.

"Ohmygodit'sAddison!" Her words rush out jumbled as she sees my text. Her eyes grow wide. "She promised nothing was going on between you two!"

I frown. "Nothing is going on."

Ashley snorts.

"What's this about Addison?" Kevin asks, leaning into the conversation. "Isn't she out of town?"

"She got back this morning," I say. "Derek had to work."

Good 'ole Derek volunteered for the holiday shift again. I invited Addison to come out with us, but she said no. She told me Ashley beat me to the invitation, but she was tired from the drive and wanted to unpack.

Ashley crosses her arms and stares at me. "You're texting her."

I smirk. "Thank you, Captain Obvious."

Ashley raises an eyebrow and turns to Kevin. "Did you see the picture of the two of them at the parade?"

"The one in front of the sculpture? Yeah." My brother looks at me. "Unless there is another one you're not telling me about."

"No, there's not," I respond. Addison forwarded the picture when I was at work, and I showed it to Kevin.

"What did you think?" Ashley questions Kevin.

"About the picture? It's a nice shot." My brother shrugs.

Ashley dramatically throws her hands in the air. "You two are frickin' clueless! How can you not see it?"

My brow furrows. "See what?"

"What's right in front of you." Ashley sighs. "Read the text again."

Confused, I do as I'm told. "She's wishing me a happy new year and she wants me to be safe. I assume she thinks I'm picking up girls. Or getting drunk. Or both."

"Bingo." Ashley points at me. "And why would she bother to tell you to stay safe?"

"Because we're friends?" I can't help the sarcastic tone in my voice.

"Let me tell you something," Ashley says and steps closer. "She's baiting you. She wants to know what you're doing without asking; she wants you to respond and tell her you're not hooking up with random chicks."

That's precisely what I was going to do, but I don't confide in Ashley. Instead, I ask, "Why would she care if I am? She's the one who's married, not me."

Ashley leans into my space. "Listen up, because I'm only going to say this once. I'm Addison's best friend, and I can read her pretty well. She may deny it, but she likes you more than she should. You need to be careful."

Wait. Is the alcohol talking or does she truly believe that?

"I mean it, Kyle. This isn't a game."

"Who said it was?" I ask. "I would never hurt Addison."

"Good." Ashley gives me a once over, apparently satisfied. "I need to piss. I'll be right back."

I grimace. "Thanks for sharing."

She kisses Kevin and leaves. My brother sits down on the stool next to me; the same one he vacated at midnight to stand and knock the breath out of his fiancée. "So what's really going on?" he asks as he reaches for a bar menu. "Do I need to worry about Derek hunting you down?"

"No," I say, annoyed. I hate that guy's name. I drain the last of my beer from the bottle, set it on the bar, and push it away. "Addison and I may flirt, but I've been permanently Friend Zoned." Not that I want to be.

"Understandable." Kevin opens the menu and starts to look over the appetizers. "Just for curiosity's sake, if she told you she wanted more, what would you say?"

"More as in what? More than friends?"

My brother meets my eyes and nods.

As awesome as it would be to hear those words fall from her lips, I don't want to have an affair with Addison. It wouldn't be enough. I want the real deal. I want her to be completely mine. There's no way in hell I'd share her with Derek. None.

"I don't think she's planning on leaving her husband any time soon," I say. "I'd have to tell her no."

"Good man." Kevin slaps my shoulder. "That's the answer I wanted to hear."

"What did you think I would say? I'm not Dad." My father's cheating still doesn't sit well with me. Not even after thirteen years.

"Love makes you do strange things. Addison wrecked you in the past. I can tell she still has a hold on you now. I just want to make sure you're thinking with your big head and not your little one."

"Who you calling little?" I scoff.

"What's little?"

Ashley comes up behind us, and I turn around. "Do you ever mind your own business?"

"Rarely." She steps between Kevin and me, draping an arm across both our shoulders. "So, who's ready for another drink?"

~ ~ ~ ~

I think I hear the doorbell ring, but that's impossible.

It's too goddamn early for any human to be awake.

I roll sideways, taking the bed sheets with me, and groan. My head throbs. I can't remember the last time I had a hangover. Damn Ashley and her shots! I haven't had that much whiskey since my twenty-first birthday.

Someone knocks on the door, and I mumble into my pillow. "Go away."

Silent seconds are followed by more knocking.

Then, the doorbell rings again.

I don't move. Just the thought of exposing my eyes to the light makes my skull ache. Thank God I scheduled Eli to be on call today for anything work related. I'm not getting out of this bed.

The next sound I hear is a key turning in my front door. I pick my head up too fast and mutter, "What the hell?"

"Kyle?"

It's my mom.

The door closes, and I hear her footsteps as she makes her way down the hall. I pull a pillow over my head, but still feel her presence when she peeks into my bedroom.

"Are you alive?" she asks from the doorway.

"Yes," I say into the pillow. "Why are you up so early?"

"It's 11:30."

Seriously? I move to the side and squint at my alarm clock. I'll be damned.

"Why are you here?" I ask, confused.

She crosses her arms and levels her motherly stare; her eyes mirror my own in their color. "Because I called and you didn't answer."

"That's because my phone is in my pants."

My mother looks around the room. "And where are your pants?"

I rub my eyes with the heel of my hand. "In the bathroom."

She sighs. "Please tell me you didn't drive home drunk."

"I didn't drive home drunk. Kevin did and he dropped me off."

"He what?!" Her voice climbs an octave. "You let your brother drink and drive?"

"No!" Man, her voice sounds shrill. "I meant he drove and dropped me off. Ashley was with us. He would never let anything happen to her."

"Oh." My mom's shoulders relax. "Well, pull yourself out of bed. I drove all the way here; I might as well make you something to eat."

The thought of her cooking versus cold cereal makes my stomach growl. "Thanks."

Her concerned look disappears, and she leaves my door. Soon, I hear the sounds of her moving around the kitchen.

Sitting up, I swing my legs off the bed and lean over to snag a t-shirt off the floor. This is not how I planned to wake up, but I won't complain. I can nap after my mom leaves. I stand and shuffle my pajama-pant covered ass across the hall. I grab a couple aspirin from the bathroom cabinet and swallow them down with a gulp of water directly from the sink faucet. Then, I find my jeans in a heap on the floor where I left them and pull my phone from the back pocket. There are no missed calls except from my mom. When I join her in the kitchen, she's busy making a bacon, ham, and cheese omelet. My favorite.

"You know you don't have to cook for me," I say as I head to the refrigerator for the orange juice. I grab the carton, stop walking, and look over her shoulder on my way to get a glass. "But, I won't stop you."

She smiles as she carefully lays strips of bacon in a pan. "Obviously."

As I pour my drink, she continues. "I'm your mother. It's my job to look out for you. Food will make you feel better."

"So, when I'm fifty and you're in your seventies, you'll still come over and take care of me?"

She shakes her head. "I hope you'll be married by then. Besides, you will probably be the one taking care of me. Pushing my wheelchair and changing my diapers."

I want to tell her none of that will happen. I won't get married, and she'll never need a wheelchair or Depends.

"How was last night?" I ask. "Did you go out with Aunt Janice?" My mom and her sister were notorious partiers back in the day. When lava lamps and disco were all the rage, Donna and Janice got into their fair share of trouble. That was before my mom became an accountant and my aunt got pregnant. She married my uncle Ian soon after.

"Yes. Janice took me to one of Ian's biker bars." My mom's expression turns wary. "Rock music and leather really aren't my thing. We didn't stay late."

I grin. I would have paid good money to see my mom sitting in the midst of a bunch of burly bikers. She must have stood out like a sore thumb with her perfect, bobbed hairstyle and standard cardigan sweater.

"Did you have a good time last night?" she asks me.

I shrug. "I've had better."

She looks confused as she pours whisked eggs into another pan. "What happened?"

"I was subjected to the Kevin and Ashley love fest."

She nods in understanding. "How many drinks did you have to block it out?"

"Not sure."

She remains focused on her task. She adds ham and shredded cheese to the eggs. "Don't worry, honey. One day that will be you. The right girl is out there."

I want to say I found the right girl and she lives about thirty minutes from me. We text each other and, despite her being married, she wants to be my friend. That she has a tattoo of the nickname I gave her when we were seventeen.

But, I don't.

My mother's opinion of Addison has never been great, especially since her disappearance turned me into the son from hell. When she found out Addison was Ashley's best friend and we would be in the wedding together, I could read the disapproval on her face. When she found out Addison was married, all was sunshine and roses again.

I finish my orange juice just as mom finishes up the omelet. She places it in front of me at the table and ruffles my hair like she used to when I was a kid. "Eat up and I'll get out of here."

I do as I'm told because I'm starving despite my aching head.

My mom runs the water in the sink and starts to wash the dishes. Between mouthfuls, I tell her to stop, relax and sit down. She gives me the stink eye, but sits in the chair opposite me anyway. We talk about the arctic winter we're having and the prediction of another snow storm this week. I remind her that I'll be over to plow her driveway, if the storm happens.

"Why were you trying to get ahold of me this morning?" I ask as I set my fork on my empty plate. "Do you need something done at the house?"

"No. I wanted to know when would be a good time to come over."

"Why?"

She stands and grabs her purse off the kitchen counter. "The reason," she says and unzips her bag, "is this."

She pulls out a plain white envelope and hands it to me. Puzzled, I take it. My name is written on the outside, and I blink in surprise as I recognize the handwriting.

It's Gram's.

"Where did you get this?"

"I found it yesterday when I was going through a box of papers from her desk," my mom says. "Evidently she had something important to tell you."

I frown. "If it was important, why didn't she just talk to me?"

My mom shrugs. "Who knows? Maybe she thought she would forget."

Gram would never forget. The woman was sharp as a tack. I run the envelope through my fingers. "What do you think is in here?"

"When you get around to opening it, let me know." My mom starts to head for her coat.

"Wait. Don't you want to see what this is?"

"Of course. But, it's a private note from your grandmother to you. I'm not going to pry. You open it and read it and let me know what she had to say." She smiles at me.

I have no idea why Gram would write me a letter. "If you say so."

I escort my mom to the door, and she gives me a quick hug goodbye. "Get some rest," she sarcastically admonishes me.

"I plan to."

Once she's gone, I stare at the envelope in my hands. I bet it's not a letter at all; most likely it's some paperwork for the cottage. As I wander over to my favorite chair and sit, I tear open the flap and pull out a few sheets of floral stationery.

June 3, 2012

Dear Kyle,

As I write this, I'm sitting in my garden on the lovely bench you made for my birthday. It's absolutely beautiful. My nosy neighbor Loretta is going to be so jealous! You, my grandson, are so very, very talented.

By the time you read this letter, time will have passed from this day. I want to remind you of how much I loved your gift and how proud I was of you for creating it; how proud I am of everything you've accomplished. There's only one thing that brings me sadness when it comes to you, and it's for that reason alone that I have decided to write this note. Today, while you were visiting, I asked you again to come up to the lake and stay with me. You refused, and it broke my heart.

Please believe me when I say I'm not telling you this to upset you. Your refusal to visit hurt not because of my feelings, but because of yours. It makes me sad to know you still miss Addison. Kyle, you and I are very much alike. While you are haunted by memories of her, I carry similar memories of my own.

When I was sixteen, I fell in love. Head over heels, just like you. Remember when I told you Addison reminded me of myself at her age? The truth is, both of you reminded me of that time in my life. A time when I was young, invincible, and infatuated with a man named Jonas Grant.

Yes. You read that right. Jonas Grant. The same Mr. Grant that lives across the lake.

When I met Jonas, he was eighteen. We ran into each other at a soda shop in town; my mother was running errands and I didn't feel like tagging along. Jonas and I had an instant connection, a moment if you will, and from that day forward our lives were consumed with one another. He was going to work for his father, I was going to finish school, and we were going to get married. Everything was perfect. Our future was written.

Until he left without saying goodbye.

Jonas used to meet me after school and walk me home. One day, he didn't show. When I went to his house, he wasn't there. No one was; the place looked ransacked and abandoned. Days went by without any word from him, and I feared the worst. I wouldn't eat; I couldn't sleep. I kept going to his house in the hopes of finding answers. I felt lost and had a very difficult time dealing with his absence. Your great-grandparents were very concerned that I was losing myself.

Almost a year later, I received a letter from Jonas. He was living in a different state, forced to move around due to some bad dealings on his father's part. He told me he loved me, apologized profusely, and said he hoped that one day I would find happiness. I was elated that he was alive, yet felt betrayed at the same time.

I met your grandfather another year later. He had to work very hard to earn my trust. Do you know he asked me on a date ten times before I agreed? Looking back, I feel terrible for what I put him through. But, in my mind, if I was going to hand over my heart, he had to prove that he would never leave me.

You know how things worked out. Your grandpa and I were married for many years; I fell deeply in love with him. Jonas became an occasional happy memory instead of a sad one. Then, when grandpa unexpectedly passed, I felt myself teetering. I didn't feel whole without my other half. A familiar sadness started to creep in, and I prayed that I wouldn't fall into a depression like I did all those years ago.

Some months later, a knock on the cottage door nearly caused me to faint. There, standing before me after some fifty years, was Jonas Grant. He walked back into my life older, wiser, a widower, and my new neighbor across the lake. The rest, as they say, is history. You know him as the elderly man who keeps chickens and comes over to complain about coyotes. I know him as my best friend who came back into my life when I needed him the most.

All of that said, I'm sure you're wondering why I decided to wait until I passed to tell you this. It's simple. No one knows about my history with Mr. Grant, except for you. Our relationship was very precious to me, and it's a secret I wanted to keep.

Fate plays funny games, Kyle. I pray that what I have said will comfort you in some way. I, without a doubt, believe that Addison will come back into your life when the time is right. She may not appear tomorrow or a year from now; she might not show up until you're old and gray like me. Just know that when she does, it will be the right time for both of you. Don't lose faith in that, but don't forget to live in the present, either.

If you ever need proof that the universe works in mysterious ways, hold this letter in your hands. Remember my story and know I'm always watching over you.

My love always,
Gram

Chapter Sixteen

I'm glad I was sitting down when I read the letter.

Gram and Mr. Grant had a past. I can't believe I didn't see it before. I guess I wouldn't have, being as I was ten or eleven when he first started coming around. I never saw the two of them touch. But, whenever Gram needed something done that Kevin and I couldn't handle, Mr. Grant was there. On Sundays, he would come over for coffee when Gram got back from church, and he would always happen to "stumble upon" a patch of daisies along the way. The more I think about it, the more I realize how dazed he appeared at Gram's funeral. At the time I was a mess, so I didn't give a second thought to the single rose he laid by her side before the service.

Now, lying on my bed with my back propped against the pillows, it's hard to believe how similar our experiences are, Gram's and mine. She was right. Addison did come back into my life. However, I'm not sure I agree with her theory that it happened at the right time. Addison has Derek. Fate must have fucked up. Or, maybe this is karma's way of teaching me a lesson; maybe the universe is trying to make me forgive my cheating father by showing me how hard it is to want something you can't have.

My phone vibrates against the top of the desk next to my bed. I lean over and pick it up, reading the message displayed on the screen.

Happy New Year.

It's from Jen.

I'm surprised. We haven't spoken since she moved out.

Thanks. Happy New Year, I respond.

My phone buzzes. *Can I call you?*

Ah, okay. *Sure.*

My cell rings a moment later. "Hello?"

"Hey." Jen sounds like she's smiling. "How are you feeling?"

That's a weird question. "Why would you ask?"

"Because I just ran into your brother at the gas station." She laughs. "He said you were looking a little green last night."

"Very funny," I say sardonically. "I'm fine."

"I just thought I'd call and give you shit. You never get wasted."

"I didn't get wasted." I sit upright. "Kevin needs to get his facts straight."

"*Riiight.*" She sounds like she doesn't believe me. "So, he told me he and Ashley picked a date."

"Yeah. May 10th."

"He said I'm invited to the wedding." Jen pauses. "Is that going to be okay?"

I frown. "Why wouldn't it be okay? You two are friends."

"I meant between us," she says. "Will it be awkward if I go?"

The thought never crossed my mind. I decide to mess with her. "Now that you mention it, maybe so. Do you plan on dancing?"

"Probably."

"Hmmm." I purse my lips. "As long as you don't clothes-line yourself doing the limbo, it should be fine."

"Ugh!" she exclaims. "You're never going to let me live that down, are you?"

"No," I laugh. "Not when you were bragging about how good you were and then fell on your ass in front of everyone."

"At least it was a room full of strangers! You want to talk about embarrassment? What about the first time you met my parents? Your fly was down!"

"Whose fault was that?" I ask. "If you'd kept your hands to yourself in the car, we wouldn't have had a problem."

"I didn't hear you complaining."

I smile. "No, there were no complaints." Only when her father shook my hand and leaned into my ear to inform me of my situation did I regret *that* decision.

Jen laughs. "I'm glad we can joke around like this."

Me too.

"You know..." she says a little quieter. "We haven't spent a New Year's Eve apart in three years. Last night was kinda..."

"Weird?" I volunteer.

"For lack of a better word, yes. I missed you."

She must be mistaken. "Are you sure you missed me or having someone to kiss at midnight?" I tease.

"Oh, I had someone to kiss."

My eyebrows shoot up.

"But, it was you that I missed."

Really? "I hope you didn't say that to your boyfriend."

"He's not my boyfriend. We only met last night."

"And you're kissing him? Wow. Who is he? James Davis?" James is a character in one of Jen's favorite book series.

"Haha. No. Just a nice guy who was all alone like me."

"You should have called Kevin and come with us. You could have met Ashley."

"That would have been all right with you?" She sounds baffled.

"Jen. Does it sound like I hate you?"

"No."

"Then stop worrying that the world's going to end if we see each other."

"I wasn't." She pauses for a few seconds. "Fine. I was. It's...I feel bad about the way I left. It was selfish of me to give you an ultimatum, especially so soon after losing Gram. I suck."

"Yes. Yes, you do."

"Kyle!"

"What?"

"You're making me feel worse!"

I laugh. "Calm down. Everything is fine. Your leaving was par for the course as far as I'm concerned. I couldn't give you what you needed and that's on me. I'm sorry, too."

"Yeah?"

"Yeah."

The line is silent for a few moments. Despite tiptoeing around the end of our relationship, I feel good about this conversation.

"So, maybe we could hang out some time?" Jen tentatively asks. "Maybe do dinner? Or a movie?"

"Are you asking me out?" I chide her.

"I'm trying to be friends with you."

There's the F word again. But, when it comes to Jen, it makes sense.

"I would love to go to dinner or a movie with you."

Jen sounds relieved. "Great."

We talk for a few minutes longer. When I hang up, I feel a weight lifted off my shoulders I didn't realize was there. It's nice when your exes don't hate you. The unfortunate thing is I have more of those than I care to count.

~~~~

Bowling tonight?

Looks that way.

I must warn you, I'm not that good.

Don't worry. I can carry us.

I'm psyched to see Addison. We talk almost every day, but it doesn't come close to laying eyes on her. When my brother told me Ashley was setting up a doubles bowling night for the wedding party, I had to hide my smile. The love birds want us to get together to discuss wedding details.

My only goal is to spend time with Sparrow.

When I walk inside the Lucky Strike, the dim lighting of the bowling alley makes me squint. There are a dozen or so lanes to my right, each one with a large screen at the end of it projecting an Andy Warhol print of Marilyn Monroe. As Marilyn morphs into a blurred cityscape, I redirect my attention. Ahead, on my left, I find the shoe desk along with a sign boasting about all the amenities the bowling alley has to offer. They have ten pool tables, an arcade, two dance floors – one which holds the largest disco ball in Michigan – and nine bars. Nine. This place is like one giant nightclub.

I step up to the desk. "Hi. Can you tell me where I can find the Dayton party?"

No sooner do I get the words out than a pair of hands tries to cover my eyes from behind. The person isn't quite tall enough to reach, and I end up with two palms pressed against my cheeks.

"Guess who?"

My heart skips.

I turn around to find Addison grinning. "Hi."

"Hey." I smile. "Are you the welcoming committee?"

"Just yours. I need shoes and you happened to be standing here."

I drink in her appearance. "Lucky me."

We step up to the counter and request our shoe sizes, hers a petite seven and mine an eleven.

"Sheesh, Sasquatch," Addison teases, looking down at my feet. "I don't remember those being so big."

I have to stop myself from joking with her and telling her something else might be bigger than she remembers.

The attendant hands us our shoes. Addison leads me in the direction of lanes eleven and twelve, explaining that Kevin and Ashley rented two of the four VIP lanes, along with the adjoining private lounge.

"We've already ordered some food," she says. "I'm starving."

When we step inside the room, I find Ashley, Kevin, Tara and Austin, along with Noah from work. Ashley is sitting next to Tara with an open binder on her lap. She looks at her wrist. "Where is Nikki?"

Tara shrugs.

"Hey." My brother comes over to me. "Couple that wins gets free beer." He looks from me to Ashley and back again. "We're going to kick your ass."

My eyes roll. "Whatever."

"No, really." Addison sits down. "Ashley used to sub on her mother's bowling league. We're toast."

Kevin laughs and then gets distracted as a waitress arrives with a tray of drinks. I sit down next to Addison and start to untie my boots. "I'm not worried about winning," I tell her. "I can afford my own beer."

She smiles. "Good because you're going to hate being stuck with me."

Never.

After a few more minutes, Ashley pipes up. "I know Nikki's not here, but let's get some stuff out of the way." She scoots to the edge of her seat and consults her binder. "Okay. You all know the wedding is May 10th. We're still deciding on a church, but the reception is going to be at the Sheraton here in Novi. That way we can all stay the night and not have to worry about driving." She flips a page. "The rehearsal dinner will be the night before." She runs her finger down the page. "As far as the bachelor party, Kyle, I'm leaving that up to you." She raises her head and gives me a pointed look. "However, Kevin and I have talked. You have been warned."

My expression twists. "We have rules?"

"A few."

"Not fair," I protest. "Addison's planning on getting you an ice sculpture of a –"

I'm cut off by a hard jab to my ribs. "Shut up!" Addison hisses. "It's a surprise!"

"That is not a surprise," I say. "That's wrong."

"Oh!" Tara's eyes light up. "What is it? Tell me!"

Addison winks at her. "Later." She redirects her attention to Ashley. "As far as your shower and bachelorette party, I have a few dates and themes in mind."

The men collectively groan.

"We don't need to go into them here," she says, annoyed. "I just wanted you to know I've been coming up with ideas."

Ashley grins, then looks back at her book. "Kevin and I will pick out the tuxes; you guys will have to go get fitted a month or so before the wedding. Us girls will do the dress thing together." She flips another page. "We're still working on the guest list, but it looks like each of you will be able to bring a date." She looks from Tara to Addison. "I already included John and Derek." Her eyes jump to me. "What about you, Kyle? Are you planning on bringing anyone?"

Her question takes me off guard. "Not that I know of. It's five months way."

"Four," she corrects me. "What about Jen? Kevin mentioned you guys were talking again."

I can feel Addison's body stiffen beside mine. My speaking to Jen shouldn't bother her, but I shoot my brother an annoyed look anyway. Apparently, he tells his woman every damn thing. "We've talked once. Besides, I thought she was already invited."

"She is," Kevin says.

"I was just trying to see if she needed a plus one," Ashley explains. "If you two came together, I could estimate two people instead of four."

Thankfully, Ashley moves on. She asks Austin and Noah if they're bringing dates, and the subject of Jen is dropped. Out of the corner of my eye, I glance at Addison. She appears extremely interested her cuticles.

Moments later, after Ashley informs me I'll be responsible for a few other things, like the rings, Nikki finally shows up. Her arrival is the distraction we need to forget the wedding talk and start bowling.

Kevin and I head to the lanes to program our names into the kiosks. One lane is guys, the other girls, paired up based on the wedding. My partner is Addison, Tara's is Austin, and Noah's is Nikki. However, before the game gets underway, the food arrives. We all dig in to an assortment of nachos, wings, and coconut shrimp. I order a beer, and Addison asks for one as well.

"I thought you only drank liquor," I say.

"You've seen me drink one time," she responds. "Get me a Redd's Apple Ale, if they have it."

They do.

When the food is gone, Kevin and Ashley are the first to bowl. They give each other a kiss over the ball return before they throw, and, no lie, they both get strikes. It's annoying.

Addison and I are up next. She selects a ball from the return, which I notice happens to be six pounds and fluorescent pink.

"You need a heavier ball," I say.

"No. I can't throw anything heavier."

"You won't be able to control that thing. It'll be all over the place."

"Kyle. I told you I suck. If I can't control this ball, I won't be able to control any ball."

She scrunches her face in frustration to prove her point, and all it does it make me want to kiss her. I take a step back. "You go first. Let me see what I'm working with here."

She sighs and walks to her lane. She takes a step, swings her arm back, and tosses the ball. It bounces loudly, twice, and proceeds to roll straight into the gutter.

She throws her hands up and turns around. "See!"

"You weren't kidding."

She walks back toward me. "No shit."

I smile. "One sec."

I leave her side to take my turn. I line up my shot, release the ball with a little curve, and bingo. Ten pins fall.

"Show off." Addison pouts as I walk back toward her.

"C'mon." I grab a heavier ball and hand it to her. "Let's see what we can do about this."

I follow her over to her lane while Austin takes his turn behind me. "See the dots on the floor?" I point. "You're going to line up your shot with the middle one."

She nods. She adjusts her stance like she's getting ready to throw, and I stop her. "Wait." I step behind her and grab her hips. "You're too far to the left. Move over."

I shift her to where I want her to stand, and it takes me a minute to realize where my hands are. I didn't give a second thought to touching her. We're standing barely an inch apart, her back to my chest, and I don't want to let her go. The electricity I felt while watching the fireworks returns, and I let my hands rest against her for a few extra seconds. Leaning over her shoulder I say, "Okay. Now try."

Addison inhales and exhales before she steps out of my grasp. She throws the ball. This time, it makes it halfway down the lane before hitting the gutter.

"Better," I concede. "Although, the point of the game is to hit the pins."

She sticks her tongue out at me. "Don't be a jerk."

Great. Now I'm thinking about kissing her again.

We rotate through our turns, and everyone appears to be an okay bowler. The next time Addison is up, I don't think twice about standing behind her and placing her body where I want it. The anticipation between us is back, and it's quickly becoming my favorite feeling. Before she throws, I reach around her and circle her wrist, holding it tight.

"Keep this straight," I say. "Don't let it bend. Pretend you're wearing a brace or my hand is supporting you."

Her skin feels soft beneath my fingers. We're standing so close that when she nods in understanding, her hair grazes the side of my chin. Gently, I squeeze her wrist and release it. As I move to the side, her eyes catch mine. She redirects her attention, then throws the ball. It reaches the end of the lane, tapping a pin before rolling away. She looks at me, surprised.

"We're getting there," I encourage her. "Let's try again."

When her ball returns, she positions herself correctly this time. I don't have an excuse to move her around; however, before she throws, I remind her of her wrist and tell her to keep her elbow locked, as well. Running two fingers from her hand to her shoulder, I explain how she should try to swing her arm like a pendulum. It takes her a few moments before she bowls, but when she does, a pin goes down.

"Yes!" she exclaims and high-fives me.

We are so going to lose this game.

And I couldn't care less.

Addison's bowling improves the longer she plays. Her aim is better and she's able to knock down several pins each time she throws. Despite this, we're no competition for Kevin and Ashley; they're blowing the rest of us out of the water. Two beers and seven frames later, I try to stay seated and just watch Addison play.

"What are you doing?" she asks when it's her turn and I don't move.

"Nothing."

"Well, come on." She gestures toward the lane.

"You're doing great. You don't need me anymore."

"Um, yes, I do." She reaches for my hand and tries to pull me to stand. "I bowl better when you're with me."

"How do you know?" I tease as she continues to yank my arm. "You haven't tried without me since I taught you a few tricks."

"Fine." She drops my hand. "I'll prove it."

She stalks away, and my brother takes a seat next to me. "You two couldn't be more obvious if you tried," he says, his voice low. "Did you forget our talk from the other day?"

I frown. "What talk?"

"The one where you said you would say no."

I scowl. "All I'm doing is helping a friend with her game."

My brother tips his bottle back and swallows. "No. You're staring at her ass and touching her every chance you get."

Well, yeah. That too.

"I'm not saying I blame you." Kevin looks at the drink in his hands. "But, just so you know, I don't think I'm the only one who's noticed."

My eyes dart to Ashley. She appears to be involved in an animated conversation with Nikki and Noah. If she's been watching us, I can't tell.

In my periphery, I catch Addison line up her shot. I turn my head to watch as she puts the ball directly into the gutter.

"She did that on purpose," I say to my brother while trying not to grin. I thrust my beer into his hand as I stand to join her.

"What was that?" I jokingly chastise her. "Have I taught you nothing?"

She turns around to look at me, uncertain.

"What's wrong? I was just teasing you."

"It's not that." She shakes her head. "I don't feel very good."

"Too much to drink?" I ask.

"I don't know. Maybe the shrimp was bad."

I feel fine, but then again, I didn't eat the seafood.

Addison retrieves her ball for her second shot when suddenly she appears pale. "Can you help me to the restroom?" she asks.

Concerned, I wrap my arm around her and she leans into my side. I walk with her toward the bathrooms. When we're steps away, she says, "We need to move faster," and leaves my side to rush into the ladies room.

As I wait outside the door, Ashley and Tara find me. "What's going on?" Ashley asks.

"Addison doesn't feel well. She thinks it might have been the shrimp."

"Oh no!" she moans. "I ate a ton of that stuff!"

The girls look at each other and then disappear behind the bathroom door. There's no point in my waiting around with her friends here, so I head back to our lanes.

"What's up?" Kevin asks as I sit down.

"Addison's sick."

"Ugh."

"Yeah. She didn't look well. She felt warm, too."

Kev raises an eyebrow. "You would know."

I choose not to respond.

After what seems like forever, the girls return. Addison walks up to me and I stand. "You okay?" I ask.

She gives me a weak smile. "I puked."

"Do you feel better?"

"A little. I'm going to call it a night and go home."

"Are you sure you can drive?"

"Yes. Tara's going to leave, too and follow me." She makes her way toward the lounge where we left our coats and shoes. "Would you walk me to my car?" she asks.

Hell yes. I'd carry her if that's what she needed.

Tara and Addison say good night to the group, and then we head to change our shoes. The girls gather their purses and coats, and I hold the door for them as they walk out into the frigid night air.

"I'm over here." Tara points to the left. "The blue Santa Fe."

Addison nods. "I'll swing around on the way out."

Tara smiles and walks away. "Have a nice night, Kyle."

"You, too."

Addison leads the way to her car, and I walk slowly by her side. "Do you think you have the flu?" I ask.

"I better not." She frowns. "I got the shot."

We walk a few more steps in silence until she looks at me. "Thanks for tonight. I'm sorry we got stuck as partners."

"I'm not."

She gives me a shy smile. "I could kinda tell."

Shit. "I'm sorry."

"No, you're not," she laughs.

She's right, and I grin. "That's not why you threw up is it?"

She laughs again. "No, Kyle. I'm not repulsed by your touch."

I let out an exaggerated sigh. "Thank God."

We make it to her Hummer, and she unlocks the door. She crawls inside and I stand there, with one hand holding the door open and the other braced against the frame. "Text me when you get home," I say.

"Will do. Then I'm going to bed."

Addison starts the car, and I back away. I move to shut her door when she stops me. "Hey." She sets her palm against the handle. "Drive safe."

"I will," I promise.

She smiles and pulls the door closed. I give her a small wave and turn to head back inside. I look over my shoulder once, to make sure Tara is following her, and they leave the parking lot together.

~~~~

The following evening, I send Addison a message to make sure she's feeling better. I've been thinking about her all day. The way she looked, the way her complexion paled, I've never seen anything like it before. Honestly, it kind of freaked me out.

167

Just checking in. How are you? I send.

Minutes later, my phone buzzes. *I'm good.*

So, I won't be getting the flu?

No. Not unless you have a uterus ;)

Um, what? *That's a relief. Last I checked I didn't have one of those.*

Funny.

Seconds pass, and I wonder what she meant. Did she get sick because she was having woman issues? My phone vibrates again as Addison sends: *Aren't you going to say congratulations?*

I frown. *For getting your period??* I can't believe I just typed that.

Ha! No.

My phone goes silent for a moment, and an uneasy feeling starts to settle in my stomach. Then, two words appear that practically gut me.

I'm pregnant.

Chapter Seventeen

It hurts.

It shouldn't, but it does.

Addison's words were like the final blow in a boxing match; the one that crowns the victor. Derek has won, and we weren't even fighting.

Wait. I take that back.

Apparently, I was. If I wasn't, this wouldn't piss me off so much.

It's been three weeks since Addison told me the news. I haven't seen her, and I don't text her anymore. She sends me messages every now and again, asking me about my day or what I've been doing. Don't get me wrong: I still respond, just not immediately and with one or two word answers. Yes, I know I'm being a selfish baby.

There's that word. Baby.

The more I think about it, the more I realize I can't be angry with her for getting pregnant. Logic says if the woman is married, she's sleeping with her husband. I'm more upset with the way she handled things. This was huge, unexpected news. Our friendship should have warranted at least a phone call. And, forgive me, but with all the mutual flirting going on, I have to admit I started to think that maybe she felt something more for me, too. I felt close to her.

I still feel close to her.

The truth is, we were dancing around forbidden lines. I hate to admit I loved the feeling. It's the only type of relationship with Addison I've ever known. When we first met, we were instantly connected and intimate. When we found each other again, we were still connected and toying with intimacy. Now, an innocent life is involved. I need to find a way to have a normal relationship with Addison if I'm going to know her at all. My stubborn self doesn't want that, and I need to man up and figure out how I'm going to pull it off. So far, the only thing I've managed to do is barely communicate with her. I think about what I've lost constantly.

Like I said, it hurts.

~~~~

"Just get your ass over here."

"I said no."

Kevin and I are arguing about the Super Bowl. He's having people over to his place for the game, and I don't feel like socializing.

"Don't make me go Dr. Phil on you again," my brother says. "It's just football. Besides, Ashley says Addison and Derek aren't coming."

This is news. Last I heard, the whole gang was headed to their apartment. "Are you sure?"

"That's what Ash said, something about Addison being really tired."

I'm quiet as I contemplate driving over there. Kevin doesn't live far from me. Plus, if I go, he'll get off my case. I'm tired of his attempts to lecture me about my mood. Working with him doesn't allow me a ton of privacy, and I'm not good at pretending things are peachy.

"I'll take your silence as a yes," he says. "Bring your own beer."

He hangs up, and I stare at the phone in my hand. If I don't show up, I know he'll keep calling me. Suddenly, I feel like Cameron from *Ferris Bueller's Day Off*, debating on caving in to his best friend's whims, despite his own better judgment.

When I arrive at Kevin's place, Noah, Eli, and Austin are already there. I also recognize John, Tara's boyfriend from the bar, seated on one end of the love seat.

"Where are the girls?" I ask Kevin as he follows me into the kitchen.

"Tara and Ash went to pick up the subs," he says. "Is that all the beer you brought?"

As I open his refrigerator door, I glance at my fingers wound around three bottle necks and shrug. "It's all I had." I place two bottles in the fridge door and keep one. Turning around, my eyes catch a tray of vegetables, a bowl of fruit, and an assortment of chips, pretzels, and dips laid out on the breakfast bar. "Nice buffet."

"My girl thinks of everything." Kevin grins.

We make our way back to the living room and the front door opens. Tara and Ashley stumble inside laughing hysterically as they try to maneuver a six-foot sub covered in plastic wrap through the door. My brother and I move to help. I grab one end of the sandwich just behind Ashley as Kevin reaches out and holds up the middle.

"What in the world?" Kevin asks.

"The deli didn't cut it," Tara laughs. "We almost lost this thing three times!"

"It tried to roll off the cart twice in the grocery store and once in the parking lot," Ashley explains. She looks over her shoulder to see who is behind her and realizes it's me. "What are you doing here?"

"Good to see you, too." I smirk.

"Kevin said you weren't coming."

"I changed my mind."

"Well," she eyes the sub, "I hope you're hungry."

By halftime I've settled comfortably into the corner of the couch with a full stomach. The game is turning out to be mostly one-sided and not that exciting to watch. No one in the room is a die-hard fan of either of the teams playing, although Austin and Eli are getting worked up over their football squares.

"I know what this game needs," John says. All eyes turn to him as he announces, "Shots."

"What do you propose?" Kevin asks.

"We do a shot every time Seattle scores."

"John!" Tara glares at him. "They've been scoring on almost every possession!"

He wiggles his eyebrows at his girlfriend. "I know."

"If you pass out your butt will spend the night here," she threatens.

John shrugs.

"I'm game," Eli says. Noah and Austin nod in agreement, and Kevin leaves the room in search of booze.

"I think we should make this a little more challenging," Noah suggests and the guys get to planning. One shot for a touchdown, two for a two-point conversion, one for a field goal, and another two if there is a turnover.

Kevin returns with a bottle of Jack and a handful of shot glasses. As we set things up on the coffee table for the second half, there's a knock on the door. Ashley stands to answer it and when she does, I don't have to turn around to know who it is.

I can feel Addison's presence without looking at her.

"Hey, guys." Ashley sounds uncertain. "I thought you decided to stay home."

"Addison was feeling up to it, so here we are," I hear Derek respond. "Better late than never."

My jaw tenses and my teeth grind together.

"Great!" Ashley's enthusiasm sounds forced. "Let me take your coats and put them in the bedroom."

I hear the shuffling of material and Addison say, "Thanks."

"There's plenty of food in the kitchen," Ashley says. "Help yourself."

I've yet to turn my head. Despite this, I swear I can feel eyes burning a hole into me. Whether they are Derek's or Addison's, I'm not sure.

"Are you hungry babe?" I hear Derek ask.

"Um, maybe," Addison answers and I can sense them move out of the room.

I allow my eyes to meet Kevin's and he mouths, "Sorry."

The back of my neck feels hot. I don't know what to do. I really, *really* don't want to sit in the same room with Derek and pretend everything is okay.

"Excuse me?" I hear Derek from the kitchen. "Whose beer is this?"

Most heads turn to look, as it's possible to see through the living room into the kitchen over the breakfast bar. "That's Kyle's," Kevin answers.

"Can I have one?"

He can't be serious.

Kevin's eyes land on me with raised brows. "Can he?" he asks.

Hell no! I think. *I only brought three.* All eyes are on me, however, and I don't want to come across as a complete dickhead. Not everyone in this room is aware of my situation, so I nod yes.

"Thanks, man," I hear Derek from behind me.

I don't acknowledge him.

The second half of the game gets under way, and I pray Seattle will do something that earns us a shot – and soon. Ashley returns to the room, and I feel our two new guests join her to stand somewhere behind the couch. I stare at the television.

No. I stare through the television. The only thing I'm truly aware of is Addison's proximity to me.

Apparently God is listening, or maybe it's Gram, because Seattle returns the opening kickoff for an 87-yard touchdown. Our group cheers, not because of Percy Harvin's run, but because our game of shots has officially begun. Hands descend on the coffee table, and I scoop up the glass closest to me. I knock back the liquor without hesitation, and it burns its way down my throat. Setting the glass down, I push it away from me with two fingers, toward Kevin, who is gathering them all to refill.

Out of the corner of my eye, I notice a pair of legs round the couch. I'm forced to look up when Derek asks, "Hey. Do you mind moving?"

My face contorts. "What?"

"Do you mind moving? Addison needs a place to sit."

"Don't get up, Kyle," Addison says stepping around Derek. "I'm fine."

"No, you're not," Derek says. "You've been nothing but exhausted and you need to sit down."

I glance around the room. Unless Addison wants to sit on the floor, the only empty seat is on the couch between me and Kevin. "I'll move over," I say and start to get up.

"Then where will I sit?" Derek asks.

My eyes narrow as I stand to my full height. His smug face is about a foot from mine. He already has my girl, my beer, and now he wants my seat too?

Unbelievable.

"Derek," Addison says in a warning tone. "I'll sit on the floor."

"You won't," he responds while staring at me.

"I'll move," Kevin volunteers, sensing the tension. He stands beside me and crosses his arms. "If I had known seating would be an issue, I would've rented chairs." He's irritated and I can tell. He'll have my back in a second if I need him.

"Thanks." Derek looks past me and at my brother. "I appreciate it."

Kevin moves out of the way, and I back up to where he was sitting. Now, it's me, Addison, and Derek sharing the couch.

Fuck my life.

Addison sits between Derek and me, causing the tense muscles in my shoulders to flex. Feeling comfortable in this situation is an impossibility. I lean away from her and set my elbow on the armrest, so as to appear casual. My body shifts, and my knee bumps against hers. Reflexively, I jerk it away.

Addison's eyes meet mine and they cloud over with hurt. My heart jumps into my throat. She thinks I don't want to touch her when the exact opposite is true. It's then I decide to set her straight. Holding her gaze, I deliberately let my knee fall to the side and rest against hers. Her eyes widen, and I turn my attention back to the game.

Throughout the third quarter, I try to concentrate on anything that doesn't involve Addison. I completely fail. Even when Seattle scores again and I take a second shot, I can still feel the warmth of her knee through the fabric of my jeans. Derek isn't helping, either. Every time he touches her, I feel like I'm going to lose it. First, he draped his arm over her shoulders. Then, he began to run his fingers over her arm and trace the top of her shoulder. The movement was all I could see out of the corner of my eye, and the thought of grabbing his fingers and breaking them brought a momentary smile to my face. After that, he pulled her close and kissed her temple. All I could do was stare straight ahead and pretend it wasn't happening.

Now, Seattle has scored in the fourth. As I reach for my shot, the feeling of Addison's knee disappears from mine. My head snaps to the right in time to catch Derek place a protective palm low on Addison's belly. He moves in close, says something into her ear, and then kisses the corner of her mouth. She gives him a tiny smile and leans back, her knee touching mine again.

It's then that I realize that's all I'll ever have with her. Small touches. It might happen once, twice, three times, possibly a million, but that's all I will ever get. I blink as the proof is laid bare before me; as it is thrown in my face. I have no idea what she is thinking, but I know what I am.

I can't do this anymore.

Throwing the shot down my throat, I slam the glass on the table. Startled, Addison looks at me with questioning eyes. Without a word, I stand and head toward the door.

"Kyle. Where are you going?" I hear Kevin ask behind me.

I don't bother to answer. I simply open the door and walk out.

~~~~

About a mile from my house, the back pocket of my jeans starts to vibrate. I'm so concentrated on pushing Addison out of my mind that I didn't even realize I was sitting on my phone.

At the next stop light, I wrestle with my cell as I try to pull it out of my pants. It's stuck. Either that or I'm more buzzed than I thought. When it finally springs free, I see that I have a message from Jen: *Are you at Kevin's?*

I start to respond, but the light turns green. I hit the gas and, before I get stopped at another light, my cell rings in my hand.

"Hello?"

"Hey!" Jen says, sounding far too bubbly on the other end. "Did you get my text?"

"Yep."

"So, are you at Kevin's?"

"Nope."

"Aw." She sounds disappointed. "He invited me over for the game, and I just got off work. I thought the party would last longer than nine o'clock."

I unintentionally snap. "It probably will."

"What's wrong?"

"Abso-fucking-lutely nothing," I respond. Yeah, I'm definitely more buzzed than I thought.

"Kyle." Jen's tone turns serious. "Are you drunk?"

"No. Maybe. Wait," I pause as I make a right-hand turn. "I'm getting there."

"What happened?"

"I told you. Nothing."

"Don't lie to me. I can tell you're upset."

"You would be, too, if someone you loved was married and pregnant and rubbing it in your face."

"Ummm..." Jen pauses, uncertain. "Care to elaborate?"

And with that, I spill my guts. I don't know how it happens; one minute I'm denying I'm pissed and the next I'm sharing all my secrets. I make it home and turn into the driveway, then sit in the truck and leave it running while I talk. I tell Jen about Addison and about her disappearance. I talk about meeting her again and finding out about the accident. I confide in her what happened at the parade and the bowling alley. And then, I tell her about tonight. It takes a while to get it all out.

A pair of headlights flash in my rearview mirror and a car pulls to a stop behind mine. I can't immediately tell who it is in the dark, so I turn off my engine and open the door.

"It's just me," Jen says in my ear.

I get out of my truck and slam the door just as she turns off her headlights. The cold winter air sobers me a bit as she gets out of her car. We walk toward one another, meeting half way.

"You didn't have to come over," I say.

"I think I did." She looks up at me. "I've never heard you talk about anything like you talk about Addison. Not even work." She regards me skeptically. "I lived with you for nearly three years, and I never knew you could be so passionate."

"Passionate?" I scowl. "I think I'm angry."

"Passion can be anger," she says. "It can also be love. It can be hate. The point is, I've never heard you get so emotional."

I look into her pale blue eyes and realize I owe her an apology. "I'm sorry. I should have told you I was haunted by Addison when we met."

"That would've been helpful," she says. "Regardless...I'm sorry you're hurting."

I shake my head. "It's not your fault. It's mine. Apparently, I have a problem accepting reality."

Jen disagrees. "You're the most down to earth person I know." She crosses her arms and looks around. "Is there any way we could go inside? I'm freezing my ass off."

"Sure."

Once inside, Jen flips the light switch by the front door. She takes off her coat, hanging it on one of the hooks on the wall, and I take off my shoes. She moves around the house like she never left. I mean, let's face it: she's only been gone a few months.

"How's your new apartment?" I ask as I toss my keys on to the counter.

"Nice," she says. "I live right above the landlord, so if I need anything he's close by."

I frown. "Doesn't that make it hard to have people over? What if you get loud?"

"Who am I going to have over?" she asks. "You know I don't throw wild parties. I get enough of that at work."

This is the perfect opportunity to tease her. "What if you have the new boyfriend over? Things might get loud." I wink.

"What new boyfriend?"

"The guy from New Year's Eve."

"Oh, him." She rolls her eyes. "He hasn't called."

"Really?"

"Yes, really. You're not the only one who doesn't feel wanted."

Her words hit me. I hate that she feels this way. Jen truly is a great girl. She's cute and funny and talented, and I'm an idiot for not being able to fall in love with her.

She places her hand against her neck and squeezes, trying to rub out the tension. My eyes roam her black bartending uniform, the tight V-neck top, thigh-high skirt, and tights. They remind me she's been on her feet all day.

"C'mere," I say and gesture for her to follow me into the living room. "Sit." I point at the couch.

With a puzzled look, she obliges. I take a seat beside her, then wrap my hands around her waist and turn her back toward me.

"What are you doing?" she asks.

I move my body closer to hers and place my hands on her shoulders. "How many hours did you work today?"

"Ugh. Ten," she sighs.

I nod and start to knead the knots from her muscles. Her chin immediately falls to her chest.

"Oh, God," she says. "That feels amazing."

"Did you forget how good I am at this?"

"Apparently," she mumbles. "Do. Not. Stop."

I laugh. Moving my thumbs in circles, I press deep into her shoulder blades, then move near her spine, and then travel up to her neck. I repeat the same pattern several times before she says, "I think I'm drooling."

"Now that's attractive," I tease. My hands glide over her back, moving from top to bottom, and when I get near her waist, she starts to wiggle.

"Stop!" She laughs. "You know that tickles!"

"Do I?" I press my fingers into her skin. "You said not to stop."

"I'm changing my mind!" She twitches beneath my touch.

I move up to her shoulders again and then lean forward to speak into her ear. "Don't you like my hands on you?"

Jen freezes. That comment sounded much more innocent in my head. But, then again, I've had a few drinks tonight.

She turns and looks over her shoulder, her mouth inches from mine. "Do you want me to answer that?" she asks.

Right then, in that moment, I want to kiss her. I'm not sure if it's the alcohol in my system, my honesty with her, or the fact that I haven't had sex in months. Most likely all three.

Jen searches my face and when her eyes settle on my mouth, she turns her body around toward me. She leans in slowly, placing her hands on my knees, and barely brushes her lips across mine. I want more than that though, and my hands move to capture her face. My mouth easily dances with hers and deepens the kiss; she moves and crawls into my lap. I'm conscious of her hands running over my shoulders, her chest pressed against mine, and her fingers weaving into my hair. She whimpers into my mouth; it's a sound I remember, and it's then that I realize this could get out of control real fast.

I break our kiss and lean back an inch. "This shouldn't happen," I breathe.

"Why?" she whispers.

"Because we're not together."

She straightens her back, sitting upright and putting another few inches of distance between us. "But, we're not with anyone else."

I'm silent. It's true. We're both unattached adults.

"Look," Jen says and moves her hands to my chest. "You and me, we've done this before. More times than I can count. We tried to have a normal relationship. It didn't work. I get that. I don't see why we can't be friends and mess around."

My eyebrows shoot up. "You want to have meaningless sex with me?"

She smiles. "I've not having it with anyone else." She zeroes in on my mouth again, and I can't stop my reaction.

I kiss her back.

My lips spend a minute on hers before leaving and traveling down her chin, along her jawline, and down her neck. Before I know it, my hands are at her waist, then under her shirt, then pulling it off over her head. Full breasts and black lace cloud my vision, and despite Jen half-dressed and straddling my lap, Addison appears in the back of mind. I start to hesitate, but the feeling is quickly forgotten when her image is replaced by one of Derek with his hand set lovingly on her stomach.

I have no place in that future.

The thought pushes me to kiss Jen harder, to shed the remaining clothes between us, and use this moment to bury the ache in my chest.

Chapter Eighteen

So began my friends with benefits relationship with Jen.

It's been a couple of weeks, and we've seen each other a handful of times. Strangely, I've yet to feel guilty about what we're doing; probably because both of us agree it isn't a permanent thing.

We've been there and tried that.

No, this is a less complicated version of us. No expectations. No pressure. No arguing. Just two relaxed friends who, more often than not, spend their time together naked. It's a pretty good gig. Given my history, it's the type of relationship I should have. Unfortunately, I still feel a sharp pang whenever I think of Addison. We haven't spoken since the Super Bowl.

It sucks.

I roll over in bed and consult the clock. Jen's going to be late. This is the first time she's stayed the night since our 'arrangement' started. I turn to look at her, and the pillow flattens beneath my head. She's lying on her stomach with her arms tucked beneath her chest. Her hair covers half her face, and the bed sheet is tangled around her legs.

"Hey," I whisper and reach over to nudge her shoulder. "It's nine o'clock."

"Hmmm," she murmurs and turns her face away from me.

I prop myself up on my elbow and lean forward. "I thought you had to meet your dad at ten."

No response.

Jen and her father have a tradition. She's one of four siblings and the only girl. Today happens to be Valentine's Day, and she's supposed to meet her dad for their annual daddy-daughter date. One year they went antiquing; one year it was a movie. Today, it's supposed to be brunch downtown at a historic hotel. If she's late, he will kick my ass. That is, if she tells him where she's been.

"Jen." I move her hair off her face and move my mouth closer to her ear. "You need to get moving."

She groans. "You're loud."

That was loud? Suddenly, I get a brilliant idea. My bare feet hardly make a sound as I roll out of bed and leave the room. I grab the guitar Jen taught me to play and return to her side. I prop one foot on the mattress, balance the instrument across my leg, and start to strum it in the hardest, most obnoxious way possible.

"What the crap?!" Jen jumps to her knees and covers her ears. When I keep playing, she tosses a pillow at me. It plunks off my hand and the guitar strings. "Are you insane?!"

"Nope." I stop strumming. "You need to get up."

She scowls. "You remember I'm not a morning person, right? Do you want me to break that over your head?" She nods toward my guitar.

"You wouldn't. You spent way too much money on this thing." It was an anniversary gift.

Jen's eyes shoot daggers at me, then fall on the clock. "It's 9:15! Why didn't you wake me sooner?" She jumps off the bed.

I give her an exasperated look. "What in the hell do you think I was trying to do?"

She gathers her clothes up off the floor. "Can I use your shower? Thanks!" She doesn't wait for my response before she sprints across the hallway and slams the bathroom door.

Rolling my eyes, I prop the guitar against my desk and then head toward the kitchen. I don't drink coffee, but Jen does. I suppose I could help her wake up in a nice way and make her some for the road.

After I scavenge the cabinets, I come up with a small plastic can of Folgers left behind from when she lived here. I open the lid and sniff the grounds. Can coffee go bad? I search for an expiration date. When I can't find one, I assume coffee is exempt from causing botulism and get to work preparing a few cups.

Jen rips open the bathroom door just as I'm pouring her liquid strength into a travel mug. She walks down the hall and into the kitchen wearing the jeans and sweater she had on last night. She snags her coat off the back of one of my dining chairs and shoves her arms through the sleeves. Pulling her purse over her wet head, she asks, "Is that for me?"

I nod as I snap the lid down. "I thought you could use a little caffeine."

She heads over to her boots. "You're a life saver."

"I wouldn't say that just yet. I don't know how old the coffee is."

She smiles. "I'm sure it's fine."

I walk over to her and wait while she ties her laces. When she stands, she grabs the door handle with one hand and holds out the other for the mug. "Thank you. I don't have time to stop anywhere. I still have to run home and change clothes."

"No thanks necessary."

As she takes the coffee, she leans forward and kisses me on the cheek. "I'll see you tomorrow?" It's a question, not a statement.

"Sure."

Jen yanks open the front door. "I'll call you after my shift."

"Sounds good."

I move around her, reaching over her head to pull the door open wide, when we both look up and stop in our tracks.

Standing on my porch, caught mid-knock, is Addison.

Her eyes travel over us, then widen and blink. Out of embarrassment or disbelief, I'm not sure. What I do know is my pulse just picked up, and it races through my veins.

"I'm so sorry," she says and starts to back away. "I'll come back later."

Jen's eyes bounce to me and, judging from my confused expression, she puts two and two together.

"No no, I was just leaving," she says as she sets one foot outside the door. "You must be Addison."

She nods.

Jen extends her free hand. "Jen. I've heard all about you. It's nice to put a name with a face."

Addison tentatively shakes her hand.

"I'd love to stay and talk, but I've got to run. I'm late for a date." Jen smiles and looks at me over her shoulder. "I'll talk to you later."

"'Kay," is all I can say.

Jen skips down the few steps of the front porch and heads to her car, digging in her purse for her keys along the way. My gaze lands on Addison, whose eyes follow my ex. I cross my arms over my chest and feel my pounding heart. It's as if I've been caught red-handed, though I've done nothing wrong. Swallowing, I say, "This is a surprise."

Addison turns to face me, her expression one of regret. "I know. It's early. I should have called."

We stare at each other. Addison's hair is piled high and messy on the top of her head. A few loose strands blow across her cheek in the cool breeze. I'm tempted to reach out and tuck them behind her ear, but I don't. She puts her hands into her coat pockets and looks down, her chin disappearing into the thick scarf she has wound around her neck. Finally, she meets my eyes and squints. "You're mad at me."

My face twists. "I'm not."

"You are," she says. "We haven't spoken in days."

"You haven't called."

"Neither have you."

Silence. I hate it when it's quiet between us, especially when I have no clue what to say.

After a few moments, Addison asks, "Are you and Jen back together?"

Uncomfortable with her question, I shift my weight. "No."

"We promised no lies," she reminds me.

"I'm not lying," I protest. "We're friends."

She lets out a sarcastic snort. "Yeah, okay. You're sleeping with her."

Her tone is accusatory and judgmental, and I don't like it. I plaster a smug look on my face and lean back against the door frame. "Yes, I am. Repeatedly. Is that a problem for you?"

Her eyes grow wide. "No."

"Because last I checked, you're sleeping with Derek." I nod toward her stomach. "We'll have proof of that in about nine months."

It takes me a second to realize I said that out loud.

Shit.

Addison's voice turns acerbic. "Yes, Kyle; I'm pregnant. God forbid I slept with my *husband*." She shakes her head in disbelief. "You know, I came here to make things right with you. Obviously, you don't care." She starts to leave, but then stops and looks over her shoulder. "Call me when you grow up."

She makes it down the steps and half way to her truck before I snap to. My bare feet barely register the snow on the frigid ground as I jog up behind her and reach for her shoulder. "Addison. Wait."

"What?" she snaps.

We stop walking, and I put my hands on my hips. "I didn't expect to see you this morning. You ambushed me."

She crosses her arms. "No, I didn't. I asked you a simple question. You're the one who threw your sex life in my face!"

I stare at her. "You haven't talked to me in weeks! You show up out of the blue. You interrogate me about Jen..." I anxiously pull my hand through my hair. "My defenses went up."

She leans toward me. "You know what? You're an ass."

"Excuse me?"

She points at her chest. "I came here to find out what was wrong between us and fix it. Why? Because that's what friends do. You haven't said shit to me since Kevin's party, so I took the first step. I assumed you were angry about what Derek did, not because I was pregnant! If I had known, I wouldn't have come. That's not something I can fix, Kyle. I didn't plan on having a baby. There's nothing I can do."

Her expression borders between anger and sadness, and I know I need to make things right if I don't want her to walk away.

"I'm not mad because you're pregnant," I say.

I'm disappointed, but I'll never admit that to her.

"Then why are you?" she asks.

"I'm upset by the way you told me. You sent a goddamn text message." My face falls and I lean in to her. "It was cold and impersonal, and I thought there was more between us. Okay? Yes, your husband went all territorial asshole on me, and I didn't like that, either. But, the main reason I've haven't called is because I don't know how to act around you anymore. What happened at that party was a wakeup call."

Her eyes soften a little. "Why don't you know how to act around me?"

I let out a breath. Standing this close to her, especially during an argument, is not a good idea. All I want to do is hold her and make sure we're okay. I know I shouldn't, but I decide to physically show her the answer to her question. Any words I could say would never come close to describing the way I feel when I'm around her.

Carefully, I bring my hand to her face and tuck the loose strands of her hair behind her ear. She doesn't move away. I trace the outside edge of her ear with my fingertips, then move along her jaw until I reach her chin. Gently, I lift her face toward mine and focus on her eyes. Their chocolate brown color swims with a million questions as I slowly move forward and place a soft kiss on her forehead. Her breath catches and her skin feels smooth beneath my lips; what I wouldn't give to continue this and taste her mouth. Instead, I lean centimeters away and confess. "I don't know how to act around you because when I see you, I want to do this. And I can't. You're not mine."

A high-pitched whine interrupts my confession. I lean away from Addison, confused.

"That wasn't me," she whispers.

"Who was it?" I start to look around. "Is Sam in the truck?"

Without asking, I move toward her vehicle and open the back passenger door. On the floor sits a small pet carrier. When I crouch down to peer inside, I'm confronted with a cute gray and white puppy face.

"You got another dog?" I ask. Then, a horrible thought crosses my mind. "Did something happen to Sam?"

Addison shakes her head as if clearing her thoughts. "No. He's fine." Stepping beside the truck, she opens the carrier and pulls out the puppy. One of her hands supports its chest, while the other holds up its butt. She nuzzles the puppy's nose before cradling the wiggly dog in her arms.

"My coworker's dog had puppies," she says. "She showed me some pictures of them at work and said how hard it was finding them homes."

I reach out and scratch behind the dog's ears. "So, you decided to adopt one?" I don't blame her. This dog is adorable. He or she looks like a malamute, like a miniature version of Sam.

"Not exactly." She looks at the puppy. "Derek won't let me get another dog."

"Why not?" I frown.

"Because Sam got ahold of his cell again and chewed the screen. This is the third time." She sighs. "I don't think he wants Derek to have a phone."

"Maybe he should put it somewhere Sam can't reach it," I suggest sarcastically.

"You think?" Addison gives me half a smile. "Anyway, as soon as I saw this little girl I thought of you. You said you always wanted a dog when you were younger, and you're great with mine. I thought maybe..." She holds the dog out toward me. "Maybe you'd like to keep her?"

"Seriously?" I look at the puppy squirming in Addison's hands. There is no way I can resist. I reach out and take her in my big paws, bringing her to my chest. She licks my chin, then burrows against me, pressing the top of her head to the side of my neck. Her little body is warm.

Which reminds me I'm standing outside in February without shoes.

Supporting the puppy with one hand, I hold out the other toward Addison. "Do you want to come inside?"

She looks uncertain. "Are you still upset with me?"

I'm not. I got what was bothering me off my chest. "Sparrow. My toes are getting frostbite. Please come inside."

She glances at my feet. "What the...! I didn't realize..." She grabs my hand and starts pulling me toward the front door.

Once in the house I set the puppy on the kitchen floor. She starts to explore, sniffing her way around the perimeter of the room. I love the way she's unsteady on the tile, her little back legs sliding a bit when she tries to run.

"So?" Addison comes up behind me. "Is she a keeper?"

I turn toward her. "I think you knew that when you brought her over here."

She smiles and it reaches her eyes. "I'm glad. I'd hate for her to end up in a shelter." She crouches down and calls the dog over. "Hey, pretty girl. Do you think you want to stay here?"

The puppy turns, trots back to Addison, and licks her hand before getting her ears scratched. "You're going to need some things." Addison looks up at me. "Want me to help you shop?"

"Right now?"

"If you're not busy." She slowly stands. "That is, if you're not still mad at me. You never answered my question."

I study her face. "No. I'm not upset. We just...we need to figure some things out." For example, I was incredibly honest with her just a few minutes ago and I have no idea how she's feels about it. I kissed her.

I kissed her. Why didn't she push me away?

"I know," she says quietly. "If we spend the afternoon together, maybe we can work those things out."

I nod. "Let me shower and we'll get out of here."

Her shoulders relax and I'm rewarded with a small smile. "Okay."

I start to walk away and she stops me. "Wait. I'm not keeping you from any Valentine's Day plans, am I?"

I turn around. "No. You?"

She shakes her head. "Derek's –"

"Working?" I guess. After all, it's a 'small' holiday.

"Yeah."

Did I imagine that or did her face just fall a little?

I rush through my shower and quickly dress afterward. I don't want Addison to be bored in my dull house, although she does have the puppy to occupy her time. The realization hits me that, even though we weren't speaking, she still thought of me when she saw the dog. I know she knew I would love it. There's no way I could turn down her offer, especially if I knew the puppy was headed to a shelter. It annoys me that Derek wouldn't allow Addison to keep the dog if she wanted. Apparently, he doesn't have a soft spot for animals.

Mentally, I add that to my list of his shitty traits.

When I walk out into the living room, I find Addison sitting on my ratty recliner with the dog at her feet. "Ready to go?"

She nods. "Just let me use the restroom before we leave. I swear I pee about fifty times a day."

I make a face. "Why do girls always talk about going to the bathroom? Ashley told me she had to piss on New Year's Eve."

"Sorry," she laughs as she walks past me.

While I wait for Addison, I decide to play with my new roommate. I sit on the floor and call her to me. When she comes, I push her body over and rub her belly. "Well, you were a surprise," I say. "What are we going to call you? We'll come up with an awesome name, I promise. You can be the Dayton Landscaping mascot." I kind of like that idea. I can bring her to work with me. The guys will get a kick out of her. She'll be spoiled rotten.

Several minutes go by before I realize Addison is taking an awfully long time in the bathroom. My legs are starting to fall asleep under me on the floor, so I stand and stretch, then decide to check on her.

"Hey." I tap one knuckle on the door. "You okay?"

It takes a second before I hear her voice. It wavers. "Can...can you bring me my phone?"

Alarms sound in my head. "Sure. Where is it?"

"In my bag. In the truck."

I make it to her truck and back in two seconds flat. I knock on the bathroom door again, winded. "I got your purse."

I watch the handle turn as she cracks the door. "Thanks," she whispers. I start to hand her the bag, but stop when I notice her face is covered in red splotches.

"What's wrong?" I ask.

She shakes her head as a tear falls from the corner of her eye. "Addison?"

She takes her purse and tries to shut the door. Worried, I put my hand out to stop it. I'm a little too forceful, because the door ends up swinging open. Addison tries to shut it again, but not before I catch a glimpse of something reflected in the mirror.

The toilet is full of blood.

My panicked eyes meet hers. I can't find words. I take a step toward her, and she pushes me back.

"I have to call my doctor." She wipes stray tears from her cheeks. "Please give me a minute."

I nod and back out of the room, closing the door behind me. My heart races. She's losing the baby.

Oh my god.

She's losing the baby. What can I do? Should I call for help?

I lean against the wall and anxiously wait. I can hear her talking, but can't make out the words. It feels like an hour has passed since she first went into the bathroom. The puppy wanders down the hallway, but I don't move. I'm frozen to this spot until Addison opens that door.

As the dog rounds the corner into my bedroom, the toilet flushes. A lump forms in my throat. I never knew that sound could represent something so final.

Tentatively, the door opens. Springing upright, I search Addison's face. "What do we do?"

Her voice is thick. "My doctor wants me to go to the hospital."

"Done," I say and leave her side to grab my keys. I'm quickly ushering her off the porch steps when her sad eyes meet mine. "You can slow down. There's nothing they can do to stop it."

I ignore her.

"Kyle." She stops walking. "What about the dog?"

Damn.

"Hold on," I say and run back inside to round up the puppy. I sprint next door to my neighbor's house, and luckily, she's home. I explain I have an emergency, and she lets me leave the dog with her.

By the time I get back, Addison is sitting in my truck. I hop up into the driver's seat. "I told you to hold on. I would have helped you."

Silent tears wind down her face making my heart feel like lead. Her eyes are rimmed in red, and her nose is the same shade. I slide over to her side and wipe her tears away with my thumbs. It does no good because they come right back.

"You'll be okay," I say. "Everything will be okay."

She nods.

"I'll drive. You call your husband."

She nods again.

I press a quick kiss to her forehead, move back over to my side of the cab, and start the engine.

Chapter Nineteen

When we make to the emergency room, I wait with Addison as she checks in at the desk. The nurse takes down her name, asks the reason she's there, and then hands her a clipboard with paperwork to complete. She tells Addison to have a seat in the waiting area, and she'll be called back as soon as someone can get to her.

Are you fucking kidding me?

Addison is literally losing a life and that's the best they can do?

I try to remain calm as I follow her over to some empty chairs. We take a seat, and Addison starts to fill out the forms. Her hand shakes as she writes. When she gets to the section regarding insurance, she balances the clipboard and her purse on her lap, while at the same time looking for her wallet. I'm just about to ask her if she needs help when the clipboard slips, hitting the floor and sending papers flying everywhere. Addison brings a shaky hand to her forehead, and I jump up to collect the mess.

"I've got it," I say as I kneel and pull the forms into a pile. When I have them all, I exchange the clipboard for her bag, so it won't happen again.

As she continues, I glance around the waiting room. It seems busy for the morning. Multiple people cough and hack behind me. One little boy looks especially green. As minutes pass, more people walk through the sliding doors and check in at the desk. I'm starting to get uncomfortable with the idea of being surrounded by sickness. I don't want Addison to catch anything, and I sure as hell don't want to, either.

When she completes the forms, I turn them in at the desk for her. As I'm walking back, I notice her pale complexion. "Are you okay?" I ask as I sit down. "Are you in pain?"

"Not really," she says. "Just a few cramps. Nothing I can't handle."

"If it gets bad, let me know. I'm not above raising hell to get you seen."

A tiny smile forms on her lips.

"Did you get ahold of Derek?" I ask.

She shakes her head no.

My face twists into a concerned scowl. On the way here, she tried to call him three times. First, she tried his cell. He didn't answer, and she left a voice message saying that she needed him, it was important, and to call her immediately. Then, she called the office where he works and spoke to the secretary. She found out he was with a patient, and she asked that he be told she was headed to the ER. After that, when we pulled into the hospital, she tried his cell again. No answer.

"How long do physical therapy appointments normally take?" I ask.

"Depends on the injury," she says.

"Still, doesn't he check his phone?"

"He doesn't take personal calls during appointments."

Whatever. If my wife was pregnant, I'd at least keep my phone on vibrate.

Forty-five minutes later, Addison adjusts her weight in the uncomfortable plastic seat. No Derek and no doctor. I feel helpless to do anything other than ask her if she's okay and hold her hand. It's killing me not to pull her into my lap and wipe away the tears that appear in her eyes. I want to kiss her and hold her and try to take away her pain. I can't believe she's had to wait this long.

Finally, Addison's name is called. I walk with her to the double doors, where we step inside and another nurse introduces himself as Brian. We're escorted into a small room where Brian takes Addison's temperature and blood pressure. After asking some general questions, he leads us further into the hospital where

Addison's shown into another small room with a bed. He instructs her to change into a hospital gown because they will be going to another floor for an ultrasound in a few minutes.

"Your husband is welcome to come along," Brian says.

"Oh, he's not my..." Addison stops.

"You're not immediate family?" he asks me.

"No. I'm a friend."

He looks at Addison. "Would you like him to be present?"

Her eyes search mine. "I...I'm not sure."

I can see the wheels turning in Brian's head. "I'll let you two discuss it privately. Press the button next to the bed when you're ready to go up."

He leaves the room, closing the door behind him. I turn to Addison. "I don't have to go, not unless you need me."

"I do need you," she says. "It's just..."

"Your husband should be here. I get it." I move around the bed. "I'll wait in the lobby. Ask the nurse if he will come and get me once the test is done. Just so I know you're all right."

She nods, but then says, "I don't want to do this alone."

Damn Derek. Where in the hell is he?

"What if I stand outside the room while you get the test? Will that help?"

Tears form in her eyes again. "Thank you," she whispers.

I step out of the room so she can change. When she's ready, Brian appears. He has her get into the bed, then pushes her out of the room and into a nearby elevator. We take a ride up to the fourth floor and, when we approach our destination, I squeeze Addison's hand. "I'll be right here."

She squeezes my hand back.

After she disappears behind the door accompanied by Brian and another woman who, I assume, is the ultrasound tech, I cross my arms and lean against the wall. Never in my wildest dreams did I expect to be standing where I am at this very moment. I woke up with Jen, fought with Addison, and now I'm in a hospital awaiting news on a baby that's not mine.

I'll never look at Valentine's Day the same way again.

Minutes pass and my vision blurs as I stare at my work boots. I blink to focus and then continue to stare at the laces. There's not much else to look at in this dreary hallway. Plain white walls and evenly spaced doorways stretch in both directions. Industrial fluorescent lighting hangs from the ceiling. A man dressed in mint green scrubs appears and walks up to a rack hanging on a door. He selects a folder, opens it, and enters the room. The door clicks shut behind him, and I'm left alone again. It's as if time has stopped, and I'm left to question if I would reverse it or speed it up. Either way, I want Addison and her baby healthy, safe, and out of here.

Just as I start to pace, movement pulls my attention to the right. When I turn to look, my entire body tenses.

Derek's eyes meet mine, and they instantly flash and harden. I can tell he's on edge by the way he walks; his body looks coiled and stiff.

"What in the hell are you doing here?" he snaps.

Standing up straight, I set my jaw. "Addison needed my help."

He stops walking a few feet in front of me. "Get the fuck out."

"What?"

"You heard me. I don't want you anywhere near my wife."

I hold his stare. "I think that's her decision. She needed help and I was there."

"Who was there eight years ago?" Derek sneers. "Me. You need to leave."

"I told Addison I'd stay."

Derek steps closer. "Don't push me."

My adrenaline spikes. "Or what?"

"Gentlemen. Is there a problem?"

Green scrubs appear in my peripheral; it's the man I saw earlier with the file folder. I break Derek's stare. "No. There's no problem."

"I disagree," Derek says. "I want this man removed. He's harassing my wife."

What the fuck?

Green Scrubs' eyes land on me. "Is his wife in this room?" He points to the door.

I nod.

"Sir, I'm going to have to ask you to leave. If there's an issue with that I can call security."

My pulse pounds behind my ears. Not because I'm afraid of Derek or being escorted out, but because Addison said she wanted me here. I'm worried about her.

"Sir?" the man says again. "The exit is this way." He extends his hand toward the elevators.

Under duress, I take a step. The last thing Addison needs is a fist fight outside her door. I shoot one last hard look at Derek before slowly making my way down the hall. Green Scrubs walks with me.

"That's not necessary," I tell him. "I can show myself out."

He nods and stops shy of entering the elevator with me. As the doors start to close, I catch a glimpse of Derek's smug ass. He's watching me. Why isn't he in the room with Addison already? I would have been by her side in a heartbeat, ex-boyfriend be damned. I hold his stare and, just as the elevator doors close, he flips me off.

Yeah.

I'm not above waiting for him in the parking lot.

~~~~

"I don't know how you handled it," Kevin says. "I would have been completely freaked out."

Reaching into the fast food bag, I pull out a burger. "I was. I still can't believe it happened." I turn over the food in my hands. "Did you have no pickle?"

"That's me." Ashley stops petting the puppy and comes over to the table. "I had the curly fries too."

I find those in the second bag and hand them to her.

"Seriously, how are you holding up?" my brother asks me.

I'm confused. "Is that why you stopped by with dinner? To ask me stupid questions?"

"It's not a stupid question." Ashley takes a bite of a fry. "Addison had a miscarriage at your house. That has to be strange."

It is. Every time I go into the bathroom my memory flashes an image of what I saw in the mirror. I'm sure it will pass; it's only been a few days. "All I care about is that Addison is okay. Have you talked to her lately?"

Ashley nods. "I called this afternoon to make sure she was up and eating. She promised me she had some fruit for breakfast."

I frown. "Has she not been eating?"

"She's sad." Ashley takes a seat. "I happen to know she doesn't eat much when she gets upset."

My frown deepens. I've only had contact with Addison once since I left her at the hospital. After my run-in with Derek, I left her a voicemail letting her know I didn't leave by choice. I asked her to contact me when she felt up to it. That night, she sent me a text message saying she had been admitted. The baby was gone, but the doctors said physically she would be okay. She said she understood why I left. She also apologized for sending me a message instead of calling. She wasn't trying to be impersonal; she was trying not to wake Derek.

"I don't know how much this will affect her," Ashley continues. "This pregnancy wasn't planned, and she's always been hesitant about having kids. She's a strong girl, but still. Addison's suffered so much loss with her parents. Now this..." She shakes her head. "She's going to need our support, guys."

My brother swallows his bite of cheeseburger. "What about her douche of a husband?" he asks.

Kevin hasn't been a fan of Derek since his actions during the Super Bowl. No doubt, it wasn't necessary for him to drink my beer and kick me out of my seat. When I told Kev that he threatened to have me removed from the hospital, it only upped his intolerance for the guy.

Ashley sighs. "I'm not saying Derek won't be there for her. It's just..." She searches for the right words. "He can be intense. He's very protective. Addison's going to need some distractions to get through this, not her husband breathing down her neck to eat five servings of vegetables a day."

"What's that supposed to mean?" I ask as I feel paws on my knee. I look down to see my dog reared up on her hind legs sniffing around for food.

Ashley chews her burger in thought. "It means that Derek has always had a say in what Addison does. When they met, she was completely dependent on him; he was her physical therapist. He helped her learn to walk again and taught her how to feed herself. He counseled her on what exercises she needed to do, what to eat, how much to sleep. It was his job." She plays with a curly fry, pulling it apart and letting it spring back together. "His tendency to tell her what to do hasn't changed."

I quit petting the puppy. "The woman I know would never let someone push her around."

"The girl you *knew* wouldn't let someone control her," she clarifies. "That person changed when she woke up from a coma without parents. Back then, she needed guidance, and Derek gave it to her."

"So, what are you saying?" Kevin asks. "Addison only does what Derek allows? It doesn't seem that way."

"Because it's not." Ashley dips her fry in ketchup. "Addison doesn't rely on him for basic needs anymore, but it doesn't stop him from suggesting she shouldn't drink or recommending she get eight hours of sleep. I swear, sometimes he acts more like her father than her husband." She turns to me and points. "I think that's part of why he doesn't like you. He can't tell her what to do where you're concerned, and it's killing him."

I try to hide my smirk and fail.

"You're confusing me," my brother says to his fiancée. "Do you like Derek or not?"

Ashley's expression twists. "He's always come across as arrogant to me. When he proposed, I told Addison marrying him was a bad idea. I told her I thought she was settling."

My eyebrows shoot up. "Then, it wasn't true love?"

"Who knows?" Ashley shrugs. "They've been married for five years. I guess whatever they have works for them."

Picking up my burger, I take a bite to hide my scowl. I wish it *didn't* work for them.

Since I'm not caving in to my puppy's begging, she moves on to Ashley and whines at her feet. Ashley looks down. "She's so cute. Can I give her a fry?"

"No," I respond, my mouth stuffed. "Let me get her some treats."

As I stand, I remember the only reason I didn't wait for Derek in the parking lot was the puppy. Well, that and Addison wouldn't have appreciated my pummeling his face, especially in her condition. Instead, I drove directly to the store to get everything the dog would need. It was a melancholy trip. I kept thinking Addison should be there with me and not in a hospital bed.

"Have you decided on a name for her yet?" Kevin asks as I pull a bag of snacks down from the top of the refrigerator. "If she's going to work with us, she needs a kick ass name."

"I know," I say as I shake a few treats into my hand. "Any suggestions?"

"Killer," Kevin says.

I shoot him a sarcastic look. "Does she look like a Killer to you?"

"No," Ashley pipes up. "I think she looks like a Smokey because of her gray fur. Or maybe a Mo, like an Eskimo. She looks like a sled dog."

Kevin's face twists. "Remind me not to let you name our kids."

Ashley throws a wadded napkin at him.

I walk back toward the table and I realize I need to come up with a name soon. The dog is going to think her name is "C'mere." I hand Ashley the treats to feed the puppy and take a seat to finish my food.

It's after ten o'clock when my guests decide to leave. I let the dog out to do her business, then change clothes and head to bed. I've been awake since five a.m. We received yet another snow storm last night, and the guys and I have been putting in our fair share of overtime plowing. Kevin may have a coronary next week when he does payroll.

As I crawl beneath the sheets, the puppy joins me and makes herself comfortable by my side. I probably shouldn't allow her on the bed...or the couch or the chair, for that matter. It's hard not to spoil her. Time passes as I run my fingers through her fur, and she manages to inch her way over me, so her entire body is lying on top of my chest. Eventually we're nose to chin, and I can't stop myself from smiling and thinking Addison should see this.

Addison should see this.

Reaching to the side, I try not to jostle the dog too much as I grab my phone off the desk. Ashley said Addison needed distractions. What's better than a puppy? I take a picture of the dog and send it to Sparrow with the message: *Look who's staring at me.* She's probably asleep and won't get the text until morning, but hopefully it will make her smile.

My cell vibrates in my hand before I have a chance to slide it back on to the desk. I touch the screen and a picture of Sam pops up; his chin resting over the edge of a bed, his eyes pleading. The message reads: *This is who I'm looking at. He wants to get into bed with me.*

Poor Sam, I think. *You and me both, buddy.*

Quickly, I think of something to send back. *Did I wake you? I'm sorry.*

No, she responds. *I haven't been sleeping much lately.*

My forehead pinches. *Everything okay?*

I can't turn my mind off :(

I don't need to ask her what she's thinking about. The last few days – hell, the last few months – have been a confusing emotional cocktail. I've gone from surprise, to happiness, to anger, to regret. Now, I've landed on worry. I assume she's feeling the same things, only heavier.

Is there anything I can do? I send.

It takes her a moment to respond. *My issues are mine. Don't worry about me.*

I scowl as I type. *Impossible. We said no lies. Tell me what I can do.*

Again, seconds pass. Just as I think she's not going to answer, she finally sends, *Keep talking to me.*

Easy enough. *Should I call?*

My phone rings. "Hello?"

"Beat you to it," she says in my ear.

I smile.

Like an idiot.

The puppy moves to get comfortable, and, suddenly, I know what to talk about. "So, I need your help," I say.

"With what?"

"Naming the dog." I scratch behind her ears. "Any thoughts?"

"You haven't named her yet?" Addison asks, surprised. "What have you come up with so far?"

"Kevin suggested Killer, and Ashley came up with Smokey and Mo. I'm not feeling any of them."

"Hmmm." I picture her biting her lip. "Her mother's name was Victoria. What about Vicky?"

I dislike Vicky, but I kind of like Vic. Wait. "What about Tori?" I suggest.

As soon as I say the name, the puppy lifts her head and flicks her ears. She pants and her tail starts to wag. It makes me laugh.

"What's funny?" Addison asks.

"I think she likes Tori. She got excited."

"Well, there you go." Addison sounds like she's smiling. "Tori Dayton."

It does have a nice ring to it. "I'm glad you called," I say. "Thanks for your help."

"No, thank you," Addison says.

"For what?"

"The other day. I don't know what I would have done without you."

I know what she would have done. She would have waited for Derek or called Ashley. As anxious as I was over what was happening, I'm glad I was with her when it did. I can't imagine what it would have been like for her to be alone.

"I told you before," I say. "I'll be whatever you need. A shoulder to cry on, an alibi, or –"

"Bar night revenge," she finishes for me. "I remember."

We spend the next hour on the phone together. Addison tells me about an upcoming spring dance recital at her work, and I tell her about how this winter is kicking Dayton Landscaping's ass but lining my pockets. We discuss dogs and vets, and then Addison lets me in on a secret: she's behind on planning Ashley's bachelorette party.

"Don't you dare tell her," she threatens me.

"I think she would understand," I say. "It's not like you haven't had other things to deal with."

"Still," she sighs. "It's one of my few jobs for this wedding. Where are you with Kevin's party?"

"Nowhere," I confess. "It's not that complicated for guys. I figure we'll hit the casino and see where the night goes from there."

"You had better remember Ashley's rules," Addison threatens. "No strippers."

"Riiiiiight," I draw out the word. "And what will you ladies be up to? Dinner and a movie?"

"Maybe."

"You're such a liar."

She laughs.

The idea of Addison watching a male review and tossing dollar bills at some chiseled dancer makes me grind my teeth. I'm such a hypocrite; I was planning on violating Ashley's rule. Strippers are expected at bachelor parties.

Addison yawns, making me realize the time. "I'd better let you go," I say. "You sound tired."

"I am," she says.

As much as I don't want to stop talking to her, she needs to sleep. "Then this is good night."

"'Night," she says before hanging up.

Setting the phone down, I roll on to my side and punch the pillow to get comfortable. Tori moves and then lies down again. I'm happy I talked to Addison. Hopefully our conversation took her mind off things for a little while.

As my eyes drift shut, my mind turns with thoughts of her. God, I wish she was here. In my house, in my bed, in my arms. Eventually, my body starts to relax. Just as I feel myself drifting, my cell vibrates against the desk. Sleepily, I roll over and grab it.

Are you still awake?

I squint at the bright screen in the dark and respond. *Yes.*

My cell rings and I answer. "Hey."

"Kyle?" Her voice sounds small.

"Sparrow?"

I hear her take a breath. "Do you...?" she drifts off. "Would you...?" she tries again.

Curious, I patiently wait.

"Just...don't hang up," she says quietly. "Okay?"

"Okay," I say, concerned. "I'm with you until morning."

"Promise?" she asks.

"I promise."

We fall silent and I don't bother to ask what's wrong. If I can't comfort her in person, I'll do it over the phone. Whatever she needs.

"Sweet dreams," I say as I lie back against the pillow.

"You too," she whispers.

Chapter Twenty

Thump thump.

My eyes abandon the winter budget to watch the office door slowly open. "Anyone home?" Jen asks as she peers inside.

"Hey." Kevin's face breaks into a smile. "Long time, no see."

My brother's desk sits across from mine, and he lowers his propped feet. Leaning forward, he tries to see around our visitor. "Is that a bag in your hand?" His eyes grow wide. "Please tell me you brought lemon bars."

"Surprise!" Jen says and produces a white paper bag from behind her back. "Norma made them this morning."

"I love you," Kevin says, his face serious. He jumps to his feet and meets Jen between our desks to grab the sweet snacks. My brother is a sucker for Norma's lemon bars. She's Jen's boss and she only makes them every few months. They are pretty damn good.

"Are you on lunch?" I ask. I didn't know she was going to drop by.

"Yes," she says and looks around the room. "Where's Tori?"

The puppy, who was sleeping by my feet, wakes to the sound of her name. "She's right here," I say, looking down as I push my chair back. "She still refuses to sleep on the dog bed."

Since I bring Tori to work with me every day, I made her an area by the filing cabinets. She has food dishes, a few toys, a kennel if we need to leave her, and a red plaid-print dog bed. She won't use it, though. It's been days and she prefers to sleep on the hard ground by my feet.

Jen scoops up the puppy as soon as she sees her. Excited to see a familiar face, Tori goes in for the kill and starts to lick Jen's chin to death. She squints and laughs. "I know, baby. I missed you, too," she coos.

Involuntarily, my eyes roll. "You saw her yesterday. I'm starting to think you're using me for the dog more than sex."

Jen raises an eyebrow and Kevin almost chokes on his lemon bar. "I am using you for the dog. When's the last time we messed around?" she asks.

"Last week," I answer.

"Okay." Kevin clears his throat and sits on the edge of his desk. "You two have the most twisted friendship I know."

"At least we can be honest with each other," Jen says as she tries to contain a wriggling Tori in her arms. "Actually, that's why I'm here." Her eyes land on me and widen. "Guess who called?"

I'm lost. "Who?"

"New Year's Eve guy."

"Seriously?"

She nods.

"What'd he say? 'I'm sorry it took me months to call'?"

"Basically." She kisses the top of Tori's head and sets her down. "I'm going out with him on Saturday."

"Why?" Kevin asks with a frown. "He sounds like a jerk."

"He's not," Jen says. "He went out of town. Now he's back."

"What did he leave for?"

She shrugs. "I don't know."

"Jen." Kevin's tone turns full-on big brother. "You can't go out with a total stranger."

She starts to laugh. "News flash! That's what dating *is*." She turns to me. "I'm sure he knew all about Ashley when he started seeing her. Am I right?"

"What time is your date?" I ask.

"Seven."

I nod. "Secret word?"

Jen tips her head in thought, and her eyes scan the room. They land on the white paper bag. "Lemon," she decides.

"Got it."

Kevin stands. "What in the hell are you two talking about?"

"If my date goes bad, I'll text Kyle the word 'lemon.' Then, he'll know to come and pick me up."

Clearly confused, my brother's eyes dart between me and my ex. "Jen works at a bar," I explain. "When we were dating, we had the secret word. If she needed me because some creep was hitting on her, she would text me the code."

Kevin's expression reflects understanding. Then, it morphs back into confusion.

After splitting another dessert with my brother, Jen finds Tori for one last cuddle before she leaves. When she finishes petting the dog, she leans over my desk. "You're okay with this, right? I mean, we're okay?" she asks.

"Of course," I say. Honestly, I'm a little surprised at my lack of jealousy over the situation. Our arrangement had to end sometime and, frankly, I'm fine with it. My thoughts are consumed with Addison, especially since we fall asleep on the phone together more often than not. I bump my fist against Jen's arm in a playful way. "Go have fun."

She smiles and plants a quick kiss on my forehead. "You're the best."

After she leaves, I feel the weight of my brother's stare. Minutes tick by before I cave in and look at him. He's leaning back in his chair with his arms crossed when I ask, "What?"

"I can't believe you did that."

My expression twists. "Did what?"

"Let an amazing woman walk out of here with plans to see another guy."

I sigh. "We're not together. She can see whoever she wants."

Kevin leans forward in his chair. "I hope you don't regret this."

Again, I shoot him a confused look.

"What if Jen moves on for real?" he asks. "Is that what you want? You two seem to be getting along great."

"I want what's best for her," I say. "If she wants to go out then she should."

My brother looks skeptical. "Tell me you didn't feel anything when she told you about the date."

"I didn't feel anything."

He shakes his head. "If I were you, I wouldn't have let her go. You're a better man than me."

I smile weakly. With the way I feel about a certain married woman, I highly doubt that.

~ ~ ~ ~

Jen never sent me the secret word. She did, however, call to let me know her date went well and she had plans to see him again. I haven't had much communication with her since. I think Tori misses her.

Who am I kidding? I miss her too.

Not in an "I-didn't-realize-what-I-had" kind of way, but more of an "I'm-bored-and-I-don't-know-what-to-do-with-myself" kind of way. Here I sit, a week later, alone with my dog, watching TV. It's not late enough for Addison to call, and Kevin went up north to check on the cottage. It's March; we haven't been up there since October, and out of nowhere Kev got a bug up his ass to visit the place. Secretly, I think I know what's going on:

He needs some space.

As the wedding date approaches, he and Ashley can't see eye to eye on anything. Their latest argument was over a seated dinner at the reception. Kevin wants a buffet instead, because it's cheaper with more food selections. Ashley, on the other hand, thinks it's rude to make people wait in line for their dinner. After listening to my brother rehash the story, I agreed with him – I would choose the buffet, too. So what if guests have to serve themselves? The option is worth saving a couple grand.

Realizing it's unacceptable to spend the night contemplating Kevin's choices, I decide to get off my ass and take Tori for a walk. We meander down three blocks and back again, with a quick stop to talk to a jogger wearing tight spandex. She thinks Tori is adorable. No, I didn't miss the batting eyelashes, the coy smile, or the subtlety in her statement that she jogs this way every evening and has never seen us. If she only knew my plan was to go home, reheat the casserole my mom dropped off, and crash into bed to wait for Addison's call, she probably would have kept jogging. Nothing screams hot bachelor like eating mom's meals and anticipating a call from your ex.

Speaking of, when midnight rolls around and I haven't heard from her, I start to wonder where she is. I could have sworn she said she would call tonight when I hung up with her this morning.

Then again, I was groggy, so it's possible I heard wrong. I'm just about to text her when the phone rings.

"Hey," I answer, relieved. "I've been waiting for your call."

"Oh, really? Do I call often?"

Shit. That's not Addison's voice. "Ashley?"

"The one and only."

"Why are you calling me from Addison's phone?"

"Because we're fucking stranded."

She sounds pissed. "What happened?" I ask as I throw my blankets aside and swing my feet to the floor.

"Girl's night gone wrong," she huffs.

My forehead pinches as I search for my jeans. "Where are you? Where's Addison?"

"We're at Necto. Hold on." I hear what sounds like a door open and music that sounded muffled grows louder. Ashley must be walking. "Sorry!" she shouts. "I had to find her. She's on the dance floor!"

Walking over to my dresser, I find a shirt and pull it over my head. It's going to take me almost an hour to get there. Assuming their car broke down, I ask, "Do you need a tow truck?"

"No!" She lets out a bitter laugh. "Derek took Addison's keys!"

I freeze. "What?"

"Just get here!" Ashley yells, the music in the background growing louder. "My buzz is wearing off and I need to keep an eye on our girl!"

"Why?"

"Let's just say she's feeling no pain!"

I head for the front door and find my shoes. "I'm on my way."

"Okay!" she shouts before hanging up.

When I arrive at the club, it's a little after one a.m. I broke multiple traffic laws to set that time record, but I wanted to get to the girls. For one, Kevin would kill me if anything happened to Ashley, and two, I don't understand why Derek caused this, but I want to find out.

Asshole.

My eyes roam the darkened room for familiar faces, and I find Ashley seated at a high-top table next to the dance floor. She raises a glass and sips from a straw. As I make my way over, I notice her gaze is fixed. I stop beside her and follow her line of vision.

My jaw drops.

The last time I saw Addison, she was lying in a hospital bed. Tonight, she's dancing with her eyes closed, oblivious to the world around her. She's wearing a black fitted mini-dress and, aside from its thigh-high length, it appears modest from the front. However, when she turns around, the back of the dress is practically non-existent. It's cut low, landing just above her ass, with thin chains draped from side to side across her back. The changing lights from the dance floor reflect off the metal, hypnotizing me. Or maybe it's the way she moves; I'm not sure. My eyes travel down her legs to her heels, which are sky-high with straps that fasten around her ankles. Unbidden, thoughts I can't control invade my mind.

Me, marching out on to the dance floor.

Me, pulling her body against mine.

Me, kissing the breath out of her.

"Enjoying the show?" Ashley asks.

My eyes snap to her face, and she smirks. She uncrosses her legs and starts to gather her purse. "Go get her so we can leave," she says.

"Why don't you?" I ask.

"Because you clearly want to." Ashley gives me a 'don't be stupid' look. "Besides, I've been trying to get her to sit down for the last hour. She won't listen to me."

I turn toward the dance floor and zero in on Addison. Her eyes are still closed. Weaving my way through a few bodies, I step up to her just as she turns to expose her back to me. Consciously, I clench my hands into fists so I won't touch her.

"Addison." I lean forward to talk over the music. "It's time to go."

She turns around and lazily opens her eyes. She blinks a few times before a slow smile creeps across her face. "You're here," she says, almost like she doesn't believe it.

I nod and shove my hands in my pockets. "Ashley's ready to leave."

Unexpectedly, she throws her body against mine. She wraps her arms around my neck and tries to bury her head beneath my chin, but her shoes make her too tall. I reach out to keep my balance and end up clutching her hips. "Dance with me," she whispers in my ear.

Swallowing hard, I glance over her head at Ashley. Our eyes meet and she points to her wrist, as if she's wearing an invisible watch.

"No, we need to go," I manage to say. I step back and reach for Addison's arms to untangle myself. "I'm here to take you home."

She leans away from me and frowns. "Because Derek took my keys?"

"Yes."

Now that I'm standing this close to her, I can see the glaze in her eyes. When she spoke, I could smell the sweet tang of alcohol on her breath.

She's drunk.

"He's mad at me," she says as I lower her arms to her sides. "He doesn't like my dress."

I love her dress, which is probably why her husband hates it. No doubt I'm not the only guy in this place who's noticed her.

I wrap my arm around her waist. "Come on," I say. "Let's get out of here."

She lets her weight fall against my side, allowing me to support her. "You smell good," she murmurs.

"What?"

"You always smell good," she says and leans closer, brushing her nose across my neck. "What cologne do you wear?"

"I don't," I say as I walk and try to calm my pulse. Her lips brushed my skin when she asked that question, and my blood is on fire.

When we reach Ashley, she hands Addison her purse and we head to the coat check. Addison leaves my side to slide into her jacket, and once we step outdoors into the cool air, my temperature returns to normal. I lead the girls in the direction of my truck, stopping once to steady Addison when she stumbles into a pothole.

"Those shoes are a death trap," I say as I hold on to Addison's elbow.

"Not when you're sober," Ashley teases.

Addison sticks her tongue out at her.

When I open the passenger side door, Ashley hops up into the cab, then reaches for Addison's hand to help pull her inside. Shutting the door behind them, I round the front of my truck and crawl into the driver's seat. I turn the ignition and pull out of the parking lot, automatically headed for Kevin and Ashley's apartment. I'm a little concerned about leaving Addison's Hummer behind, but, in truth, it's none of my business.

No more than ten minutes into the drive I glance over and see Addison's head resting on her best friend's shoulder. She's passed out. Ashley moves to support her, which prompts me to ask, "So, what happened?"

Ashley frowns. "Derek got pissed after he found out where we were. He showed up at the club and took Addison's keys because he said she was too drunk to drive."

"Was she?"

"Not at that point." Addison's head rolls forward and Ashley gently pushes it back. "She got there real quick after he left, though."

"Didn't you try to stop him?"

"Of course! I told him she was fine and we didn't have a ride. He told me to call a cab."

I grow angry and merge into another lane on the expressway. "If he was that concerned, he should have stayed and drove you home."

"You think?" Ashley asks sarcastically. "I know the two of them are going through some stuff right now, but you don't leave your wife and her best friend stranded at a bar. You don't criticize her outfit in front of strangers, and you certainly don't walk away when she's near tears. Those are dick moves."

My eyes narrow and I clutch the steering wheel. "Agreed," I mutter.

We fall silent the rest of the way to the apartment. I can't stop thinking about Derek. Where does he get off treating Addison that way? Or Ashley, for that matter? When Kevin finds out, he's not going to be happy. I need to talk to Addison when she's sober and find out what she sees in this man. She needs to help me understand why she loves him.

Because she deserves better.

When I pull in and park in front of Kevin's building, I ask Ashley if Addison is staying with her.

"No," Addison mumbles, surprising us. She sits up slowly, her hair a mess across one side of her face. "I want to go home."

"Are you sure?" Ashley asks, concerned. "You can stay with me. Kevin's up north. He won't be back until Monday."

Addison nods. "I want my own bed." She looks at me. "And Sam."

I get it.

The girls hug goodbye, and I follow Ashley to her door to make sure she gets inside safely.

"I'm sorry we had to bother you," she says. "If Kevin were home, I would have called him."

"Don't worry about it," I say. "I'm glad I could help."

She opens the door, then stands on her toes to wrap an arm around my neck. "I always wanted a big brother," she says into my shoulder. "Thank you."

I pat her back. "You're welcome."

When I return to my truck, I find Addison in probably one of the strangest positions possible. She's got her leg pulled up beside her on the seat. Her knee is twisted awkwardly with her heel to her butt as she fumbles with the buckle on her ankle.

"What are you doing?" I ask.

"Taking off these damn shoes." She lets out an irritated breath.

Sliding over on the seat a few inches, I hold out my hand. "Give me your foot."

Her eyes meet mine before she turns and unwinds herself. She props her back against the door and extends her leg toward me. As I reach for her ankle, my eyes fall on a scar that extends over her knee, the skin slightly raised and faded from time. I hesitate, looking at it, and she notices.

"That's where they put the rod in my leg," she says.

I want to kiss that scar.

Immediately, I move my focus to her shoe, unfastening the small strap. Her skin is red and indented where the leather was. "Does it hurt?" I ask.

"My knee?"

"No, your ankle," I say as I remove her shoe and motion for her to give me her other foot.

"A little."

Heels off, I concentrate on her pink-painted toenails and try to rub the red spots away. The dome light in the truck times out, leaving us in the dark. I continue to massage her skin, and she sighs. I look up. "Feel good?"

Her face is shadowed, but I can still see her features. "Everything about you feels good."

211

My hands stop moving. "What?"

She rests her head against the passenger window and stares at me. "I can't stop thinking about you." She closes her eyes. "The sound of your voice. The touch of your hands. The way you look." She lets her head roll to the side along the glass. "I'm drowning in you."

My throat goes dry. "What does that mean?"

She opens her eyes. "It means I can't breathe, but you make my heart beat."

Holding her gaze, I move closer. "Why can't you breathe?"

"The guilt takes my air," she confesses. "It's so heavy. It sits on my chest and crushes my lungs. It whispers to me and says I shouldn't care about you."

She cares about me.

I reach for her hand, and she weaves her fingers through mine. I can't believe she's being so honest. "Your guilt and mine have been hanging out together," I say. "They tell us the same things."

She runs her thumb over my knuckles. "Assholes," she mutters.

I laugh.

"I wish I could give you more, Kyle."

I want that. I so fucking do.

Suddenly, she pulls her hand from mine. "I'm sorry. Ignore me. I'm drunk." She moves, sitting up straight and putting distance between us. "I shouldn't have said those things."

She's not that drunk.

"We shouldn't hang out," she says, nervously straightening her dress.

Oh, no you don't, I think. "Listen." I lean toward her. "A very wise woman told me you would come back into my life when the time was right. Promise me we'll stick together long enough to find out if that's true."

Addison's eyes grow wide. "Gram?"

I nod, and her eyes turn glassy with unshed tears.

"You're not getting rid of me that easily." Now that I know she's battling the same feelings as me I feel lighter. It's almost as if we're a team, fighting against the same thing.

Our hearts.

Silent seconds pass before she takes a breath. "Okay. I can handle it. We're friends."

"Right," I say. "Friends who in secret really, really like each other, but won't act on it because the girl is married. Although, the guy wants it noted that he thinks the husband is a royal jackass and doesn't deserve the girl."

Addison's mouth falls open and she starts to laugh. She slaps her free hand over her mouth in remorse. "I'm so going to hell," she says.

I squeeze her knee. "I'll meet you there."

Chapter Twenty-One

I stare at myself in the dressing room mirror. The last time I wore a tux, I was fourteen and forced.

I remember the sleeves of the jacket were too long and the collar of my shirt too tight. I remember standing at the altar, between my dad and my brother, fidgeting. I remember my father elbowing me to stop when Lydia started to walk down the aisle, and I remember spending most of that night with a scowl on my face.

It's funny how one image can bring back so many memories.

With a little more than a month to go before the big day, Kevin, Austin, Noah, and I are at the mall getting fitted for our monkey suits. As I fasten the jacket at my waist, I realize something I never wanted to: my dad and I share similar choices. No, Addison and I aren't having a physical affair. And no, I'm not planning to break up her marriage. But, we know how we feel about one another. We're having an emotional affair, with plans to see how things play out.

And damn it if it doesn't feel right.

I pull the bottom of the jacket down to straighten it and hear Kevin outside my door.

"How does it fit?"

"Good," I say. At least I can breathe. "How much is the deposit again?"

"Seventy-five, but don't worry about it. It's on the etiquette list that the groom covers the best man's tux."

Since when does my brother care about etiquette? Opening the door, I come face-to-face with Kevin. "Dude. Don't do shit like that."

"Like what?"

"Pay for my suit."

He rolls his eyes. "I'm supposed to."

"Don't."

My brother places his hand against the doorframe. "Think about it. I work for you. You sign my paycheck. Therefore, my money is your money." He raises his eyebrows. "You're really paying for your own tux."

I frown. When he puts it that way, I'm shelling out for more than a rental. "I'm footing the bill for half this wedding, aren't I?"

Kevin grins. "Thanks, big brother."

Shithead.

Once the four of us have reserved our sizes, we make our way out of the mall. Since we're all together, I decide to share the bachelor party details. The other guys already know the plan, but my brother has been kept in the dark.

"So," I set my hand on Kev's shoulder, "plan on being indisposed the Saturday before the wedding."

"Why?"

"Because we're kidnapping you," Austin says, wagging his eyebrows. "It's your final celebration as a free man."

My brother smiles. "Where are we headed?"

"It's a secret," I say. "Just plan on leaving Saturday and coming home on Sunday."

"Ashley's not going to like that."

"No worries," I reassure him. "She'll be indisposed too."

Over the last few days, Addison and I discussed our respective parties and decided to plan them for the same weekend. That way, both Ashley and Kevin would be too busy to worry about what the other one was doing. Unfortunately, I know Addison's plans for Ashley.

Yeah, it bugs me.

My phone rings as we exit the mall. I simultaneously answer it and wave goodbye to our friends as Kevin and I head toward his Wrangler. "Hello?"

"Hey there, Kyle. How ya' doin'?"

It's Brady, my former boss. "Not too bad. Yourself?"

"Can't complain," he says, and I imagine him hitching up his pants. He always did that.

"Are you and Estelle still tearing up the States in the motorhome?" I ask.

He chuckles. "Not since last summer. 'Stell fell and messed up her back, so we've been taking it easy this winter."

"I'm sorry to hear that."

"S'okay," he says. "It gave me some time to get other things done. Like clean out that storage I've been meaning to get to."

"Storage?"

"You know, that place over on Elm. The last of the property."

Now I remember. "Ah. You finally got your antiques moved."

"I'm sorry it took so long," he apologizes. "The wife couldn't decide what she wanted to keep."

I laugh. "It's no big deal. We haven't needed it."

When I bought Brady Landscape, I initially purchased the main garage. Brady also had a few off-site storage buildings where he kept things, like old equipment and paperwork. He used the Elm Street address to store personal items; he and his wife are big antique collectors. Over time, as part of our deal, I bought all the storage space, too. Even though I technically own it, I've let him take his time clearing out the Elm Street place.

"Well, it's clean and it's empty," Brady says. "You still have a key?"

Since I never messed with the original key ring when he handed it to me, I say yes.

"It looks like you're all set then." He pauses for a second. "Business been good?"

"Better than ever," I tell him honestly. "All that snow sure helped this winter."

"I bet it did, I bet it did," he repeats himself. He had a habit of doing that too, along with the pants thing.

We talk for a few more seconds and when I hang up, Kevin looks at me. "About damn time."

My expression twists. "Brady's an old man. Cut him some slack. It's not like we needed the space."

As we get into his car, my brother says, "You're right, but we're still paying on it. We should swing by and see what we're working with. If we're not going to use the building, we should think about selling it."

That's not a bad idea.

A half hour later, we're standing outside an old storefront downtown about a ten minute drive from the main garage. It's located on the back side of a historical building, almost like it was the rear entrance at some point. The windows are covered in aged brown paper, which is secured with yellowed strips of masking tape that have lost their tack and are starting to hang. Finding the only key on my key ring I don't use regularly, I open the door and step inside.

"Huh," Kevin says as he follows me. "I didn't expect it to be this nice."

"Right," I agree as I walk further inside. The last time I was here, the place was packed to the rafters with musty collectibles. There was so much stuff, only one aisle existed down the center of the room.

Brady wasn't kidding when he said he cleaned, either. He must have hired a service. Very little dust exists anywhere and the drywall looks freshly painted. Kevin takes off toward the back of the store as I circle the perimeter of the room. It's basically one large area, with a few doors in the back.

"Did you know there was a bathroom here?" My brother pops out of one of the doorways. "Looks like it needs work, though."

I make it to the other doorway and stick my head through. "This could be an office," I say.

Kevin joins me and eyes the smaller space. "Think we'll ever use it?"

I shrug. "Your guess is as good as mine."

Crossing my arms, I turn and stare into the large empty room. Sunlight streams through the paper-covered windows, and the weathered hardwood floor looks like an angry mob danced across it.

It's then the idea hits me, hard and square in the chest.

I know what I'm going to do with this building.

~~~~

"Keep your eyes closed."

"Okay."

"I'm serious."

"Okay."

"Don't open them until I tell you to."

"I said okay!" Addison huffs. "You're starting to freak me out."

It's been a couple of days since I came up with my idea. Despite my ability to do whatever the hell I want, I ran it by Kevin just to gauge his reaction. He didn't fight me, but he asked me to sleep on it. He's not one hundred percent sure about my plan, although he says he understands. Especially after I reminded him about what an asshole Derek is.

"Stand right here." My voice echoes as I position Sparrow by her shoulders in the center of the room.

"Where are we?" she asks.

"That's the surprise." I let go of her and take a few steps back. "All right. Open your eyes."

She complies and blinks a few times to adjust her vision to the light. She glances around the vacant room that used to hold antiques, then turns her body to see what's behind her. When all she's greeted with is empty space, she pins me with a confused look. "You brought me to an abandoned building?"

"Does it look abandoned?" I ask. "I thought it was in pretty decent shape."

She starts to walk backward, away from me. "I guess." Before she makes it too far, she shoots me a sly smile. "Bringing a girl to a strange place. Are you planning to kidnap me?"

Now there's an interesting thought. My eyes light up. "No. But I think you'll be spending a lot of time here."

She stops walking. "Why?"

I head over to the wall nearest to me and set my palm against it. "How would this wall look covered in mirrors?"

Her face registers confusion.

I set my hands on my hips and look down. "The floor will need to be refinished," I say as I run my foot across it. Then, I take a few steps and point to the opposite side of the room. "I thought that spot would make a good place for the barre, but it's up to you. You're the expert."

Yeah. I've been doing some research.

Addison's eyes grow wide as I continue. "I talked to Kevin, and his buddy Austin is into sound systems. He can wire the place, and I know a good plumber." I gesture over my shoulder with my thumb. "The bathroom back there is in pretty sad shape."

Her mouth falls open. "What are you saying?"

I smile. "Welcome to your studio."

It takes a moment for my statement to register. Her eyes bounce around the room before landing on me. "Are you serious?" she breathes.

I nod.

Suddenly, she launches herself across the room and jumps into my arms. She wraps her hands around my neck and her legs around my waist. Thankfully, I catch her with only a small stumble. I turn us around once to catch my balance.

"How?" she asks with her cheek pressed to my neck.

"I own this place."

She leans back so we're face-to-face and gives me a questioning look. Quickly, I explain Brady, his hobby, and what happened a few days ago.

"Are you sure?" she asks. "What about rent? How much do I owe you?"

"You don't owe me anything. I was paying on this building when it was stuffed with Brady's antiques. What's the difference if it's your studio?"

"Kyle." Her expression turns serious. "I'm not using this building for free."

"It won't be free," I protest. "There's work to be done and utilities to pay. But, we won't worry about it until things are up and running."

She removes her hand from the back of my neck and sets it against my jaw. "Are you sure?" she asks again, quietly this time.

Turning my head, I kiss the inside of her wrist. "I've never been more positive. This is your dream."

Her eyes soften and lock on mine. She stares at me in disbelief, as if she couldn't possibly have heard me right. After a second or two, her eyes dart to my mouth, and I realize she's barely breathing. "What will happen if I kiss you?" she whispers.

Only a million amazing things.

She leans forward and brushes her nose against mine, causing my heart to pound wildly in my chest. My lips are a centimeter from hers; they tingle with anticipation. Conscious of her legs wrapped around my body, of my hands holding on to the backs of her thighs, I grip them tighter. We stay like this, hovering, breathing each other's air, until I answer her question.

"I won't want to stop."

She closes her eyes and lets her forehead fall against mine.

"Not the answer you wanted to hear?" I murmur.

She shakes her head. "No. It's perfect."

"Then why aren't we kissing?" Like I don't know the reason. *Guilt, thy name is Derek.*

She lifts her head and looks at me. "Because I don't think I'll want to stop, either."

The last thing we need is to regret this moment. My decision to bring her here was innocent; this is supposed to be the realization of her dream. I know, without a doubt, if something happens between us now, her guilt will crush her.

And mine will commiserate with it.

Slowly, I relax my hold beneath her legs and set her feet back on the ground. Her hands fall to land on my chest, and I keep mine wrapped around her waist.

"I'm sorry," she says. "I should never have led you on that way."

"It's fine."

"No, it's not." She focuses on my shirt and plays with the buttons. "I just...I..." she stutters.

"You don't have to explain it."

"I do." She meets my eyes. "You gave me an unbelievable gift. You understand how important this is to me. No one has ever given my goals value. Not my parents with Julliard, not Derek with my business." She pauses. "Only you."

I set my feet and smile. "So, let me get this straight. If I do something nice for you, you'll throw yourself at me. Is there any way I can get that in writing?"

"Stop!" She rolls her eyes. "I'm trying to justify my actions."

"And I said you didn't have to." I lean toward her. "Years ago, a girl I knew gave me some good advice. I'd forgotten it until recently, until she reappeared in my life. Do you remember what it was?"

Suspicious, Addison narrows her eyes. "Maybe."

"She told me that, as long as I followed my heart, no one had the right to tell me what I did was wrong."

Her face relaxes.

"Do you still believe your own words?"

"I want to."

"What changed?"

"The addition of a third party." She steps out of my arms. "Any normal, sane person would have simply thanked you for your offer. But, no, not me." She gets sarcastic. "What do I do? I jump on you, then try to kiss you."

"Do you see me complaining?"

"That's not the point. I need to do better." She crosses her arms and puts another few feet between us. Then, she takes a deep breath, plasters a fake smile on her face, and looks me in the eye. "Thank you so much for the building. Thank you for thinking of me and for giving me this opportunity."

I scowl at her. "What the fuck was that?"

"That, Potty Mouth, is called acting like an adult."

"I don't like it."

"Tough shit."

My eyebrows shoot up. "Who's got the potty mouth now?"

She laughs, and I walk toward her. "Can we rewind this conversation? Let's go back to the part where you were excited about the studio."

"Okay." She smiles. "But, I'm not jumping on you."

With an exaggerated pout, I reach for her hand. "Let me take you on a tour instead. You can tell me what you see. I need to get a better idea of how much work I have to do."

"Why?"

"This is our project. Yours and mine. I'm good with my hands, but you have the vision."

Addison's bright smile fades into one of sincerity. "Thank you, Kyle. Truly. I don't think I have the words to tell you how much this means to me."

I squeeze her hand. "Don't worry. I'm pretty sure I know how you feel."

"Yeah?"

"When I signed the papers to buy Brady's, I felt liberated. I felt in charge of my life for once. I was finally making my own path. A path you set me on." I wink. "It's a good feeling."

"Damn good," she agrees.

As we start to head toward the back of the room, I ask, "So, what do you think your husband will say about this?"

She frowns. "I'm sure he'll be pissed. Lately, that's all he ever is."

"Was he upset when I brought you home the other night?"

"He doesn't know." She shrugs one shoulder. "He was asleep when I came in the door."

Nice. Apparently he wasn't worried if she made it home safe.

"Do you want to come up with a story?" I ask. "You could tell him Ashley found the building. Or maybe some distant relative left it in their will. Do you have any aunts or uncles?"

"No." She shakes her head. "No lies. I've told enough of those already."

"To who?"

We stop walking next to the room I thought could be an office. "To myself," she says.

Before I can ask what that means, she lets go of my hand and reaches through the doorway to find the light switch. When she flips it on, she steps inside the little room. "What was this used for?"

"I don't know." I look around with her. "I thought it could be your office."

She looks at me and grins. "I'm going to have my own office?"

Her smile is contagious. "If that's what you want."

She grabs my arm with both hands and starts to bounce on her toes. "I'm going to have my own office!"

The more time we spend walking around the room and tossing around ideas, the more enthusiastic Addison becomes. Her gestures get more animated, her smile grows brighter, and her eyes dance. You can tell she's put some deep thought into what she hoped to have one day. Eventually, I lean against the wall to let her exist in her own world. As she takes pictures with her phone to send to her sister, I realize I made the right choice in doing this. Kevin thought she might feel as if I was trying to show up Derek and buy her affections. I don't think that thought crossed her mind at all. I'm trying to show her I support her future; that I value the person she has become. She's more than just a girl from my past.

Besides, her smile is gorgeous.

I'd do anything to keep it on her face.

Chapter Twenty-Two

"Pizza's here!"

Paintbrushes and rollers drop to the tarp-covered floor.

"It's about time."

"I'm starving."

"Did you have to make it yourself?"

Addison gives me half a smile as our grumbling volunteers make their way toward Kevin, his arms stacked to his chin with boxes.

"I got here as fast as I could," he says as Ashley, Tara, Noah, and Austin take turns unloading my brother's burden. "Our order wasn't ready yet. I had to wait."

"Kevin!" Ashley says as she opens the pizza box in her hands. "Two slices of this one are missing!"

"I got hungry on the way back," he says with a shrug. "What's the big deal?"

Addison clears off one end of the table we set up for our weekend painting party. "Did they give you any plates?"

Kevin's face falls. "Uh, no."

"We don't need them. We can use these," Tara says as she grabs an unopened box of disposable rags. "We're so hungry, the food wouldn't have touched the plates anyway. We'll only need to wipe our hands."

SPARROW

"You guys act like you haven't eaten in days." Kevin shuffles toward the table with the last box. "It's only painting."

"Our friends are soft," I say and elbow my brother's arm. "They're not used to manual labor."

Tara eyes me as she reaches for the cheese and mushroom pie. "This place is huge. I wasn't expecting ladders and stretching."

I look around the room. She has a point. The studio ceiling doesn't look very high until you're trying to paint the walls to reach it.

Lifting a breadstick to her mouth, Addison says, "I'm feeling worn out, too. As thanks for your help, I'll make us all appointments for a massage."

The girls make some sort of squeely noise and the guys all stare at each other.

"The only way I'm getting a massage is if a hot chick does it," Austin states as he shoves his mouth full of food. "I nowf geffng rudbed by som dud."

"What was that?" I ask with a smile. "You like getting rubbed by dudes?"

"No!" he says as he swallows. "I'm not getting rubbed by some dude."

I laugh. I've actually had a few massages in the past; once, in high school, I jacked up my shoulder in a game. Then, a couple of years ago, I pulled something in my back out on a job. The chiropractor I went to did a massage after adjusting me. It felt great, and the least of my concerns was that Dr. Murphy was a man.

"If you want an exotic rub down," Addison points at Austin, "you're on your own. I'm not paying for that."

I frown at her. "Wait a minute. You won't pay for a girly massage, but you'll pay for –"

"Shhhhh!" She puts her hand over my mouth. "It's a secret!"

She read my mind. I nearly outed some of her bachelorette party plans.

"Hold on." Kevin gets involved. "What are you two talking about? There had better be no rubbing of anything, anywhere, at any time during any upcoming parties."

Addison and Tara giggle as Ashley gives them a curious look.

"There's no rubbing that I know of," I reassure my brother. "I was going to say something else."

What I was going to reveal were Addison's plans to follow through on her ice sculpture purchase. She requested Rick's catalog and, while she's not wasting money on a replication of the male genitalia, she is getting an ice recreation of a chest. A chest ripped with six-pack abs that you can do shots off of, like a luge. I told her if she wanted to do body shots, all she had to do was ask. She laughed and said, "You wish."

She was right. I do wish.

"Don't worry, baby." Ashley walks over to Kevin and wraps her arm around his waist. "Addison will follow the rules. Just like Kyle. Right, brother-in-law?" She raises an eyebrow at me.

Addison's eyes dart to mine, and we bite our tongues. In a few weeks we are so busted.

Quickly, I grab a slice of pizza from the nearest box and take a bite. "Right," I mumble as I chew, hoping Ashley will believe me. Then, the taste in my mouth registers and I gag. *Olives!* I can't stand olives!

I nearly knock Addison out of my way to reach for a rag. I need to get this taste out of my mouth *now*. I turn and try to spit out my food as inconspicuously as possible, and Kevin laughs. He's well aware of my aversion.

"That's called karma," he says behind my back.

Addison appears at my side and leans around me. "Are you okay?"

"I don't like olives."

"Are you allergic?"

"No. I just don't like them."

She starts to laugh and disappears from my side. After I wipe my mouth and turn back around, she's holding a can of Coke for me.

"Thanks." I take it and down half.

"So, Addison, why purple?" Noah asks. He turns his paint-splattered hands over. "I hope this comes off."

"It's not purple, it's lavender," Addison says. "It's soothing. It's also my favorite color."

"It is?" I ask. How did I not know this?

She nods. "We had a bunch of lilac bushes by my house when I was little, and I loved the smell. I think I was six when I made my parents make my room lavender. Walls, bedspread, curtains, sheets...just about anything that could be was light purple."

"It's true," Ashley says. "It was like Barney threw up in her bedroom."

"Hey!" Addison exclaims.

"Have you seen her master bathroom now?" Ashley asks me.

"No."

"Same thing."

"Some friend you are." Addison narrows her eyes. "You never said my bathroom looked like kiddie dinosaur vomit!"

Ashley shrugs. "You never asked."

Unexpectedly, the door to the studio opens, and every one of us turns to see who's here. When Derek steps inside, it's like all the oxygen has been sucked out of the room. The fun atmosphere evaporates.

Derek removes his sunglasses and lets the door close behind him. He looks at Addison. "You ready to go?"

"Sure." Addison finds a rag and wipes her fingers. "Just give me a second."

Wait a minute. Why is she leaving? I want to ask, but I'm sure that won't sit well with present company. My eyes dart questioningly to Kevin, and he understands.

"Hey, Derek." He extends his hand for a handshake. "How's it going?"

Derek pumps his hand twice. "Fine."

Addison rounds the table to pick up her purse and jacket where she left them by the wall.

"Where you off to?" Ashley asks, beating Kevin to the punch.

"We have that appointment, remember? I told you."

Ashley's eyes get big. "That's today?"

Addison nods, then looks around the group. "Thanks for all your help, guys. We really made a lot of progress. I wasn't kidding about the massages." She smiles and then focuses on me. "Is the floor guy still coming on Wednesday?"

I nod.

"Great. I'll bring the deposit."

Frowning, I say, "No. We talked about this. You don't have –
"

"I want to," she cuts me off. She waves at us over her shoulder as she turns toward Derek. "Gotta run. See you later."

Without so much as a goodbye, her husband ushers her out the door. When it closes, my attention jumps to Ashley. She gives me a resigned look while, out of the corner of my eye, I see Tara and Noah start to pick up empty boxes for the trash. Austin shoves another piece of pizza into his mouth.

Ashley rounds the table and walks up to me. "Tell me again how this layout is going to work."

"What?"

"Walk with me," she whispers.

I follow by her side as she moves to stand in front of the one wall we haven't started working on yet. Completely unsure I want to know the answer, I ask, "What's going on?"

Ashley looks at her shoes, then at me. "Addison and Derek are going to marriage counseling."

My brow furrows. "Since when?"

"Since now," she says. "Tonight is their first session."

I'm confused. "She didn't tell me."

"She told me yesterday," Ashley sighs. "Although, I thought they weren't starting until next week. I guess I got my dates mixed up."

"Who sees patients this late on a Sunday?" I ask. "It's after five."

"One of Derek's colleagues, apparently. The counseling office is in the same building as his."

I stare at my brother's fiancée, my mind spinning. "Am I not supposed to know?"

She shrugs. "Addison didn't tell me *not* to tell you. Honestly, I figured she would."

I start to pace. I would have thought she would have told me, too.

"Ask her about it," Ashley continues. "You can tell her you heard it from me. I don't care."

I stop in my tracks. "Do you think Derek pushed her into this?"

"Hell yes." Ashley smirks. "You know how he reacted when she told him about this place." She gestures around the studio. "He's all kinds of insecure right now."

Addison was right when she said Derek would be pissed; she said he stormed out of the house when she told him. When he finally came back, he was ready to discuss the situation. Addison said they talked about the pros and cons, namely money, and he seemed to calm down a bit.

"You really think he's insecure?" I ask Ashley.

"Wouldn't you be? A man from your wife's past shows up and hands her her dream. Don't you think that raises a few red flags?"

It does. I knew it would, too, but I didn't care. All I cared about was Addison's happiness.

"Look at it this way," Ashley interrupts my thoughts. "This could be a good thing. The two of them might realize they don't belong together anymore."

I raise an eyebrow. "So, you're on my team?"

She gives me a pointed look. "We're about to be family. There is no other team."

~~~~

Unlocking the door to the studio Wednesday morning, I impatiently await the arrival of two people. One, Jim, the floor refinisher.

The other, Addison.

We haven't spoken since the painting party. It's true we don't talk every single day, but now that I know she and Derek are consciously working on their marriage, I question her silence. Did the counselor, an outside third party, sway her into believing that my gift was wrong? Did he denounce our friendship? Was I even discussed? I hate that part of me wonders about this, and I pray the counselor can remain unbiased, since he knows Derek professionally. I'm sure if he took sides it would breach some sort of ethical client/patient privilege. I've spent the last few days worrying, probably for nothing. Odds are they didn't discuss me at all.

At least, not at the first meeting.

When eleven o'clock rolls around, Jim shows up right on time. We make small talk while we wait for Addison. I ask him about his business, and he asks me about mine. After a half hour passes and she doesn't show, I tell him to go ahead and do the estimate. While he takes his measurements, I call Sparrow. When I get her voicemail, I hang up and send her a text message.

The floor guy is here. Where are you?

I want to add *"Business Ownership 101: Keep all of your appointments,"* but I don't. There's no need to get shitty just because I'm on edge.

When Jim completes his quote and hands it to me, I have no problem putting down the ten percent required to get him started on the job. As he swipes my credit card through his cell phone, the door to the studio opens.

"Wait!"

Both of us turn as Addison rushes through the door. "I don't have the deposit," she says, her cheeks flushed.

"Too late," I tease, relieved to see her and a little pissed at the same time. "Don't worry, I've got it. Jim's estimate was more than fair."

Addison hangs by the door with her hands in her pockets while I set up a date with the refinisher to get started. Once those details are finalized, he bids us farewell and we're left alone.

"Did you forget about today," I ask as I walk toward her. "Where were you?"

"Packing."

I freeze and stare at her. Now that I'm closer, I can see, along with her pink cheeks, the tops of her ears are red. Also, her hair looks tangled, like she's pushed it behind her ears one too many times. "What's going on?"

"This," she says and pulls a piece of paper out of her pocket. She hands it to me. It's a bank receipt.

"I don't −" I examine the slip closer. The balance reads $0.00. Concerned, I meet her eyes. "Talk to me."

"I went to the bank this morning to get the money for the floor," she says, her voice unsteady. "I tried to withdraw it from the savings, but the account was empty."

My eyes narrow.

"The teller told me Derek withdrew the money a couple days ago." She looks at me in disbelief. "All twenty grand. Gone."

My mouth falls open. Twenty grand? I look at the paper. "Was this the account −?"

"Yes," she cuts me off. "The one that held my parent's life insurance money."

I remember our conversation from last fall, when she told me about the in vitro versus studio savings. There has to be some mistake. "Did you talk to Derek?"

Anxiously, she runs her fingers through her hair. "I just left home," she says. "He was there, I confronted him. He said he moved the money so I couldn't have it." Her eyes swim and focus on mine. "He said he thought about it, and if he can't have his dream, I can't have mine."

My hands ball into fists, crushing the paper. There is no way those words left her lips. "Does he have a death wish?" I growl.

Addison wipes her cheek. "That's why I'm leaving," she says. "I threw some things in a suitcase, grabbed Sam, and came here. I tried to stop you before you spent any money –"

She's leaving? As in leaving him? I step forward and wrap my arms around her. "The money doesn't matter."

"Yes, it does." She moves away from me. "I can't do this right now. Sell the building. I'm not ready."

"What?"

She takes a deep breath. "I'm going up north to stay with my sister. I need some time to myself. I can't start a business."

"Addison." I rest my hands on her shoulders. "Don't give up on this because of him. Don't run away. You didn't do anything wrong."

"I'm not running," she says. "I need to get my head straight, and I can't do it if I stay here."

My expression twists. "Why?"

"Because my head and my heart are fighting." She backs away from me. "What Derek did...when I found out...I was so angry. My first reaction was to run to you, which isn't right."

"I disagree." It is *so* right.

She sighs. "Every time I look at you I see the future I lost. It's messing with my reality."

Good. Her reality sucks.

"Sparrow," I say and step toward her. "Is this the reality you want? One where you deny your dreams because your husband tries to bully you? You already spend countless nights and holidays alone. He abandoned you at a club because he didn't like what you were wearing. Now, he's hidden money that's rightfully yours. What's next?"

Addison looks down. "Logic says I should fight for my marriage. I made a promise."

"So that means you have to put up with his shit?"

"No!" Her head snaps up. "That's why I'm leaving! I'm hurt, and he needs to realize it."

Catching her eyes with mine, I say, "I would never hurt you."

I don't know why those words chose to leave my mouth just now, but they did. Addison's whole body reacts; her expression softens and her shoulders sag. Even her stance looks defeated.

"I know," she says. "My heart knows it, too. But I can't just walk away from the man who rebuilt me. I'm walking, dancing, *feeding myself*, because of him. The weight of what he's done for me is enormous."

I take another step closer to her. "That doesn't give him the right to make you miserable."

She hesitates. "Still...it doesn't lessen the guilt I feel."

I hate this. So much.

Running my hand into my hair, I ask, "So, what do we do? You stay married, we stay friends, and I go on hating the man who hurts you?"

She shakes her head. "I hope when I come back from Meagan's I'll have figured some things out. I'm going to stay with her until the bachelorette party."

Three weeks? I think.

"Hopefully being with my sister will bring some clarity."

I get it. She needs space. I don't like it, but I understand.

I reach for her hands and run my thumbs over the back of them when she places her palms in mine. The thought of getting rid of something we've just started to create hurts, but it's her call. "I won't sell the building. Take all the time you need to think things through. When you make up your mind, just say the word. If you don't want it, you don't have to use it."

"Thank you," she says quietly.

We end up walking hand in hand to her truck. The only time I let go of her is to pet Sam when he sticks his head outside the back window. I grab both sides of his face, stare at him and say, "Take care of our girl."

He licks me.

When Addison reaches for the door handle, I stop her by placing my hand on her wrist. "Can I call you?"

She sighs. "How am I supposed to keep a clear head with your voice in my ear?"

"I don't want you to forget me."

"Like that's possible. You're part of the reason I need to take this trip."

Suddenly, I feel like this is a do or die moment. What if she, in her solitude, decides to side with Derek? What if she rationalizes his behavior and kicks me to the curb completely? I don't want to lose her again.

I wrap my fingers around her wrist and gently pull her toward me. She gives me a confused look, but steps forward just the same.

"Do you remember the night your dad made me come to dinner," I ask.

She rewards me with a smile. "Yes."

"What were we doing that got us into trouble?"

"Kissing."

"Where?"

Before she can answer, I move forward, which pushes her back. Her hip brushes the side of her truck.

"Where?" I ask again.

"Kind of where we are now," she finally says.

"Close your eyes."

"Kyle."

"Just do it," I say.

She lets out a breath and squeezes her eyes shut.

My heart races. I press her back a little more and bring my body to within an inch of hers. We're not touching, except for the hold I have on her wrist. I lean forward, like I'm going to kiss her, but stop short. I memorize her face instead. The way her eyes move beneath her eyelids, searching in the dark for what I'm going to do next. The way her lashes sit on her cheeks, the way her nose flares as her breathing picks up, and the way her lips part the longer we stand like this. Her pulse quickens beneath my fingertips, and, still, I don't move.

While she's gone, I want her to remember. I want her to remember the summer we had all those years ago. I want her to remember this moment: the tension between us, the way spring air feels heavy, and the way her heartbeat matches mine. She needs to know that she can trust me; I'll never push her, and I'll never hurt her with actions or words.

Shifting slightly, I bring my mouth to her ear. My cheek grazes hers, stubble against soft skin, and her breath catches. "Do you remember what I was supposed to tell you when I saw you again? The first words you wanted to come out of my mouth?"

She swallows and nods.

"I missed my chance when I saw you at the lake. I had a hard time believing you were real. While you're gone, will you consider giving me another shot?"

I need to tell you I love you, I think. *Without either of us feeling guilty about it.*

"Yes," she whispers.

My body relaxes. I rest my forehead on her shoulder for a moment before releasing her wrist and backing away.

Her eyes pop open in surprise. They comb over me with unanswered questions, and I give her a crooked smile. "What?"

"You..." Her brow furrows. "You didn't kiss me."

I cross my arms. "No."

Her face registers confusion.

"Although, I think that was just as good as a kiss. Don't you?"

She doesn't answer. Slowly, she turns and pulls the truck door open. She starts to get inside, but stops. She looks at me over her shoulder. "It might have been better."

Chapter Twenty-Three

The first week without Addison went by faster than I expected. Due to warmer temperatures, many of our clients got spring fever and called Dayton Landscaping to clean up their yards from the harsh winter. In addition to more snowfall than normal, our area also had one hell of an ice storm in December that took out hundreds of branches and large trees. Many homeowners didn't realize the amount of the damage, or didn't want to deal with it, until the snow melted. I spent the majority of the week with a chainsaw in my hands, which reminded me of ice angel Piggy. One day, I attempted to carve a bird out of a tree stump, only to end up with a butchered piece of wood that Eli said looked like a mangled letter W.

I spent the second week dividing my time between real work and making progress on Addison's studio. Even though she's undecided on keeping it, I still met Jim for the floor appointment. Once the hardwood was shiny and sealed, I devoted a few days to painting the walls that weren't finished during our painting party. I even went out and bought the trim for the floor and around the doorways. I painted it white, as Addison and I discussed, and then asked Kevin to come by and help me put it up. Each night I fell into bed with Tori, exhausted, but still laid awake, half expecting Addison to call. Most of me knew she wouldn't; she hadn't contacted anyone but Ashley since she left. Through my brother and soon-to-be-sister-in-law I knew she was doing okay, but my ears still wanted to hear Addison's voice on their own.

It's now the beginning of the third week, and work has let up enough for me to get busy in my own yard. It's relatively small. I only have to clean up a few things, so I decide to get creative and design an area just for Tori. By the time I lay it out in my head and then on paper, I'm looking at the equivalent of a doggie playground. Forcing myself to backtrack, I end up with a pretty amazing little area, one that combines a new flower garden, her doghouse, and a flagstone path that leads to my existing patio. Eventually, I'd like to recreate this on a larger scale, when I build a new house on another piece of property. Then, I can weave it around bigger features, like a pond and a pergola, or a maybe a gazebo and a hot tub. Or, a hot tub that looks like a natural pond. There are so many possibilities.

I'm in the middle of digging holes for my new plants when, unexpectedly, I get a visitor. As Jen rounds the corner of my house, Tori takes off running. I drop my shovel, wipe the sweat off my face with the bottom of my t-shirt, and follow her. When I get within a few feet of the girl canoodling my dog, I say, "This is a surprise."

Jen smiles up at me as she scratches Tori. "I have a favor to ask."

"What?" I tease her. "Is the new boyfriend not enough for you?"

"Ha ha," she says and stands. "He's more than enough, thank you very much."

My eyebrows shoot up. "Really? So, you've done the deed?"

She blushes. "That's none of your business!"

"I'll take that as a yes."

She huffs. "We've been together almost two months."

"Hey, I'm not judging." I grin and cross my arms. "What did you need?"

"Your help."

My dog is practically crawling up Jen's leg for attention, so she reaches down to pet her again. "What are you getting Kevin and Ashley for a wedding present?"

"I planned on giving them a card with a check in it. Why?"

"I want to give them something different."

"I think they're registered at Bed, Bath, & Body."

Jen laughs. "It's Bed, Bath, & *Beyond*."

Oh.

"I don't want to get them the same thing everyone else does," she says. "You know I don't operate that way."

This is true. Jen has always been one to stress over giving original gifts. Last year, she made wind chimes out of wine bottles for my mom's birthday.

"So, you need ideas?" I ask.

She shakes her head. "I have the idea. I need your cooperation."

Instantly, I frown.

"I wrote a song for them," she says and stands upright again. "I thought maybe you could perform it with me. I need your harmony."

I stare at her like she's lost her mind. "You want me to play guitar with you in front of a room full of people?"

She enthusiastically nods.

"No." I'm defiant. "I suck."

She scowls. "You do not suck! You can play the whole first half of "Freebird"!"

"Not well."

"Yes, well! How many hours did I spend teaching you that song?"

"Probably hundreds."

"And why is that?"

"Because it's the only song Addison and I ever danced to."

Jen blinks and her mouth falls open. "You're telling me I taught you a song that reminded you of your ex? I thought it was your favorite!"

Oh shit.

Her eyes grow wide as she puts two and two together. "That's why it's your favorite," she says in disbelief.

"You taught me other songs," I say, trying not to look like a total ass.

She crosses her arms and cocks an eyebrow. "Not like "Freebird"."

Fuck.

I'm about to apologize when she gets sarcastic. "You are *so* lucky."

"Why?"

She takes a step forward and jabs her finger into my chest. "You're lucky I'm happy with a new guy and writing love songs! I should be seriously pissed at you!"

I hold my hands up in surrender. "I know."

"You owe me big time." She's quiet for a moment before shooting me an evil smile. "You have no choice now. You're playing with me at the reception."

"Ugh!" I throw my head back and stare at the sky. "Can't I do something else? I haven't played in a year!"

She grins. "My song is easy. Your part is basically three chords. We can practice until the wedding gets here."

My expression twists as I turn to walk back to what I was doing. "You know, *you're* the one who's lucky."

"How's that?"

"You're lucky I feel bad."

She laughs.

With Tori at our heels, Jen follows me further into the backyard. "What are you working on?" she asks.

"Sprucing up the yard and making a place for Tori," I say as I bend over to pick up the shovel.

"These are nice." Jen walks over to the bushes I bought and touches some of the leaves. "What are they?"

I push the shovel into one of the holes to make it bigger. "Lilacs," I say.

"Oooo, my grandma used to have a bunch of these," she says. "They smell so good."

I nod, knowing full well the real reason for planting them.

As Jen leans over to check out some hostas, Tori circles her feet. "You must not pay this dog enough attention," she jokes. "She acts deprived."

"She loves company," I say.

"I take it Addison comes to visit her a lot?"

"No, we don't share custody."

My dog collapses on her back at Jen's feet, begging for a belly rub. "Do you mind if I take her for a walk?" she asks.

"Not at all." I stop digging. "Knock yourself out."

Jen smiles and races Tori to the house. They disappear inside and I focus on getting lost in my outdoor project. I plan to drag the work out until the weekend, so I can keep myself busy until a certain someone returns. As I continue to dig, I start to hum.

Great. The song that runs through my mind won't help me forget Addison.

Thanks for bringing up Skynyrd, Jen.

~~~~

Later that night, after Jen brought Tori back and I grabbed a quick dinner from the Chinese place, I'm finding it hard to fall asleep. Jen brought up that stupid song, and now all I can think about is Addison. Not that I wasn't thinking about her before, but this is constant. Sparrow will be back in a few days, and I'm not prepared to face what she may tell me.

Not by a long shot.

I'm not normally a sentimental guy; ask any of my ex-girlfriends and they'll tell you the same. I never told any of them I loved them. Not one. There's only one girl who brings out those types of feelings in me, the only girl to whom I've wanted to say those three words. The connection I have with Addison...I can't explain it. I can't rationalize it, and I can't make it go away. If she decides to end things with me to make things easier with Derek, it's going to hurt. Bad. I need to prepare myself now, just in case, but my stubborn side won't let me.

I want what Gram said to be true, and I want it to be our truth now, not when we're eighty. Call me impatient, but we've already spent enough time apart. Addison said she sees the future she lost when she looks at me. Does she realize she holds the power to find it again? Or is she too wrapped up in her guilt over Derek to see it? Was three weeks enough time to figure it out?

Before I can overthink things any more, I grab my phone to send her a message. I don't know if it will help or hurt my case, but I have to do something. She said not to call, but she needs to know I'm thinking about her. She needs to know I want her here with me.

Texting isn't the same as calling. You need to know I miss you.

I pause as I think of what to send next. I think of all the things that remind me of her and try to put them into words.

Every time I see a sparrow, and every time I smell lilacs.

Every time I taste rocky road ice cream, and every time I touch Tori.

Every time I hear Freebird.

You've stolen my senses, and I miss you like crazy.
So much. Every day.
With all that is me.

~~~~

Ping.

God, I fell asleep late. Tori walks over my legs and jumps off the bed. I pull a pillow over my face.

Ping.

What time is it? What day is it? Right. It's Wednesday.

Ping.

My phone. I reach for it blindly, remembering the message I sent to Addison. She never responded.

I open my eyes and squint at the screen to see who is trying to get ahold of me. Instantly, I'm awake. The message is from Addison, and it is only one word:

Mailbox?

I throw off the blankets and leap to my feet, texting her back with my thumb.

What's at the mailbox?

I can barely breathe as I wait for her answer, remembering this same conversation from years ago. It was early morning, just like now, when we stood on separate docks and faced each other with the lake between us.

Ping.

Me.

I toss my phone aside and race to the front door. Ripping it open, my eyes find Addison immediately. She's at the end of the driveway, pacing, with Sam. Her gaze snaps to mine when she realizes I'm watching her, and her expression softens into a smile.

I make it to her in seconds. She throws her arms around my neck and buries her head beneath my chin. I pick her up off the ground and hold her body tight. "You're back early," I murmur against her hair.

"I got your message," she says.

"It's six in the morn –"

"I drove straight here."

I set her down. "All it took was a text? If I had known, I would have sent one sooner."

"It wasn't just any text." She stands up on her toes to level her face with mine. "It was the most romantic thing anyone has ever said to me."

My pulse accelerates as I stare into her chocolate brown eyes. I notice there's more flecks of gold in them this morning. Actually, there's more gold in them than I've seen in weeks. Despite driving all night, she looks rested; hell, she looks gorgeous. As my heart continues to hammer, I silently pray that her absence did her – did us – some good.

"How was your trip?" I whisper.

She leans toward me and tentatively brushes her lips against mine. "Can I show you?"

Did that just happen? I barely breathe.

Her hands tighten around my neck, so I pull her closer, my hands at her waist. Her mouth finds mine again, and I close my eyes.

Time stops.

Everything that is wrong rights itself.

Addison's kiss feels the same as it did all those years ago. I'm transported back in time, yet I'm clearly in the present. I haven't forgotten her, and she hasn't forgotten me. What starts out slow and gentle quickly turns hungry. My hand leaves her waist to find the nape of her neck, and I hold her there, my fingers twisting in her hair. Memories slam into me: the shape of her mouth, the smell of her skin, and the way we move together. Blood pounds behind my ears as she presses her body against mine. Our lips dance before she pulls back and finishes our kiss with a second, softer one.

I rest my forehead against hers, refusing to let her go. "Your visit went well then?"

She looks at me from beneath her lashes. "I'd say so."

Lifting my head, I move my hand to cradle her face. I run my thumb across her cheek and stare, trying to process her presence. I want to pinch myself to make sure I'm not dreaming. I lower my lips to hers again and kiss her slowly; I can't help it. It's been so long.

A bump to my hip distracts me, and I glance down to find Sam looking at us.

"I think he feels left out," Addison says.

"Hey, buddy." I kneel down to scratch behind his ears. He leans into my hand, then looks toward the house. I follow his gaze and, through the screen door, I can see my dog prancing around impatiently.

"Do you want to meet Tori?" I ask Sam.

He looks between Addison and me, as if asking for permission.

"C'mon," I say as I stand.

I reach for Addison's hand, and she weaves her fingers through mine. The three of us walk together toward my house and when we get to the porch, Tori is almost jumping out of her skin with excitement. I open the door and try to let Sam in without letting her out. It's a tangle of legs and fur for a minute before we're all inside.

As the dogs playfully get to know one another, I wind my hands around Addison's waist. "Do you want anything?" *Like me naked?*

"Um...do you have any tea?" she asks.

I wink. "You're in luck. My mother drinks tea."

I let go of her to walk into the kitchen. Pulling the drawer open next to the stove, I rummage through it and find a box of assorted kinds. "Take your pick."

"Great." She plucks the box from my fingers.

In that moment, I look down at myself. "You have a habit of showing up when I'm in my pajamas."

She laughs. "Sorry."

After I show her where the mugs are, I leave the kitchen to change. Dressing in jeans and a t-shirt, I forego the socks and wander back into the living room. There I find Addison sitting on the couch with her legs curled to the side, drink in hand, while she watches Tori try to wrestle with Sam on the floor. One side of my mouth quirks up. "You're still here."

She sighs. "For as long as I can put off the inevitable."

I frown and gesture for her to move her legs. She does and I catch them, picking them up so I can sit down beside her. She turns to face me, leaning her back against the armrest of the couch, and I drape her legs over my lap. "I was being facetious."

"I know," she says and takes a sip. "I'm hoping this tea will calm me for what I have to do."

"What's that?"

"Leave my husband."

My heart skips a beat, then starts to race. "Are you sure?"

She focuses on the mug in her hands and nods. "I'm not happy. He's not happy. Why suffer?"

Those words don't sound like hers. I reach forward and lift her chin. "Who told you that?"

Her eyes meet mine. "Meagan."

Don't get me wrong. I want this. So damn much. But, I want to make sure she's making this decision on her own. It's too important. I don't want her to look back and say her sister or anyone else swayed her, including me. I know it's hypocritical to think now; I've wanted her to leave Derek this entire time. However, she's standing on the edge of a cliff, ready to jump. Even though I can, I won't push her. Our relationship won't survive if she ends up regretting her decision.

"Is it what *you* believe though?" I quietly ask.

"Yes." She wraps her hand around my wrist. "Now that I've had time to put things in perspective...it should have been obvious for a while now."

"How long?"

"Since before you and I met again," she says. "Do you remember last fall when I told you I brought Derek to the lake to talk about things? Our relationship had already begun to crumble. I just didn't see it clearly at the time."

Removing my hand from her chin, I hold on to her legs and shift closer to her. "Do you love him?" I ask.

"I think, in some convoluted way, I do, because of everything he's done for me. But, it's not a romantic love. I don't think it ever was, it was more of a...a grateful love. We were around each other constantly. I think it grew comfortable. Does that make sense?"

I nod.

"Then, when I saw you again, all these feelings came rushing back. Feelings I'd forgotten existed or could be felt. I was so overwhelmed by them, it scared me. Seeing you reminded me of who I used to be. A girl who didn't take no for an answer. A girl who had dreams. You make me want to be that person again. Then, when I tried to be, Derek didn't like her. He flat out told me I'm not the same woman he married."

"He's not the same either, is he?" I ask. "I mean, was he always absent? Always controlling?"

"Controlling, yes. Absent, no." Addison reaches over to set her tea on the coffee table. I take the mug from her hand to help her. "When my sister asked me what was going on, I told her everything. She got pissed, stopped me, and asked me to reverse the situation. She said to remove myself and put her in my place and Marc in Derek's. What would it look like? What advice would I give her? I said I would be livid if her husband ever treated her that way."

"What did she say?"

"She said she felt the same for me. She's mad at Derek and asked if what we have is worth saving."

I rub her leg. "And you decided the answer was no?"

Her eyes lock on mine and start to glaze over. "While I was gone, he never called Meagan to see how I was doing. He didn't even check to see if I arrived okay. He never tried to contact Ashley either. It's like I don't exist. Ashley told me you asked about me every chance you got. You sent me that amazing message yesterday." She pauses. "I know where I belong."

My eyes widen, and I lean forward, only to stop when our faces are centimeters apart. "Please say that place is with me."

Instead of speaking, she sets her hand against my cheek. She leaves a slow, soft kiss on my lips, and when she leans back, she stares at me. "More green today," she finally says.

"What?"

"Your eyes." She smiles. "If you'll let me, I'd like to get lost in those more often."

I grin. "Like every morning?"

She tips her head. "Eventually."

My expression falls.

"I plan to move out of my house as soon as I can find a place that will let me have Sam."

I look around the room in an exaggerated way. "Gee. Lemme think where that might be."

She laughs. "I'm not moving in with you, Kyle."

"Why the hell not?"

"Because." She playfully nudges my shoulder with her palm. "How would that look? I need to do everything the right way. I don't want to give Derek any more ammunition when it comes to us separating. He's already hidden my money. I'd like it back."

I give her a defeated look.

"Besides, when I was up north, I realized something. I've never lived on my own. Ever. Before the accident, I lived with my parents. After, with Meagan, then Derek. I'd like to give it a try."

My mouth twists. "Fine." I sit back a little. "I'll help you move."

"Thank you." She covers her mouth as she yawns.

I glance toward the television to catch the time and notice our dogs have curled up together into a comfortable ball. Tori has wedged her body next to Sam, and they're sleeping near the couch.

"Hey." I look at Addison. "Check out our kids."

She leans around me to see, and her face softens. "Awww. How cute."

"I think they have the right idea," I say. "It is only seven a.m."

She raises an eyebrow at me.

Moving over, I slide my arm under her waist and pull her toward me. I lie down beside her and stretch out on the couch. She does the same, facing me. The top of her head lands beneath my chin, and I wrap one arm over her waist to pull her as tight to me as possible. She relaxes into me and sighs. "This is so much better than falling asleep on the phone."

I smile. "It's not better. It's heaven."

I kiss her hair, and she settles into me. I run my fingers up and down her arm slowly, until we both fall asleep together.

Chapter Twenty-Four

When Addison left that day, I didn't want her to go. I wanted to monopolize her time for a few selfish reasons:

One, I couldn't stop kissing her.

And two, to save her from the fight I knew was coming.

Of course I wanted her to end things with Derek, but I didn't want her hurt or made to feel guilty. Who knew what his reaction might be? I doubted it would be an easy acceptance; this is the real world, not a movie.

Guess what?

I was right.

From what Addison said, she tried her best to break things off amicably. She sat Derek down and explained she knew they weren't in a good place. She told him he had changed from the man she met and she had changed, too. Addison said if she knew anything, life was short and the unexpected could happen in the blink of an eye. She didn't want to spend any of that time unhappy, and he neither should he. She told him she was leaving, that it was a fresh start for both of them, and she would move out as soon as she found a place.

Derek, true to his asshole self, wouldn't let her stay. He blamed everything on me, saying I was the one who talked her into leaving him. He accused her of having an affair with me all along, even going as far as to insinuate the baby she lost wasn't his. He told her she was the one who had changed, not him, and he couldn't believe she was doing this after everything he had done for her. He said he couldn't stand to look at her and told her she had until Saturday to pack her shit and get out.

That gave us two days to find her a new place to live.

Luckily, the house hunt kept me from finding Derek and giving him a piece of my mind – or my fist. My brother was all for joining me in showing Derek he messed with the wrong woman, but Addison and Ashley convinced us otherwise. Ashley didn't want her fiancé in jail a week before their wedding, and Addison didn't want to give her ex the satisfaction of pissing us off.

"Forget him," she said before kissing me. "He's my past. You're my future."

Eventually, we found an available rental about ten minutes away from my house. It's a condo in a relatively new development that allows pets. After touring the unit, Addison jumped at the chance to sign the lease and beamed when the property manager handed her the keys. "Thank God for twenty-four-hour background checks," she said.

Once that happened, Operation Move Out went into full effect. With reluctance, I let the girls borrow my truck, so they could go to Addison's house and load her things. Since Ashley and Sparrow want us to stay away from Derek, Kevin and I got busy at the new place, watching the dogs and putting furniture together.

"Addison's lucky we didn't put this stuff on Craig's List," my brother says as he screws together one corner of the bed frame. "Ash and I were just talking about it the other day."

Ashley had her own apartment before moving in with Kevin, and she put a few things in storage when they combined households. Addison's best friend generously donated a queen size bed, two bean bag chairs, a microwave, a coffee table, and an entertainment center, not to mention a box of kitchen utensils and a DVD player. There's no television, but I'll remedy that.

"I'm sure once Addison's on her feet you can have your stuff back," I say as I hold the next two sides of the frame together.

"Doesn't bother me any," Kevin says as he crawls across the floor on his knees. "It actually saves me from meeting the creepy people who respond to the ad."

When everything is where we think it should go, Kevin and I drag the bean bag chairs out on to the small cement slab that is Addison's new patio. We toss sticks to the dogs and drink a few beers while we wait for the girls to return. It's a warm day for the beginning of May, and the sun shines down on us. I close my eyes for a few seconds and soak up the warmth. I'm not sad to see winter go. Plowing parking lots and driveways gets old after a while. This is the season I look forward to most, as far as work goes.

"Hey."

I open my eyes and look at Kevin. He's holding the neck of his bottle out toward me.

"Here's to new beginnings. For the both of us."

Smiling, I tap my bottle against his. "I'll drink to that."

An hour later, the girls stumble through the front door. Ashley carries bags of groceries, while Addison's arms are loaded with clothes still on their hangers. Kevin and I bring the chairs and the dogs back inside so we can help.

"How'd it go?" I ask. "Did you get everything you needed?"

"I think so." Addison blows her hair out of her face. "Derek's working, but I still wanted to move quickly."

I reach for the clothes and she hands them to me. "Just throw those in the bedroom," she says. "I'll organize later."

I deposit her things on the bed and when I return, my brother, Ashley, and Addison abruptly stop talking. Ashley avoids my eyes, Kevin smirks, and Addison looks pensive.

"You guys aren't obvious at all," I say sarcastically. "What's going on?"

Addison steps forward, twisting her fingers together. "I kinda hit something with your truck."

My eyes widen. "Like what?"

"Garbage cans," she says sheepishly and squints one eye.

What the hell? My eyes snap to Kevin, who is trying to suppress a laugh. "How bad is it?"

"Some paint may need to be fixed."

"Did you run them over or scrape against them or what?"

Addison bites her lip. "Um, both."

She holds her hand out to me, and I take it. She pulls me toward the door.

"We'll stay inside so you two can have a moment." Kevin grins.

Jackass. He's in for it tomorrow at his bachelor party.

Addison leads me outside, down the steps, and over to where she parked my baby in the driveway. She keeps her head down the entire time. How awful can it be? Aren't most garbage cans made out of plastic?

As we round the back of the truck, I see it. I drop her hand and fall to my knees beside the back quarter panel. Running my fingers over the scrapes, my mouth falls open. Some of them go as deep as the metal. I look up at her. "Were the garbage cans made out of cement?"

"Aluminum," she says quietly.

I stare at the damage. This has to be fixed or it will rust. My truck will be in the shop for at least a week.

"I'm so sorry," Addison says. "I was backing up. I heard this horrible crunching noise and I got out and the cans were crushed between the rocks by the garage and–"

She's babbling. It's cute.

"You'll have to pay for this," I say while trying to look stern.

"I know!" she whines and holds her head in both hands. "How much do you think it will cost?"

I rest my chin between my forefinger and thumb, pretending to think it over. "A least a grand. Maybe more."

"What?!" Her eyes get huge.

She looks like she's about to panic. I smile and stand to pull her into my arms. "I'm kidding! It was an accident. You don't have to pay for anything."

"But it's my fault," she says into my chest. "I feel terrible. Aren't you mad?"

"No." I squeeze her tight. "It's a good thing I love you."

Addison stills in my arms. She remains silent, and I realize what I've just said.

Shit! Could I have been any less romantic? I want to kick myself.

A few seconds pass before Addison lifts her head. She looks into my eyes and runs her fingers over the back of my neck. "I love you, too."

The words slip effortlessly from her lips, causing my heart to pound against my ribs. I feel invincible. I want to run down the street shouting. An odd energized calm settles over me, and I realize I haven't felt this *right* in a long, long time.

Eight years to be exact.

My mouth finds hers and I kiss her hard. Probably too hard, but she feels so damn good in my arms. To my surprise, instead of receiving my kiss, she leans in and gives it back. Her tongue teases mine and I let it; my hands travel from her waist to her ass. Not that our other kisses haven't been great, but this one puts those to shame. This is the girl I remember: the bold one from the lake.

"Jesus!"

I hear Ashley from behind us.

"We're not going to get anything done with you two attached at the mouth!"

Both Addison and I turn to look at Ashley. "In case you've forgotten, we have some very important parties tomorrow. I need my beauty sleep and my Maid of Honor does, too. We can't be up all night."

I roll my eyes. God forbid the bachelorette doesn't get enough rest before her last fling.

Addison laughs and moves away from me.

"Hey," I protest.

"The sooner we unload, the sooner they'll leave." She winks.

That's all the motivation I need.

~~~~

The following evening, I find myself sitting between Austin and Eli in the back of a black Escalade limousine. Across from us are Noah and two other guys from work, Chase and Ben. We've cracked a bottle of Jack, added a splash of Coke, and we're on our way to pick up the groom for his last night out as a single man. Addison is on her way, too, in an identical limo, with the girls to pick up Ashley. When we planned these parties, we thought it would be cool to arrive at the same time to pick up the happy couple, since they live together. This way, they get to see the other is in good hands and receiving equal treatment. In fact, we're all going to end up at the Motor City Hotel and Casino, but on different floors. Because the limos will pick us up in the morning, Addison thought it would be nice if Kevin and Ashley went home alone in one, while the rest of us take the other.

As we pull up in front of my brother's apartment, I send him a text to let him know we're here. When the car stops, all six of us pile out just in time to see the girls turn into the parking lot behind us. Their limo pulls to the curb, and the driver gets out to open the door for them. He catches my eye as he rounds the vehicle, giving me a professional nod, and instantly, I'm suspicious. I look over my shoulder and compare our driver to theirs. Ours is a stodgy, balding man named Theo. He seems like a laid back guy who chauffeurs to ward off the boredom of retirement. Glancing back at the girls' driver again, I realize he looks like he just stepped off the pages of GQ.

The guys start to clap and whistle, redirecting my attention. I join in as my brother and Ashley make their way toward us with their overnight bags, grinning like fools. I'm glad Kevin took my advice and dressed up a little; I told him jeans would be fine, but he should at least wear a nice dress shirt. The other guys and I are mostly dressed in dark denim and button downs, and Kevin fits right in. Ashley stands out, however, and I get why the other guys are whistling. She's wearing an extremely tight, low-cut, white sequined mini-dress with matching heels. Her blonde hair falls in messy waves around her face. I know it's a party in her honor, but damn. Isn't she overdressed just a little?

It's then that I hear deep bass echo from the limo behind us. I turn to see that Captain GQ has opened the door. He extends his hand and, one by one, he helps the girls exit the car. Collectively, all the male mouths around me drop.

Holy hell.

Each of the girls – Addison, Tara, Nikki, and four more I don't recognize – are identically dressed in the same super-small sequined dresses as Ashley, except in black. It's hard not to focus on their assets: it's a cluster of bare legs, swollen tits, and tight asses. With their perfect hair and smoky eyes I feel like I stepped into a music video. Of course Addison is my favorite, and suddenly I'm not so sure I want her out in public looking the way she does.

"Love you, babe!" Ashley kisses Kevin on the cheek and walks over to meet her entourage. They laugh and fawn over her dress and hair before Addison places a white sash over her head. On the front, in silver glitter, is the word "Bride." Then, Tara places a tiny tiara on Ashley's head.

Are you kidding me?

Kevin elbows me in the ribs. "Where's my crown?"

"In the car in a bottle. It's labeled with the word Royal," I say sarcastically.

Once Ashley is pimped out, the girls start to get back into the car. Addison excuses herself and makes her way over to me with a smile. "Hi."

I wrap my arms around her waist and look her over from head to toe. "Are you sure we can't combine these parties? I'd much rather look at you all night than this bunch." I nod over my shoulder.

"You ain't kidding," Austin says from beside me. "Is there room for one more in that limo?"

Addison laughs. "You guys are going to have a great time." She turns to me and kisses my chin. "Have fun."

"You too, but not too much."

She rolls her eyes, then turns to see the driver waiting for her to get in the car. She starts to walk away.

"Hey." I pull her back. "What's up with him? Why do we get old man chauffeur and you get Magic Mike?"

She grins and leans into me conspiratorially. "Funny you should call him that. His name is Jonathan," she whispers.

"So?"

"He's part of the show."

I'm confused. "What show?"

She looks at me like I've bumped my head. "He's a dancer."

My eyebrows jump. "Why is he driving?!"

"Ssshhh!" she whisper-yells. "I don't want your brother to hear!"

For the second time tonight, my mouth falls open. "How...why..." I stutter. I thought the guys were showing up at the hotel.

Quickly, she leans into my ear. "It's part of his act. He pretends to have car trouble and he has to get in the back with us to check things out."

I nearly choke. *Oh, hell no!*

"Addison..." I say uncertainly.

"Gotta go. I'll call you later. Love you!"

She blows me a kiss as she rushes away. Jonathan holds her hand as he helps her into the car and then shuts the door behind her. He rounds the front of the limo, shoots a smile in my general direction, and gets behind the wheel.

I really, *really* do not like him.

Once the girls leave the lot, the guys get into our car. Crawling in behind them, I find my drink and down it in two swallows. I can't help but wonder when the girls' fake car trouble will occur. Halfway to Detroit? Just before they get there? Will we pass them on the side of the road?

Ugh. I wish she hadn't said anything.

"So, I've been kept in the dark for days," my brother says. "Where are we going?"

"Comerica Park," I answer. "We're hitting the Tigers game first, then Motor City to do a little gambling."

"Nice." He nods approvingly.

"Speaking of," Austin reaches into his pocket, "we took up a collection. You won't be losing your own money tonight." My brother's best friend hands him a wad of bills. "Although, I do plan to win my fifty bucks back at the Blackjack table."

"As if," Kevin taunts him.

We make it to the baseball game where we fill up on brats and soft pretzels, peanuts and overpriced draft beer. The competitive atmosphere keeps my mind off what the girls are doing...for the most part. When it's clear the Tigers are going to beat Kansas City, we decide to head to the casino early. Even though we aren't driving, the idea of six guys stuck in traffic after eating a bunch of junk food doesn't sit well with any of us. Sometimes immaturity is unavoidable.

When we arrive at the hotel, my mind turns to Addison again. As I check our group in at the desk, I consult my watch. While we were at the game, they were at dinner. Afterward, they were supposed to go dancing so we could arrive first and disappear on the casino floor. While we gamble, the girls will start the "sleepover" part of their party. Addison decided to get all the girls matching sleep shirts and have an old school pajama party – except with adult activities. Our entertainment isn't due to arrive until one a.m. This gives the guys plenty of time to lose their money and take advantage of the casino's all-you-can-eat buffet.

An hour later, I'm holding my own at the poker table. Granted, I'm playing against Noah and Chase and some other guy who looks like he could be sixteen years old, but it would be nice to walk away with some cash in my pocket. Speaking of pockets, mine vibrates and I pull out my cell.

We're here. Where are you? Not near the eleventh floor I hope.

No, I send back to Addison. *Half of us are losing to me at poker, while the other half is playing roulette.*

Excellent!

I can't help my curiosity. *How was your "ride" to the play?*

She responds with one word. *Hot.*

Really?! I scowl.

But not as hot as you ;) she sends.

Humph. I know it's stupid, but I feel like sulking. *How do you know?*

Because I've seen you naked.

Good answer, but that was eons ago. *Not recently,* I respond.

The dealer reveals her cards and defers to Noah. He folds. As I consult my hand, my phone buzzes again.

No, not recently. Just not yet <3

Hmm. Now I'm trying to figure out how to ditch this party and find her.

Shortly before one, I round up the guys so they can help me get Kevin upstairs. They are well aware of who we're expecting and have no problem leaving the tables. Honestly, now that this final part of the night is here, I wish it would be over. I have no desire to watch these girls dance, although, the look on Kevin's face should be priceless.

Just as everyone is getting settled in our suite, there's a knock at the door. I look through the peep hole, then step outside.

"Are you Kyle?"

One of the girls, the blonde, smiles at me. She has tan skin and perfect teeth; her hair is swept up smooth and business-like on the top of her head. She wears dark rimmed glasses, diamond stud earrings, and her fitted black suit jacket and barely-there skirt give me a naughty librarian vibe.

I nod. "That's me. You are?"

"Stacie." She shakes my hand. "This is Brielle."

I shake Brielle's hand, too and notice her raven hair is braided. She's wearing a plaid skirt and white knee highs. She's totally playing bad school girl.

"Nice to meet you," I say. "My brother, the groom, is the one sitting in the middle of the couch. He has dark hair like me."

They nod.

I start to open the door, and Stacie stops me. "You've paid for two hours, but we'll stay longer if the price is negotiable. You've already given us a generous tip."

Well, yeah. The entertainment service required it. "That's up to the other guys," I say. I've dropped enough money on this night.

I hold the door open and let the girls walk in ahead of me. They drop the bags they're carrying and saunter to the center of the room. Immediately, they zero in on Kevin, and I wish I had thought to record his reaction. The other guys whistle and cheer as my brother's eyes consume his face. Suppressing a smile, I try not to laugh as he looks between the two women like he's never seen strippers before.

Brielle takes an obnoxiously close seat next to my brother on the couch. She wraps one arm around his shoulders and plays with his hair as Stacie stands in front of both of them. She bends over at the waist, blatantly sticking out her ass, and playfully says, "Someone told us you're getting married."

Kevin stares.

She tries again. "Are you getting married?"

Slowly, he nods. Stacie smiles. "Well, it looks like we arrived just in time then."

The girls introduce themselves and make a flirtatious show of learning everyone's name. Brielle sets the ground rules as Stacie walks to their bags and pulls out a Beats Pill speaker. While she sets up, Kevin catches my eyes.

"I'm going to kill you," he mouths.

I laugh.

About ten minutes into their routine, I decide I've had enough. Not that they aren't good-looking and...ah...talented, but I'm just not as into this as the other guys. I'm hanging by the edge of the room anyway, so I take the opportunity to slip out the door and into the hall. Leaning against the wall, I slide down it until I'm sitting on the floor. After playing around on my phone for a few minutes, I decide to call Addison. When she doesn't answer, I hang up. She's probably busy with manicures or mud masks...or men.

"Why are you sitting on the floor?"

My head snaps up. Addison is two doors down and walking toward me. She's wearing a long black sleep shirt that reads, "Last Fling before the Ring" in hot pink letters.

"Stacie and Brielle couldn't hold my attention." I smile and stand.

She sighs. "Same goes for Dante and Lance." She reaches me and winds her arms around my neck. "They just didn't do it for me."

"No?" I raise an eyebrow. "Is that why you're in my hallway?"

She nods. "I was going to see if you could leave the party for a minute."

"Why?" I tease.

She looks around, then grabs the front of my shirt with one hand. She smiles and walks backward, pulling me along, until we reach the stairwell door. She backs into it, opening it with her hip, then clutches my shirt with both hands to pull me through. At the same time the door clicks shut behind us, her mouth lands on mine.

I place my hands around the tops of her arms and press forward, pushing her back. We bump up against the wall next to the stairs, and she lets go of my shirt, splaying her fingers across my chest. My teeth find her bottom lip and play with it before my mouth leaves hers to find her neck. I kiss my way down her throat and she arches into me, tipping her head back and sliding her hands down to my waist. She lifts my shirt, untucking the one beneath it, and I feel her touch against my bare skin. She runs her hands over my stomach, and I let go of her arms to trail my fingers the length of her body. I find the bottom of her sleep shirt and hitch it up just enough to work my hands beneath it. My thumbs trace circles on her hips and her breath catches until I decide to cover her mouth with mine again.

We make out like teenagers until I realize I've been gone long enough for someone to notice. My pulse throbs in every inch of my body, and I think Addison feels the same. She hangs on to my shoulders as we catch our breath; if this continues we're going to need a room. Resting my forehead against hers I say, "I wish we were home."

She gives me a lazy smile and agrees. "Come over tomorrow," she says. "We can have dinner and...dessert."

I grin and lean into her. "I like the way you think." Our kiss is slow and deep and promising, and tomorrow can't get here soon enough.

With reluctance, we separate. Addison smooths her shirt, and I tuck mine in. She kisses me one last time before we head for the door. She opens it and peeks outside to make sure the coast is clear. Headed separate ways, we sneak back into the hallway with our friends none the wiser.

Chapter Twenty-Five

When I arrive at Addison's the following evening, I'm greeted at the door by Sam. The smell of something Italian drifts through the screen, and my stomach growls. After our late night, I haven't had much of an appetite today.

Until right now.

I peer through the door to find Addison and when I don't see her, I knock. Sam's tail stops wagging, and he looks at me expectantly. His eyebrows shift, as if asking, "Why don't you just come in?"

"Is it unlocked, buddy?" I ask and try the handle. It is, so I let myself inside.

Rounding the corner into the kitchen, I expect to find Sparrow there. She's not, but a fresh loaf of sliced bread sits on a cutting board on the counter. The fantastic aroma I caught at the door is stronger and radiating from the oven. I dare to peek and crack the door open an inch to see what's inside. It looks like some sort of lasagna.

"Damn it!"

I jump, thinking I've been caught. When I turn around, I realize Addison isn't behind me. Frowning, I walk into the living room and finally see her through the open patio door. She's standing outside, on the cement, with a large black pot at her feet.

And it's on fire.

What the hell?

I'm at the door in seconds. "What's going on?"

Addison's eyes snap to mine. She pulls the pad of her thumb out of her mouth. "I burnt myself."

I step out on to the patio and grab her hand to look at it. Her thumb is red, but it doesn't look blistered. "Why are you setting things on fire?"

She looks to a box on the other side of the pot. It's full of pictures and papers. "I'm incinerating my past," she spits.

Okay. This wasn't the attitude I expected when I came over tonight. "Do you want to tell me why?"

"Sure," she says matter-of-factly. She releases my hand to bend over and reach into the box. She pulls out a picture and shows it to me. It's a candid shot of her and Derek somewhere tropical. They're sitting at what looks like a tiki bar holding umbrella drinks. Once I've had a look, she tosses it into the fire where it instantly curls and shrivels.

"I stopped at the house this afternoon," she says. "In my rush to move I forgot my recipe book. I needed it to make dinner. All my mother's recipes are in there."

She selects a greeting card from the box. On the outside it reads, "For My Beautiful Wife." She throws it into the pot and it disappears.

"Was Derek there?" I ask.

"No." She scowls. "But, I did find some other interesting things."

"Such as?"

She reaches for another picture. "Two dirty wine glasses in the sink. One with pink lipstick on the rim." She rips the photo in half before tossing it into the flames.

"So, Derek had a date." I shrug. "Does that bother you?"

She lets out a sarcastic laugh. "No."

A handwritten note turns to ash.

"Addison. Stop." I reach for her shoulders. "Talk to me. What's wrong?"

"He's been cheating on me," she says, her tone toxic. "After I found the glasses, I went into the bathroom. Her razor was in the shower."

I'm struggling to comprehend this. They're separated. I don't consider Derek's actions cheating. I mean, no one likes to be replaced so quickly, but –

"I only left four days ago," Addison interrupts my thoughts.

"I'll admit he moves fast," I say, trying to commiserate with her. "But, what does it matter? Maybe it was a one-night stand."

"Or maybe it started before I left."

My eyes narrow. "You think so?"

"I know so."

She reaches into her back pocket and pulls out a receipt. "I decided to dig around in his desk drawer." She shows the paper to me. It's from a jewelry store. "That's our credit card number," she says. "He bought these in March...and he didn't give them to me."

I stare at the print. He bought earrings, expensive ones at that. "Five hundred dollars?" I ask.

She nods, and then produces another receipt. This time it's for lingerie. In April.

From the time she was gone.

"There's more, too," she says as she throws the papers into the fire. "I didn't take them all."

I didn't think it was possible to hate Derek more. I was wrong. My jaw clenches. "I'm sorry he did this to you."

"Don't be," she says and turns out of my grasp. "I'm the one who's sorry." She crouches down and picks up the box, then stands and dumps it out over the fire. "I'm sorry for not noticing it sooner. I'm sorry for giving him the benefit of the doubt. I'm sorry I beat myself up over you. Obviously, I didn't have to."

"It's all right," I tell her. "You didn't know. We're together now. Everything's fine."

"No, it's not," she says and tosses the box aside. "Think about it. How long has he been cheating? Was this girl the only one? What if he gave me something?"

I'm not following her. "What do you mean?"

"What if I'm sick, Kyle? We didn't use protection."

A hard lump forms in my throat. "Do you feel sick?"

"I didn't until I discovered this." Her anger subsides and worry starts to take over. "I can't...we can't..." she falters. "I won't put you at risk. Not until I see a doctor."

Again, I want to murder Derek. I pull Addison into my arms. "Everything's going to be fine," I reassure her. "You'll see."

Her voice is muffled against my chest. "That's easy for you to say. You're not the one who feels dirty."

I step back and stare into her eyes. "Don't ever say that. Even if you do have something – which you don't – it's not your fault."

"What if I do?" she whispers.

"Then we'll work through it," I say without blinking an eye. "I love you."

Addison gives me a desperate look. "You wouldn't leave?"

"Hell, no." My eyes search her face. "I've waited too damn long for you. I'm never letting you go."

She steps forward and kisses me, leaving a slow, meaningful taste of her on my lips. "God, I love you," she says when we part. "I'm sorry our night won't go as planned."

"It's not a total bust," I say as I move my hands low on her waist. "There is something amazing cooking in your oven."

"Chicken Parmesan." She smiles for the first time tonight. "I hope you're hungry."

"Starved," I say.

She backs away from me and looks at the fire.

"Are you done with that?" I ask.

Her expression twists, and she nods. "I'll get some water to put it out." She walks toward the patio door and stops. "I hope he felt it," she says.

"What?"

"The burn."

"Like a voodoo doll?" I ask.

"Yes." She scowls and enters the house.

~~~~

Over the next few days, my frustration grows. Kevin won't stop talking, Jen won't stop nagging, and I can't touch Addison the way I want. Not to mention I've had two dreams about running over Derek with my truck.

I think I'm stressed.

My brother is getting married on Saturday, which means he'll be gone the following week on his honeymoon. He's been grilling me to make sure I understand everything he's been working on at the office just in case something comes up while he's away. He won't stop detailing every little thing; it's incessant. I think part of it is pre-wedding jitters, and it's driving me nuts.

If Kevin's OCD isn't enough in one ear, I have Jen in the other. She's on my case about learning her damn wedding song. She's emailed me the music and the lyrics, but we have yet to practice together. I know she's starting to panic, but after I leave work the last thing on my mind is picking up a guitar. Addison's been working on the studio, and I want to spend time with her.

Speaking of, Sparrow has decided to go ahead with the business. I couldn't be more proud. She's been brainstorming studio names, developing a price scale, comparing advertising strategies, and ordering the things she needs to complete the renovation of the space. She's really hit the ground running. At first she admitted her drive was to keep her mind off Derek and his douchebaggery. But, as the days go by, she grows more focused on what this means for her. I want to be there to share in the experience. Also, she should get word from her doctor any day. We've been sitting on pins and needles, waiting.

By the end of the week, I'm more than ready to fast-forward time. Instead, I'm forced to be patient and deal with Jen.

"The wedding is *two days away!*" she shrieks into my ear. "We have to get together tonight! Practicing over the phone is not an option!"

"Calm down," I say.

"Calm down? This is my *gift*. You're supposed to be helping me!"

"Okay. I know." I let out a heavy sigh. "You can come over. Addison's with Ashley working on some stuff for the rehearsal dinner anyway."

"Thank God. I'll be there around seven."

Jen is not late. She's also not stupid. When she arrives, she comes armed with her guitar, a grocery bag full of snacks, and a case of beer. "We're in for the long-haul," she says.

While Jen says hi to Tori for a few minutes, I set the food she brought on the coffee table. Digging into the bag, I pull out some pretzels and open them. I take a handful and shove a few into my mouth as I go retrieve my instrument. When I return, Jen is sitting on the couch tuning her guitar and holding a piece of red licorice between her teeth.

"Ofay," she says as she chews. "Lemme hear wat you got."

I start to play and she stops me. She gestures toward my guitar. "Hand it over."

I concede and give it to her. As she tweaks the tuners, I say, "It's fine. You need to relax. When is the last time you got laid?"

I thought my comment would make her laugh but instead she grumbles. "Last weekend."

Oh. "Something go wrong?"

She shakes her head. "We had a great time, or I thought we did." She hands my guitar back to me. "I haven't been able to connect with Ross since."

"Ross?"

"New Year's Eve Guy," she explains.

"So, he has a name," I muse. "Aren't you bringing him to the wedding? You can connect there."

"No. He said he would be out of town, so I never brought it up." Jen positions her guitar across her knee. "You ready?"

"Are we done talking about Ross?"

"Yes."

"Are you sure?"

"Yes!"

Playfully, I bump her shin with my foot. "Don't let him hurt you. I already have one man on my hit list, don't make me add another."

"Let me guess." She smiles. "You and Derek aren't getting along?"

"We will never get along."

We practice and eat, drink and practice. The song isn't complicated, but Jen makes us work on it for hours. By eleven o'clock, we start to get a little slap-happy. During the last run-through, I screw up transitioning from the first verse to the second, which earns me a peanut to the face that nearly hits my eye. Jen thinks that's funny, so I retaliate with a handful of M&M's, which she blocks with her guitar. She picks up the few that land in her lap, eats them, then decides to stand and grab the bag of pretzels. She tosses it at me, and I laugh, swatting it away. Pretzels fly everywhere, and Tori is in heaven. As my dog scavenges, I stand and reach for the spoon in the chip dip, pulling it back like I'm going to launch it at Jen.

"You wouldn't," she laughs.

"Watch me."

She grabs an unopened bottle of beer and shakes it. "I will spray you," she threatens.

At this point, I don't care. I let go of the spoon and a clump of green onion dip splats against her belly.

"You're such an ass!" she yells as she looks down at herself. With an evil glint in her eye, she shakes the bottle harder. "You should probably run."

There's no doubt in my mind she will douse me, so I decide the kitchen is the best way to go. However, instead of running, I shove my hands in my pockets and lazily stroll backwards, taunting her, like I couldn't care less if I get wet. She's fast though, faster than I expected, and she twists off the bottle cap before I can cover my face.

"Shit!" I curse. Beer runs down my forehead and stings my eyes.

Jen laughs as she walks up to me. Her fingers brush my cheeks as she tries to help wipe the liquid away.

"Am I interrupting?"

My head snaps around. Addison is standing in my kitchen, just inside the door. I wipe the foam from my lashes and blink, trying to focus. I walk toward her and she backs away. It's then I see hurt and confusion on her face.

I look from Addison to Jen and back again, realizing what this looks like. I never told her Jen and I were working on a gift for Kevin. My stomach drops.

"We're rehearsing," I say.

"Rehearsing what?"

"A song." Jen walks up behind me. "I asked Kyle if he would perform with me at the wedding."

Addison pins me with hard eyes. "On the guitar? You said you barely play."

"That's right," I say as I stand there and drip. "But, Jen didn't want to give Kevin and Ashley a regular gift, so she wrote a song and recruited me."

Addison looks between me and my ex. Silent seconds pass as she assesses us. I know I told her Jen had moved on with someone else. She has to believe there's nothing going on here.

Without a word, Addison turns to leave.

"Wait." I step toward her.

She looks at me and keeps walking.

I pick up my pace and step around her, blocking the door. "Listen. It's not what you think. We're really rehearsing."

Addison crosses her arms. Finally, she says, "Prove it."

Jen leaves to pick up her guitar, and I head to the kitchen to wipe my eyes with a dish towel. When I make it back to the living room, Addison is sitting on the edge of my recliner with a "this-better-be-good-or-I'm-going-to-kill-you" look on her face. I take my original seat across from Jen and get comfortable. She meets my eyes and counts us down.

"Three, two, one..."

We strum the opening chords, and Jen sings the first verse. When it's time for the chorus, I join in:

The day we met
I'll never forget
Your smile
Your eyes
Your hand in mine

My heart always knew
I'd choose you

Baby, you know
My pulse beats for you
Yearns for you
Turns for you
Loves you
I do

Your laugh
Your tears
Your beautiful face
There's nothing you have
That I would replace

My heart always knew
I'd choose you

Your head on my shoulder
Your hand on my chest
Another year older
Another year best
You're mine
I'm yours
I love you
I do

My heart always knew

I'd choose you

We finish strong; it's probably the best rendition we've done. Each time I sang the chorus I focused on Addison and caught her eyes with mine. Those words mean so much more when I sing them to her:

My heart always knew I'd choose you.

"What did you think?" I ask, wondering if her blank stare bears good or bad news.

"I..." She blinks. "That was really good," she says quietly.

"Yeah?" Jen smiles. "See." She shoves my shoulder. "I told you that you don't suck."

My eyes roll.

"Jen?" Addison stands. "Is there any way I can talk to you in private?"

Wait. What?

"Um...sure." Jen's eyes dart to me before she sets down her guitar. The two girls disappear down the hallway, and I hear a door shut. I'm left alone in the living room with my dog.

I don't know what to do with myself, so I start to pick up the mess on the table. I bag the food and clear off the crumbs before I realize I'm still covered in beer. I head to the bathroom to clean up and stop short when I hear muffled voices behind my guest room door. I know I shouldn't eavesdrop, but I'm a little nervous. What are they talking about? I step as close as I dare to the closed door, acting as if it will shock me if I touch it.

"...three years," I hear Jen. "In all that time, he never once told me he loved me. What we have isn't love. It's friendship."

"Are you positive?" Addison asks. "You two look pretty close. Look, you don't know me from Adam, but I need to be sure about what I'm getting involved with here. I don't know how much more I can take."

"Trust me," Jen reassures Addison, "that man is head over heels, fall down and get back up, in love with *you*. You should hear him talk about you. Damn. Do you walk on water?"

Addison doesn't respond.

"Let me put it this way," Jen says. "I've never seen Kyle like this before. He's way more fun and relaxed. When I was here, it was the business 24/7. There were no food fights. There was no dog. Hell, I swear he acted like he was seventy."

Really? Seventy? I would say I acted no older than thirty.

269

"He's a good guy," Jen says. "I swear there's nothing going on between us."

"Okay," I hear Addison sigh. "Thank you for being honest. I just...I don't want anything to screw this up. You know?"

"I get it," Jen says, her voice closer to the door. "And, for what it's worth, I appreciate you not attacking me. I wasn't sure what was going to happen when you brought me in here."

The doorknob starts to turn, and I skip to my original destination – the bathroom. I grab a washcloth and look at myself in the mirror. The rims of my eyes are red from the beer. Nice. I look like I've been on an all-night bender.

I hear the girls walk past the bathroom, and I quickly wash my face. Then, I head to my dresser to put on a clean t-shirt.

When I make it back to the living room, Jen is gone. Addison is sitting on my favorite chair with a sleepy Tori curled in her lap.

"She's getting too big for that, you know." I nod toward my dog.

"She'll never be too big." Addison pets her. "I still cuddle with Sam."

"Not on a chair," I say.

"No, not on a chair."

I stop in front of the recliner and crouch down in front of Addison. "Everything okay?"

She nods.

"Did you find out what you wanted to know?"

She nods again.

"I'm sorry I forgot to tell you about the song. You were up north when Jen conned me into helping her. I kept putting off practice because I wanted to spend time with you."

Addison's face twists. "How did she con you into it?"

I groan. "She brought up "Freebird". I admitted it was the only song you and I ever danced to. She was upset because she spent countless hours teaching me to play it. She said I owed her."

Sparrow's eyes get big. "I agree. You do owe her."

I smirk.

"And, now, you owe me."

"What?"

"I caught you with your ex-girlfriend singing a love song. I want to hear "Freebird"."

"No, you don't."

"Yes, I do." Addison shifts Tori off her lap and stands. "You played beautifully earlier." She raises an eyebrow. "And, since when do you sing? Your voice is hot."

It is?

Pulling her hair over her shoulder, she turns and exposes her tattoo. "It's our song," she says. "Please play it for me."

I can't argue with that.

I reach for her hand and lead her to where I left my guitar. She sits next to me on the couch, then folds her legs beneath her and faces me. I pluck at the strings, remembering where to start, then warn her, "I don't know the whole song."

"It doesn't matter."

Okay. I take a breath and start to play.

I concentrate more on my fingers than Addison since it's been awhile since I've played Skynyrd. I know the words by heart, though, and they roll off my tongue. When I finish the last chord, my eyes meet hers. She looks like she might cry.

"Are you upset?"

She shakes her head and reaches for the neck of my guitar. I let her take it, and she sets it on the floor. Then, she crawls into my lap, presses her chest to mine, and cradles my face in both hands.

"I love you, Kyle Dayton," she whispers.

I smile before my lips meet hers. "I love you, too."

Chapter Twenty-Six

"What is going on with you?"

I watch my brother loosen his collar *again*. His skin is turning red from where he's been messing with it. He turns to face a mirror hanging on the vestibule wall, and I slide two fingers between his shirt and the back of his neck. "You have plenty of room," I say.

He shrugs his tuxedoed shoulders and steps out of my reach. "Dude. Keep your hands to yourself."

I roll my eyes, then check my watch. "Five minutes until show time."

Kevin lets out a pent up breath and mumbles to his reflection. "Five minutes."

His reaction reminds me of how we used to mentally prepare for our football games in high school. Coach would have the team take a few minutes to pump ourselves up before taking the field. Some of us would mutter, others would pray. Some just sat there, like me, going over the game plan in our heads. As I glance around the waiting area inside the church, I'm sure Kevin is contemplating the biggest play of his life:

In half an hour, he'll be a married man.

Since it's almost do or die time, I step beside him. "So. Should I bring the car around?"

He shoots me a confused look.

"Now would be the time to bail," I say. "Are you sure you want to go through with this?"

His expression grows more twisted. "Are you serious?"

"I think it's my job as your Best Man to offer."

Kev gives me a lopsided smile. "Thanks, but no thanks."

I expected his answer, but I thought I should check just in case. Especially with the way he's been yanking on his shirt collar like he can't breathe. "Are you nervous?" I ask.

"Hell, yes," he says and runs his hand through his hair. "If it were Addison walking down that aisle, how would you feel?"

"If she were marrying you?" I raise an eyebrow. "I'd be pissed."

"You know what I mean," he says. "How would you feel if it was your wedding day?"

I pause to think about his question. Seconds pass before I finally answer. "Psyched."

"Exactly," he says. "I still can't believe Ashley said yes." Taking a few steps to pace, he adds, "I just hope she doesn't change her mind."

Ashley would never do that. It is possible that Addison is having this same discussion with her right now, but I know she would never leave my brother.

"Hey." I reach out and grab his shoulder to stop his pacing. "Ashley is in love with you. Even I can see it. You two were meant to be together, so stop worrying."

Kevin stares at me and waves his hand in front of my face. "What did you do with my brother?"

I scowl. "What?"

"Just a few months ago you were telling me I was moving too fast. Now, Ashley and I are meant to be?"

"Don't be stupid. You know you are. She won't change her mind any more than you will change yours."

Kevin looks skeptical. "Do you mean that?"

I can't believe he has doubts. "One hundred percent."

"Gentlemen?"

The priest speaks from behind us, and I turn around to look at him. He's a thin, elderly man with short gray hair.

"It's time," he says with smiling eyes. "Do you have any questions?"

I look at Kev. "Any questions?"

He shakes his head, and I notice him swallow.

"We're all set," I say on his behalf.

The priest nods. "Then, let's get started. You have a full house out there."

Kevin walks around me to stand behind Father Frank, and I follow him, just as we rehearsed. When we step out of the vestibule at the front of the church, we're feet from the altar and immediately on display. As the priest leads us to our marks, I clasp my hands in front of me and concentrate on Kevin's shoulders. Even though I haven't looked out over the crowd yet, I can feel hundreds of eyes on us. It's a little unnerving. How many people did they invite to this wedding?

The music cueing the bridal party begins, and my eyes sweep over the church to land on the rear doors. I catch a glimpse of my mom, dad, and my step-mother, Lydia; they're all seated in the first row in front of us. Being the landscaper that I am, I recognize the flowers that decorate the end of each pew. They're a combination of blue hydrangeas and Lily of the Valley. Last night at the rehearsal, I was told the wedding colors are Tiffany blue, pink, and cream. I have no idea what Tiffany blue is, but I have to say that the florist did an excellent job in selecting spring flowers.

Shadows appear through the frosted glass that separates the back of the church from the entrance, and I realize how excited I am to see Addison. She stayed with Ashley last night at the apartment, while Kevin crashed at my house. Although this day is about the newlyweds, I plan on having one hell of a time with my girl. Amongst all the things to celebrate, the fact that Addison is here with me and not Derek tops my list. This is our first event as a couple, and I'm ready to brag about it.

When the doors at the back of the church open, Nikki and Noah appear. They take their sweet time walking down the aisle arm in arm, with Tara and Austin following them. Then, Addison steps into view and my world stops.

I doubt anyone is paying attention to me, but if they are, they would know in an instant how much I love this woman. I can feel it written all over my face. My eyes focus solely on her, and the rest of the church blurs around us. She looks at me with a knowing smile, and it's almost as if we're practicing for our own future. Today, she wears a light blue strapless dress that hugs her waist and falls to her knees. The next time I see her walking down an aisle, I know she'll be the one in white. For the first time in my life I can see this happening for me. For us.

One day, I'm going to make Addison my wife.

She makes it to the front of the church and walks to the opposite side of the altar to stand with the girls. The music fades and all eyes shift to watch the bride make her entrance. Once the congregation stands, the string quartet starts to play, and Ashley appears on the arm of her father. Her dress mirrors Addison's except it's a cream color, floor length, gauzy and glittery. Her blonde hair is piled on top of her head, which makes me think of a princess. While the bride looks beautiful, my eyes skip to the woman standing across from me. I'm so completely and utterly biased. No one, not even Ashley, compares to her.

The closer the bride gets to my brother, the more I feel the anticipation around Kevin fade. Just before Ashley reaches us, I lean forward and whisper, "Feel better now?"

Without taking his eyes off her, he smiles and says, "One hundred percent."

Ashley and her father reach the altar, and Father Frank begins the ceremony. He welcomes everyone to the church and then asks who gives this woman to be wed. Ashley's father states, "Her mother and I do," then kisses his daughter on the cheek. He shakes my brother's hand before placing Ashley's inside it, and when everyone is seated, the bride and groom step forward. Now, nothing is left between Addison and me except empty space. She catches my eye from across the aisle and winks. I wink back at her.

The ceremony goes off without a hitch. Aside from my brother and Ashley looking like two lovesick kids, they remember their lines, repeat their vows, and lay one hell of a kiss on each other when announced as husband and wife. Everyone in the church stands and applauds when they head down the aisle, and I try not to appear too eager as I walk toward Addison and extend my arm. When she loops hers through mine, she says, "Hi, handsome."

I squeeze her arm against my side and lean over a little bit. "You look amazing."

She smiles.

When we're about a halfway down the aisle, I whisper, "I've been dying to touch you since you walked into this church."

She squeezes my arm this time and quietly says, "Good. I have some news."

"Yeah?"

We reach the end of the aisle and step into the lobby. She pulls me over to the side, away from Kevin and Ashley. She looks up into my eyes and says, "I heard from my doctor."

"And?"

She stands on her toes and leans in to my ear. "We're good to go. The tests were negative."

Hell yes! I grin at her. "I told you so."

She smiles and plants a kiss on my lips before we're called to duty.

"Hey! You two making out in the corner!" Ashley chastises us. "C'mon. We have a receiving line to get through."

Grudgingly, I pull away from Addison and take her hand to lead her outside. As we walk, I check my watch.

Damn. It's only four o'clock.

I have to wait eight hours until this party is over. Then, I can have her all to myself.

~~~~

"Is this thing on?" I tap the microphone and hear two static thuds. "Good evening everyone."

The conversation in the hotel ballroom starts to quiet as all eyes at the reception swing to me. I'm standing behind the head table next to Kevin, ready to deliver my Best Man speech. As soon as I do, we can eat and get this night started.

The photographer steps in front of the table and takes my picture, blinding me. What is with this guy? Ashley must have requested the paparazzi package. I've posed for more pictures between the ceremony and arriving at the Sheraton than I've ever taken in my life. Every time I tried to escape with Addison for a minute, we were pulled into another photo.

Blinking to focus, I clear my throat, pick up my glass, and begin my not-so-well-rehearsed toast. "As many of you know, the groom is my baby brother."

Kevin immediately hangs his head as laughter trickles throughout the room.

"I could stand here all night and tell you embarrassing stories about him, but I won't." I gesture with my drink toward the bride. "I'll save those for Ashley when she needs blackmail."

The crowd politely laughs again as she gives me a thumbs up.

"No, tonight I thought I would share an embarrassing moment of my own."

The room gets quieter, and I focus on my brother and his new wife. "Kevin, when you told me you were falling for Ashley, I didn't believe you."

He nods.

"And then, when you told me you had proposed, I thought you were moving too fast."

He nods again.

"Now, don't get used to this, but..." I pause. "I'm embarrassed to say I was wrong."

My brother and Ashley grin. Addison smiles, too, from her seat next to the bride.

"I think everyone here will agree you two share something special. Despite the short time you've been together, it's hard to picture one of you without the other. You two put smiles on each other's faces I've never seen before. What you have will last a lifetime, and I'm glad you didn't listen to me." *Especially since it brought Addison back into my life,* I silently add.

I raise my glass and address the room. "A toast. To the bride and groom. Congratulations on your happily ever after."

Glasses clink, and I tap my glass against Kevin's and then Austin's before taking a drink. My speech gets applause when I sit down.

As the DJ starts the dinner music, the waiters begin to serve salads. My brother leans over to me and says, "That was really nice."

I smirk. "Don't get used to it."

After dinner, I finally get a few minutes with Addison. I want to introduce her to my parents, and I figure this is the best time to do it. The short time we have between now and the bridal dance should be just long enough to avoid awkward conversation. As I walk up to her, her eyes light up.

"Come with me," I say as I reach for her hand.

"Where are we going?"

"I want to introduce you to my family."

She looks surprised. "Really?"

"Yes, really." I scan the room to look for my mom and find her talking to my Aunt Janice. Two tables over, I see my dad and Lydia having coffee and cake. "You're not a secret," I say as I start to lead her in their direction.

"I didn't think I was," she replies and wraps her other hand over mine. "But, we've only been together a week. I didn't think you would want to announce it yet."

I stop walking and pull her close. "We've been together a hell of a lot longer than a week."

Her eyes search mine before she asks, "How long? Just so I have my story straight."

"Eight years," I respond automatically, then correct myself. "Wait. It's 2014. Nine years."

She grins and rewards me with a slow kiss.

When we step up to my father, he has a questioning glint in his eye. He must have been watching us. "Kyle," he says as he stands. "You did a nice job with your speech."

"Thanks." I release Sparrow's hand and weave my arm around her waist. "I'd like you to meet someone. Addison, this is my dad, Colin. Dad, this is my girlfriend, Addison."

It feels weird to call her my girlfriend. She's so much more.

My father's eyes widen infinitesimally. He may or may not remember her name. I'm sure my mom brought it up all those years ago when she was having trouble with me. "It's a pleasure to meet you," he says and shakes her hand. "This is my wife, Lydia." He gestures to his right.

Lydia smiles and hugs Addison. "I'm happy to meet you."

"Likewise," Addison says. She looks between me and my father. "I can see the resemblance."

I study my dad. We are the same height and we have the same hair color; although his is graying at the temples. He keeps his face clean shaven, and I think Kevin inherited his more chiseled features. Gram always said my dad reminded her of Cary Grant in *An Affair to Remember*. I don't think I resemble Nickie Ferrante.

Yes. One summer, Gram made us watch the movie.

The ladies exchange a few more pleasantries about the wedding before I lead Addison over to my mother. My mom is talking to a man I don't recognize until he turns around.

"Mr. Grant?" I ask, surprised. Kevin didn't tell me he invited our grandmother's first love to his wedding.

"Hello, Kyle." The corners of his eyes crinkle when he smiles. "It's good to see you again."

"You, too," I respond.

"Jonas was just telling me how much the lake has changed," my mother says. "I think I might have to spend some time there this summer."

My mom's comment strikes me as odd. The last time I remember her staying at Gram's was when she was still married to my father.

Mr. Grant's attention shifts to my girl. "If I'm not mistaken, I think we've met before."

Addison blushes. "Well, you met my dog."

"Ah." His smile grows bigger.

"Mr. Grant, Mom," I say as I move behind Sparrow. "This is Addison." I place my hands around her waist and pull her against my chest. I want to make it clear we're together without calling her my girlfriend again. It sounds juvenile.

My mother's demeanor immediately changes. Her shoulders tense and her smile turns plastic. Her eyes ask, *"What?"* while her voice says, "Oh. I've heard a lot about you."

"All good, I'm sure," Addison laughs.

Mr. Grant steps forward. "Everything I've heard about you is fantastic." He looks at me with understanding eyes. "Your grandmother was a big talker."

From the way his expression softens, I'm sure he's referencing the letter she wrote exposing their past. "I know," I say with a hint of a smile.

"There you are!"

I turn my head to find Jen at my side. "I talked to the DJ. We're on at ten."

"Okay." I nod.

"Hi, Donna!" Jen greets my mom with a one-armed hug. "Long time, no see."

My mother relaxes. "I'm so glad you came."

"Of course!" Jen says. "I wouldn't miss it." Keeping her arm around my mom's shoulders, she steps beside her. "Can you believe these two?" She points at Addison and me. "Are they cute or what?"

My mom shoots her a befuddled look.

"Speaking of cute," Addison steps out of my arms and toward Jen, "where did you get that dress?"

"Macy's." My ex smoothes her blue skirt over her hip. "It was on sale!"

"Is it chiffon?" Addison asks.

As the girls get lost in conversation, my mom walks away from Jen and up to me. "Are they friends?" she whispers.

I shrug. "They've met a couple of times."

"You three don't have some weird thing going on, do you?"

I'm confused. "What kind of weird thing?"

"Like a ménage a trois."

"Mom!"

"Well, I just finished reading *Fifty Shades of Grey*. I know all kinds of things go on these days –"

"No!" I cut her off. "Please stop talking. Addison is it for me. She's the only one."

"What about her husband?"

"They're separated."

Mr. Grant clears his throat, and I focus on him. He looks uncomfortable. I'm about to apologize for what he overheard when the DJ calls the bridal party to the dance floor.

"I'll talk to you later," I tell my mom. Smiling over her head, I say, "Thanks for coming, Mr. Grant. I'm sure we'll run into each other up north sometime."

"I'm sure we will," he says.

Reaching for Addison's hand, I pull her away from the group. We walk to the edge of the dance floor. "Your mom doesn't like me," she says.

Damn. I was hoping she didn't notice her hesitation. "You're wrong," I say. "She's just worried. Once she gets to know you, she'll love you."

Addison squeezes my fingers. "I hope so."

After the newlyweds dance for the first time, the rest of us are called on to the floor. As I take Addison in my arms, I'm reminded of our first dance together. This time feels just as good, if not better. My hands rest on the small of her back and hers are wound around my neck. I want to pull her against me, so I can feel more of her, but the other couples around us are keeping a respectful distance. Leaning down, I whisper in her ear. "I wish we were somewhere private."

She smiles. "After you play Jen's song we can be."

My thoughts jump to the room we've reserved upstairs. Just like Ashley planned months ago, the bridal party and some other guests are staying overnight at the hotel. I rest my forehead against Addison's. "I can skip it."

She leans away from me. "No! Jen would be upset and I want to hear you sing."

"Why?"

"I told you your voice was hot." She tips her head flirtatiously. "Singing now will only benefit you later."

My eyebrows arch in surprise. I'm tempted to pick her up and carry her out of the room. Instead, I hold her tighter and bring her closer. "Promise?"

"Cross my heart," she says before kissing me.

We spend the next few hours enjoying the night. We get a couple of drinks, she dances with Ashley and the girls, and I eventually lose my jacket and tie. I catch up with some family members and get one more slow dance with Addison before it's gift-giving time.

"Hello." Jen's voice echoes through the room. "If Kevin and Ashley could join his brother and me in front of the DJ booth that would be perfect."

Kev and Ashley are on opposite sides of the reception when Jen makes her request. They both shoot us curious looks when they see us seated with our guitars.

"Don't look so worried, guys," I say into the mic.

They laugh as they make their way toward us, and Jen explains what's going on. "Kevin and I have been friends for...what? Five years now?" She directs her question toward my brother. He nods and she continues. "I wanted to give him and his wife a special gift today, one that didn't fit in a card." Jen looks at me and smiles. "Kyle here was generous enough to help."

"She bribed me," I say into the microphone and the guests chuckle.

Jen swats my arm. "Regardless, we'd like to play a song I wrote for my friend and his bride."

When Kevin and Ashley meet in front of us they join hands and step aside. "Make it good," my brother teases.

Jen clears her throat. "This song is called 'I Choose You'."

Silence falls over the room, and Jen plucks her guitar strings. She meets my eyes, nods, and we start the song together.

Everything goes as planned. I look at Addison every time I join the chorus. She's standing on the far side of the dance floor with Tara, and I notice they whisper to each other several times during the performance. After we finish, the guests burst into applause as Kevin and Ashley descend upon us. As I stand, I notice Ashley brush tears from her cheeks.

"You..." She tries to give me a stern look. "You made me cry!"

"I didn't mean to," I say as she hugs me.

"That was the sweetest gift ever. Thank you so much."

Kevin steps up next. "Wow." He glances between Jen and me. "You two should take that act on the road."

When the attention is no longer on us, Jen throws her arms around my neck. "Thank you for your help! I think they really liked it."

"You had doubts?" I ask.

"That was so much fun! I'll always remember tonight."

As I pat her back, I know I will, too. I'm glad we were able to do this for Kevin, and I'm glad we could do it together as friends.

Suddenly, her body goes rigid in my arms.

"How does Addison know Ross?" she asks over my shoulder.

"Who?"

"My boyfriend, Ross."

Stepping back, I turn around just in time to see Addison yank her arm out of Derek's grasp. "That's not Ross," I say through gritted teeth. "That's Derek." What in the hell is he doing here?

"No."

I hear Jen's quiet protest and turn to look at her. Her face is pale and twisted with confusion. "That's...he's..." she stutters. "Oh my God."

I look at Addison once more. It appears she and Derek are arguing. Anger builds in my chest, and I point in their direction. "Are you telling me Derek is Ross?" I ask.

Slowly, Jen nods.

Oh. Hell. No.

It feels like I reach Derek in two strides. I come up behind him and shove his shoulder. "What the fuck are you doing?"

He looks me over with hard eyes. "I could ask you the same thing."

"Derek is leaving," Addison says. "We can talk another time."

"Not when you won't answer your goddamn phone!" he spits.

"I hate to interrupt," Jen appears by my side, "but, I thought your name was Ross." Despite her acerbic tone, her eyes shimmer with unshed tears.

Derek blinks and stares. "Jen?"

She crosses her arms. "The one and only."

Addison's eyes dart between my ex and hers. I can tell when the realization hits. Her mouth falls open and she takes a step back. "You've been cheating on me with *Jen?!*" she exclaims.

Derek gets defensive. "How do you even know her?"

"She's Kyle's ex!"

Derek moves toward Addison and I step in his way. "I wouldn't if I were you."

He scoffs. "Who do you think you are? You were screwing my wife before I even met Jen!"

I grab Derek's collar. Clutching it, I twist and pull. "Say one more word. I dare you."

His eyes narrow. "How do I always end up with your sloppy seconds?"

My fist connects with his jaw.

Chapter Twenty-Seven

Derek stumbles into the table behind him. Drinks spill and guests jump out of their seats.

"Get out of here," I snarl.

He rights himself and shoves my chest. "Make me."

"Stop!" Addison steps between us. "Derek, go home." She focuses on his face. "Don't ruin this night for Ashley."

"Do you think I give a fuck about Ashley?" His hand flies out and grabs Addison's elbow. "You're the only one I care about."

I see red. I'm about to pull Addison to my side when Jen steps forward. "Thanks a lot, asshole!" she spits.

She throws something at Derek and it bounces off his chest. I don't know what it is until I see her pull at her ear and rip the jewelry out of it. She chucks the other earring at him. "You're a piece of work, you know that?" She gets in his face. "Why the fake name? Were you worried you would get caught? Karma sure is a funny bitch."

"I don't have time for you right now," Derek snaps.

"Perfect!" Jen exclaims. "Because I don't have any more time for you." She pulls Addison's arm out of Derek's grasp and starts to lead her away. "I suggest you leave before the Dayton brothers kick your ass."

Jen's eyes focus on something behind me, and I turn my head. Kevin is headed in our direction. I lean toward Derek. "Find the door."

His eyes jump from me to my brother, and he takes a step back. I'm done wasting my time with this prick. I start to walk toward Addison.

Until a fist meets the side of my face.

I trip over my feet, but quickly get my balance. I turn just in time to block another punch and land one of my own. Derek staggers back, crashing into a different table. The few people seated there gasp and scatter.

Before he can react, I lunge forward and grab his shirt with both hands. I slam him against the tabletop, then pull him off and shove him away. Kevin catches him from behind and pins his arms to his sides. As Derek struggles, Austin and Eli appear.

"What in the hell is going on?" Austin asks.

"Help me get him out of here!" Kevin grunts.

He doesn't have to ask twice.

As they lead him out, Tara's boyfriend, John, finds me. "Let me see if I can talk some sense into him," he says.

Good luck with that, I think.

"Kyle." Addison touches my arm. "Are you okay? Your cheek is swelling."

I know. I can feel it. I haven't been hit like that in years.

She reaches up and runs her fingers over my face. "This is my fault."

"No." I move her hand away and hold on to it. "I hit Derek and he hit me back. You had nothing to do with it."

"I have everything to do with it! The only reason he was here was because of me." Her face falls. "I should have answered his stupid calls."

I had no idea he was calling. "Why didn't you tell me he was bothering you?"

Addison gives me a knowing look. "It wasn't worth making you angry. He only called a few times and I let them go to voice mail. He said we needed to talk, but I'm done. Nothing he can say will make me change my mind."

I squeeze her hand that I'm still holding.

Addison glances around the room. People are looking at us out of the corners of their eyes, and I refuse to turn around to see if my parents are staring, too. I'm sure my mom is and I don't want to hear her opinion.

"Guys." Ashley walks up to us. "Is everything all right? I was in the bathroom and missed it! Where's Kevin?"

I look over her head to see my brother, Austin, and Eli return to the reception. "Over there." I nod. "Everything's fine."

"I'm so sorry, Ash," Addison says. She lets go of me and hugs her best friend. "I didn't mean for this to happen."

"What are you worried about?" Ashley frowns over Addison's shoulder. "Derek should have known better than to show up here."

Addison steps back. "Your families must think we're insane."

"Please," Ashley scoffs. "At my cousin Kimmie's wedding, her sister Kendra got caught having sex in the linen closet with one of the wait staff. Oh, and two of my aunts got caught smoking pot in the parking lot. I think my family would be upset if something *didn't* happen."

From across the room, I notice Jen walk over to Kevin. He holds on to her arms and looks her in the eye as she talks; I'm sure she is filling him in on what happened. I feel terrible for her. Just a few days ago she was so happy.

"Wow, Kyle," Ashley says. "You should really get some ice."

I raise my hand to my cheek. "I've had worse."

Addison turns to me. "Not on my watch you haven't." She inspects my face again. "Please get some ice."

You know, a drink wouldn't hurt either. "C'mon." I take her hand and pull her toward the bar. On our way there, we pass my brother and Jen.

"You don't have to leave," I hear him say as we walk by.

"I know, but I need to."

We stop walking. Jen and Addison face each other. After silent seconds, Jen says, "I don't know what to say. I didn't know."

"It's okay," Addison responds. "He gave you his middle name. Even if he was honest, what were the odds of your Derek being the same as mine?"

Jen looks down. "We met on New Year's Eve, but he didn't call for months. We've been seeing each other since the end of February."

"You don't have to explain." Addison steps forward. "My marriage was hurting well before New Year's Eve."

Jen sighs. "Still. I feel awful. I just...I just want to go home."

"Do you want me to walk you to your car?" I volunteer. Not that I can fix this, but I feel like I should try to do something.

"No," she says. "I'm a big girl." She looks at Kevin. "It was a beautiful wedding. Have fun on your honeymoon."

He gives her a hug. "Thank you for my present. I want a copy of it, okay?"

"Talk to your brother," she says. "He'll have to agree to perform it again."

Jen says goodbye. After she leaves, Kevin lets out a heavy breath. "It took everything I had not to punch that guy before I knew about Jen. I want another shot."

I'm just about to agree when a man dressed in a suit and tie approaches. "Mr. Dayton?"

Both Kevin and I respond. "Yes?"

The man looks confused. "I'm looking for the groom."

"Right here." Kevin raises his hand.

"I'm Anthony Towner, general manager. There's a gentleman out front causing a commotion. Our valets saw you remove him from the premises, but he's back. Security would like to have a word with you."

"Looks like you might get your shot," I say. "I'll come with you."

"No." Addison steps in front of me. "He's just trying to make us mad. Don't give him the satisfaction. Let Ashley and Kevin have their night without our mess." She turns to my brother. "Tell him we left and you don't know where we went. We'll disappear. If he wants to come in and check, let him. He won't find us."

"Where are we going?" I ask.

"Upstairs." She looks at Kevin again. "It's okay if we leave the party, right?"

"It's fine," he says. "We're only here for another hour anyway."

Satisfied, Addison heads across the room to the opposite doors and I follow. Once we're outside the ballroom, we find a set of elevators and head up to the seventh floor. Inside the small space, I pull her close.

"We're going to have to deal with him eventually," I say.

"Yes, but not tonight." She buries her head against my chest. "I don't want to ruin the wedding any more than it has been."

"Ashley and Kevin aren't upset."

"It doesn't matter. It doesn't feel right to involve them."

I have to agree. Their night should not be about us.

When the elevator stops we exit and find our room. I fish the key card out of my wallet. Earlier, while the girls were taking more photos, I checked us in and brought up our bags. As I hold the door open for Addison, she brushes past me and heads straight for the counter that holds the coffee pot and over-priced bottles of water. She grabs the ice bucket.

"What are you doing?" I ask.

"Helping you," she says. "I'll be right back."

She leaves, and I flip the door lock so she can get back in. Headed toward the bed, I kick off my shoes and decide to look in the mirror hanging over the desk. My face is sore, but it doesn't look very swollen. I pause, thinking of all the fights I got into in high school. If Addison had seen me after those, she would have lost her shit. This is nothing.

When she returns, she puts some ice in a washcloth from the bathroom and hands it to me. "For your cheek."

"It's not that bad," I protest and plop down on the edge of the bed. "You're worrying for nothing."

She steps out of her heels and kicks them behind her. "Humor me. I know bad when I see it."

I laugh. "No, you don't."

She moves to stand in front of me and raises an eyebrow. She lifts her knee and points to her scar. "Yes, I do."

"You want to compare scars?" I ask. I set down her makeshift ice pack, unbutton my cuff, and roll up my sleeve. "See that? That's what happens when your brother turns around holding a weed whipper."

She scrutinizes the permanent line on my skin. I remember the day Kevin accidentally cut me. It hurt like hell and the gash needed twenty stitches.

Addison's unimpressed eyes meet mine. "I'll see your arm and raise you a thigh." Reaching down, she grabs the bottom of her dress and hikes it to her hip. The top of her left leg is covered in faded marks. It looks like she walked through a plate glass window.

"Plane crash," she says matter-of-factly.

My eyes meet hers. There's no way any of my past split lips, cut eyebrows, or banged up fingers trump what she's been through. I start to reach for her, but she steps back.

"Uh uh." She smiles. "You started this. What else you got?"

I accept her challenge and stand, untucking my shirt. Lifting it, I point to a tiny scar. "Appendix," I say. "I had it out when I was nineteen."

She squints. "I can barely see that."

I shrug and drop my shirt, then gesture for her to go next. To my surprise, she turns around and starts to lower the zipper on the back of her dress.

"Hey." I step forward. "That's my job."

She grins over her shoulder and her hand stops moving. "A little help here?"

Gladly, I oblige. With her back exposed, Addison holds on to the top of her dress and says, "On the left."

I have to push the fabric aside to see. My eyes widen when I find the lines etched into the surface of her skin. They extend from her thigh over her hip and run outside the waistline of her lacey boy shorts. Tempted, I trace one of them with my finger, trailing it along her lower back before her skin breaks out in goose bumps.

"I know they're not pretty," she says. "I wasn't lying. I know what bad looks like."

She's wrong.

Sliding my hand inside her dress, I weave it around her waist. I press my palm against her stomach and pull her to me, wrapping my free hand over her shoulder. As her back settles against my chest, my lips gently tease her ear. "There is not one part of you that isn't beautiful," I whisper.

Addison's breath hitches. I can feel it with her body pressed to mine. I leave a trail of open-mouthed kisses down the side of her neck and she leans further into me. Her hands move, letting the front of her dress fall, and one of them finds its way into my hair while the other covers mine at her waist. I don't know why I didn't notice earlier, but she's not wearing anything under the dress other than the boy shorts. I can't stop the groan that leaves my throat. What I see is perfect and better than my memory. My hand leaves her shoulder and teases her breasts before reaching her hip and pushing down.

"Can we get rid of this?" I breathe.

She murmurs a "yes" before helping me. We push her dress to her feet and then I pull her back to my chest again. My lips find her shoulder and my hands roam her skin. I take my time exploring every soft inch of her. When my fingers find the top of her shorts, I'm dying to dive inside. But, this is our first time – again. We've been waiting for this moment and I don't want to rush it. Instead, I slowly trace the lace across her waist, over her hip, and down her backside.

She grabs my hands and stills them against her body as she turns her face toward me. She catches my mouth in a kiss that pulls the air from my lungs. When we stop she says, "If you don't touch me, I'm going to explode."

I laugh against her temple. "I thought I was touching you."

"You know what I mean." She lifts my hand from her ass and places it between her legs. "You need to move fast...*ter*," she stutters as I move before she finishes her sentence.

"Like that?" I ask.

All I get is an "uhm hmm" as her head falls back against my shoulder. Since she's not worried about taking things slow, I pause to fully undress her. She protests with a disappointed sigh when my hands leave her body, then gasps when they return. The sound makes me smile and urges me on. I want her to feel good beneath my touch. It doesn't take long for her breath to race and her body to tremble; her knees give out and I hold her tighter. As she falls over the edge, my eyes land on her tattoo. I kiss behind her ear then down her neck. As her breathing slows, my heart swells. Only two words echo in my mind. The first is Sparrow.

The second is *mine.*

Addison turns and plants a deep kiss on my mouth. She blindly unbuttons my shirt and pushes it off my shoulders. When she steps back, her eyes rake over my chest. "Damn," she murmurs before kissing me again. "Your turn," she says against my lips.

Her mouth slides to my jaw to my neck to my collarbone. She continues south, over my chest and down my stomach. My hands find their way into her hair. What she's doing is driving me crazy; it's been far too long since I've had the right to her body. When her tongue runs along the waistline of my pants, I know I need to slow her down. I understand she's trying to give me what I gave her, but when I fall, I want to look into her eyes.

Grasping her arms, I pull her up to me. She looks confused. "Not tonight," I say and then turn her around. I back her toward the bed. Her legs hit the edge and she sits down. I go for the button on my pants and she helps. Once those are off, she pushes herself up the mattress and I start to crawl over her.

"Do you know how long I've waited for you?" I ask.

Her eyes widen. "Too long," she whispers.

I kiss the scar on her knee. "I thought I'd lost you forever." Working my way up, I stop at the marks on her thigh. There must be a dozen, and I kiss every one. "I thought you'd never be mine again."

Her breath catches and my heart pounds. I move to her hip, kissing and licking along the permanent lines there. Then, I move over her belly and higher still. My eyes meet hers. "I'm going to worship you every chance I get."

Her expression softens, and I place a kiss in the center of her chest.

"Starting with your heart."

~~~~

Hazy sunlight filters through the hotel curtains. Addison moves against my side, her body snaked around me. We're in the same position we fell asleep in last night. Her head rests on my shoulder, her arm across my chest, and her bare legs are intertwined with mine.

We still fit together like two puzzle pieces.

Lightly, I run my fingers down her spine and back up again. Her breathing picks up in her sleep. As I study her, I remember the first night we spent together. It was under the stars on the dock at Buhl Lake. I never thought I'd feel that calm again.

I was wrong.

Addison's eyes blink open with a lazy smile. She stretches her legs and I can feel her toes flex against my skin. "Good morning," she says softly.

"Good morning."

She stretches again, this time rolling on to her back and pushing her arms above her head. I shift my weight to my side and watch her.

"What?" she asks.

My eyes comb over her body and she notices. She smirks, reaches for the sheet, and pulls it over her chest.

"Awww." I frown.

She giggles and rolls on her side, facing me. "Didn't you get enough of that last night?"

I lift the blanket at my waist and raise an eyebrow. "Nope."

She laughs. I reach for her and she moves close, her nose nearly touching mine. "I love you," I say.

"I love you, too."

She tips her head and gives me a slow, sweet good morning kiss. When she leans back, I push her hair behind her ear. "You know something?"

"What?"

"This is only the second time we've spent the whole night together."

Her brow furrows then smooths. "You're right. That's weird." She props herself on her elbow and leans over me. "I never want to spend another night away from you."

I run my fingers over her shoulder and down her arm. "You're in luck. I have a really big bed."

She grins. "Oh yeah? So do I." She kisses me again, then stops and groans. "Hang on a sec. Nature calls."

My face twists. "Really?"

Her eyes dance. "Don't worry. I'll make it up to you."

She slides out of bed and heads for the bathroom. While she's busy, I rub my eyes and yawn. My thoughts jump to Kevin. He and Ashley should be on a plane to Cabo by now. I assume nothing else happened with Derek because no one contacted me. Then again, I was a little preoccupied last night. Would I have paid attention if my phone rang?

A self-satisfied smile creeps across my face.

Eh...probably not.

I hear water running as minutes pass. When Addison doesn't return from the bathroom, I start to wonder if she fell asleep in there.

Finally, the door opens. My eyes nearly jump out of my head when she appears wearing nothing but my tuxedo shirt. Only the bottom few buttons are fastened. She raises her arm above her head and casually leans against the door frame. One side of the shirt hangs open revealing everything she has to offer.

"Could I interest you in a shower?" she asks and bites her lip.

I want to leap out of the bed. "Is this you making it up to me?"

She nods. "Unless you'd rather do something else."

Everything I want to do with her can be done in the shower. In less than a second, I'm standing in front of her. "I'll help you get clean even though I like you dirty."

She smiles and drapes her arms around my neck. "I thought you might."

She kisses me and her mouth tastes like mint; she must have brushed her teeth. I lift her off the ground and carry her into the bathroom. I don't bother to undress her; I walk right into the shower with her legs wrapped around my waist.

She laughs as water rains down on us. "You're impatient!"

I set her feet on the floor and find her eyes. "You're mine."

Her laughter fades. "I am," she says. Water drips off her lashes as she reaches behind her ear and touches her tattoo. "I always have been."

The invincible feeling I had when she told me she loved me is back. It wells up in my chest so fast I can barely contain it. I cradle her face with both hands and kiss her. I kiss her until my lips feel swollen. I kiss her for all the years we missed and all the years we'll have.

I kiss her until the water runs cold.

Chapter Twenty-Eight

"Are you Kyle Dayton?"

It's the Monday following the wedding, and I slide lazily from beneath the tractor I'm working on. Two police officers stand over me, tall and intimidating. They stand out like sore thumbs in my garage.

"Yeah." I frown. "Can I help you?"

"You're under arrest," the officer on my left says. He reaches for my arm and hauls me to my feet. "You have the right to remain silent. Anything you say can be used against you in a court of law."

He pulls my hands behind my back as the second officer cuffs me.

"You have the right to an attorney. If you cannot afford an attorney, one will be provided for you."

The words fade. What in the hell is going on? I look around the garage and catch Eli staring at me. Confusion is written all over his face.

"Mr. Dayton," the officer says. "Do you understand?"

I must have missed something. I look over my shoulder and stare at him. "What is this about?"

"Assault and battery. Let's go."

He hooks his hand around my elbow and starts to pull me to the door. Through it, I can see a police cruiser parked outside. My vision blurs for a second. I'm being arrested. What the fuck for? Assault of whom?

I try to stop walking, but they nudge me forward. I want to ask questions but I know they won't answer specifics. Looking over my shoulder, I find Eli. "Call Kevin!" I shout to him.

He nods and heads for the office. I have no idea if my brother will pick up his cell on his honeymoon; hopefully he will listen to his messages.

When we get to the car, the officers put me in the back seat. They shut the door and crawl into the front. I glance out the window to see Noah and Chase rush out of the garage. They look at me and I can barely hear Noah's voice. "What's going on?" he asks. All I can do is shrug and shake my head.

The officer pulls out of the parking lot and on to the main road. Slowly, we drive through town. *What? No sirens?* I think as my pulse races faster than the car I'm riding in. What just happened? Who would –?

Derek.

My jaw clenches and my breath comes in short spurts.

Son of a bitch.

~~~~

Once we get to the station, I'm booked and fingerprinted. My mug shot is taken, and one of the officers – Perkins, his badge reads – informs me I'm being charged with assault and battery of one Derek R. Cole.

Fucker.

I have to give up my cell and my wallet, along with the keys to my truck. Then, I'm led to a desk with a phone.

"You get one call," Officer Perkins says. He hands me the receiver and I almost laugh. This is surreal.

Staring at the numbers on the keypad, I reluctantly dial Addison. My mind races with ways to tell what's going on without freaking her out. She picks up on the third ring.

"Um, hello?" She sounds hesitant.

"Hey, Sparrow."

"Kyle?" Her tone sounds worried. "Why are you calling me from the police department?"

The name must have shown up on her caller ID. Before I can say anything, she takes a startled breath. "Are you hurt?"

"No. I'm fine."

"Thank god," she says. "I thought there was an accident."

"No. No accident." I run my hand through my hair. "I've been arrested."

I can picture her frown. "Arrested for what?"

"Assault."

"Of who?"

"Derek."

The thought must take a second to sink in because she doesn't say anything. "Addison?"

Silence. I glance at Perkins. He's thumbing through a magazine and doesn't look the least bit interested in me.

Finally, I hear Addison's voice. It's toxic. "I *hate* him," she breathes. "What do you need from me?"

"Call Ashley and talk to Kevin. I need him to get ahold of the lawyer we use for Dayton Landscaping."

"Done," she says. "Then what?"

I have no idea. "I assume after I talk to the lawyer there's bail or something. I'm not sure."

"I can't believe Derek did this!" she spits. "You weren't the only one throwing punches!"

"No shit."

"I want you home." Her tone is adamant, yet pleading. "How long will you have to stay there? Can I come see you?"

Again, I have no clue.

"Okay," she sounds anxious. "I'm hanging up and calling Ashley. The sooner we get you help, the sooner we'll know what's what." She pauses. "I love you."

"I love you, too."

The line goes dead and I immediately feel hollow. That was the last time I'll hear her voice until who-knows-when. I look around the small town police station and realize I'm at the mercy of these people. Right now that only includes Perkins, his buddy Oliver, and a receptionist, but I'm sure there are more officers on duty. I feel trapped, and I'm not even behind bars. I pray my brother or Ashley answers their phone. I want out of here *now*.

"All set?" Perkins asks and steps away from the desk.

I nod and hang up the receiver. "What happens next?"

"You get to spend some time in our luxury accommodations," he says.

My stomach feels like lead. "Do I have to stay overnight?"

"Maybe." Perkins pushes me ahead of him by my elbow. We walk a short distance down a hallway to a small empty cell. He slides open the door and gestures for me to step inside. I do, and the door clangs shut.

"We'll let you know if you get any visitors," he says through the bars. "Oh, and if I were you, I'd get comfortable and claim the bench." He nods to the left. "Monday nights usually bring us a few patrons from the Moose Lodge. It might get crowded in there."

I stare at the tiny seat and curse under my breath as Perkins walks away. Even so, I take his advice and park my ass on the seat.

After I call Derek every name in the book and create a few of my own, I lean my head against the cement wall and close my eyes. Now what do I do?

~~~~

Hours later, I hear my name.

"Dayton!"

I open one eye. It's Perkins.

"Your lawyer is here."

I sit up. Addison or Eli must have gotten through to the newlyweds.

Ron Crispin steps to the side of Officer Perkins to be let into the cell. I like Ron; Brady used his law office when he owned the business and I followed suit. When I first bought the place, we worked together to set up contracts and liability clauses. I also needed a course on the legalities of hiring and firing employees. Ron was patient with me then, just as he is with Kevin now, since it's my brother he deals with more these days.

"Kyle." Ron shakes my hand when steps in front of me. "I never thought I'd see you in here."

"You and me both." I scoot over on the bench so he can have a seat. "So. How do I fight this?"

"Well," Ron shuffles a file folder and some papers in his hands, "the first step is your arraignment hearing tomorrow morning. It's scheduled for..." He flips over a paper. "Ten a.m. We'll be at the municipal court. The magistrate will explain the charges and then set bail."

I groan. "How much? And what's a magistrate?"

"A judge. He will determine the bail amount."

"Fuck." I rub my eyes.

"There's a chance he'll let you go on your own recognizance. However, looking at the redacted police report, several witnesses state they saw you punch this Derek first. The judge may think you'll go after him again and set bail to deter that."

"What witnesses?"

Ron opens the file folder and pulls out a paper. "Looks like hotel staff. A bartender and a few waitresses. Security also corroborated an incident." Ron eyes me. "Did you hit him first?"

"Yes, but then he hit me."

He looks at the report again. "And then you punched him a second time?"

"Yes."

"Why?"

"Because he punched me!"

"No. Why did you hit him in the first place?"

I sigh. "He accused me of sleeping with his wife before she left him. I didn't. I also found out he was cheating on Addison with my ex-girlfriend, Jen. We were all at the wedding."

Ron blinks. "Is this "Days of Our Lives"?"

"Funny."

"Who's Addison?" he asks and pulls out a pen.

"I'm seeing her. She's Derek's ex-wife."

"Are they divorced?"

"Separated."

"When did you get involved with her?"

"When I was seventeen."

Ron stares at me again.

"Look, bottom line, I was standing up for two women I care about," I say. "I told Derek not to say another word. He did. So, I hit him."

Ron nods. "Have you and Derek fought before?"

I shake my head. "We've exchanged words. That's it."

Ron closes the folder. "Okay. I'll meet you in the morning at the courthouse." He stands. "Only speak when spoken to and look apologetic. Once the judge sets bail, we'll go from there."

I stand with him and my stomach growls.

"Have you eaten?" he asks.

"No. What time is it anyway?"

He looks at his watch. "It's going on four o'clock. I'll talk to the officers on my way out. They should at least bring you a sandwich or something."

"I'm staying here?"

"Unfortunately, yes." Ron frowns. "Since there are witnesses to back Derek's story, they won't release you until you see the judge. I'm sorry."

Feeling tense, I lace my fingers and press them against the back of neck. Other than complicating my life, what does Derek hope to get out of this? Does he think Addison will come back to him if I'm sent to jail?

Wait.

I bet that's exactly what he thinks.

"What's the penalty?" I ask Ron.

"If you're convicted? Up to ninety-three days in jail or a fine. Or both."

"I can't spend three months in here," I argue. "I have a business to run." *And a girl I'm in love with.* Not that I think Addison would go back to Derek, but he can sure make her life hell while I'm gone.

Ron steps toward the door. "You wouldn't be here. You'd be in a larger facility."

I fucking hate this.

"Will you let Kevin know what's happening?" I ask.

"Will do. He sounded a little panicked when he called."

Great. Now I'm ruining his sun and fun in Cabo.

"All right," Ron says. "I'm going to take off and get things in order. Try to get some sleep."

I extend my hand and he shakes it. "Thanks for your help."

"I'd like to say it's my pleasure, but..." He smiles. "Try not to worry too much."

Like that's possible.

Ron calls for Perkins, and he's let out of the cell. As they walk away, I hear him mention getting his client some food.

~~~~

The next morning, I'm up early.

Late last night they delivered a Moose Lodge member to the cell. If I had to guess I would say it was around two a.m., because that's when the Lodge closes. Dave must be a regular, because the officers called him by his first name and told him to sleep it off. He glanced at me before curling up in the far corner of the cell. He was snoring almost instantly. I tried to drown out his noise by thinking about Addison, Tori, landscape design, *anything*, but it didn't work. Soon, I could smell the unmistakable scent of piss. I couldn't sleep after that. Not after getting company.

So, I started to pace. I counted the bars that made up the cell walls. I counted the ceiling tiles. I counted the tiles on the floor. I took my time to estimate the number Dave was lying on. I came up with twenty-four.

Tiles beneath Dave.

Not for the whole room.

That number was 144. Easy math. Twelve by twelve.

"Dayton? Time to go."

An officer interrupts my internal monologue. I've never been so sick of my own voice. I jump up, more than ready to leave this joint. An officer named Dwight leads me out of the cell and down the same hallway I came through yesterday. We stop to collect my things and then head out a side door to a waiting police car. Once I'm seated in the back, another officer joins him for the drive. He hands him a small paper bag that he then hands to me.

"Bagel?" Dwight asks.

I take it. "Thanks."

The clock on the dash of the car tells me it's eight in the morning. We make it to the courthouse a half hour later. I'm led into a full waiting room and when I see Ron, the police escort me to him and remain by my side.

"You look terrible," he says. "I told you to get some sleep."

"I had to spend the night with a loud, pissy drunk," I say. "Sleep wasn't happening."

"Well, I brought you a change of clothes," he says. "That will help."

He hands me a clean, red polo shirt that's not mine. "Where did you get this?"

"My closet," he says. "Put it on."

I take off my dirty t-shirt and pull on the polo while sitting in the middle of the room. Ron flips me some deodorant, and I use that, too. Then, he hands me a stick of gum.

"Okay. Our magistrate is Harrison," he says while consulting some papers. "Let's hope she sets bail for a minimal amount. That way, you can pay it and be home by noon."

That sounds amazing.

As I chew on my Doublemint, case after case is called ahead of mine. Finally, the bailiff appears and calls, "Kyle Dayton."

I swallow my gum.

We walk into the courtroom. I follow Ron because I don't know where to go. Based on the movies I've watched, I think the defendant stands to the right side of the judge, but hell if I know. My nerves are starting to kick in. The faces of the people sitting in the courtroom blend together until I happen to focus on one.

Addison.

Her eyes lock on mine and she gives me a confident nod. *"It's okay,"* she mouths. She looks so sure.

Seeing her makes me feel better. It calms me some, and I return her confidence with a wink. It's then that I see who she's sitting with.

Mr. Grant.

How is that possible?

I don't have a lot of time to think about it before Ron and I make it to a table with a small podium. It's to the right of the judge, just like I thought. I glance around the room looking for Derek. It surprises me that he's not here. I thought for sure he would want to witness my humiliation.

The bailiff hands the judge a file. "State of Michigan vs. Dayton, 14-1014201. Assault and battery."

Judge Harrison adjusts her glasses and peers at the file. She looks like a nice woman; she reminds me of Judge Judy without the scowl. I hope she's in a good mood today.

I clasp my hands in front of me and shift my weight. Silence reigns and you could hear a pin drop in this place. Then, whispering begins at the rear of the courtroom. I look behind me and see a man has entered. He strides toward the bench with a paper in his hand.

"Your Honor," he holds up one finger as he walks. "The State has decided to drop the charges."

Judge Harrison looks up annoyed. "Excuse me Detective Hoskins?"

"I just received a signed affidavit from Mr. Cole. The State won't be filing a case."

Ron's surprised eyes lock on mine.

"Bring it here," she says.

Detective Hoskins approaches the bench and hands over the paper. My pulse accelerates in the hope it's legit. I don't know why Derek would change his mind, and I really don't care. All that matters is if he did.

After a minute or two, Judge Harrison puts the affidavit in the file folder and thrusts it at the bailiff. "You people are wasting my time," she says under her breath. She looks at me. "You're free to go."

Ron gathers his things. "That went better than expected," he says.

"You're not kidding."

We make our way out of the courtroom and meet up with Addison and Mr. Grant just before the rear doors. Addison throws her arms around my neck and squeezes tight. "I missed you," she says into my neck.

"It was only twenty-four hours," I say, trying to make light of a shitty situation I don't care to repeat.

"That's too long," she says and backs away. "I'm glad I ran into Mr. Grant. He kept me sane."

My eyes jump to Gram's old flame. "I was wondering why you were here."

"Guys," Ron interrupts us. "Let's continue this conversation outside."

We make it to the front steps of the courthouse where the sun is shining so bright it blinds me. I have to squint. "So, where did you two find each other?" I ask.

"At your house," Addison explains. "I went to get Tori when Mr. Grant stopped by."

"Your grandmother asked me to check in on you boys from time to time." Jonas rocks back on his heels. "It looks like I picked the right day."

Gram asked him to look out for us? "Thanks, but we're adults," I say. "You shouldn't feel obligated."

"It's no trouble."

"Mr. Grant told me an amazing story." Addison's eyes light up. "I think you know it."

"You told her about Gram?" I ask, surprised. "I thought it was a secret."

Jonas smiles. "Can I talk to you privately for a moment?"

His request is odd, but I follow him anyway. We walk down a few steps and out of earshot of Addison and Ron. They strike up a conversation as Mr. Grant turns to me.

"Kyle. I told Addison the story because she needed to hear it," he says. "She needed to know you two are supposed to be together and what you have is worth fighting for. I think my history with

Agnes drove that home. Your girl actually thought you might be better off without her."

My forehead pinches. "She said that?"

"She thinks everything Derek does is her fault. She's worried you might wake up one day and realize she's not worth the hassle."

"That will never happen," I say seriously. "I don't blame her for anything. Addison and me...we're forever."

Mr. Grant nods. "I want you two to have the chance your grandmother and I never got. That's why I took care of Derek. He won't be bothering you anymore."

My eyes grow wide. "I'm sorry?"

Mr. Grant leans toward me. "I'm only going to say this once. Did your grandmother mention why I disappeared all those years ago?"

My brain tries to remember her letter. "She said it was because of your father. Something about bad business."

"That's right. The apple doesn't fall far from the tree." He meets my eyes. "I had a few associates pay Derek a visit. He had two choices. Sign the affidavit or potentially lose the use of his legs. He chose option number one."

My mind is blown. "Are you involved with –?"

"Subject closed," Mr. Grant says. "I said nothing and Derek will say nothing."

"Does Addison know?" I whisper.

Mr. Grant shakes his head. "And she shouldn't."

I get it. My lips are sealed.

"I don't know what to say other than thank you."

"Say you'll visit an old man at the lake from time to time." He gives me a crooked smile.

"Will do."

We make our way over to Addison and my lawyer again. Ron says my case was so short I don't need to pay him; he'll trade me for some yard work. He leaves and then Mr. Grant follows, saying he needs to get on the road. Addison gives him a big hug goodbye.

Left alone, Sparrow turns to me. She wraps her arms around my waist, and I wrap mine around hers. "I love you," she says. "I'm so sorry for all of this. I have the shittiest soon-to-be-ex-husband ever."

"I'm sure he's near the top of the list," I say. "But nothing he does will ever come between us. You know that, right? I love you.

I've loved you since I was seventeen. Nothing – not him or anyone or anything else – can ruin us."

Her shoulders relax and she tucks her head beneath my chin. "I know."

I hold her tight. Does she know? It's hard for me to put into words how I feel, but I try. My need to be with her, take care of her – love her – is ridiculous. After she disappeared, I never thought I could feel this way.

And I didn't.

Until I found her again.

She takes a step back. "Let's celebrate. What do you want to do today?"

"You."

She raises an eyebrow.

I grin and she laughs. "C'mon," she says and takes my hand. "We won't leave the house. Let's spend the day together."

I follow her down the steps and change her words in my mind.

No. Let's spend forever together.

Epilogue

So, I'm nervous.

I shouldn't be because I know the answer to the question I'm going to ask. However, so much thought has been put into this night that I want it to be perfect.

Addison deserves perfect.

"Is the blindfold really necessary?" she complains from the seat beside me. "You're not fooling me. I know where we're going."

"Do you now?" I lift our entwined fingers and kiss the back of her hand. "Are you psychic?"

"No. I just know three left turns from the cottage means we're headed to the farm."

She's right. I am taking her to the old farm property up north. We've been staying at the cottage, vacationing, for nearly two weeks. It's the end of summer, late August, and I knew it was now or never to get some uninterrupted time away from our everyday lives. Addison's divorce was finalized before we left, the grand opening of her studio is scheduled for next week, and the start of the fall season is catch-up time for Dayton Landscaping.

As I pull up to our destination, I see my brother and Ashley have been busy. When I requested their help they jumped at the chance. Minutes ago they called to tell me everything was set and they were on their way to Mr. Grant's place. Addison has no idea they are even in the same zip code.

"Okay. We're here," I say as I cut the engine.

"Can I take this off now?" She gestures to the blindfold.

"Not yet. I'll help you down."

"Ugh!" she groans. "I know we're at the farm."

"Yeah, but I want you to get the full effect."

Her face registers confusion.

I release her hand, jump out of my truck, and then dive back inside to grab her waist. She feels around to find my shoulders, smacking me in the face.

"Hey!"

"What?" she asks innocently. "I can't see."

Smartass.

Instead of setting her feet on the ground like I planned, I slide one arm beneath her knees and the other around her back. "Hold on," I say. "I'm going to carry you."

I swing her up into my arms and she laughs. She clutches my neck, and I use her feet to shut the door behind us. "Don't drop me," she says as I walk out into the field.

"Never."

I head toward the white lights I asked Ashley and Kevin to put in a tall oak tree, the same one beneath which Addison and I had our picnic years ago. It sparkles in the twilight, especially when the wind moves the leaves. On the ground is the same blanket we used back then, too. Other than that, I gave Ashley creative license. I guess there's this website called Pinter-something where she gets ideas. Scattered on the ground around the blanket are Mason jars lit with candles. There has to be at least fifty of them, and the flames flicker in the glass. They radiate out from the blanket, sporadically spaced. To me, it looks as if there are stars on the ground.

I walk to the outer edge of the candles and stop.

"Are we there?" Addison asks.

"Yep." I set her down then turn her back to my chest. I reach up and untie the blindfold. "Ready?" I ask.

She nods enthusiastically.

I pull off the blindfold and she gasps. She takes a step back, bumping into me.

"Do you like it?" I whisper in her ear.

She turns to me with wide eyes. "It's gorgeous."

I take her hand.

"When did you have time to do all this?" she asks.

"I had help." I smile at her.

As I lead her to the blanket, I see the picnic basket I asked my brother to bring. I also see Ashley got creative here, too. I told her I wanted lilacs somewhere, because they're Addison's favorite flower. I thought a vase of them would do because they're out of season. However, Ashley went all out. I don't know where she got them, but the entire border of the blanket is covered in lilacs.

"Oh, wow," Addison says as we step over them. She inhales the scent of the flowers. "This is beautiful."

I'm still holding her hand, so I pull her to me. "No," I say as I wind my free hand around her waist. "You're beautiful."

She smiles before I lower my mouth to hers and catch her lips in a greedy kiss. She lets go of my hand and runs both of hers over my chest; she hangs on to my shoulders and kisses me back. There's nothing else like kissing Addison, every time it's like she's breathing life into me. I can never get enough.

When we finally separate, she asks, "Did you bring me out here just to kiss?"

I run my fingers up and down her back. "Would you be disappointed if I said yes?"

"No," she laughs. "I like kissing you here."

"Good," I say. "There's something I want to tell you. Well, two things, actually."

She tips her head, curious.

"Do you remember when I told you how much I love this place?"

"Yes. It's because of us."

"Exactly. I liked it before we met, but after, it held so much more meaning. That's why..." I hesitate with a mischievous grin.

"Spit it out!"

"I bought it."

"You did?" Her mouth falls open. "I thought you didn't know who owned it!"

"Turns out I do. It's Mr. Grant's property."

After the whole mess with the arrest, Jonas and I kept in touch. He said he was just fulfilling his promise to Gram to check in, but I got the vibe he was lonely. We got to talking one day about jobs and work, and I confided in him that the farm property was always a favorite of mine. I told him I wished I could own it, not only because it inspired me, but because Addison and I had memories there. He told me it was the place he grew up, the place he kissed Gram for the first time, and the place he wished he never had to leave. He offered to sell it to me for one whole dollar. I agreed.

"You're kidding me," Addison says. "He doesn't want it?"

"Does it look like he's been using it?"

She looks around. "Well, no."

It's then that I drop to one knee in front of her. She looks confused before the realization sets in. One hand flies up to cover her mouth.

"Sparrow," I take her other hand, "I love you. I want to spend the rest of our lives together in the place where you stole my heart. I want to build a home here where we can escape, and I want to fill it with babies, be they on four legs or two."

Tears start to well in her eyes as I reach into my pocket and pull out her ring. I had it made just for her. A round, brown diamond sits on a platinum band surrounded by smaller white stones. It's not a traditional ring, but Addison is not a traditional girl.

"This is a promise," I say as I slide it on her finger. "I won't leave your side unless you tell me to go. And even then, I'll still fight like hell to stay." I look up into her eyes. "Addison Renee Parks. Will you marry me?"

She takes a deep breath as a few tears fall. She moves to her knees, so we're eye to eye, and takes my face in her hands. She stares at my mouth and gently traces my bottom lip with her thumb. "Ask me again," she whispers.

I lean forward so our lips are centimeters apart. "Will you marry me?" I breathe.

"A million times yes," she says before bringing her mouth down on mine.

When our breathing slows, she moves and plants tiny kisses all over my face. I laugh and fall backward, pulling her on top of me. I settle into the blanket and she curls against my side. We stare above us into the tree filled with lights. It's as if we're the only people in the universe.

Just the two of us together.

As it was always meant to be.

Acknowledgements

I can't tell you how happy I am that Sparrow is in your hands! Kyle and Addison have been driving me crazy for over a year ~ I had a hard time keeping their hands off each other! Although they are fictional, Buhl Lake is a real place. Last year, while riding backward on a jet ski to spot my kids tubing, inspiration hit. Kyle invaded my mind and he wouldn't leave me alone. I had to tell his story. I hope you enjoyed reading it as much as I enjoyed writing it.

With that said, there are a few people I need to thank for their support and encouragement along the way:

My family. Thank you to my husband for allowing me a peek into the male mind. Thank you for answering my questions and not laughing...too much. Thank you for pushing me and reminding me I'm not writing this book for "fourteen-year-olds" (see Chapter 27). Super thanks to my daughter for naming Tori, and to my son for playing his video games alongside my typing fingers.

My betas. Tara, Koz, Erica, Aubrey, and Breena. Thank you for your patience as you received Sparrow chapter by chapter. Thank you for questioning me and wanting more. I honestly thought Koz was going to have a stroke in the beginning of the book! And Tara, wow. Just wow. Now that you (and your husband, John) are immortalized in print, I hope you know you've signed a life-long beta ~ I mean, friendship ~ contract.

My Street Team. Jenn L., Lisa, Jennifer, Barbie, Tracey, Joelle, Lindsey, Shawanda, Lynn, Kelsey, Linda, Tiffany, Deanna, Sarah, Jordan, Tami, Charlotte, Nathanie, Christina, Jenn C., Sandy, Shawna, Leann, Stacie, Alissa, Ricky, Kristina, Kelly, Tracy H., Leslie, Michele, Ann, Lori, Gloria, Jessica, Miranda, Carla, Angela, Kristi, Paige, and Sonya. Thank you so much for promoting my work and loving my characters! You keep me going. And, last but not least, Ms. Whitney. Thank you for our long Facebook chats and volunteering your husband as my editor. Or, maybe he was coerced? Either way, I hope my overuse of adverbs and semi-colons didn't scar him! Chris, thank you for helping me keep Kyle direct ("Why can't you just say...") while maintaining his charm.

About the Author

Sara Mack is a Michigan native who grew up with her nose in books. She is a wife and a hockey mom on top of being trapped in an office forty hours a week. Her spare time is spent one-clicking on Amazon and devouring books on her Kindle, cleaning up after her kids and two elderly cats, attempting to keep her flower garden alive, and, of course, writing. She has an unnatural affinity for dark chocolate, iced tea, and bacon.

Connect with Sara:

On Facebook:
https://www.facebook.com/AuthorSaraMack

On Twitter:
http://twitter.com/smackwrites

Website and Email:
http://smackwrites.wix.com/saramackauthor

smackwrites@gmail.com

Other books by Sara Mack:

The Guardian Trilogy
Guardian
Allegiant
Reborn

Available on Amazon
http://www.amazon.com/Sara-Mack

21736483R00180